WHO ARE
THE PEOPLE?

"**The People** are the descendants of the survivors of a spaceship from another planet which crashed on Earth long, long ago. **The People** were scattered, and their children have lost the knowledge of their origins. Since they possess special powers of telepathy, telekinesis, etc., which would be regarded with horror and terror by normal terrene natives, theirs is a story of the conflict between their desire to conform to Earth standards, and their slow recognition and acceptance of their special identity."

Alfred Bester, <u>Fantasy and Science Fiction</u>

PILGRIMAGE is one of the most remarkable creations of science fiction and has earned for **ZENNA HENDERSON** an important name in imaginative writing.

Other Avon books by
Zenna Henderson

Zenna Henderson's

PILGRIMAGE

AVON
PUBLISHERS OF BARD, CAMELOT AND DISCUS BOOKS

To all my cherubs—
and the Bells of Couvron

AVON BOOKS
A division of
The Hearst Corporation
959 Eighth Avenue
New York, New York 10019

First Avon Printing, November, 1963
Fourteenth Printing

I

THE WINDOW of the bus was a dark square against the featureless night. Lea let her eyes focus slowly from their unthinking blur until her face materialized, faint and fragmentary, highlighted by the dim light of the bus interior. "Look," she thought, "I still have a face." She tilted her head and watched the wan light slide along the clean soft line of her cheek. There was no color except darkness for the wide eyes, the crisp turn of short curls above her ears and the curve of her brows—all were an out-of-focus print against the outside darkness. "That's what I look like to people," she thought impersonally. "My outside is intact—an eggshell sucked of life."

The figure in the seat next to her stirred.

"Awake, deary?" The plump face beamed in the dusk. "Must have had a good nap. You've been so quiet ever since I got on. Here, let me turn on the reading light." She fumbled above her. "I think these lights are cunning. How'd they get them to point just in the right place?" The light came on and Lea winced away from it. "Bright, isn't it?" The elderly face creased into mirth. "Reminds me of when I was a youngster and we came in out of the dark and lighted a coal-oil lamp. It always made me squint like that. By the time I was your age, though, we had electricity. But I got my first two before we got electricity. I married at seventeen and the two of them came along about as quick as they could. You can't be much more than twenty-two or three. Lordee! I had four by then and buried another. Here, I've got pictures of my grandbabies. I'm just coming back from seeing the newest one. That's Jennie's latest. A little girl after three boys. You remind me of her a little, your eyes being dark and the color your hair is. She wears hers longer but it has that same kinda red tinge to it." She fumbled in her bag. Lea felt as though words were washing over her like a warm frothy flood. She automatically took the bulging billfold the woman tendered her and watched unseeingly as the glassine windows flipped. ". . . and this is Arthur and Jane. Ah, there's Jennie. Here, take a good look and see if she doesn't look like you."

Lea took a deep breath and came back from a long painful distance. She stared down at the billfold.

"Well?" The face beamed at her expectantly.

"She's—" Lea's voice didn't work. She swallowed dryly. "She's pretty."

"Yes, she is," the woman smiled. "Don't you think she looks a little like you, though?"

"A little—" Her repetition of the sentence died, but the woman took it for an answer.

"Go on, look through the others and see which one of her kids you think's the cutest."

Lea mechanically flipped the other windows, then sat staring down into her lap.

"Well, which one did you pick?" The woman leaned over. "Well!" She drew an indignant breath. "That's my driver's license! I didn't say snoop!" The billfold was snatched away and the reading light snapped off. There was a good deal of flouncing and muttering from the adjoining seat before quiet descended.

The hum of the bus was hypnotic and Lea sank back into her apathy, except for a tiny point of discomfort that kept jabbing her consciousness. The next stop she'd have to do something. Her ticket went no farther. Then what? Another decision to make. And all she wanted was nothing—nothing. And all she had was nothing—nothing. Why did she have to do anything? Why couldn't she just *not*—? She leaned her forehead against the glass, dissolving the nebulous reflection of herself, and stared into the darkness. Helpless against habit, she began to fit her aching thoughts back into the old ruts, the old footprints leading to complete futility—leading into the dark nothingness. She caught her breath and fought against the horrifying—threatening . . .

All the lights in the bus flicked on and there was a sleepy

6

stirring murmur. The scattered lights of the outskirts of town slid past the slowing bus.

It was a small town. Lea couldn't even remember the name of it. She didn't even know which way she turned when she went out the station door. She walked away from the bus depot, her feet swift and silent on the cracked sidewalk, her body appreciating the swinging rhythm of the walk after the long hours of inactivity. Her mind was still circling blindly, unnoticing, uncaring, unconcerned.

The business district died out thinly and Lea was walking up an incline. The walk leveled and after a while she wavered into a railing. She clutched at it, waiting for a faintness to go away. She looked out and down into darkness. "It's a bridge!" she thought. "Over a river." Gladness flared up in her. "It's the answer," she exulted. "This is it. After this—nothing!" She leaned her elbows on the railing, framing her chin and cheeks with her hands, her eyes on the darkness below, a darkness so complete that not even a ripple caught a glow from the bridge lights.

The familiar, so reasonable voice was speaking again. *Pain like this should be let go of. Just a momentary discomfort and it ends. No more breathing, no more thinking, no aching, no blind longing for anything.* Lea moved along the walk, her hand brushing the railing. "I can stand it now," she thought, "Now that I know there is an end. I can stand to live a minute or so longer—to say good-by." Her shoulders shook and she felt the choke of laughter in her throat. Good-by? To whom? Who'd even notice she was gone? One ripple stilled in all a stormy sea. Let the quiet water take her breathing. Let its impersonal kindness hide her—dissolve her—so no one would ever be able to sigh and say, That was Lea. Oh, blessed water!

There was no reason not to. She found herself defending her action as though someone had questioned it. "Look," she thought. "I've told you so many times. There's no reason to go on. I could stand it when futility wrapped around me occasionally, but don't you remember? Remember the morning I sat there dressing, one shoe off and one shoe on, and couldn't think of one good valid reason why I should put the other shoe on? Not one reason! To finish dressing? Why? Because I had to work? Why? To earn a living? Why? To get something to

7

eat? Why? To keep from starving to death? Why? because you have to *live!* Why? *Why? Why!*

"And there were no answers. And I sat there until the grayness dissolved from around me as it did on lesser occasions. But then—" Lea's hands clutched each other and twisted painfully. "Remember what came then? The distorted sky wrenched open and gushed forth all the horror of a meaningless mindless universe—a reasonless existence that insisted on running on like a faceless clock—a menacing nothingness that snagged the little thread of reason I was hanging onto and unraveled it and unraveled it." Lea shuddered and her lips tightened with the effort to regain her composure. "That was only the beginning.

"So after that the depths of futility became a refuge instead of something to run from, its negativeness almost comfortable in contrast to the positive horror of what living has become. But I can't take either one any more." She sagged against the railing. "And I don't have to." She pushed herself upright and swallowed a sudden dry nausea. "The middle will be deeper," she thought. "Deep, swift, quiet, carrying me out of this intolerable—"

And as she walked she heard a small cry somewhere in the lostness inside her. "But I could have loved living so much! Why have I come to this pass?"

Shhh! the darkness said to the little voice. *Shhh! Don't bother to think. It hurts. Haven't you found it hurts? You need never think again or speak again or breathe again past this next inhalation. . . .*

Lea's lungs filled slowly. *The last breath!* She started to slide across the concrete bridge railing into the darkness—into finishedness—into The End.

"You don't really want to." The laughing voice caught her like a splash of water across her face. "Besides, even if you did, you couldn't here. Maybe break a leg, but that's all.

"Break a leg?" Lea's voice was dazed and, inside, something broke and cried in disappointment, "*I've spoken again!*"

"Sure." Strong hands pulled her away from the railing and nudged her to a seat in a little concrete kiosk sort of thing. "You must be *very* new here, like on the nine-thirty bus tonight."

"Nine-thirty bus tonight," Lea echoed flatly.

" 'Cause if you'd been here by daylight you'd know this bridge is a snare and a delusion as far as water goes. You couldn't drown a gnat in the river here. It's dammed up above. Sand and tamarisks here, that's all. It's dammed up above. Sand and tamarisks here, that's all. Besides you don't want to die, especially with a lovely coat like that—almost new!"

"Want to die," Lea echoed distantly. Then suddenly she jerked away from the gentle hands and twisted away from the encircling arm.

"I *do* want to die! Go *away*!" Her voice sharpened as she spoke and she almost spat the last word.

"But I *told* you!" The dim glow from the nearest light of the necklace of lights that pearled the bridge shone on a smiling girl-face, not much older than Lea's own. "You'd goof it up good if you tried to commit suicide here. Probably lie down there in the sand all night, maybe with a sharp stub of a tamarisk stuck through your shoulder and your broken leg hurting like mad. And tomorrow the ants would find you, and the flies—the big blowfly kind. Blood attracts them, you know. Your blood, spilling onto the sand."

Lea hid her face, her fingernails cutting into her hairline with the violence of the gesture. *This—this creature had no business peeling the oozing bleeding scab off,* she thought. *It's so easy to think of jumping into darkness—into nothingness, but not to think of blowflies and blood—your own blood.*

"Besides—" the arm was around her again, gently leading her back to the bench, "you can't want to die and miss out on everything."

"Everything is nothing," Lea gasped, grabbing for the comfort of a well-worn groove. "It's nothing but gray chalk writing gray words on a gray sky in a high wind. There's nothing! There's nothing!"

"You must have used that carefully rounded sentence often and often to have driven yourself such a long way into darkness," the voice said, unsmiling now. "But you must come back, you know, back to wanting to live."

"No, no!" Lea moaned, twisting. "Let me go!"

"I can't." The voice was soft, the hands firm. "The Power sent me by on purpose. You can't return to the Presence with

9

your life all unspent. But you're not hearing me, are you? Let me tell you.

"Your name is Lea Holmes. Mine, by the way, is Karen. You left your home in Clivedale two days ago. You bought a ticket for as far as your money would reach. You haven't eaten in two days. You're not even quite sure what state you're in, except the state of utter despair and exhaustion—right?"

"How—how did you know?" Lea felt a long-dead something stir inside her, but it died again under the flat monotone of her voice. "It doesn't matter. Nothing matters. You don't know anything about it!" A sick anger fluttered in her empty stomach. "You don't know what it's like to have your nose pressed to a blank wall and still have to walk and walk, day after day, with no way to get off the treadmill—no way to break through the wall—nothing, nothing, nothing! Not even an echo! Nothing!"

She snatched herself away from Karen's hands and, in a mad flurry of motion, scraped her way across the concrete railing and flung herself over into the darkness.

Endlessly tumbling—endlessly turning—slowly, slowly. Did it take so long to die? Softly the sand received her.

"You see," Karen said, shifting in the sand to cradle Lea's head on her lap. "I can't let you do it."

"But—I—I—jumped!" Lea's hands spatted sideways into the sand, and she looked up to where the lights of the passing cars ran like sticks along a picket fence.

"Yes, you did." Karen laughed a warm little laugh. "See, Lea, there *is* some wonder left in the world. Not everything is bogged down in hopelessness. What's that other quote you've been using for an anesthesia?"

Lea turned her head fretfully and sat up. "Leave me alone."

"What *was* that other quote?" Karen's voice was demanding now.

" 'There is for me no wonder more,' " Lea whispered into her hands, " 'Except to wonder where my wonder went, And why my wonder all is spent—' " Hot tears stung her eyes but could not fall. " '—no wonder more—' " The big emptiness that was always waiting, stretched and stretched, distorting—

"No wonder?" Karen broke the bubble with her tender laughter. "Oh, Lea, if only I had the time! No wonder, indeed!

10

But I've *got* to go. The most incredibly wonderful—" There was a brief silence and the cars shh-ed by overhead, busily, busily. "Look!" Karen took Lea's hands. "You don't care what happens to you any more, do you?"

"No!" Lea said dully, but a faint voice murmured protest somewhere behind the dullness.

"You feel that life is unlivable, don't you?" Karen persisted. "That nothing could be worse?"

"Nothing," Lea said dully, squelching the murmur.

"Then listen." Karen hunched closer to her in the dark. "I'll take you with me. I really shouldn't, especially right now, but they'll understand. I'll take you along and then—*then*—if when it's all over you still feel there's no wonder left in the world, I'll take you to a much more efficient suicide-type place and *push* you over!"

"But where—" Lea's hands tugged to release themselves.

"Ah, ah!" Karen laughed. "Remember, you don't care! You don't care! Now I'll have to blindfold you for a minute. Stand up. Here, let me tie this scarf around your eyes. There, I guess that isn't too tight, but tight enough—" Her chatter poured on and Lea grabbed suddenly, feeling as though the world were dissolving around her. She clung to Karen's shoulder and stumbled from sand to solidness. "Oh, does being blindfolded make you dizzy?" Karen asked. "Well, okay. I'll take it off then." She whisked the scarf off. "Hurry, we have to catch the bus. It's almost due." She dragged Lea along the walk on the bridge, headed for the far bank, away from the town.

"But—" Lea staggered with weariness and hunger, "how did we get up on the bridge again? This is crazy! We were down—"

"Wondering, Lea?" Karen teased back over her shoulder. "If we hurry we'll have time for a hamburger for you before the bus gets here. My treat."

A hamburger and a glass of milk later, the InterUrban roared up to the curb, gulped Lea and Karen in and roared away. Twenty minutes later the driver, expostulating, opened the door into blackness.

"But, lady, there's nothing out there! Not even a house for a mile!"

"I know," Karen smiled. "But this is the place. Someone's

11

waiting for us." She tugged Lea down the steps. "Thanks!" she called. "Thanks a lot!"

"Thanks!" the driver muttered, slamming the doors. "This isn't even a *corner*! Screwballs!" And roared off down the road.

The two girls watched the glowworm retreat of the bus until it disappeared around a curve.

"Now!" Karen sighed happily. "Miriam is waiting for us somewhere around here. Then we'll go—"

"I won't." Lea's voice was flatly stubborn in the almost tangible darkness. "I won't go another inch. Who do you think you are, anyway? I'm going to stay here until a car comes along—"

"And jump in front of it?" Karen's voice was cold and hard. "You have no right to draft someone to be your executioner. Who do you think *you* are that you can splash your blood all over someone else?"

"Stop talking about blood!" Lea yelled, stung to have had her thoughts caught from her. "Let me die! Let me die!"

"It'd serve you right if I did," Karen said unsympathetically. "I'm not so sure you're worth saving. But as long as I've got you on my hands, shut up and come on. Cry babies bore me."

"But—you—don't—know!" Lea sobbed tearlessly, stumbling miserably along, towed at arm's length behind Karen, dodging cactus and greasewood, mourning the all-enfolding comfort of nothingness that could have been hers if Karen had only let her go.

"You might be surprised," Karen snapped. "But anyway God knows, and you haven't thought even once of Him this whole evening. If you're so all-fired eager to go busting into His house uninvited you'd better stop bawling and start thinking up a convincing excuse."

"You're mean!" Lea wailed, like a child.

"So I'm mean." Karen stopped so suddenly that Lea stumbled into her. "Maybe I *should* leave you alone. I don't want this most wonderful thing that's happening to be spoiled by such stupid goings on. Good-by!"

And she was gone before Lea could draw a breath. Gone completely. Not a sound of a footstep. Not a rustle of brush. Lea cowered in the darkness, panic swelling in her chest, fear catching her breath. The high arch of the sky glared at her starrily

12

and the suddenly hostile night crept closer and closer. There was nowhere to go—nowhere to hide—no corner to back into. Nothing—nothing!

"Karen!" she shrieked, starting to run blindly. "Karen!"

"Watch it." Karen reached out of the dark and caught her. "There's cactus around here." Her voice went on in exasperated patience. "Scared to death of being alone in the dark for two minutes and fourteen seconds—and yet you think an eternity of it would be better than living—

"Well, I've checked with Miriam. She says she can help me manage you, so come along.

"Miriam, here she is. Think she's worth saving?"

Lea recoiled, startled, as Miriam materialized vaguely out of the darkness.

"Karen, stop sounding so mean," the shadow said. "You know wild horses couldn't pull you away from Lea now. She needs healing—not hollering at."

"She doesn't even *want* to be healed," Karen said.

"As though I'm not even here," Lea thought resentfully. "Not here. Not here." The looming wave of despair broke and swept over her. "Oh, let me go! Let me die!" She turned away from Karen, but the shadow of Miriam put warm arms around her.

"She didn't want to live either, but you wouldn't accept that—no more than you'll accept her not wanting to be healed."

"It's late," Karen said. "Chair-carry?"

"I suppose so," Miriam said. "It'll be shock enough, anyway. The more contact the better."

So the two made a chair, hand clasping wrist, wrist clasped by hand. They stooped down.

"Here, Lea," Karen said, "sit down. Arms around our necks."

"I can walk," Lea said coldly. "I'm not all that tired. Don't be silly."

"You can't walk where we're going. Don't argue. We're behind schedule now. Sit."

Lea folded her lips but awkwardly seated herself, clinging tightly as they stood up, lifting her from the ground.

"Okay?" Miriam asked.

"Okay," Karen and Lea said together.

13

"Well?" Lea said, waiting for steps to begin.

"Well," Karen laughed, "don't say I didn't warn you, but look down."

Lea looked down. And down! And *down!* Down to the scurrying sparks along a faded ribbon of a road. Down to the dew-jeweled cobweb of street lights stretching out flatly below. Down to the panoramic perfection of the whole valley, glowing magically in the night. Lea stared, unbelieving, at her two feet swinging free in the air—nothing beneath them but air—the same air that brushed her hair back and tangled her eyelashes as they picked up speed. Terror caught her by the throat. Her arms convulsed around the two girls' necks.

"Hey!" Karen strangled. "You're choking us! You're all right. Not so tight! Not so tight!"

"You'd better Still her," Miriam gasped. "She can't hear you."

"Relax," Karen said quietly. "Lea, relax."

Lea felt fear leave her like a tide going out. Her arms relaxed. Her uncomprehending eyes went up to the stars and down to the lights again. She gave a little sigh and her head drooped on Karen's shoulder.

"It did kill me," she said. "Jumping off the bridge. Only it's taken me a long time to die. This is just delirium before death. No wonder, with a stub of a tamarisk through my shoulder." And her eyes closed and she went limp.

Lea lay in the silvery darkness behind her closed eyes and savored the anonymous unfeeling between sleep and waking. Quietness sang through her, a humming stillness. She felt as anonymous as a transparent seaweed floating motionless between two layers of clear water. She breathed slowly, not wanting to disturb the mirror-stillness, the transparent peace. If you breathe quickly you think, and if you think— She stirred, her eyelids fluttering, trying to stay closed, but awareness and the growing light pried them open. She lay thin and flat on the bed, trying to be another white sheet between two muslin ones. But white sheets don't hear morning birds or smell breakfasts. She turned on her side and waited for the aching burden of life to fill her, to weigh her down, to beset her with its burning futility.

"Good morning." Karen was perched on the window sill,

reaching out with one cupped hand. "Do you know how to get a bird to notice you, short of being a crumb? I wonder if they do notice anything except food and eggs. Do they ever take a deep breath for the sheer joy of breathing?" She dusted the crumbs from her hands out the window.

"I don't know much about birds." Lea's voice was thick and rusty. "Nor about joy either, I guess." She tensed, waiting for the heavy horror to descend.

"Relax," Karen said, turning from the window. "I've Stilled you."

"You mean I'm—I'm healed?" Lea asked, trying to sort out last night's memories.

"Oh, my, no! I've just switched you off onto a temporary siding. Healing is a slow thing. You have to do it yourself, you know. I can hold the spoon to your lips but you'll have to do the swallowing."

"What's in the spoon?" Lea asked idly, swimming still in the unbeset peace.

"What have you to be cured of?"

"Of life." Lea turned her face away. "Just cure me of living."

"*That* line again. We could bat words back and forth all day and arrive at nowhere—besides I haven't the time. I must leave now." Karen's face lighted and she spun around lightly. "Oh, Lea! Oh, Lea!" Then, hastily: "There's breakfast in the other room. I'm shutting you in. I'll be back later and then— well, by then I'll have figured out something. God bless!" She whisked through the door but Lea heard no lock click.

Lea wandered into the other room, a restlessness replacing the usual sick inertia. She crumbled a piece of bacon between her fingers and poured a cup of coffee. She left them both un- tasted and wandered back into the bedroom. She fingered the strange nightgown she was wearing and then, in a sudden breathless skirl of action, stripped it off and scrambled into her own clothes.

She yanked the doorknob. It wouldn't turn. She hammered softly with her fists on the unyielding door. She hurried to the open window and sitting on the sill started to swing her legs across it. Her feet thumped into an invisible something. Startled she thrust out a hand and stubbed her fingers. She pressed both hands slowly outward and stared at them as they splayed against a something that stopped them.

She went back to the bed and stared at it. She made it up, quickly, meticulously, mitering the corners of the sheets precisely and plumping the pillow. She melted down to the edge of the bed and stared at her tightly clasped hands. Then she slid slowly down, turning and catching herself on her knees. She buried her face in her hands and whispered into the arid grief that burned her eyes, "Oh, God! Oh, God! Are You really there?"

For a long time she knelt there, feeling pressed against the barrier that confined her, the barrier that, probably because of Karen, was now an inert impersonal thing instead of the malicious agony-laden frustrating, deliberately evil creature it had been for so long.

Then suddenly, incongruously, she heard Karen's voice. "You haven't eaten." Her startled head lifted. No one was in the room with her. "You haven't eaten," she heard the voice again, Karen's matter-of-fact tone. "You haven't eaten."

She pulled herself up slowly from her knees, feeling the smart of returning circulation. Stiffly she limped to the other room. The coffee steamed gently at her although she had poured it out a lifetime ago. The bacon and eggs were still warm and uncongealed. She broke the warm crisp toast and began to eat.

"I'll figure it all out sometime soon," she murmured to her plate. "And then I'll probably scream for a while."

Karen came back early in the afternoon, bursting through the door that swung open before she reached it.

"Oh, Lea!" she cried, seizing her and whirling her in a mad dance. "You'd never guess—not in a million years! Oh, Lea! Oh, Lea!" She dumped the two of them onto the bed and laughed delightedly. Lea pulled away from her.

"Guess what?" Her voice sounded as dry and strained as her tearless eyes.

Karen sat up quickly. "Oh, Lea! I'm so sorry. In all the mad excitement I forgot.

"Listen, Jemmy says you're to come to the Gathering tonight. I can't tell you—I mean, you wouldn't be able to understand without a lengthy explanation, and even then—" She

16

looked into Lea's haunted eyes. "It's bad, isn't it?" she asked softly. "Even Stilled, it comes through like a blunt knife hacking, doesn't it? Can't you cry, Lea? Not even a tear?"

"Tears—" Lea's hands were restless. " 'Nor all your tears wash out a word of it.' " She pressed her hands to the tight constriction in her chest. Her throat ached intolerably. "How can I bear it?" she whispered. "When you let it come back again how can I even bear it?"

"You don't have to bear it alone. You need never have borne it alone. And I won't release you until you have enough strength.

"Anyway—" Karen stood up briskly, "food again—then a nap. I'll give sleep to you. Then the Gathering. *There* will be your new beginning."

Lea shrank back into her corner, watching with dread as the Gathering grew. Laughter and cries and overtones and undercurrents swirled around the room.

"They won't bite!" Karen whispered. "They won't even notice you, if you don't want them to. Yes," she answered Lea's unasked question. "You must stay—like it or not, whether you can see any use in it or not. I'm not quite sure myself why Jemmy called this Gathering, but how appropriate can you get —having us meet in the schoolhouse? Believe it or not, this is the where that I got my education—and this is where— Well, teachers have been our undoing—or doing according to your viewpoint. You know, adults can fairly well keep themselves to themselves and not let anyone else in on their closely guarded secrets—but the kids—" She laughed. "Poor cherubs —or maybe they're wiser. They pour out the most personal things quite unsolicited to almost any adult who will listen— and who's more apt to listen than a teacher? Ask one sometime how much she learns of a child's background and everyday family activities from just what is let drop quite unconsciously. Kids are the key to any community—which fact has never been more true than among us. That's why teachers have been so involved in the affairs of the People. Remind me sometime when we have a minute to tell you about—well, Melodye, for instance. But now—"

17

The room suddenly arranged itself decorously and stilled itself expectantly and waited attentively.

Jemmy half sat on one corner of the teacher's desk in front of the Group, a piece of paper clutched in one hand. All heads bowed. "We are met together in Thy Name," Jemmy said. A settling rustle filled the room and subsided. "Out of consideration for some of us the proceedings here will be vocal. I know some of the Group have wondered that we included all of you in the summons. The reasons are twofold. One, to share this joy with us—" A soft musical trill of delight curled around the room, followed by faint laughter. "Francher!" Jemmy said. "The other is because of the project we want to begin tonight.

"In the last few days it has become increasingly evident that we all have a most important decision to make. Whatever we decide there will be good-bys to say. There will be partings to endure. There will be changes."

Sorrow was tangible in the room, and a soft minor scale mourned over each note as it moved up and down, just short of tears. "The Old Ones have decided it would be wise to record our history to this point. That's why all of you are here. Each one of you holds an important part of our story within you. Each of you has influenced indelibly the course of events for our Groups. We want your stories. Not reinterpretations in the light of what you now know, but the original premise, the original groping, the original reaching—" There was a murmur through the room. "Yes," Jemmy answered. "Live it over, exactly the same—aching and all.

"Now," he smoothed out his piece of paper, "chronologically —Oh, first, where's Davey's recording gadget?"

"Gadget?" someone called. "What's wrong with our own memories?"

"Nothing," Jemmy said, "but we want this record independent of any of us, to go with whoever goes and stay with whoever stays. We share the general memories, of course, but all the little details—well, anyway. Davey's gadget." It had arrived on the table unobtrusively, small and undistinguished. "Now chronologically—Karen, you're first—"

"Who, me?" Karen straightened up, surprised. "Well, yes," she answered herself, settling back, "I guess I am."

"Come to the desk," Jemmy said. "Be comfortable."

18

Karen squeezed Lea's hand and whispered, "Make way for wonder!" and, after threading her way through the rows of desks, sat behind the table.

"I think I'll theme this beginning," she said. "We've remarked on the resemblance before, you know.

" 'And the Ark rested . . . upon the mountains of Ararat.' Ararat's more poetical than Baldy, anyway!

"And now," she smiled, "to establish Then again. Your help, please?"

Lea watched Karen, fascinated against her will. She saw her face alter and become younger. She saw her hair change its part and lengthen. She felt years peel back from Karen like thin tissue and she leaned forward, listening as Karen's voice, higher and younger, began. . . .

ARARAT

WE'VE HAD trouble with teachers in Cougar Canyon. It's just an accommodation school anyway, isolated and so unhandy to anything. There's really nothing to hold a teacher. But the way the People bring forth their young, in quantities and with regularity, even our small Group can usually muster the nine necessary for the county superintendent to arrange for the schooling for the year.

Of course I'm past school age, Canyon school age, and have been for years, but if the tally came up one short in the fall I'd go back for a postgraduate course again. But now I'm working on a college level because Father finished me off for my high-school diploma two summers ago. He's promised me that if I do well this year I'll get to go Outside next year and get my training and degree so I can be the teacher and we won't have to go Outside for one any more. Most of the kids would just as soon skip school as not, but the Old Ones don't hold with ignorance and the Old Ones have the last say around here.

Father is the head of the school board. That's how I get in on lots of school things the other kids don't. This summer when he wrote to the county seat that we'd have more than our nine again this fall and would they find a teacher for us, he got back a letter saying they had exhausted their supply of teachers who hadn't heard of Cougar Canyon and we'd have to dig up our own teacher this year. That "dig up" sounded like a dirty crack to me since we have the graves of four past teachers in the far corner of our cemetery. They sent us such old teachers, the homeless, the tottering, who were trying to piece out the end of their lives with a year here and a year there in jobs no one else wanted because there's no adequate pension system in the state and most teachers seem to die in harness. And their oldness and their tottering were not sufficient in the Canyon where there are apt to be shocks for Outsiders—unintentional as most of them are.

We haven't done so badly the last few years, though. The Old Ones say we're getting adjusted, though some of the non-conformists say that the Crossing thinned our blood. It might be either or both or the teachers are just getting tougher. The last two managed to last until just before the year ended. Father took them in as far as Kerry Canyon and ambulances took them on in. But they were all right after a while in the sanatorium and they're doing okay now. Before them, though, we usually had four teachers a year.

Anyway Father wrote to a teachers' agency on the coast, and after several letters each way he finally found a teacher.

He told us about it at the supper table.

"She's rather young," he said, reaching for a toothpick and tipping his chair back on its hind legs.

Mother gave Jethro another helping of pie and picked up her own fork again. "Youth is no crime," she said, "and it'll be a pleasant change for the children."

"Yes, though it seems a shame." Father prodded at a back tooth and Mother frowned at him. I wasn't sure if it was for picking his teeth or for what he said. I knew he meant it seemed a shame to get a place like Cougar Canyon so early in a career. It isn't that we're mean or cruel, you understand. It's only that they're Outsiders and we sometimes forget—especially the kids.

"She doesn't *have* to come," Mother said. "She could say no."

"Well, now—" Father tipped his chair forward. "Jethro,

20

no more pie. You go on out and help Kiah bring in the wood. Karen, you and Lizbeth get started on the dishes. Hop to it, kids."

And we hopped, too. Kids do to fathers in the Canyon, though I understand they don't always Outside. It annoyed me because I knew Father wanted us out of the way so he could talk adult talk to Mother, so I told Lizbeth I'd clear the table and then worked as slowly as I could, and as quietly, listening hard.

"She couldn't get any other job," Father said. "The agency told me they had placed her twice in the last two years and she didn't finish the year either place."

"Well," Mother said, pinching in her mouth and frowning. "If she's that bad why on earth did you hire her for the Canyon?"

"We have a choice?" Father laughed. Then he sobered. "No, it wasn't for incompetency. She was a good teacher. The way she tells it they just fired her out of a clear sky. She asked for recommendations and one place wrote, 'Miss Carmody is a very competent teacher but we dare not recommend her for a teaching position.' "

" 'Dare not'?" Mother asked.

" 'Dare not,' " Father said. "The agency assured me that they had investigated thoroughly and couldn't find any valid reasons for the dismissals, but she can't seem to find another job anywhere on the coast. She wrote me that she wanted to try another state."

"Do you suppose she's disfigured or deformed?" Mother suggested.

"Not from the neck up!" Father laughed. He took an envelope from his pocket. "Here's her application picture."

By this time I'd got the table cleared and I leaned over Father's shoulder.

"Gee!" I said. Father looked back at me, raising one eyebrow. I knew then that he had known all along that I was listening.

I flushed but stood my ground, knowing I was being granted admission to adult affairs, if only by the back door.

The girl in the picture was lovely. She couldn't have been many years older than I and she was twice as pretty.

21

She had short dark hair curled all over her head and apparently that poreless creamy skin which seems to have an inner light of its own. She had a tentative look about her as though her dark eyebrows were horizontal question marks. There was a droop to the corners of her mouth—not much, just enough to make you wonder why, and want to comfort her.

"She'll stir the Canyon for sure," Father said.

"I don't know." Mother frowned thoughtfully. "What will the Old Ones say to a marriageable Outsider in the Canyon?"

"*Adonday Veeah!*" Father muttered. "That never occurred to me. None of our other teachers was ever of an age to worry about."

"What *would* happen?" I asked. "I mean if one of the Group married an Outsider?"

"Impossible," Father said, so like the Old Ones that I could see why his name was approved in Meeting last spring.

"Why, there's even our Jemmy," Mother worried. "Already he's saying he'll have to start trying to find another Group. None of the girls here pleases him. Supposing this Outsider—how old is she?"

Father unfolded the application. "Twenty-three. Just three years out of college."

"Jemmy's twenty-four." Mother pinched her mouth together. "Father, I'm afraid you'll have to cancel the contract. If anything happened—well, you waited overlong to become an Old One to my way of thinking and it'd be a shame to have something go wrong your first year."

"I can't cancel the contract. She's on her way here. School starts next Monday." Father ruffled his hair forward as he does when he's disturbed. "We're probably making a something of a nothing," he said hopefully.

"Well, I only hope we don't have any trouble with this Outsider."

"Or she with us," Father grinned. "Where are my cigarettes?"

"On the bookcase," Mother said, getting up and folding the tablecloth together to hold the crumbs.

Father snapped his fingers and the cigarettes drifted in from the front room.

Mother went on out to the kitchen. The tablecloth shook itself over the wastebasket and then followed her.

Father drove to Kerry Canyon Sunday night to pick up our new teacher. She was supposed to have arrived Saturday afternoon but she didn't make bus connections at the county seat. The road ends at Kerry Canyon. I mean for Outsiders. There's not much of the look of a well-traveled road very far out our way from Kerry Canyon, which is just as well. Tourists leave us alone. Of course *we* don't have much trouble getting our cars to and fro, but that's why everything dead-ends at Kerry Canyon and we have to do all our own fetching and carrying—I mean the road being in the condition it is.

All the kids at our house wanted to stay up to see the new teacher, so Mother let them, but by seven thirty the youngest ones began to drop off and by nine there was only Jethro and Kiah, Lizbeth and Jemmy and me. Father should have been home long before and Mother was restless and uneasy. But at nine fifteen we heard the car coughing and sneezing up the draw. Mother's wide relieved smile was reflected on all our faces.

"Of course!" she cried. "I forgot. He has an Outsider in the car. He had to use the *road* and it's terrible across Jackass Flat."

I felt Miss Carmody before she came in the door. Already I was tingling all over from anticipation, but suddenly I felt her, so plainly that I knew with a feeling of fear and pride that I was of my grandmother, that soon I would be bearing the burden and blessing of her Gift—the Gift that develops into free access to any mind, one of the People or an Outsider, willing or not. And besides the access, the ability to counsel and help, to straighten tangled minds and snarled emotions.

And then Miss Carmody stood in the doorway, blinking a little against the light, muffled to the chin against the brisk fall air. A bright scarf hid her hair, but her skin *was* that luminous matte-cream it had looked. She was smiling a little but scared, too. I shut my eyes and—I went in, just like that. It was the first time I had ever sorted anybody. She was all fluttery with tiredness and strangeness, and there was a

23

question deep inside her that had the wornness of repetition, but I couldn't catch what it was. And under the uncertainty there was a sweetness and dearness and such a bewildered sorrow that I felt my eyes dampen. Then I looked at her again (sorting takes such a little time) as Father introduced her. I heard a gasp beside me and suddenly I went into Jemmy's mind with a stunning rush.

Jemmy and I have been close all our lives and we don't always need words to talk with each other, but this was the first time I had ever gone in like this and I knew he didn't know what had happened. I felt embarrassed and ashamed to know his emotion so starkly. I closed him out as quickly as possible, but not before I knew that now Jemmy would never hunt for another Group; Old Ones or no Old Ones, he had found his love.

All this took less time than it takes to say how-do-you-do and shake hands. Mother descended with cries and drew Miss Carmody and Father out to the kitchen for coffee, and Jemmy swatted Jethro and made him carry the luggage instead of snapping it to Miss Carmody's room. After all we didn't want to lose our teacher before she even saw the schoolhouse.

I waited until everyone was bedded down. Miss Carmody in her cold cold bed, the rest of us of course with our sheets set for warmth—how I pity Outsiders! Then I went to Mother.

She met me in the dark hall and we clung together as she comforted me.

"Oh, Mother," I whispered, "I sorted Miss Carmody tonight. I'm afraid."

Mother held me tight again. "I wondered. It's a great responsibility. You have to be so wise and clear-thinking. Your grandmother carried the Gift with graciousness and honor. You are of her. You can do it."

"But, Mother! To be an Old One!"

Mother laughed. "You have years of training ahead of you before you'll be an Old One. Councilor to the soul is a weighty job."

"Do I have to tell?" I pleaded. "I don't want anyone to know yet. I don't want to be set apart."

"I'll tell the Oldest. No one else need know." She hugged me again and I went back, comforted, to bed.

I lay in the darkness and let my mind clear, not even knowing how I knew how to. Like the gentle reachings of quiet fingers I felt the family about me. I felt warm and comfortable as though I were cupped in the hollow palm of a loving hand. Someday I would belong to the Group as I now belonged to the family. Belong to others? With an odd feeling of panic I shut the family out. I wanted to be alone—to belong just to me and no one else. I didn't *want* the Gift.

I slept after a while.

Miss Carmody left for the schoolhouse an hour before we did. She wanted to get things started a little before schooltime, her late arrival making it kind of rough on her. Kiah, Jethro, Lizbeth and I walked down the lane to the Armisters' to pick up their three kids. The sky was so blue you could taste it, a winy fallish taste of harvest fields and falling leaves. We were all feeling full of bubbly enthusiasm for the beginning of school. We were lighthearted and light-footed, too, as we kicked along through the cottonwood leaves paving the lane with gold. In fact Jethro felt too light-footed, and the third time I hauled him down and made him walk on the ground I cuffed him good. He was still sniffling when we got to Armisters'.

"She's pretty!" Lizbeth called before the kids got out to the gate, all agog and eager for news of the new teacher.

"She's young," Kiah added, elbowing himself ahead of Lizbeth.

"She's littler'n me," Jethro sniffed, and we all laughed because he's five six already even if he isn't twelve yet.

Debra and Rachel Armister linked arms with Lizbeth and scuffled down the lane, heads together, absorbing the details of teacher's hair, dress, nail polish, luggage and night clothes, though goodness knows how Lizbeth found out about all that.

Jethro and Kiah annexed Jeddy and they climbed up on the rail fence that parallels the lane, and walked the top rail. Jethro took a tentative step or two above the rail, caught my eye and stepped back in a hurry. He knows as well as any child in the Canyon that a kid his age has no business lifting along a public road.

We detoured at the Mesa Road to pick up the Kroginold boys. More than once Father has sighed over the Kroginolds.

You see, when the Crossing was made the People got separated in that last wild moment when air was screaming past and the heat was building up so alarmingly. The members of our Group left their ship just seconds before it crashed so devastatingly into the box canyon behind Old Baldy and literally splashed and drove itself into the canyon walls, starting a fire that stripped the hills bare for miles. After the People gathered themselves together from the life slips, and founded Cougar Canyon they discovered that the alloy the ship was made of was a metal much wanted here. Our Group has lived on mining the box canyon ever since, though there's something complicated about marketing the stuff. It has to be shipped out of the country and shipped in again because everyone knows that it isn't found in this region.

Anyway our Group at Cougar Canyon is probably the largest of the People, but we are reasonably sure that at least one Group and maybe two survived along with us. Grandmother in her time sensed two Groups but could never locate them exactly, and, since our object is to go unnoticed in this new life, no real effort has ever been made to find them. Father can remember just a little of the Crossing, but some of the Old Ones are blind and crippled from the heat and the terrible effort they put forth to save the others from burning up like falling stars.

But getting back, Father often mourned that of all the People who could have made up our Group we had to get the Kroginolds. They're rebels and were even before the Crossing. It's their kids who have been so rough on our teachers. The rest of us usually behave fairly decently and remember that we have to be careful around Outsiders.

Derek and Jake Kroginold were wrestling in a pile of leaves by the front gate when we got there. They didn't even hear us coming, so I leaned over and whacked the nearest rear end, and they turned in a flurry of leaves and grinned up at me for all the world like pictures of Pan in the mythology book at home.

26

"What kinda old bat we got this time?" Derek asked as he scrabbled in the leaves for his lunch box.

"She's not an old bat," I retorted, madder than need be because Derek annoys me so. "She's young and beautiful."

"Yeah, I'll bet!" Jake emptied the leaves from his cap onto the trio of squealing girls.

"She is so!" Kiah retorted. "The nicest teacher we ever had."

"She won't teach me nothing!" Derek yelled, lifting to the top of the cottonwood tree at the turnoff.

"Well, if she won't I will," I muttered, and reaching for a handful of sun I platted the twishers so quickly that Derek fell like a rock. He yelled like a catamount, thinking he'd get killed for sure, but I stopped him about a foot from the ground and then let go. Well, the stopping and the thump to the ground pretty well jarred the wind out of him, but he yelled:

"I'll tell the Old Ones! You ain't supposed to platt twishers!"

"Tell the Old Ones," I snapped, kicking on down the leafy road. "I'll be there and tell them why. And then, old smarty pants, what will be your excuse for lifting?"

And then I was ashamed. I was showing off as bad as a Kroginold, but they make me so mad!

Our last stop before school was at the Clarinades'. My heart always squeezed when I thought of the Clarinade twins. They just started school this year, two years behind the average Canyon kid. Mrs. Kroginold used to say that the two of them, Susie and Jerry, divided one brain between them before they were born. That's unkind and untrue—thoroughly a Kroginold remark—but it is true that by Canyon standards the twins were retarded. They lacked so many of the attributes of the People. Father said it might be a delayed effect of the Crossing that they would grow out of, or it might be advance notice of what our children will be like here—what is ahead for the People. It makes me shiver, wondering.

Susie and Jerry were waiting, clinging to each other's hands as they always were. They were shy and withdrawn, but both were radiant because of starting school. Jerry, who did almost all the talking for the two of them, answered our greetings with a shy hello.

27

Then Susie surprised us all by exclaiming, "We're going to school!"

"Isn't it wonderful?" I replied, gathering her cold little hand into mine. "And you're going to have the prettiest teacher we ever had."

But Susie had retired into blushing confusion and didn't say another word all the way to school.

I was worried about Jake and Derek. They were walking apart from us, whispering, looking over at us and laughing. They were cooking up some kind of mischief for Miss Carmody. And more than anything I wanted her to stay. I found right then that there *would* be years ahead of me before I became an Old One. I tried to go into Derek and Jake to find out what was cooking, but try as I might I couldn't get past the sibilance of their snickers and the hard flat brightness of their eyes.

We were turning off the road into the school yard when Jemmy, who should have been up at the mine long since, suddenly stepped out of the bushes in front of us, his hands behind him. He glared at Jake and Derek and then at the rest of the children.

"You kids mind your manners when you get to school," he snapped, scowling. "And you Kroginolds—just try anything funny and I'll lift you to Old Baldy and platt the twishers on you. This is one teacher we're going to keep."

Susie and Jerry clung together in speechless terror. The Kroginolds turned red and pushed out belligerent jaws. The rest of us just stared at a Jemmy, who never raised his voice and never pushed his weight around.

"I mean it, Jake and Derek. You try getting out of line and the Old Ones will find a few answers they've been looking for—especially about the bell in Kerry Canyon."

The Kroginolds exchanged looks of dismay and the girls sucked in breaths of astonishment. One of the most rigorously enforced rules of the Group concerns showing off outside the community. If Derek and Jake *had* been involved in ringing that bell all night last Fourth of July—*well!*

"Now you kids, scoot!" Jemmy jerked his head toward the schoolhouse, and the terrified twins scudded down the leaf-strewn path like a pair of bright leaves themselves, followed by the rest of the children, with the Kroginolds look-ing sullenly back over their shoulders and muttering.

Jemmy ducked his head and scowled. "It's time they got civilized anyway. There's no sense to our losing teachers all the time."

"No," I said noncommittally.

"There's no point in scaring her to death." Jemmy was intent on the leaves he was kicking with one foot.

"No," I agreed, suppressing my smile.

Then Jemmy smiled ruefully in amusement at himself. "I should waste words with you? Here." He took his hands from behind him and thrust a bouquet of burning-bright autumn leaves into my arms. "They're from you to her. Something pretty for the first day."

"Oh, Jemmy!" I cried through the scarlet and crimson and gold. "They're beautiful. You've been up on Baldy this morning."

"That's right. But she won't know where they came from." And he was gone.

I hurried to catch up with the children before they got to the door. Suddenly overcome with shyness, they were milling around the porch steps, each trying to hide behind the others.

"Oh, for goodness' sakes!" I whispered to our kids. "You ate breakfast with her this morning. She won't bite. Go on in."

But I found myself shouldered to the front and leading the subdued group into the schoolroom. While I was giving the bouquet of leaves to Miss Carmody the others with the ease of established habit slid into their usual seats, leaving only the twins, stricken and white, standing alone.

Miss Carmody, dropping the leaves on her desk, knelt quickly beside them, pried a hand of each gently free from their frenzied clutching and held them in hers.

"I'm so glad you came to school," she said in her warm rich voice. "I need a first grade to make the school work out right and I have a seat that must have been built on purpose for twins."

And she led them over to the side of the room, close enough to the old potbellied stove for Outside comfort later

29

and near enough to the window to see out. There, in dusted glory, stood one of the old double desks that the Group must have inherited from some ghost town out in the hills. There were two wooden boxes for footstools for small dangling feet and, spouting like a flame from the old inkwell hole, a spray of vivid red leaves—matchmates to those Jemmy had given me.

The twins slid into the desk, never loosening hands, and stared up at Miss Carmody, wide-eyed. She smiled back at them and, leaning forward, poked her fingertip into the deep dimple in each round chin.

"Buried smiles," she said, and the two scared faces lighted up briefly with wavery smiles. Then Miss Carmody turned to the rest of us.

I never did hear her introductory words. I was too busy mulling over the spray of leaves and how she came to know the identical routine, words and all, that the twins' mother used to make them smile, and how on earth she knew about the old desks in the shed. But by the time we rose to salute the flag and sing our morning song I had it figured out. Father must have briefed her on the way home last night. The twins were an ever-present concern of the whole Group, and we were all especially anxious to have their first year a successful one. Also, Father knew the smile routine and where the old desks were stored. As for the spray of leaves, well, some did grow this low on the mountain and frost is tricky at leaf-turning time.

So school was launched and went along smoothly. Miss Carmody was a good teacher and even the Kroginolds found their studies interesting.

They hadn't tried any tricks since Jemmy had threatened them. That is, except that silly deal with the chalk. Miss Carmody was explaining something on the board and was groping sideways for the chalk to add to the lesson. Jake deliberately lifted the chalk every time she almost had it. I was just ready to do something about it when Miss Carmody snapped her fingers with annoyance and grasped the chalk firmly. Jake caught my eye about then and shrank about six inches in girth and height. I didn't tell Jemmy, but Jake's fear that I might kept him straight for a long time.

The twins were really blossoming. They laughed and played with the rest of the kids, and Jerry even went off occasionally with the other boys at noontime, coming back as disheveled and wet as the others after a dam-building session in the creek.

Miss Carmody fitted so well into the community and was so well liked by us kids that it began to look like we'd finally keep a teacher all year. Already she had withstood some of the shocks that had sent our other teachers screaming. For instance . . .

The first time Susie got a robin-redbreast sticker on her bookmark for reading a whole page—six lines—perfectly, she lifted all the way back to her seat, literally walking about four inches in the air. I held my breath until she sat down and was caressing the glossy sticker with one finger, then I sneaked a cautious look at Miss Carmody. She was sitting very erect, her hands clutching both ends of her desk as though in the act of rising, a look of incredulous surprise on her face. Then she relaxed, shook her head and smiled, and busied herself with some papers.

I let my breath out cautiously. The last teacher but two went into hysterics when one of the girls absentmindedly lifted back to her seat because her sore foot hurt. I had hoped Miss Carmody was tougher, and apparently she was.

That same week, one noon hour, Jethro came pelting up to the schoolhouse where Valancy—that's her first name and I call her by it when we are alone; after all she's only four years older than I—was helping me with that gruesome tests and measurements I was taking by extension from teachers' college.

"Hey, Karen!" he yelled through the window. "Can you come out a minute?"

"Why?" I yelled back, annoyed at the interruption just when I was trying to figure what was normal about a normal grade curve.

"There's need," Jethro yelled.

I put down my book. "I'm sorry, Valancy. I'll go see what's eating him."

"Should I come, too?" she asked. "If something's wrong—"

"It's probably just some silly thing," I said, edging out fast.

When one of the People says, "There's need," that means Group business.

"*Adonday Veeah!*" I muttered at Jethro as we rattled down the steep rocky path to the creek. "What are you trying to do? Get us all in trouble? What's the matter?"

"Look," Jethro said, and there were the boys standing around an alarmed but proud Jerry, and above their heads, poised in the air over a half-built rock dam, was a huge boulder.

"Who lifted that?" I gasped.

"I did," Jerry volunteered, blushing crimson.

I turned on Jethro. "Well, why didn't you platt the twishers on it? You didn't have to come running—"

"On *that?*" Jethro squeaked. "You know very well we're not allowed to *lift* anything that big, let alone platt it. Besides," shamefaced, "I can't remember that dern girl stuff."

"Oh, Jethro! You're so stupid sometimes!" I turned to Jerry. "How on earth did you ever lift anything that big?"

He squirmed. "I watched Daddy at the mine once."

"Does he let you lift at home?" I asked severely.

"I don't know." Jerry squashed mud with one shoe, hanging his head. "I never lifted anything before."

"Well, you know better. You kids aren't allowed to lift anything an Outsider your age can't handle alone. And not even that if you can't platt it afterward."

"I know it." Jerry was still torn between embarrassment and pride.

"Well, remember it." And taking a handful of sun I platted the twishers and set the boulder back on the hillside where it belonged.

Platting does come easier to the girls—sunshine platting, that is. Of course only the Old Ones do the sun-and-rain one, and only the very Oldest of them all would dare the moonlight-and-dark, which can move mountains. But that was still no excuse for Jethro to forget and run the risk of having Valancy see what she mustn't see.

It wasn't until I was almost back to the schoolhouse that it dawned on me. Jerry had lifted! Kids his age usually lift play stuff almost from the time they walk. That doesn't need platting because it's just a matter of a few inches and a few seconds, so gravity manages the return. But Jerry and Susie never had.

They were finally beginning to catch up. Maybe it *was* just the Crossing that slowed them down—and maybe only the Clarinades. In my delight I forgot and lifted to the school porch without benefit of the steps. But Valancy was putting up pictures on the high old-fashioned molding just below the ceiling, so no harm was done. She flushed from her efforts and asked me to bring the step stool so she could finish them. I brought it and steadied it for her—and then nearly let her fall as I stared. How had she hung those first four pictures before I got there?

The weather was unnaturally dry all fall. We didn't mind it much because rain with an Outsider around is awfully messy. We have to let ourselves get wet. But when November came and went and Christmas was almost upon us and there was practically no rain and no snow at all, we all began to get worried. The creek dropped to a trickle and then to scattered puddles and then went dry. Finally the Old Ones had to spend an evening at the Group reservoir doing something about our dwindling water supply. They wanted to get rid of Valancy for the evening, just in case, so Jemmy volunteered to take her to Kerry to the show. I was still awake when they got home long after midnight. Since I began to develop the Gift I have had long periods of restlessness when it seems I have no apartness but am of every person in the Group. The training I should start soon will help me shut out the others except when I want them. The only thing is that we don't know who is to train me. Since Grandmother died there has been no Sorter in our Group, and because of the Crossing we have no books or records to help.

Anyway I was awake and leaning on my window sill in the darkness. They stopped on the porch—Jemmy is bunking at the mine during his stint there. I didn't have to guess or use a Gift to read the pantomime before me. I closed my eyes and my mind as their shadows merged. Under their strong emotion I could have had free access to their minds, but I had been watching them all fall. I knew in a special way what passed between them, and I knew that Valancy often went to bed in tears and that Jemmy spent too many lonely hours on the crag that juts out over the canyon from high on Old Baldy, as though he were trying to make his heart as inaccessible to Outsiders as the crag is. I knew what he felt, but oddly enough I had never been able to sort Valancy since that first night. There was something very un-Outsiderish and also very un-Groupish about her mind and I couldn't figure what.

I heard the front door open and close and Valancy's light steps fading down the hall and then I felt Jemmy calling me outside. I put my coat on over my robe and shivered down the hall. He was waiting by the porch steps, his face still and unhappy in the faint moonlight.

"She won't have me," he said flatly.

"Oh, Jemmy! You asked her—"

"Yes. She said no."

"I'm so sorry." I huddled down on the top step to cover my cold ankles. "But, Jemmy—"

"Yes, I know!" he retorted savagely. "She's an Outsider. I have no business even to want her. Well, if she'd have me I wouldn't hesitate a minute. This purity-of-the-Group deal is—"

"Is fine and right," I said softly, "as long as it doesn't touch you personally? But think for a minute, Jemmy. Would you be able to live a life as an Outsider? Just think of the million and one restraints that you would have to impose on yourself —and for the rest of your life, too, or lose her after all. Maybe it's better to accept 'no' now than to try to build something and ruin it completely later. And if there should be children—" I paused. "*Could* there be children, Jemmy?"

I heard him draw a sharp breath.

"We don't know," I went on. "We haven't had the occasion to find out. Do you want Valancy to be part of the first experiment?"

Jemmy slapped his hat viciously down on his thigh, then he laughed.

"You have the Gift," he said, though I had never told him. "Have you any idea, sister mine, how little you will be liked when you become an Old One?"

"Grandmother was well liked," I answered placidly. Then I cried, "Don't *you* set me apart, darn you, Jemmy. Isn't it enough to know that among a different people *I* am different? Don't *you* desert me now!" I was almost in tears.

34

Jemmy dropped to the step beside me and thumped my shoulder in his old way. "Pull up your socks, Karen. We have to do what we have to do. I was just taking my mad out on you. What a world!" He sighed heavily.

I huddled deeper in my coat, cold of soul.

"But the other one is gone," I whispered. "The Home."

And we sat there sharing the poignant sorrow that is a constant undercurrent among the People, even those of us who never actually saw the Home. Father says it's because of a sort of racial memory.

"But she didn't say no because she doesn't love me," Jemmy went on at last. "She does love me. She told me so."

"Then why not?" As his sister I couldn't imagine anyone turning Jemmy down.

Jemmy laughed—a short unhappy laugh. "Because she is different."

"*She's* different?"

"That's what she said, as though it was pulled out of her. 'I can't marry,' she said. 'I'm different!' That's pretty good, isn't it, coming from an Outsider!"

"She doesn't know we're the People. She must feel that she is different from everyone. I wonder why?"

"I don't know. There's something about her, though. A kind of shield or wall that keeps us apart. I've never met anything like it in an Outsider or in one of the People either. Sometimes it's like meshing with one of us and then *bang!* I smash the daylights out of me against that stone wall."

"Yes, I know. I've felt it, too."

We listened to the silent past-midnight world and then Jemmy stood.

"Well, g'night, Karen. Be seeing you."

I stood up, too. "Good night, Jemmy." I watched him start off in the late moonlight. He turned at the gate, his face hidden in the shadows.

"But I'm not giving up," he said quietly. "Valancy is my love."

The next day was hushed and warm, unusually so for December in our hills. There was a kind of ominous stillness among the trees, and, threading thinly against the milky sky, the slender smokes of little brush fires pointed out the dryness of the whole country. If you looked closely you could see piling behind Old Baldy an odd bank of clouds, so nearly the color of the sky that it was hardly discernible, but puffy and summer-thunderheady.

All of us were restless in school, the kids reacting to the weather, Valancy pale and unhappy after last night. I was bruising my mind against the blank wall in hers, trying to find some way I could help her.

Finally the thousand and one little annoyances were climaxed by Jerry and Susie scuffling until Susie was pushed out of the desk onto an open box of wet water colors that Debra for heaven only knows what reason had left on the floor by her desk. Susie shrieked and Debra sputtered and Jerry started a high silly giggle of embarrassment and delight. Valancy, without looking, reached for something to rap for order with and knocked down the old cracked vase full of drooping wild-flowers and three-day-old water. The vase broke and flooded her desk with the foul-smelling deluge, ruining the monthly report she had almost ready to send in to the county school superintendent.

For a stricken moment there wasn't a sound in the room, then Valancy burst into half-hysterical laughter and the whole room rocked with her. We all rallied around doing what we could to clean up Susie's and Valancy's desks, and then Valancy declared a holiday and decided that it would be the perfect time to go up-canyon to the slopes of Baldy and gather what greenery we could find to decorate our schoolroom for the holidays.

We all take our lunches to school, so we gathered them up and took along a square tarp the boys had brought to help build the dam in the creek. Now that the creek was dry they couldn't use it, and it'd come in handy to sit on at lunchtime and would serve to carry our greenery home in, too, stretcher fashion.

Released from the schoolroom, we were all loud and jubilant and I nearly kinked my neck trying to keep all the kids in sight at once to nip in the bud any thoughtless lifting or other Group activity. The kids were all so wild, they might forget.

We went on up-canyon past the kids' dam and climbed the bare dry waterfalls that stair-step up to the mesa. On the mesa we spread the tarp and pooled our lunches to make it more picnicky. A sudden hush from across the tarp caught my attention. Debra, Rachel and Lizbeth were staring horrified at Susie's lunch. She was calmly dumping out a half dozen *koomatka* beside her sandwiches.

Koomatka are almost the only plants that lasted through the Crossing. I think four *koomatka* survived in someone's personal effects. They were planted and cared for as tenderly as babies, and now every household in the Group has a *koomatka* plant growing in some quiet spot out of casual sight. Their fruit is eaten not so much for nourishment as Earth knows nourishment but as a last remembrance of all other similar delights that died with the Home. We always save *koomatka* for special occasions. Susie must have sneaked some out when her mother wasn't looking. And there they were—across the table from an Outsider!

Before I could snap them to me or say anything Valancy turned, too, and caught sight of the softly glowing bluey-green pile. Her eyes widened and one hand went out. She started to say something and then she dropped her eyes quickly and drew her hand back. She clasped her hands tightly together, and the girls, eyes intent on her, scrambled the *koomatka* back into the sack and Lizbeth silently comforted Susie, who had just realized what she had done. She was on the verge of tears at having betrayed the people to an Outsider.

Just then Kiah and Derek rolled across the picnic table fighting over a cupcake. By the time we salvaged our lunch from under them and they had scraped the last of the chocolate frosting off their T-shirts, the *koomatka* incident seemed closed. And yet as we lay back resting a little to settle our stomachs, staring up at the smothery low-hanging clouds that had grown from the milky morning sky, I suddenly found myself trying to decide about Valancy's look when she had seen the fruit. Surely it couldn't have been recognition!

At the end of our brief siesta we carefully buried the remains of our lunch—the hill was much too dry to think of burning it—and started on again. After a while the slope got steeper and the stubborn tangle of manzanita tore at out clothes and scratched our legs and grabbed at the rolled-up tarp until we all looked longingly at the free air above it. If

37

Valancy hadn't been with us we could have lifted over the worst and saved all this trouble. But we blew and panted for a while and then struggled on.

After an hour or so we worked out onto a rocky knoll that leaned against the slope of Baldy and made a tiny island in the sea of manzanita. We all stretched out gratefully on the crumbling granite outcropping, listening to our heart beats slowing.

Then Jethro sat up and sniffed. Valancy and I alerted. A sudden puff of wind from the little side canyon brought the acrid pungency of burning brush to us. Jethro scrambled along the narrow ridge to the slope of Baldy and worked his way around out of sight into the canyon. He came scrambling back, half lifting, half running.

"Awful!" he panted. "It's awful! The whole canyon ahead is on fire and it's coming this way fast!"

Valancy gathered us together with a glance.

"Why didn't we see the smoke?" she asked tensely. "There wasn't any smoke when we left the schoolhouse."

"Can't see this slope from school," he said. "Fire could burn over a dozen slopes and we'd hardly see the smoke. This side of Baldy is a rim fencing in an awful mess of canyons."

"What'll we do?" Lizbeth quavered, hugging Susie to her.

Another gust of wind and smoke set us all to coughing, and through my streaming tears I saw a long lapping tongue of fire reach around the canyon wall.

Valancy and I looked at each other. I couldn't sort her mind, but mine was a panic, beating itself against the fire and then against the terrible tangle of manzanita all around us. Bruising against the possibility of lifting out of danger, then against the fact that none of the kids was capable of sustained progressive self-lifting for more than a minute or so, and how could we leave Valancy? I hid my face in my hands to shut out the acres and acres of tinder-dry manzanita that would blaze like a torch at the first touch of fire. If only it would rain! You can't *set* fire to wet manzanita, but after these long months of drought—!

I heard the younger children scream and looked up to see Valancy staring at me with an intensity that frightened me even as I saw fire standing bright and terrible behind her at the mouth of the canyon.

Jake, yelling hoarsely, broke from the group and lifted a yard or two over the manzanita before he tangled his feet and fell helpless into the ugly angled branches.

"Get under the tarp!" Valancy's voice was a whiplash. "All of you get under the tarp!"

"It won't do any good," Kiah bellowed. "It'll burn like paper!"

"Get—under—the—tarp!" Valancy's spaced icy words drove us to unfolding the tarp and spreading it to creep under. Hoping even at this awful moment that Valancy wouldn't see me, I lifted over to Jake and yanked him back to his feet. I couldn't lift with him, so I pushed and prodded and half carried him back through the heavy surge of black smoke to the tarp and shoved him under. Valancy was standing, back to the fire, so changed and alien that I shut my eyes against her and started to crawl in with the other kids.

And then she began to speak. The rolling terrible thunder of her voice shook my bones and I swallowed a scream. A surge of fear swept through our huddled group and shoved me back out from under the tarp.

Till I die I'll never forget Valancy standing there tense and taller than life against the rolling convulsive clouds of smoke, both her hands outstretched, fingers wide apart as the measured terror of her voice went on and on in words that plagued me because I should have known them and didn't. As I watched I felt an icy cold gather, a paralyzing unearthly cold that froze the tears on my tensely upturned face.

And then lightning leaped from finger to finger of her lifted hands. And lightning answered in the clouds above her. With a toss of her hands she threw the cold, the lightning, the sullen shifting smoke upward, and the roar of the racing fire was drowned in a hissing roar of down-drenching rain.

I knelt there in the deluge, looking for an eternal second into her drained despairing hopeless eyes before I caught her just in time to keep her head from banging on the granite as she pitched forward, inert.

Then as I sat there cradling her head in my lap, shaking with cold and fear, with the terrified wailing of the kids behind me, I heard Father shout and saw him and Jemmy and Darcy Clarinade in the old pickup, lifting over the steaming streaming manzanita, over the trackless mountainside through the rain to us. Father lowered the truck until one of the wheels brushed a branch and spun lazily; then the three of them lifted all of us up to the dear familiarity of that beat-up old jalopy.

Jemmy received Valancy's limp body into his arms and crouched in back, huddling her in his arms, for the moment hostile to the whole world that had brought his love to such a pass.

We kids clung to Father in an ecstasy of relief. He hugged us all tight to him; then he raised my face.

"Why did it rain?" he asked sternly, every inch an Old One while the cold downpour dripped off the ends of my hair and he stood dry inside his shield.

"I don't know," I sobbed, blinking my streaming eyes against his sternness. "Valancy did it—with lightning—it was cold— she talked—" Then I broke down completely, plumping down on the rough floor boards and, in spite of my age, howling right along with the other kids.

It was a silent solemn group that gathered in the schoolhouse that evening. I sat at my desk with my hands folded stiffly in front of me, half scared of my own People. This was the first official meeting of the Old Ones I'd ever attended. They all sat in desks, too, except the Oldest who sat in Valancy's chair. Valancy sat stony-faced in the twins' desk, but her nervous fingers shredded one Kleenex after another as she waited.

The Oldest rapped the side of the desk with his cane and turned his sightless eyes from one to another of us.

"We're all here," he said, "to inquire—"

"Oh, stop it!" Valancy jumped up from her seat. "Can't you fire me without all this rigmarole? I'm used to it. Just say go and I'll go!" She stood trembling.

"Sit down, Miss Carmody," said the Oldest. And Valancy sat down meekly.

"Where were you born?" the Oldest asked quietly.

"What does it matter?" Valancy flared. Then resignedly, "It's in my application. Vista Mar, California."

"And your parents?"

40

"I don't know."

There was a stir in the room.

"Why not?"

"Oh, this is so unnecessary!" Valancy cried. "But if you *have* to know, both my parents were foundlings. They were found wandering in the streets after a big explosion and fire in Vista Mar. An old couple who lost everything in the fire took them in. When they grew up, they married. I was born. They died. Can I go now?"

A murmur swept the room.

"Why did you leave your other jobs?" Father asked.

Before Valancy could answer the door was flung open and Jemmy stalked defiantly in.

"Go!" the Oldest said.

"Please," Jemmy said, deflating suddenly. "Let me stay. It concerns me, too."

The Oldest fingered his cane and then nodded. Jemmy half smiled with relief and sat down in a back seat.

"Go on," the Oldest One said to Valancy.

"All right then," Valancy said. "I lost my first job because I—well—I guess you'd call it levitated—to fix a broken blind in my room. It was stuck and I just—went up—in the air until I unstuck it. The principal saw me. He couldn't believe it and it scared him so he fired me." She paused expectantly.

The Old Ones looked at one another, and my silly confused mind began to add up columns that only my lack of common sense had kept from giving totals to long ago.

"And the other one?" The Oldest leaned his cheek on his doubled up hand as he bent forward.

Valancy was taken aback and she flushed in confusion.

"Well," she said hesitantly, "I called my books to me—I mean they were on my desk—"

"We know what you mean," the Oldest said.

"You know!" Valancy looked dazed.

The Oldest stood up.

"*Valancy Carmody, open your mind!*"

Valancy stared at him and then burst into tears.

"I can't, I can't," she sobbed. "It's been too long. I can't let anyone in. I'm different. I'm alone. Can't you understand? They all died. I'm alien!"

"You are alien no longer," the Oldest said. "You are home now, Valancy." He motioned to me. "Karen, go in to her."

So I did. At first the wall was still there; then with a soundless cry, half anguish and half joy, the wall went down and I was with Valancy. I saw all the secrets that had cankered in her since her parents died—the parents who were of the People.

They had been reared by the old couple who were not only of the People but had been the Oldest of the whole Crossing.

I tasted with her the hidden frightening things—the need for living as an Outsider, the terrible need for concealing all her differences and suppressing all the extra Gifts of the People, the ever-present fear of betraying herself and the awful lostness that came when she thought she was the last of the People.

And then suddenly *she* came in to *me* and my mind was flooded with a far greater presence than I had ever before experienced.

My eyes flew open and I saw all of the Old Ones staring at Valancy. Even the Oldest had his face turned to her, wonder written as widely on his scarred face as on the others.

He bowed his head and made the Sign. "The lost Persuasions and Designs," he murmured. "She has them all."

And then I knew that Valancy, Valancy who had wrapped herself so tightly against the world to which any thoughtless act might betray her that she had lived with us all this time without our knowing about her or her knowing about us, was one of us. Not only one of us but such a one as had not been since Grandmother died, and even beyond that. My incoherent thoughts cleared to one.

Now I would have someone to train me. Now I could become a Sorter, but only second to her.

I turned to share my wonder with Jemmy. He was looking at Valancy as the People must have looked at the Home in the last hour. Then he turned to the door.

Before I could draw a breath Valancy was gone from me and from the Old Ones and Jemmy was turning to her outstretched hands.

Then I bolted for the outdoors and rushed like one possessed down the lane, lifting and running until I staggered up our porch steps and collapsed against Mother, who had heard me coming.

"Oh, Mother! She's one of us! She's Jemmy's love! She's wonderful!" And I burst into noisy sobs in the warm comfort of Mother's arms.

So now I don't have to go Outside to become a teacher. We have a permanent one. But I'm going anyway. I want to be as much like Valancy as I can and she has her degree. Besides I can use the discipline of living Outside for a year.

I have so much to learn and so much training to go through, but Valancy will always be there with me. I won't be set apart alone because of the Gift.

Maybe I shouldn't mention it, but one reason I want to hurry my training is that we're going to try to locate the other People. None of the boys here please me.

II

It was as though silver curtains were shimmering back across some magic picture, warm with remembered delight. Lea took a deep breath and, with a realization as sudden as the bursting of a bubble, became aware that she had completely forgotten herself and her troubles for the first time in months and months. And it felt good—oh, so good—so smooth, so smilingly relaxing. "If only," she thought wistfully. "*If only!*" And then shivered under the bare echoless *thunk* as things-as-they-are thudded against the blessed shelter Karen had loaned her. Her hands tightened bitterly.

Someone laughed softly into the silence. "Have you found him yet, Karen? You started looking long enough ago—"

"Not so long," Karen smiled, still entangled in the memories she had relived. "And I *have* got my degree now. Oh, I had forgotten so much—the wonder—the terror—" She dreamed a moment longer, then shook her head and laughed.

"There, Jemmy, I seen my duty and I done it. Whose hot little hands hold the next installment?"

Jemmy smoothed out his crumpled paper. "Well, Peter's next, I guess. Unless Bethie wants to—"

"Oh no, oh no!" Bethie's soft voice protested. "Peter, Peter can do it better—he was the one—I mean—Peter!"

Everyone laughed. "Okay, Bethie, okay!" Jemmy said. "Cool down. Peter it will be. Well, Peter, you have until tomorrow evening to get organized. I think after the excitement of the day, one—well—installment will be enough."

The crowd stood up and swirled and moved. The soft murmur of their voices and laughter washed over Lea like a warm ocean.

44

"Lea." It was Karen. "Here's Jemmy and Valancy. They want to meet you."

Lea struggled to her feet, feeling impaled by their interested eyes. She felt welcome enwrapping her—a welcome far beyond any words. She felt a pang catch painfully somewhere in her chest, and to her bewilderment tears began to wash down her cheeks. She turned her head aside and groped for a handkerchief. Someone tucked a huge white one into her hands and someone's shoulder was strong and steady for a moment and someone's arms were deft and sure as they lifted her and bore her, blind with sobless weeping, away from the schoolhouse.

Later—oh, much later—she suddenly sat up in her bed. Karen was there instantly, noiselessly.

"Karen, was that supposed to be real?"

"Was what supposed to be real?"

"That story you told. It wasn't true, was it?"

"But of course. Every word of it."

"But it can't be!" Lea cried. "People from space! Magic people! It can't be true."

"Why don't you want it to be true?"

"Because—because! It doesn't fit. There's nothing outside of what is—I mean, you go around the world and come back to where you started from. Everything ends back where it started from. There are boundaries beyond which—" Lea groped for words. "Anything outside the bounds isn't true!"

"Who defines the boundaries?"

"Why, they're just there. You get trapped in them when you're born. You have to bear them till you die."

"Who sold *you* into slavery?" Karen asked wonderingly. "Or did you volunteer? I agree with you that everything comes back to where it started, but where did everything start?"

"No!" Lea shrieked, clenching her fists over her eyes and writhing back on her pillow. "Not back to that muck and chaos and mindless seething!"

The blackness rolled and flared and roared its insidious whimper—the crowded emptiness, the incinerating cold—the impossibility of all possibilities. . . .

"Lea, Lea." Karen's voice cut softly but authoritatively through the tangled horror. "Lea, sleep now. Sleep now, knowing that everything started with the Presence and all things can return joyfully to their beginning."

Lea ate breakfast with Karen the next morning. The wind was blowing the short ruffled curtains in and out of the room.

"No screens?" Lea asked, carrying the armed truce with darkness as carefully as a cup of water, not to brim it over.

"No, no screens," Karen said. "We keep the bugs out another way."

"A way that works for keeping bugs in, too," Lea smiled. "I tried to leave yesterday."

"I know." Karen held a slice of bread in her hand and watched it brown slowly and fragrantly. "That's why I blocked the windows a little more than usual. They aren't that way today."

"You trust me?" Lea asked, feeling the secret slop of terror in the balanced cup.

"This isn't jail! Yesterday you were still clinging to the skirts of death. Today you can smile. Yesterday I put the lye up on the top shelf. Today you can read the label for yourself."

"Maybe I'm illiterate," Lea said somberly. Then she pushed her cup back. "I'd like to go outside today, if it's okay. It's been a long time since I looked at the world."

"Don't go too far. Most of the going around here is climbing—or lifting. We haven't many Outside-type trails. Only don't go beyond the schoolhouse. Right now we'd rather you didn't—the flat beyond—" She smiled softly. "Anyway there's lots of other places to go."

"Maybe I'll see some of the children," Lea said. "Davy or Lizbeth or Kiah."

Karen laughed. "It isn't very likely—not under the circumstances, and 'the children' would be vastly insulted if they heard you. They've grown up—at least they think they have. My story was years ago, Lea."

"Years ago! I thought it just happened!"

"Oh, my golly, no! What made you think—?"

"You remembered so completely! Such little things. And the way Jemmy looked at Valancy and Valancy at him—"

"The People have their special memory. And Jemmy was only looking love at Valancy. Love doesn't die—"

"Love doesn't—" Lea's mouth twisted. "Come, then, let us

46

define love—" She stood up briskly. "I do want to walk a little—" She hesitated. "And maybe wade a little? In real wet water, free-running—"

"Why, sure," Karen said. "The creek is running. Wade to your heart's content. Lunch will be here for you and I'll be back by supper. We'll go to the school together for Peter's installment."

Lea came upon the pool, her bare feet bruised, her skirt hem dabbled with creek water, and her stomach empty of the lunch she had forgotten.

The pool was wide and quiet. Water murmured into it at one end and chuckled out at the other. In between the surface was like a mirror. A yellow leaf fell slowly from a cottonwood tree and touched so gently down on the water that the resultant rings ran as fine as wire out to the sandy edge. Lea sighed, gathered up her skirts and stepped cautiously into the pool. The clean cold bite of the water caught her breath, but she waded deeper. The water crept up to her knees and over them. She stood under the cottonwood tree, waiting, waiting so quietly that the water closed smoothly around her legs and she could feel its flow only in the tiny crumblings of sand under her feet. She stood there until another leaf fell, brushed her cheek, slipped down her shoulder and curved over her crumpled blouse, catching briefly in the gathered-up folds of her skirt before it turned a leisurely circle on the surface of the shining water.

Lea stared down at the leaf and the silver shadow behind it that was herself, then lifted her face to the towering canyon walls around her. She hugged her elbows tightly to her sides and thought, "I am becoming an entity again. I have form and proportion. I have boundaries and limits. I should be able to learn how to manage a finite being. The burden of being a nothing in infinite nothingness was too much—too much—"

A restless stirring that could turn to panic swung Lea around and she started for shore. As she clambered up the bank, hands encumbered by her skirt, she slipped and, flailing wildly for balance, fell backward into the pool with a resounding splat. Dripping and gasping she scrambled wetly to a sitting position, her shoulders barely out of the water. She blinked the water out of her eyes and saw the man.

He had one foot in the water, poised in the act of starting toward her. He was laughing. She spluttered indignantly, and the water sloshed up almost to her chin.

"I might have drowned!" she cried, feeling very silly and very wet.

"If you go on sitting there you can drown yet!" he called. "High water comes in October."

"At the rate you're helping me out," she answered, "I'll make it! I can't get up without getting my head all wet."

"But you're already wet all over," he laughed, wading toward her.

"That was accidental," she sputtered. "It's different, doing it on purpose!"

"Female logic!" He grabbed her hands and hoisted her to her feet, pushed her to shore and shoved her up the bank.

Lea looked up into his smiling face and, smiling back, started to thank him. Suddenly his face twisted all out of focus—and retreated a thousand miles away. Faintly, faintly from afar, she heard his voice and her own gasping breath. Woodenly she turned away and started to grope away from him. She felt him catch her hand, and as she tugged away from him she felt all her being waver and dissolve and nothingness roll in, darker and darker.

"Karen!" she cried. "Karen! Karen!" And she lost herself.

"I won't go." She turned fretfully away from Karen's proffered hand. The bed was soft.

"Oh, yes, you will," Karen said. "You'll love Peter's installment. And Bethie! You *must* hear about Bethie."

"Oh, Karen, please don't make me try any more," Lea pleaded. "I can't bear the slipping back after—after—" She shook her head mutely.

"You haven't even started to try yet," Karen said, coolly. "You've got to go tonight. It's lesson two for you, so you'll be ready to go on."

"My clothes," Lea groped for an excuse. "They must be a mess."

"They are," Karen said, undisturbed. "You're about Lizbeth's size. I brought you plenty. Choose."

"No." Lea turned away.

"Get up." Karen's voice was still cool but Lea got up. She fumbled wordlessly into the proffered clothes.

"Hmm!" Karen said. "You're taller than I thought. You slump around so since you gave up."

Lea felt a stir of indignation but stood still as Karen knelt and tugged at the hem of the dress. The material stretched and stayed stretched, making the skirt a more seemly length for Lea.

"There," Karen said, standing and settling the dress smoothly around Lea's waist by pinching a fullness into a pleat. Then, with a stroke of her hand, she deepened the color of the material. "Not bad. It's your color. Come on now or we'll be late."

Lea stubbornly refused to be interested in anything. She sat in her corner and concentrated on her clasped hands, letting the ebb and flow of talk and movement lap around her, not even looking. Suddenly, after the quiet invocation, she felt a pang of pure homesickness—homesickness for strong hands holding hers with the coolness of water moving between them. She threw back her head, startled, just as Jemmy said, "I yield the desk to you, Peter. It's yours, every decrepit splinter of it."

"Thanks," Peter said. "I hope the chair's comfortable. This'll take a while. I've decided to follow Karen's lead and have a theme, too. It could well have been my question at almost any time in those long years.

" 'Is there no balm in Gilead; is there no physician there? Why then is not the health of the daughter of my people recovered?' "

In the brief pause Lea snatched at a thought that streaked through her mind. "I forgot all about the pond! Who was it? Who was it?" But she found no answer as Peter began. . . .

I don't know when it was that I found out that our family was different from other families. There was nothing to point it out. We lived in a house very like the other houses in Socorro. Our pasture lot sloped down just like the rest through arrowweed and mesquite trees to the sometime Rio Gordo that looped around town. And on occasion our cow bawled just as loudly across the river at the Jacobses' bull as all the other cows in all the other pasture lots. And I spent as many lazy days as any other boy in Socorro lying on my back in the thin shade of the mesquites, chewing on the beans when work was waiting somewhere. It never occurred to me to wonder if we were different.

I suppose my first realization came soon after I started to school and fell in love—with the girl with the longest pigtails and the widest gap in her front teeth of all the girls in my room. I think she was seven to my six.

My girl and I had wandered down behind the school woodshed, under the cottonwoods, to eat our lunch together, ignoring the chanted "Peter's got a gir-ul! Peter's got a gir-ul!" and the whittling fingers that shamed me for showing my love. We ate our sandwiches and pickles and then lay back, arms doubled under our heads, and blinked at the bright sky while we tried to keep the crumbs from our cupcakes from falling into our ears. I was so full of lunch, contentment and love that I suddenly felt I just had to do something spectacular for my lady-love. I sat up, electrified by a great idea and by the knowledge that I could carry it out.

"Hey! Did you know that I can fly?" I scrambled to my feet, leaving my love sitting gape-mouthed in the grass.

"You can't neither fly! Don't be crazy!"

"I can too fly!"

"You can not neither!"

"I can so! You just watch!" And lifting my arms I swooped

up to the roof of the shed. I leaned over the edge and said, "See there? I can, too!"

"I'll tell teacher on you!" she gasped, wide-eyed, staring up at me. "You ain't supposed to climb up on the shed."

"Oh, poof," I said, "I didn't climb. Come on, you fly up, too. Here, I'll help you."

And I slid down the air to the ground. I put my arms around my love and lifted. She screamed and wrenched away from me and fled shrieking back to the schoolhouse. Somewhat taken aback by her desertion, I gathered up the remains of my cake and hers and was perched comfortably on the ridgepole of the shed, enjoying the last crumbs, when teacher arrived with half the school trailing behind her.

"Peter Merrill! How many times have you been told not to climb things at school?"

I peered down at her, noting with interest that the spit curls on her cheeks had been jarred loose by her hurry and agitation and one of them was straightening out, contrasting oddly with the rest of her shingled bob.

"Hang on tight until Stanley gets the ladder!"

"I can get down," I said, scrambling off the ridgepole. "It's easy."

"Peter!" teacher shrieked. "Stay where you are!"

So I did, wondering at all the fuss.

By the time they got me down and teacher yanked me by one arm back up to the schoolhouse I was bawling at the top of my voice, outraged and indignant because no one would believe me, even my girl denying obstinately the evidence of her own eyes. Teacher, annoyed at my persistence, said over and over, "Don't be silly, Peter. You can't fly. Nobody can fly. Where are your wings?"

"I don't need wings," I bellowed. "People don't need wings. I ain't a bird!"

"Then you can't fly. Only things with wings can fly."

So I alternately cried and kicked the schoolhouse steps for the rest of the noon hour, and then I began to worry for fear teacher would tattle to Dad. After all I had been on forbidden territory, no matter how I got there.

As it turned out she didn't tell Dad, but that night after I was put to bed I suddenly felt an all-gone feeling inside me.

51

Maybe I *couldn't* fly. Maybe teacher was right. I sneaked out of bed and cautiously flew up to the top of the dresser and back. Then I pulled the covers up tight under my chin and whispered to myself, "I can so fly," and sighed heavily. Just another fun stuff that grownups didn't allow, like having cake for breakfast or driving the tractor or borrowing the cow for an Indian-pony-on-a-warpath.

And that was all of that incident except that when teacher met Mother and me at the store that Saturday she ruffled my hair and said, "How's my little bird?" Then she laughed and said to Mother, "He thinks he can fly!"

I saw Mother's fingers tighten whitely on her purse, and she looked down at me with all the laughter gone from her eyes. I was overflooded with incredulous surprise mixed with fear and dread that made me want to cry, even though I knew it was Mother's emotions and not my own that I was feeling.

Mostly Mother had laughing eyes. She was the laughingest mother in Socorro. She carried happiness inside her as if it were a bouquet of flowers and she gave part of it to everyone she met. Most of the other mothers seemed to have hardly enough to go around to their own families. And yet there were other times, like at the store, when laughter fled and fear showed through—and an odd wariness. Other times she made me think of a caged bird, pressing against the bars. Like one night I remember vividly.

Mother stood at the window in her ankle-length flannel nightgown, her long dark hair lifting softly in the draft from the rattling window frames. A high wind was blowing in from a spectacular thunderstorm in the Huachucas. I had been awakened by the rising crescendo and was huddled on the sofa wondering if I was scared or excited as the house shook with the constant thunder. Dad was sitting with the newspaper in his lap.

Mother spoke softly, but her voice came clearly through the tumult.

"Have you ever wondered what it would be like to be up there in the middle of the storm with clouds under your feet and over your head and lightning lacing around you like hot golden rivers?"

Dad rattled his paper. "Sounds uncomfortable," he said.

But I sat there and hugged the words to me in wonder. I knew! *I remembered!* " 'And the rain like icy silver hair lashing across your lifted face,' " I recited as though it were a loved lesson.

Mother whirled from the window and stared at me. Dad's eyes were on me, dark and troubled.

"How do you know?" he asked.

I ducked my head in confusion. "I don't know," I muttered.

Mother pressed her hands together, hard, her bowed head swinging the curtains of her hair forward over her shadowy face. "He knows because I know. I know because my mother knew. She knew because our People used to—" Her voice broke. "Those were her words—"

She stopped and turned back to the window, leaning her arm against the frame, her face pressed to it, like a child in tears.

"Oh, Bruce, I'm sorry!"

I stared, round-eyed in amazement, trying to keep tears from coming to my eyes as I fought against Mother's desolation and sorrow.

Dad went to Mother and turned her gently into his arms. He looked over her head at me. "Better run on back to bed, Peter. The worst is over."

I trailed off reluctantly, my mind filled with wonder. Just before I shut my door I stopped and listened.

"I've never said a word to him, honest." Mother's voice quivered. "Oh, Bruce, I try so hard, but sometimes—oh sometimes!"

"I know, Eve. And you've done a wonderful job of it. I know it's hard on you, but we've talked it out so many times. It's the only way, honey."

"Yes," Mother said. "It's the only way, but—oh, be my strength, Bruce! Bless the Power for giving me you!"

I shut my door softly and huddled in the dark in the middle of my bed until I felt Mother's anguish smooth out to loving warmness again. Then for no good reason I flew solemnly to the top of the dresser and back, crawled into bed and relaxed. And remembered. Remembered the hot golden rivers, the clouds over and under and the wild winds that buffeted like foam-frosted waves. But with all the sweet remembering was the reminder, *You can't because you're only eight. You're only eight. You'll have to wait.*

And then Bethie was born, almost in time for my ninth birthday. I remember peeking over the edge of the bassinet at the miracle of tiny fingers and spun-sugar hair. Bethie, my little sister. Bethie, who was whispered about and stared at when Mother let her go to school, though mostly she kept her home even after she was old enough. Because Bethie was different—too.

When Bethie was a month old I smashed my finger in the bedroom door. I cried for a quarter of an hour, but Bethie sobbed on and on until the last pain left my finger.

When Bethie was six months old our little terrier, Glib, got caught in a gopher trap. He dragged himself, yelping, back to the house dangling the trap. Bethie screamed until Glib fell asleep over his bandaged paw.

Dad had acute appendicitis when Bethie was two, but it was Bethie who had to be given a sedative until we could get Dad to the hospital.

One night Dad and Mother stood over Bethie as she slept restlessly under sedatives. Mr. Tyree-next-door had been cutting wood and his ax slipped. He lost a big toe and a pint or so of blood, but as Doctor Dueff skidded to a stop on our street it was into our house that he rushed first and then to Mr. Tyree-next-door who lay with his foot swathed and propped up on a chair, his hands pressed to his ears to shut out Bethie's screams.

"What can we do, Eve?" Dad asked. "What does the doctor say?"

"Nothing. They can do nothing for her. He hopes she will outgrow it. He doesn't understand it. He doesn't know that she—"

"What's the matter? What makes her like this?" Dad asked despairingly.

Mother winced. "She's a Sensitive. Among my People there were such—but not so young. Their perception made it possible for them to help sufferers. Bethie has only half the Gift. She has no control."

"Because of me?" Dad's voice was ragged.

54

Mother look at him with steady loving eyes. "Because of us, Bruce. It was the chance we took. We pushed our luck after Peter."

So there we were, the two of us—different—but different in our differences. For me it was mostly fun, but not for Bethie.

We had to be careful for Bethie. She tried school at first, but skinned knees and rough rassling and aching teeth and bumped heads and the janitor's Monday hangover sent her home exhausted and shaking the first day, with hysteria hanging on the flick of an eyelash. So Bethie read for Mother and learned her numbers and leaned wistfully over the gate as the other children went by.

It wasn't long after Bethie's first day in school that I found a practical use for my difference. Dad sent me out to the woodshed to stack a cord of mesquite that Delfino dumped into our back yard from his old wood wagon. I had a date to explore an old fluorspar mine with some other guys and bitterly resented being sidetracked. I slouched out to the wood-pile and stood, hands in pockets, kicking the heavy rough stove lengths. Finally I carried in one armload, grunting under the weight, and afterward sucking the round of my thumb where the sliding wood had peeled me. I hunkered down on my heels and stared as I sucked. Suddenly something prickled inside my brain. If I could fly why couldn't I make the wood fly? *And I knew I could!* I leaned forward and flipped a finger under half a dozen sticks, concentrating as I did so. They lifted into the air and hovered. I pushed them into the shed, guided them to where I wanted them and distributed them like dealing a pack of cards. It didn't take me long to figure out the maximum load, and I had all the wood stacked in a wonderfully short time.

I whistled into the house for my flashlight. The mine was spooky and dark, and I was the only one of the gang with a flashlight.

"I told you to stack the wood." Dad looked up from his milk records.

"I did," I said, grinning.

"Cut the kidding," Dad grunted. "You couldn't be done already."

"I am, though," I said triumphantly. "I found a new way to do it. You see—" I stopped, frozen by Dad's look.

"We don't need any new ways around here," he said evenly. "Go back out there until you've had time to stack the wood right!"

"It *is* stacked," I protested. "And the kids are waiting for me!"

"I'm not arguing, son," said Dad, white-faced. "Go back out to the shed."

I went back out to the shed—past Mother, who had come in from the kitchen and whose hand half went out to me. I sat in the shed fuming for a long time, stubbornly set that I wouldn't leave till Dad told me to.

Then I got to thinking. Dad wasn't usually unreasonable like this. Maybe I'd done something wrong. Maybe it was bad to stack wood like that. Maybe—my thoughts wavered as I remembered whispers I'd overheard about Bethie. Maybe it—it was a crazy thing to do—an insane thing.

I huddled close upon myself as I considered it. Crazy means not doing like other people. Crazy means doing things ordinary people don't do. Maybe that's why Dad made such a fuss. Maybe I'd done an insane thing! I stared at the ground, lost in bewilderment. What *was* different about our family? And for the first time I was able to isolate and recognize the feeling I must have had for a long time—the feeling of being on the outside looking in—the feeling of apartness. With this recognition came a wariness, a need for concealment. If something was wrong no one else must know—I must not betray . . .

Then Mother was standing beside me. "Dad says you may go now," she said, sitting down on my log.

"Peter—" She looked at me unhappily. "Dad's doing what is best. All I can say is: remember that whatever you do, wherever you live, different is dead. You have to conform or—or die. But Peter, don't be ashamed. Don't ever be ashamed!" Then swiftly her hands were on my shoulders and her lips brushed my ear. "Be different!" she whispered. "Be as different as you can. But don't let anyone see—don't let anyone know!" And she was gone up the back steps, into the kitchen.

As I grew further into adolescence I seemed to grow further

and further away from kids my age. I couldn't seem to get much of a kick out of what they considered fun. So it was that with increasing frequency in the years that followed I took Mother's whispered advice, never asking for explanations I knew she wouldn't give. The wood incident had opened up a whole vista of possibilities—no telling what I might be able to do—so I got in the habit of going down to the foot of our pasture lot. There, screened by the brush and greasewood, I tried all sorts of experiments, never knowing whether they would work or not. I sweated plenty over some that didn't work—and some that did.

I found that I could snap my fingers and bring things to me, or send them short distances from me without bothering to touch them as I had the wood. I roosted regularly in the tops of the tall cottonwoods, swan-diving ecstatically down to the ground, warily, after I got too ecstatic once and crash-landed on my nose and chin. By headaching concentration that left me dizzy, I even set a small campfire ablaze. Then blistered and charred both hands unmercifully by confidently scooping up the crackling fire.

Then I guess I got careless about checking for onlookers because some nasty talk got started. Bub Jacobs whispered around that I was "doing things" all alone down in the brush. His sly grimace as he whispered made the "doing things" any nasty perversion the listeners' imaginations could conjure up, and the "alone" damned me on the spot. I learned bitterly then what Mother had told me. Different is dead—and one death is never enough. You die and die and die.

Then one day I caught Bub cutting across the foot of our wood lot. He saw me coming and hit for tall timber, already smarting under what he knew he'd get if I caught him. I started full speed after him, then plowed to a stop. Why waste effort? If I could do it to the wood I could do it to a blockhead like Bub.

He let out a scream of pure terror as the ground dropped out from under him. His scream flatted and strangled into silence as he struggled in midair, convulsed with fear of falling and the terrible thing that was happening to him. And I stood and laughed at him, feeling myself a giant towering above stupid dopes like Bub.

Sharply, before he passed out, I felt his terror, and an echo of his scream rose in my throat. I slumped down in the dirt, sick with sudden realization, knowing with a knowledge that went beyond ordinary experience that I had done something terribly wrong, that I had prostituted whatever powers I possessed by using them to terrorize unjustly.

I knelt and looked up at Bub, crumpled in the air, higher than my head, higher than my reach, and swallowed painfully as I realized that I had no idea how to get him down. He wasn't a stick of wood to be snapped to the ground. He wasn't me, to dive down through the air. I hadn't the remotest idea how to get a human down.

Half dazed, I crawled over to a shaft of sunlight that slit the cottonwood branches overhead and felt it rush through my fingers like something to be lifted—and twisted—and fashioned and *used! Used on Bub!* But how? *How?* I clenched my fist in the flood of light, my mind beating against another door that needed only a word or look or gesture to open, but I couldn't say it, or look it, or make it.

I stood up and took a deep breath. I jumped, batting at Bub's heels that dangled a little lower than the rest of him. I missed. Again I jumped and the tip of one finger flicked his heel and he moved sluggishly in the air. Then I swiped the back of my hand across my sweaty forehead and laughed—laughed at my stupid self.

Cautiously, because I hadn't done much hovering, mostly just up and down, I lifted myself up level with Bub. I put my hands on him and pushed down hard. He didn't move.

I tugged him up and he rose with me. I drifted slowly and deliberately away from him and pondered. Then I got on the other side of him and pushed him toward the branches of the cottonwood. His head was beginning to toss and his lips moved with returning consciousness. He drifted through the air like a waterlogged stump, but he moved and I draped him carefully over a big limb near the top of the tree, anchoring his arms and legs as securely as I could. By the time his eyes opened and he clutched frenziedly for support I was standing down at the foot of the tree, yelling up at him.

"Hang on, Bub! I'll go get someone to help you down!"

So for the next week or so people forgot me, and Bub

58

squirmed under "Who treed you, feller?" and "How's the weather up there?" and "Get a ladder, Bub, get a ladder!"

Even with worries like that it was mostly fun for me. Why couldn't it be like that for Bethie? Why couldn't I give her part of my fun and take part of her pain?

Then Dad died, swept out of life by our Rio Gordo as he tried to rescue a fool Easterner who had camped on the bone-dry white sands of the river bottom in cloudburst weather. Somehow it seemed impossible to think of Mother by herself. It had always been Mother and Dad. Not just two parents but Mother-and-Dad, a single entity. And now our thoughts must limp to Mother-and, Mother-and. And Mother—well, half of her was gone.

After the funeral Mother and Bethie and I sat in our front room, looking at the floor. Bethie was clenching her teeth against the stabbing pain of Mother's fingernails gouging Mother's palms.

I unfolded the clenched hands gently and Bethie relaxed. "Mother," I said softly, "I can take care of us. I have my part-time job at the plant. Don't worry. I'll take care of us."

I knew what a trivial thing I was offering to her anguish, but I had to do something to break through to her.

"Thank you, Peter," Mother said, rousing a little. "I know you will—" She bowed her head and pressed both hands to her dry eyes with restrained desperation. "Oh, Peter, Peter! I'm enough of this world now to find death a despair and desolation instead of the solemnly sweet calling it is. Help me, help me!" Her breath labored in her throat and she groped blindly for my hand.

"If I can, Mother," I said, taking one hand as Bethie took the other. "Then help me remember. Remember with me."

And behind my closed eyes I remembered. Unhampered flight through a starry night, a flight of a thousand happy people like birds in the sky, rushing to meet the dawn—the dawn of the Festival. I could smell the flowers that garlanded the women and feel the quiet exultation that went with the Festival dawn. Then the leader sounded the magnificent opening notes of the Festival song as he caught the first glimpse of the rising sun over the heavily wooded hills. A thousand voices took up the song. A thousand hands lifted in the Sign. . . .

I opened my eyes to find my own fingers lifted to trace a sign I did not know. My own throat throbbed to a note I had never sung. I took a deep breath and glanced over at Bethie. She met my eyes and shook her head sadly. She hadn't seen. Mother sat quietly, eyes closed, her face cleared and calmed.

"What was it, Mother?" I whispered.

"The Festival," she said softly. "For all those who had been called during the year. For your father, Peter and Bethie. We remembered it for your father."

"Where was it?" I asked. "Where in the world—?"

"Not in this—" Mother's eyes flicked open. "It doesn't matter, Peter. You are of this world. There is no other for you."

"Mother," Bethie's voice was a hesitant murmur, "what do you mean, 'remember'?"

Mother looked at her and tears swelled into her dry burned-out eyes.

"Oh, Bethie, Bethie, all the burdens and none of the blessings! I'm sorry, Bethie, I'm sorry." And she fled down the hall to her room.

Bethie stood close against my side as we looked after Mother.

"Peter," she murmured, "what did Mother mean, 'none of the blessings'?"

"I don't know," I said.

"I'll bet it's because I can't fly like you."

"Fly!" My startled eyes went to hers. "How do you know?"

"I know lots of things," she whispered. "But mostly I know we're different. Other people aren't like us. Peter, what made us different?"

"Mother?" I whispered. "Mother?"

"I guess so," Bethie murmured. "But how come?"

We fell silent and then Bethie went to the window where the late sun haloed her silvery blond hair in fire.

"I can do things, too," she whispered. "Look."

She reached out and took a handful of sun, the same sort of golden sun-slant that had flowed so heavily through my fingers under the cottonwoods while Bub dangled above me. With flashing fingers she fashioned the sun into an intricate glowing pattern. "But what's it for?" she murmured, "except for pretty?"

"I know," I said, looking at my answer for lowering Bub. "I know, Bethie." And I took the pattern from her. It strained between my fingers and flowed into darkness.

The years that followed were casual uneventful years. I finished high school, but college was out of the question. I went to work in the plant that provided work for most of the employables in Socorro.

Mother built up quite a reputation as a midwife—a very necessary calling in a community which took literally the injunction to multiply and replenish the earth and which lay exactly seventy-five miles from a hospital, no matter which way you turned when you got to the highway.

Bethie was in her teens and with Mother's help was learning to control her visible reactions to the pain of others, but I knew she still suffered as much as, if not more than, she had when she was smaller. But she was able to go to school most of the time now and was becoming fairly popular in spite of her quietness.

So all in all we were getting along quite comfortably and quite ordinarily except—well, I always felt as though I were waiting for something to happen or for someone to come. And Bethie must have, too, because she actually watched and listened—especially after a particularly bad spell. And even Mother. Sometimes as we sat on the porch in the long evenings she would cock her head and listen intently, her rocking chair still. But when we asked what she heard she'd sigh and say, "Nothing. Just the night." And her chair would rock again.

Of course I still indulged my differences. Not with the white fire of possible discovery that they had kindled when I first began, but more like the feeding of a small flame just "for pretty." I went farther afield now for my "holidays," but Bethie went with me. She got a big kick out of our excursions, especially after I found that I could carry her when I flew, and most especially after we found, by means of a heart-stopping accident, that though she couldn't go up she could control her going down. After that it was her pleasure to have me carry her up as far as I could and she would come down, sometimes taking an hour to make the descent, often weaving about her the intricate splendor of her sunshine patterns.

It was a rustling russet day in October when our world

61

ended—again. We talked and laughed over the breakfast table, teasing Bethie about her date the night before. Color was high in her usually pale cheeks, and, with all the laughter and brightness the tingle of fall, everything just felt good.

But between one joke and another the laughter drained out of Bethie's face and the pinched set look came to her lips.

"Mother!" she whispered, and then she relaxed.

"Already?" asked Mother, rising and finishing her coffee as I went to get her coat. "I had a hunch today would be the day. Reena would ride that jeep up Peppersauce Canyon this close to her time."

I helped her on with her coat and hugged her tight.

"Bless-a-mama," I said, "when are you going to retire and let someone else snatch the fall and spring crops of kids?"

"When I snatch a grandchild or so for myself," she said, joking, but I felt her sadness. "Besides she's going to name this one Peter—or Bethie, as the case may be." She reached for her little black bag and looked at Bethie. "No more yet?"

Bethie smiled. "No," she murmured.

"Then I've got plenty of time. Peter, you'd better take Bethie for a holiday. Reena takes her own sweet time and being just across the road makes it bad on Bethie."

"Okay, Mother," I said. "We planned one anyway, but we hoped this time you'd go with us."

Mother looked at me, hesitated and turned aside. "I—I might sometime."

"Mother! Really?" This was the first hesitation from Mother in all the times we'd asked her.

"Well, you've asked me so many times and I've been wondering. Wondering if it's fair to deny our birthright. After all there's nothing wrong in being of the People."

"What people, Mother?" I pressed. "*Where* are you from? Why *can*—?"

"Some other time, son," Mother said. "Maybe soon. These last few months I've begun to sense—yes, it wouldn't hurt you to know even if nothing could ever come of it; and perhaps soon something *can* come, and you will have to know. But no," she chided as we clung to her. "There's no time now. Reena might fool us after all and produce before I get there. You kids scoot, now!"

We looked back as the pickup roared across the highway and headed for Mendigo's Peak. Mother answered our wave and went in the gate of Reena's yard, where Dalt, in spite of this being their sixth, was running like an anxious puppy dog from Mother to the porch and back again.

It was a day of perfection for us. The relaxation of flight for me, the delight of hovering for Bethie, the frosted glory of the burning-blue sky, the russet and gold of grasslands stretching for endless miles down from the snow-flecked blue and gold Mendigo.

At lunchtime we lolled in the pleasant warmth of our favorite baby box canyon that held the sun and shut out the wind. After we ate we played our favorite game, Remembering. It began with my clearing my mind so that it lay as quiet as a hidden pool of water, as receptive as the pool to every pattern the slightest breeze might start quivering across its surface.

Then the memories would come—strange un-Earthlike memories that were like those Mother and I had had when Dad died. Bethie could not remember with me, but she seemed to catch the memories from me almost before the words could form in my mouth.

So this last lovely "holiday" we remembered again our favorite. We walked the darkly gleaming waters of a mountain lake, curling our toes in the liquid coolness, loving the tilt and sway of the waves beneath our feet, feeling around us from shore and sky a dear familiarity that was stronger than any Earth ties we had yet formed.

Before we knew it the long lazy afternoon had fled and we shivered in the sudden chill as the sun dropped westward, nearing the peaks of the Huachucas. We packed the remains of our picnic in the basket, and I turned to Bethie, to lift her and carry her back to the pickup.

She was smiling her soft little secret smile.

"Look, Peter," she murmured. And flicking her fingers over her head she shook out a cloud of snowflakes, gigantic whirling tumbling snowflakes that clung feather-soft to her pale hair and melted, glistening, across her warm cheeks and mischievous smile.

"Early winter, Peter!" she said.

"Early winter, punkin!" I cried and snatching her up,

boosted her out of the little canyon and jumped over her, clearing the boulders she had to scramble over. "For that you walk, young lady!"

But she almost beat me to the car anyway. For one who couldn't fly she was learning to run awfully light.

Twilight had fallen before we got back to the highway. We could see the headlights of the scurrying cars that seldom even slowed down for Socorro. "So this is Socorro, wasn't it?" was the way most traffic went through.

We had topped the last rise before the highway when Bethie screamed. I almost lost control of the car on the rutty road. She screamed again, a wild tortured cry as she folded in on herself.

"Bethie!" I called, trying to get through to her. "What is it? Where is it? Where can I take you?"

But her third scream broke off short and she slid limply to the floor. I was terrified. She hadn't reacted like this in years. She had never fainted like this before. Could it be that Reena hadn't had her child yet? That she was in such agony—but even when Mrs. Allbeg had died in childbirth Bethie hadn't— I lifted Bethie to the seat and drove wildly homeward, praying that Mother would be . . .

And then I saw it. In front of our house. The big car skewed across the road. The kneeling cluster of people on the pavement.

The next thing I knew I was kneeling, too, beside Dr. Dueff, clutching the edge of the blanket that mercifully covered Mother from chin to toes. I lifted a trembling hand to the dark trickle of blood that threaded crookedly down from her forehead.

"Mother," I whispered. "Mother!"

Her eyelids fluttered and she looked up blindly. "Peter." I could hardly hear her. "Peter, where's Bethie?"

"She fainted. She's in the car," I faltered. "Oh, Mother!"

"Tell the doctor to go to Bethie."

"But, Mother!" I cried. "You—"

"I am not called yet. Go to Bethie."

We knelt by her bedside, Bethie and I. The doctor was gone. There was no use trying to get Mother to a hospital. Just moving her indoors had started a dark oozing from the corner

64

of her mouth. The neighbors were all gone except Gramma Reuther who always came to troubled homes and had folded the hands of the dead in Socorro from the founding of the town. She sat now in the front room holding her worn Bible in quiet hands, after all these years no longer needing to look up the passages of comfort and assurance.

The doctor had quieted the pain for Mother and had urged sleep upon Bethie, not knowing how long the easing would last, but Bethie wouldn't take it.

Suddenly Mother's eyes were open.

"I married your father," she said clearly, as though continuing a conversation. "We loved each other so, and they were all dead—all my People. Of course I told him first, and oh, Peter! He believed me! After all that time of having to guard every word and every move I had someone to talk to—someone to believe me. I told him all about the People and lifted myself and then I lifted the car and turned it in mid-air above the highway—just for fun. It pleased him a lot but it made him thoughtful and later he said, 'You know, honey, your world and ours took different turns way back there. We turned to gadgets. You turned to the Power.'"

Her eyes smiled. "He got so he knew when I was lonesome for the Home. Once he said, 'Homesick, honey? So am I. For what this world could have been. Or maybe—God willing—what it may become.'

"Your father was the other half of me." Her eyes closed, and in the silence her breath became audible, a harsh straining sound. Bethie crouched with both hands pressed to her chest, her face dead white in the shadows.

"We discussed it and discussed it," Mother cried. "But we had to decide as we did. We thought I was the last of the People. I had to forget the Home and be of Earth. You children had to be of Earth, too, even if— That's why he was so stern with you, Peter. Why he didn't want you to—experiment. He was afraid you'd do too much around other people if you found out—" She stopped and lay panting. "Different is dead," she whispered, and lay scarcely breathing for a moment.

"I knew the Home." Her voice was heavy with sorrow. "I remember the Home. Not just because my People remem-

65

bered it but because I saw it. I was born there. It's gone now. Gone forever. There is no Home. Only a band of dust between the stars!" Her face twisted with grief and Bethie echoed her cry of pain.

Then Mother's face cleared and her eyes opened. She half propped herself up in her bed.

"You have the Home, too. You and Bethie. You will have it always. And your children after you. Remember, Peter? Remember?"

Then her head tilted attentively and she gave a laughing sob. "Oh, Peter! Oh, Bethie! Did you hear it? I've been called! I've been called!" Her hand lifted in the Sign and her lips moved tenderly.

"Mother!" I cried fearfully. "What do you mean? Lie down. Please lie down!" I pressed her back against the pillows.

"I've been called back to the Presence. My years are finished. My days are totaled."

"But Mother," I blubbered like a child, "what will we do without you?"

"Listen!" Mother whispered rapidly, one hand pressed to my hair. "You must find the rest. You must go right away. They can help Bethie. They can help you, Peter. As long as you are separated from them you are not complete. I have felt them calling the last year or so, and now that I am on the way to the Presence I can hear them clearer, and clearer." She paused and held her breath. "There is a canyon—north. The ship crashed there, after our life slips—here, Peter, give me your hand." She reached urgently toward me and I cradled her hand in mine.

And I saw half the state spread out below me like a giant map. I saw the wrinkled folds of the mountains, the deceptively smooth roll of the desert up to the jagged slopes. I saw the blur of timber blunting the hills and I saw the angular writhing of the narrow road through the passes. Then I felt a sharp pleasurable twinge, like the one you feel when seeing home after being away a long time.

"There!" Mother whispered as the panorama faded. "I wish I could have known before. It's been lonely—

"But you, Peter," she said strongly. "You and Bethie must go to them."

66

"Why should we, Mother?" I cried in desperation. "What are they to us or we to them that we should leave Socorro and go among strangers?"

Mother pulled herself up in bed, her eyes intent on my face. She wavered a moment and then Bethie was crouched behind her, steadying her back.

"They are not strangers," she said clearly and slowly. "They are the People. We shared the ship with them during the Crossing. They were with us when we were out in the middle of emptiness with only the fading of stars behind and the brightening before to tell us we were moving. They, with us, looked at all the bright frosting of stars across the blackness, wondering if on one of them we would find a welcome.

"You are woven of their fabric. Even though your father was not of the People—"

Her voice died, her face changed. Bethie moved from in back of her and lowered her gently. Mother clasped her hands and sighed.

"It's a lonely business," she whispered. "No one can go with you. Even with them waiting it's lonely."

In the silence that followed we heard Gramma Reuther rocking quietly in the front room. Bethie sat on the floor beside me, her cheeks flushed, her eyes wide with a strange dark awe.

"Peter, it didn't hurt. It didn't hurt at all. It—healed!"

But we didn't go. How could we leave my job and our home and go off to—where? Looking for—whom? Because—why? It was mostly me, I guess, but I couldn't quite believe what Mother had told us. After all she hadn't said anything definite. We were probably reading meaning where it didn't exist. Bethie returned again and again to the puzzle of Mother and what she had meant, but we didn't go.

And Bethie got paler and thinner, and it was nearly a year later that I came home to find her curled into an impossibly tight ball on her bed, her eyes tight shut, snatching at breath that came out again in sharp moans.

I nearly went crazy before I at last got through to her and uncurled her enough to get hold of one of her hands. Finally, though, she opened dull dazed eyes and looked past me.

"Like a dam, Peter," she gasped. "It all comes in. It should—it should! I was born to—" I wiped the cold sweat from her forehead. "But it just piles up and piles up. It's supposed to go somewhere. I'm supposed to do something! Peter Peter Peter!" She twisted on the bed, her distorted face pushing into the pillow.

"What does, Bethie?" I asked, turning her face to mine. "What does?"

"Glib's foot and Dad's side and Mr. Tyree-next-door's toe—" and her voice faded down through the litany of years of agony.

"I'll go get Dr. Dueff," I said hopelessly.

"No." She turned her face away. "Why build the dam higher? Let it break. Oh, soon soon!"

"Bethie, don't talk like that," I said, feeling inside me my terrible aloneness that only Bethie could fend off now that Mother was gone. "We'll find something—some way—"

"Mother could help," she gasped. "A little. But she's gone. And now I'm picking up mental pain, too! Reena's afraid she's got cancer. Oh, Peter Peter!" Her voice strained to a whisper. "Let me die! Help me die!"

Both of us were shocked to silence by her words. Help her die? I leaned against her hand. Go back into the Presence with the weight of unfinished years dragging at our feet? For if she went I went, too.

Then my eyes flew open and I stared at Bethie's hand. What Presence? Whose ethics and mores were talking in my mind?

And so I had to decide. I talked Bethie into a sleeping pill and sat by her even after she was asleep. And as I sat there all the past years wound through my head. The way it must have been for Bethie all this time and I hadn't let myself know.

Just before dawn I woke Bethie. We packed and went. I left a note on the kitchen table for Dr. Dueff saying only that we were going to look for help for Bethie and would he ask Reena to see to the house. And thanks.

I slowed the pickup over to the side of the junction and slammed the brakes on.

"Okay," I said hopelessly. "You choose which way this time. Or shall we toss for it? Heads straight up, tails straight down! I can't tell where to go, Bethie. I had only that one little glimpse that Mother gave me of this country. There's a million canyons and a million side roads. We were fools to leave Socorro. After all we have nothing to go on but what Mother said. It might have been delirium."

"No," Bethie murmured. "It can't be. It's got to be real."

"But, Bethie," I said, leaning my weary head on the steering wheel, "you know how much I want it to be true, not only for you but for myself, too. But look. What do we have to assume if Mother was right? First, that space travel is possible —was possible nearly fifty years ago. Second, that Mother and her People came here from another planet. Third, that we are, bluntly speaking, half-breeds, a cross between Earth and heaven knows what world. Fourth, that there's a chance—in ten million—of our finding the other People who came at the same time Mother did, presupposing that any of them survived the Crossing.

"Why, any one of these premises would brand us as crazy crackpots to any normal person. No, we're building too much on a dream and a hope. Let's go back, Bethie. We've got just enough gas money along to make it. Let's give it up."

"And go back to what?" Bethie asked, her face pinched. "No, Peter. Here."

I looked up as she handed me one of her sunlight patterns, a handful of brilliance that twisted briefly in my fingers before it flickered out.

"Is that Earth?" she asked quietly. "How many of our friends can fly? How many—" she hesitated, "how many can Remember?"

"Remember!" I said slowly, and then I whacked the steering wheel with my fist. "Oh, Bethie, of all the stupid—! Why, it's Bub all over again!"

I kicked the pickup into life and turned on the first faint desert trail beyond the junction. I pulled off even that suggestion of a trail and headed across the nearly naked desert toward a clump of ironwood, mesquite and catclaw that marked a sand wash against the foothills. With the westering sun making shadow lace through the thin foliage we made camp.

I lay on my back in the wash and looked deep into the arch of the desert sky. The trees made a typical desert pattern of warmth and coolness on me, warm in the sun, cool in the shadow, as I let my mind clear smoother, smoother, until the soft intake of Bethie's breath as she sat beside me sent a bright ripple across it.

And I remembered. But only Mother-and-Dad and the little campfire I had gathered up, and Glib with the trap on his foot and Bethie curled, face to knees on the bed, and the thin crying sound of her labored breath.

I blinked at the sky. I *had* to Remember. I just had to. I shut my eyes and concentrated and concentrated, until I was exhausted. Nothing came now, not even a hint of memory. In despair I relaxed, limp against the chilling sand. And all at once unaccustomed gears shifted and slipped into place in my mind and there I was, just as I had been, hovering over the life-sized map.

Slowly and painfully I located Socorro and the thin thread that marked the Rio Gordo. I followed it and lost it and followed it again, the finger of my attention pressing close. Then I located Vulcan Springs Valley and traced its broad rolling to the upsweep of the desert, to the Sierra Cobreña Mountains. It was an eerie sensation to look down on the infinitesimal groove that must be where I was lying now. Then I hand-spanned my thinking around our camp spot. Nothing. I probed farther north, and east, and north again. I drew a deep breath and exhaled it shakily. There it was. The Home twinge. The call of familiarity.

I read it off to Bethie. The high thrust of a mountain that pushed up baldly past its timber, the huge tailings dump across the range from the mountain. The casual wreathing of smoke from what must be a logging town, all forming sides of a slender triangle. Somewhere in this area was the place.

I opened my eyes to find Bethie in tears.

"Why, Bethie!" I said. "What's wrong? Aren't you glad—?"

Bethie tried to smile but her lips quivered. She hid her face in the crook of her elbow and whispered. "I saw, too! Oh, Peter, this time I saw, too!"

We got out the road map and by the fading afternoon light we tried to translate our rememberings. As nearly as we could figure out we should head for a place way off the highway called Kerry Canyon. It was apparently the only inhabited spot anywhere near the big bald mountain. I looked at the little black dot in the kink in the third-rate road and wondered if it would turn out to be a period to all our hopes or the point for the beginning of new lives for the two of us. Life and sanity for Bethie, and for me . . . In a sudden spasm of emotion I crumpled the map in my hand. I felt blindly that in all my life I had never known anyone but Mother and Dad and Bethie. That I was a ghost walking the world. If only I could see even one other person that felt like our kind! Just to know that Bethie and I weren't all alone with our unearthly heritage!

I smoothed out the map and folded it again. Night was on us and the wind was cold. We shivered as we scurried around looking for wood for our campfire.

Kerry Canyon was one business street, two service stations, two saloons, two stores, two churches and a handful of houses flung at random over the hillsides that sloped down to an area that looked too small to accommodate the road. A creek which was now thinned to an intermittent trickle that loitered along, waited for the fall rains to begin. A sudden speckling across our windshield suggested it hadn't long to wait.

We rattled over the old bridge and half through the town. The road swung up sharply over a rusty single-line railroad and turned left, shying away from the bluff that was hollowed just enough to accommodate one of the service stations.

We pulled into the station. The uniformed attendant came alongside.

"We just want some information," I said, conscious of the thinness of my billfold. We had picked up our last tankful of gas before plunging into the maze of canyons between the main highway and here. Our stopping place would have to be soon whether we found the People or not.

"Sure! Sure! Glad to oblige." The attendant pushed his cap back from his forehead. "How can I help you?"

I hesitated, trying to gather my thoughts and words—and some of the hope that had jolted out of me since we had left the junction. "We're trying to locate some—friends—of ours. We were told they lived out the other side of here, out by Baldy. Is there anyone—?"

"Friends of *them* people?" he asked in astonishment. "Well,

71

say, now, that's interesting! You're the first I ever had come asking after them."

I felt Bethie's arm trembling against mine. Then there *was* something beyond Kerry Canyon!

"How come? What's wrong with them?"

"Why, nothing, Mac, nothing. Matter of fact they're dern nice people. Trade here a lot. Come in to church and the dances."

"Dances?" I glanced around the steep sloping hills.

"Sure. We ain't as dead as we look," the attendant grinned. "Come Saturday night we're quite a town. Lots of ranches around these hills. Course, not much out Cougar Canyon way. That's where your friends live, didn't you say?"

"Yeah. Out by Baldy."

"Well, nobody else lives out that way." He hesitated. "Hey, there's something I'd like to ask."

"Sure. Like what?"

"Well, them people pretty much keep themselves to themselves. I don't mean they're stuck-up or anything, but—well, I've always wondered. Where they from? One of them overrun countries in Europe? They're foreigners, ain't they? And seems like most of what Europe exports any more is DP's. Are them people some?"

"Well, yes, you might call them that. Why?"

"Well, they talk just as good as anybody and it must have been a war a long time ago because they've been around since my Dad's time, but they just—feel different." He caught his upper lip between his teeth reflectively. "Good different. Real nice different." He grinned again. "Wouldn't mind shining up to some of them gals myself. Don't get no encouragement, though.

"Anyway, keep on this road. It's easy. No other road going that way. Jackass Flat will beat the tar outa your tires, but you'll probably make it, less'n comes up a heavy rain. Then you'll skate over half the county and most likely end up in a ditch. Slickest mud in the world. Colder'n hell—beg pardon, lady—out there on the flat when the wind starts blowing. Better bundle up."

"Thanks, fella," I said. "Thanks a lot. Think we'll make it before dark?"

"Oh, sure. 'Tain't so awful far but the road's lousy. Oughta

72

make it in two-three hours, less'n like I said, comes up a heavy rain."

We knew when we hit Jackass Flat. It was like dropping off the edge. If we had thought the road to Kerry Canyon was bad we revised our opinions, but fast. In the first place it was choose your own ruts. Then the tracks were deep sunk in heavy clay generously mixed with sharp splintery shale and rocks as big as your two fists that were like a gigantic gravel as far as we could see across the lifeless expanse of the flat.

But to make it worse, the ruts I chose kept ending abruptly as though the cars that had made them had either backed away from the job or jumped over. Jumped over! I drove, in and out of ruts, so wrapped up in surmises that I hardly noticed the rough going until a cry from Bethie aroused me.

"Stop the car!" she cried. "Oh, Peter! Stop the car!"

I braked so fast that the pickup swerved wildly, mounted the side of a rut, lurched and settled sickeningly down on the back tire which sighed itself flatly into the rising wind.

"What on earth!" I yelped, as near to being mad at Bethie as I'd ever been in my life. "What was that for?"

Bethie, white-faced, was emerging from the army blanket she had huddled in against the cold. "It just came to me. Peter, supposing they don't want us?"

"Don't want us? What do you mean?" I growled, wondering if that lace doily I called my spare tire would be worth the trouble of putting it on.

"We never thought. It didn't even occur to us. Peter, we—we don't belong. We won't be like them. We're partly of Earth —as much as we are of wherever else. Supposing they reject us? Supposing they think we're undesirable—?" Bethie turned her face away. "Maybe we don't belong anywhere, Peter, not anywhere at all."

I felt a chill sweep over me that was not of the weather. We had assumed so blithely that we would be welcome. But how did we know? Maybe they *wouldn't* want us. We weren't of the People. We weren't of Earth. Maybe we didn't belong—not anywhere.

"Sure they'll want us," I forced out heartily. Then my eyes wavered away from Bethie's and I said defensively, "Mother said they would help us. She said we were woven of the same fabric—"

"But maybe the warp will only accept genuine woof. Mother couldn't know. There weren't any—half-breeds—when she was separated from them. Maybe our Earth blood will mark us—'

"There's nothing wrong with Earth blood," I said defiantly. "Besides, like you said, what would there be for you if we went back?"

She pressed her clenched fists against her cheeks, her eyes wide and vacant. "Maybe," she muttered, "maybe if I'd just go on and go completely insane it wouldn't hurt so terribly much. It might even feel good."

"Bethie!" my voice jerked her physically. "Cut out that talk right now! We're going on. The only way we can judge the People is by Mother. She would never reject us or any others like us. And that fellow back there said they were good people."

I opened the door. "You better try to get some kinks out of your legs while I change the tire. By the looks of the sky we'll be doing some skating before we get to Cougar Canyon."

But for all my brave words it wasn't just for the tire that I knelt beside the car, and it wasn't only the sound of the lug wrench that the wind carried up into the darkening sky.

I squinted through the streaming windshield, trying to make out the road through the downpour that fought our windshield wiper to a standstill. What few glimpses I caught of the road showed a deceptively smooth-looking chocolate river, but we alternately shook like a giant maraca, pushed out sheets of water like a speedboat, or slithered aimlessly and terrifyingly across sudden mud flats that often left us yards off the road. Then we'd creep cautiously back until the soggy squelch of our tires told us we were in the flooded ruts again.

Then all at once it wasn't there. The road, I mean. It stretched a few yards ahead of us and then just flowed over the edge, into the rain, into nothingness.

"It couldn't go there," Bethie murmured incredulously. "It can't just drop off like that."

"Well, I'm certainly not dropping off with it, sight unseen," I said, huddling deeper into my army blanket. My jacket was packed in back and I hadn't bothered to dig it out. I hunched

74

my shoulders to bring the blanket up over my head. "I'm going to take a look first."

I slid out into the solid wall of rain that hissed and splashed around me on the flooded flat. I was soaked to the knees and mud-coated to the shins before I slithered to the drop-off. The trail—call that a road?—tipped over the edge of the canyon and turned abruptly to the right, then lost itself along a shrub-grown ledge that sloped downward even as it paralleled the rim of the canyon. If I could get the pickup over the rim and onto the trail it wouldn't be so bad. But—I peered over the drop-off at the turn. The bottom was lost in shadows and rain. I shuddered.

Then quickly, before I could lose my nerve, I squelched back to the car.

"Pray, Bethie. Here we go."

There was the suck and slosh of our turning tires, the awful moment when we hung on the brink. Then the turn. And there we were, poised over nothing, with our rear end slewing outward.

The sudden tongue-biting jolt as we finally landed, right side up, pointing the right way on the narrow trail, jarred the cold sweat on my face so it rolled down with the rain.

I pulled over at the first wide spot in the road and stopped the car. We sat in the silence, listening to the rain. I felt as though something infinitely precious were lying just before me. Bethie's hand crept into mine and I knew she was feeling it, too. But suddenly Bethie's hand was snatched from mine and she was pounding with both fists against my shoulder in most un-Bethie-like violence.

"I can't stand it, Peter!" she cried hoarsely, emotion choking her voice. "Let's go back before we find out any more. If they should send us away! Oh, Peter! Let's go before they find us! Then we'll still have our dream. We can pretend that someday we'll come back. We can never dream again, never hope again!" She hid her face in her hands. "I'll manage somehow. I'd rather go away, hoping, than run the risk of being rejected by them."

"Not me," I said, starting the motor. "We have as much chance of a welcome as we do of being kicked out. And if they can help you—say, what's the matter with you today? I'm supposed to be the doubting one, remember? You're the mustard seed of this outfit!" I grinned at her, but my heart sank at the drawn white misery of her face. She almost managed a smile.

The trail led steadily downward, lapping back on itself as it worked back and forth along the canyon wall, sometimes steep, sometimes almost level. The farther we went the more rested I felt, as though I were shutting doors behind or opening them before me.

Then came one of the casual miracles of mountain country. The clouds suddenly opened and the late sun broke through. There, almost frighteningly, a huge mountain pushed out of the featureless gray distance. In the flooding light the towering slopes seemed to move, stepping closer to us as we watched. The rain still fell, but now in glittering silver-beaded curtains; and one vivid end of a rainbow splashed color recklessly over trees and rocks and a corner of the sky.

I didn't watch the road. I watched the splendor and glory spread out around us. So when, at Bethie's scream, I snatched back to my driving all I took down into the roaring splintering darkness was the thought of Bethie and the sight of the other car, slanting down from the bobbing top branches of a tree, seconds before it plowed into us broadside, a yard above the road.

I thought I was dead. I was afraid to open my eyes because I could feel the rain making little puddles over my closed lids. And then I breathed. I was alive, all right. A knife jabbed itself up and down the left side of my chest and twisted itself viciously with each reluctant breath I drew.

Then I heard a voice.

"Thank the Power they aren't hurt too badly. But, oh, Valancy! What will Father say?" The voice was young and scared.

"You've known him longer than I have," another girl-voice answered. "You should have some idea."

"I never had a wreck before, not even when I was driving instead of lifting."

"I have a hunch that you'll be grounded for quite a spell," the second voice replied. "But that isn't what's worrying me, Karen. Why didn't we know they were coming? We always can sense Outsiders. We should have known—"

"Q. E. D. then," said the Karen-voice.

" 'Q. E. D.'?"

"Yes. If we didn't sense them, then they're not Outsiders—"
There was the sound of a caught breath and then, "Oh, what I
said, Valancy! You don't suppose!" I felt a movement close to
me and heard the soft sound of breathing. "Can it really be
two more of us? Oh, Valancy, they must be second generation
—they're about our age. How did they find us? Which of our
Lost Ones were their parents?"

Valancy sounded amused. "Those are questions they're certainly in no condition to answer right now, Karen. We'd better
figure out what to do. Look, the girl is coming to."

I was snapped out of my detached eavesdropping by a moan
beside me. I started to sit up. "Bethie—" I began, and all the
knives twisted through my lungs. Bethie's scream followed my
gasp.

My eyes were open now, but good, and my leg was an
agonized burning ache down at the far end of my consciousness.
I gritted my teeth but Bethie moaned again.

"Help her, help her!" I pleaded to the two fuzzy figures
leaning over us as I tried to hold my breath to stop the jabbing.

"But she's hardly hurt," Karen cried. "A bump on her head.
Some cuts."

With an effort I focused on a luminous clear face—Valancy's
—whose deep eyes bent close above me. I locked the rain from
my lips and blurted foolishly, "You're not even wet in all this
rain!" A look of consternation swept over her face. There was
a pause as she looked at me intently and then said, "Their shields
aren't activated, Karen. We'd better extend ours."

"Okay, Valancy." And the annoying sibilant wetness of the
rain stopped.

"How's the girl?"

"It must be shock or maybe internal—"

I started to turn to see, but Bethie's sobbing cry pushed me
flat again.

"Help her," I gasped, grabbing wildly in my memory for
Mother's words. "She's a—a Sensitive!"

"A Sensitive?" The two exchanged looks. "Then why doesn't
she—?" Valancy started to say something, then turned swiftly.
I crooked my arm over my eyes as I listened.

"Honey—Bethie—hear me!" The voice was warm but authoritative. "I'm going to help you. I'll show you how, Bethie."

There was a silence. A warm hand clasped mine and Karen squatted close beside me.

"She's sorting her," she whispered. "Going into her mind. To teach her control. It's so simple. How could it happen that she doesn't know—?"

I heard a soft wondering "Oh!" from Bethie, followed by a breathless "Oh, thank you, Valancy, thank you!"

I heaved myself up onto my elbow, fire streaking me from head to foot, and peered over at Bethie. She was looking at me, and her quiet face was happier than smiles could ever make it. We stared for the space of two relieved tears, then she said softly, "Tell them now, Peter. We can't go any farther until you tell them."

I lay back again, blinking at the sky where the scattered raindrops were still falling, though none of them reached us. Karen's hand was warm on mine and I felt a shiver of reluctance. If they sent us away . . . ! But then they couldn't take back what they had given to Bethie, even if—I shut my eyes and blurted it out as bluntly as possible.

"We aren't of the People—not entirely. Father was not of the People. We're half-breeds."

There was a startled silence.

"You mean your mother married an Outsider?" Valancy's voice was filled with astonishment. "That you and Bethie are—?"

"Yes she did and yes we are!" I retorted. "And Dad was the best—" My belligerence ran thinly out across the sharp edge of my pain. "They're both dead now. Mother sent us to you."

"But Bethie is a Sensitive—" Valancy's voice was thoughtful.

"Yes, and I can fly and make things travel in the air and I've even made fire. But Dad—" I hid my face and let it twist with the increasing agony.

"Then we *can!*" I couldn't read the emotion in Valancy's voice. "Then the People and Outsiders—but it's unbelievable that you—" Her voice died.

In the silence that followed, Bethie's voice came fearful and tremulous, "Are you going to send us away?" My heart twisted to the ache in her voice.

"Send you away! Oh, my people, my people! Of course not!

As if there were any question!" Valancy's arm went tightly around Bethie, and Karen's hand closed warmly on mine. The tension that had been a hard twisted knot inside me dissolved, and Bethie and I were home.

Then Valancy became very brisk.

"Bethie, what's wrong with Peter?"

Bethie was astonished. "How did you know his name?" Then she smiled. "Of course. When you were sorting me!" She touched me lightly along my sides, along my legs. "Four of his ribs are hurt. His left leg is broken. That's about all. Shall I control him?"

"Yes," Valancy said. "I'll help."

And the pain was gone, put to sleep under the persuasive warmth that came to me as Bethie and Valancy came softly into my mind.

"Good," Valancy said. "We're pleased to welcome a Sensitive. Karen and I know a little of their function because we are Sorters. But we have no full-fledged Sensitive in our Group now."

She turned to me. "You said you know the inanimate lift?"

"I don't know," I said. "I don't know the words for lots of things."

"You'll have to relax completely. We don't usually use it on people. But if you let go all over we can manage."

They wrapped me warmly in our blankets and lightly, a hand under my shoulders and under my heels, lifted me carrying-high and sped with me through the trees, Bethie trailing from Valancy's free hand.

Before we reached the yard the door flew open and warm yellow light spilled out into the dusk. The girls paused on the porch and shifted me to the waiting touch of two men. In the wordless pause before the babble of question and explanation I felt Bethie beside me draw a deep wondering breath and merge like a raindrop in a river into the People around us.

But even as the lights went out for me again, and I felt myself slide down into comfort and hunger-fed belongingness, somewhere deep inside of me was a core of something that couldn't quite—no, *wouldn't* quite dissolve—wouldn't yet yield itself completely to the People.

I sank into the kitchen, my stiff hands clutching at the doorknob. I huddled in a chair, gratefully leaning over the hot

III

Lea slipped soundlessly toward the door almost before Peter's last words were said. She was halfway up the steep road that led up the canyon before she heard the sound of Karen coming behind her. Lifting and running, Karen caught up with her.

"Lea!" she called, reaching for her arm.

With a twist of her shoulder Lea evaded Karen and wordlessly, breathlessly ran on up the road.

"Lea!" Karen grabbed both her shoulders and stopped her bodily. "Where on earth are you going!"

"Let me go!" Lea shouted. "Sneak! Peeping Tom! Let me go!" She tried to wrench out of Karen's hands.

"Lea, whatever you're thinking it isn't so."

"Whatever I'm thinking!" Lea's eyes blazed. "Don't you *know* what I'm thinking? Haven't you done enough scrabbling around in all the muck and mess—?" Her fingernails dented Karen's hands. "Let me go!"

"Why do you *care*, Lea?" Karen's cold voice jabbed mercilessly. "Why should you care? What difference does it make to you? You left life a long time ago."

"Death—" Lea choked, feeling the dusty bitterness of the word she had thought so often and seldom said. "Death is at least private—no one nosing around—"

"Can you be so sure?" It was Karen's quiet voice. "Anyway, believe me, Lea, I haven't gone in to you even once. Of course I could if I wanted to and I will if I have to, but I never would without your knowledge—if not your consent. All I've learned of you has been from the most open outer part of your mind. Your inner mind is sacredly your own. The People are taught reverence for individual privacy. Whatever powers we have are

80

for healing, not for hurting. We have health and life for you if you'll accept it. You see, there *is* balm in Gilead! Don't refuse it, Lea."

Lea's hands drooped heavily. The tension went out of her body slowly.

"I heard you last night," she said, puzzled. "I heard your story and it didn't even occur to me that you could—I mean, it just wasn't real and I had no idea—" She let Karen turn her back down the road. "But then when I heard Peter—I don't know—he seemed more true. You don't expect men to go in for fairy tales—" She clutched suddenly at Karen. "Oh, Karen, what shall I do? I'm so mixed up that I can't—"

"Well, the simplest and most immediate thing is to come on back. We have time to hear another report and they're waiting for us. Melodye is next. She saw the People from quite another angle."

Back in the schoolroom Lea fitted herself self-consciously into her corner again, though no one seemed to notice her. Everyone was busy reliving or commenting on the days of Peter and Bethie. The talking died as Melodye Amerson took her place at the desk.

"Valancy's helping me," she smiled. "We chose the theme together, too. Remember—?

" 'Behold, I am at a point to die and what profit shall this birthright do to me? And he sold his birthright for bread and pottage.'

"I couldn't do the recalling alone, either. So now, if you don't mind, there'll be a slight pause while we construct our network."

She relaxed visibly and Lea could feel the receptive quietness spread as though the whole room were becoming mirror-placid like the pool in the creek, and then Melodye began to speak. . . .

POTTAGE

You GET tired of teaching after a while. Well, maybe not of teaching itself, because it's insidious and remains a tug in the blood for all of your life, but there comes a day when you look down at the paper you're grading or listen to an answer you're giving a child and you get a *boinnng!* feeling. And each reverberation of the *boing* is a year in your life, another set of children through your hands, another beat in monotony, and it's frightening. The value of the work you're doing doesn't enter into it at that moment and the monotony is bitter on your tongue.

Sometimes you can assuage that feeling by consciously savoring those precious days of pseudofreedom between the time you receive your contract for the next year and the moment you sign it. Because you *can* escape at that moment, but somehow —you don't.

But I did, one spring. I quit teaching. I didn't sign up again. I went chasing after—after what? Maybe excitement—maybe a dream of wonder—maybe a new bright wonderful world that just *must* be somewhere else because it isn't here-and-now. Maybe a place to begin again so I'd never end up at the same frightening emotional dead end. So I quit.

But by late August the emptiness inside me was bigger than boredom, bigger than monotony, bigger than lusting after freedom. It was almost terror to be next door to September and not care that in a few weeks school starts—tomorrow school starts —first day of school. So, almost at the last minute, I went to the placement bureau. Of course it was too late to try to return to my other school, and besides, the mold of the years there still chafed in too many places.

"Well," the placement director said as he shuffled his end-of-the-season cards, past Algebra and Home Ec and PE and High-School English, "there's always Bendo." He thumbed out a battered-looking three-by-five. "There's *always* Bendo."

And I took his emphasis and look for what they were intended and sighed.

"Bendo?"

"Small school. One room. Mining town, or used to be. Ghost town now." He sighed wearily and let down his professional hair. "Ghost people, too. Can't keep a teacher there more than a year. Low pay—fair housing—at someone's home. No community activities—no social life. No city within fifty or so miles. No movies. No nothing but children to be taught. Ten of them this year. All grades."

"Sounds like the town I grew up in," I said. "Except we had two rooms and lots of community activities."

"I've been to Bendo." The director leaned back in his chair, hands behind his head. "Sick community. Unhappy people. No interest in anything. Only reason they have a school is because it's the law. Law-abiding anyway. Not enough interest in anything to break a law, I guess."

"I'll take it," I said quickly before I could think beyond the feeling that this sounded about as far back as I could go to get a good running start at things again.

He glanced at me quizzically. "If you're thinking of lighting a torch of high reform to set Bendo afire with enthusiasm, forget it. I've seen plenty of king-sized torches fizzle out there."

"I have no torch," I said. "Frankly I'm fed to the teeth with bouncing bright enthusiasm and huge PTA's and activities until they come out your ears. They usually turn out to be the most montonous kind of monotony. Bendo will be a rest."

"It will that," the director said, leaning over his cards again. "Saul Diemus is the president of the board. If you don't have a car the only way to get to Bendo is by bus—it runs once a week."

I stepped out into the August sunshine after the interview and sagged a little under its savage pressure, almost hearing a hiss as the refrigerated coolness of the placement bureau evaporated from my skin.

I walked over to the quad and sat down on one of the stone benches I'd never had time to use, those years ago when I had been a student here. I looked up at my old dorm window and, for a moment, felt a wild homesickness—not only for years that were gone and hopes that had died and dreams that had had grim awakenings, but for a special magic I had found in that room. It was a magic—a true magic—that opened such vistas to me that for a while anything seemed possible, anything feasible—if not for me right now, then for others, someday. Even now, after the dilution of time, I couldn't quite believe that magic, and even now, as then, I wanted fiercely to believe it. If only it could be so! If only it could be so!

I sighed and stood up. I suppose everyone has a magic moment somewhere in his life and, like me, can't believe that anyone else could have the same—but mine *was* different! No one else *could* have had the same experience! I laughed at myself. Enough of the past and of dreaming. Bendo waited. I had things to do.

I watched the rolling clouds of red-yellow dust billow away from the jolting bus, and cupped my hands over my face to get a breath of clean air. The grit between my teeth and the smothering sift of dust across my clothes was familiar enough to me, but I hoped by the time we reached Bendo we would have left this dust plain behind and come into a little more vegetation. I shifted wearily on the angular seat, wondering if it had ever been designed for anyone's comfort, and caught myself as a sudden braking of the bus flung me forward.

We sat and waited for the dust of our going to catch up with us, while the last-but-me passenger, a withered old Indian, slowly gathered up his gunny-sack bundles and his battered saddle and edged his Levied velveteen-bloused self up the aisle and out to the bleak roadside.

We roared away, leaving him a desolate figure in a wide desolation. I wondered where he was headed. How many weary miles to his hogan in what hidden wash or miniature greenness in all this wilderness.

Then we headed straight as a die for the towering redness of the bare mountains that lined the horizon. Peering ahead I could see the road, ruler straight, disappearing into the distance. I sighed and shifted again and let the roar of the motor and the weariness of my bones lull me into a stupor on the border between sleep and waking.

A change in the motor roar brought me back to the jouncing bus. We jerked to a stop again. I looked out the window through the settling clouds of dust and wondered who we could be picking up out here in the middle of nowhere. Then a clot of dust dissolved and I saw

BENDO POST OFFICE
GENERAL STORE
Garage & Service Station
Dry Goods & Hardware
Magazines

in descending size on the front of the leaning, weather-beaten building propped between two crumbling smoke-blackened stone ruins. After so much flatness it was almost a shock to see the bare tumbled boulders crowding down to the roadside and humping their lichen-stained shoulders against the sky.

"Bendo," the bus driver said, unfolding his lanky legs and hunching out of the bus. "End of the line—end of civilization —end of everything!" He grinned and the dusty mask of his face broke into engaging smile patterns.

"Small, isn't it?" I grinned back.

"Usta be bigger. Not that it helps now. Roaring mining town years ago." As he spoke I could pick out disintegrating buildings dotting the rocky hillsides and tumbling into the steep washes. "My dad can remember it when he was a kid. That was long enough ago that there was still a river for the town to be in the bend o'."

"Is *that* where it got its name?"

"Some say yes, some say no. Might have been a feller named Bendo." The driver grunted as he unlashed my luggage from the bus roof and swung it to the ground.

"Oh, hi!" said the driver.

I swung around to see who was there. The man was tall, well built, good-looking—and old. Older than his face—older than years could have made him because he was really young, not much older than I. His face was a stern unhappy stillness, his hands stiff on the brim of his Stetson as he held it waist high.

In that brief pause before his "Miss Amerson?" I felt the same feeling coming from him that you can feel around some highly religious person who knows God only as a stern implacable vengeful deity, impatient of worthless man, waiting only for an unguarded moment to strike him down in his sin. I wondered who or what his God was that prisoned him so cruelly. Then I was answering, "Yes, how do you do?" And he touched my hand briefly with a "Saul Diemus" and turned to the problem of my two large suitcases and my record player.

I followed Mr. Diemus' shuffling feet silently, since he seemed to have slight inclination for talk. I hadn't expected a reception committee, but kids must have changed a lot since I was one, otherwise curiosity about teacher would have lured out at least a couple of them for a preview look. But the silent two of us walked on for a half block or so from the highway and the post office and rounded the rocky corner of a hill. I looked across the dry creek bed and up the one winding street that was residential Bendo. I paused on the splintery old bridge and took a good look. I'd never see Bendo like this again. Familiarity would blur some outlines and sharpen others, and I'd never again see it, free from the knowledge of who lived behind which blank front door.

The houses were scattered haphazardly over the hillsides and erratic flights of rough stone steps led down from each to the road that paralleled the bone-dry creek bed. The houses were not shacks but they were unpainted and weathered until they blended into the background almost perfectly. Each front yard had things growing in it, but such subdued blossoming and unobtrusive planting that they could easily have been only accidental massings of natural vegetation.

Such a passion for anonymity . . .

"The school—" I had missed the swift thrust of his hand.

"Where?" Nothing I could see spoke school to me.

"Around the bend." This time I followed his indication and suddenly, out of the featurelessness of the place, I saw a bell tower barely topping the hill beyond the town, with the fine pencil stroke of a flagpole to one side. Mr. Diemus pulled himself together to make the effort.

"The school's in the prettiest place around here. There's a spring and trees, and—" He ran out of words and looked at me as though trying to conjure up something else I'd like to hear. "I'm board president," he said abruptly. "You'll have ten children from first grade to second-year high school. You're the boss in your school. Whatever you do is your business. Any discipline you find desirable—use. We don't pamper our children. Teach them what you have to. Don't bother the parents with reasons and explanations. The school is yours."

"And you'd just as soon do away with it and me, too," I smiled at him.

He looked startled. "The law says school them." He started across the bridge. "So school them."

I followed meekly, wondering wryly what would happen if I asked Mr. Diemus why he hated himself and the world he was in and even—oh, breathe it softly—the children I was to "school."

"You'll stay at my place," he said. "We have an extra room."

I was uneasily conscious of the wide gap of silence that followed his pronouncement, but couldn't think of a thing to fill it. I shifted my small case from one hand to the other and kept my eyes on the rocky path that protested with shifting stones and vocal gravel every step we took. It seemed to me that Mr. Diemus was trying to make all the noise he could with his shuffling feet. But, in spite of the amplified echo from the hills around us, no door opened, no face pressed to a window. It was a distinct relief to hear suddenly the happy unthinking rusty singing of hens as they scratched in the coarse dust.

I hunched up in the darkness of my narrow bed trying to comfort my uneasy stomach. It wasn't that the food had been bad—it had been quite adequate—but such a dingy meal! Gloom seemed to festoon itself from the ceiling and unhappiness sat almost visibly at the table.

I tried to tell myself that it was my own travel weariness that slanted my thoughts, but I looked around the table and saw the hopeless endurance furrowed into the adult faces and beginning faintly but unmistakably on those of the children. There were two children there. A girl, Sarah (fourth grade, at a guess), and an adolescent boy, Matt (seventh?)—too silent, too well mannered, too controlled, avoiding much too pointedly looking at the empty chair between them.

My food went down in lumps and quarreled fiercely with the coffee that arrived in square-feeling gulps. Even yet—long difficult hours after the meal—the food still wouldn't lie down to be digested.

Tomorrow I could slip into the pattern of school, familiar no matter where school was, since teaching kids is teaching kids no matter where. Maybe then I could convince my stomach that all was well, and then maybe even start to thaw those frozen unnatural children. Of course they well might be little demons away from home—which is very often the case. Anyway I felt, thankfully, the familiar September thrill of new beginnings.

I shifted in bed again, then stiffening my neck, lifted my ears clear of my pillow.

It was a whisper, the intermittent hissing I had been hearing. Someone was whispering in the next room to mine. I sat up and listened unashamedly. I knew Sarah's room was next to mine, but who was talking with her? At first I could get only half words and then either my ears sharpened or the voices became louder.

". . . and did you hear her laugh? Right out loud at the table!" The quick whisper became a low voice. "Her eyes crinkled in the corners and she laughed."

"Our other teachers laughed, too." The uncertainly deep voice must be Matt.

"Yes," Sarah whispered. "But not for long. Oh, Matt! What's wrong with us? People in our books have fun. They laugh and run and jump and do all kinds of fun stuff and nobody—" Sarah faltered, "no one calls it evil."

"Those are only stories," Matt said. "Not real life."

"I don't believe it!" Sarah cried. "When I get big I'm going away from Bendo. I'm going to see—"

"Away from Bendo!" Matt's voice broke in roughly. "Away from the Group?"

I lost Sarah's reply. I felt as though I had missed an expected step. As I wrestled with my breath the sights and sounds and smells of my old dorm room crowded back upon me. Then I caught myself. It was probably only a turn of phrase. This futile desolate unhappiness couldn't possibly be related in any way to *that* magic. . . .

"Where *is* Dorcas?" Sarah asked, as though she knew the answer already.

"Punished." Matt's voice was hard and unchildlike. "She jumped."

"Jumped!" Sarah was shocked.

"Over the edge of the porch. Clear down to the path. Father saw her. I think she let him see her on purpose." His voice was defiant. "Someday when I get older I'm going to jump, too—all I want to—even over the house. Right in front of Father."

"Oh, Matt!" The cry was horrified and admiring. "You wouldn't! You couldn't. Not so far, not right in front of Father!"

"I would so," Matt retorted. "I could so, because I—" His words cut off sharply. "Sarah," he went on, "can you figure any way, *any* way, that jumping could be evil? It doesn't hurt anyone. It isn't ugly. There isn't any law—"

"Where is Dorcas?" Sarah's voice was almost inaudible. "In the hidey hole again?" She was almost answering Matt's question instead of asking one of her own.

"Yes," Matt said. "In the dark with only bread to eat. So she can learn what a hunted animal feels like. An animal that is different, that other animals hate and hunt." His bitter voice put quotes around the words.

"You see," Sarah whispered. "You see?"

In the silence following I heard the quiet closing of a door and the slight vibration of the floor as Matt passed my room. I eased back onto my pillow. I lay back, staring toward the ceiling. What dark thing was here in this house? In this community? Frightened children whispering in the dark. Rebellious children in hidey holes learning how hunted animals feel. And a Group . . . ? No it couldn't be. It was just the recent reminder of being on campus again that made me even consider that this darkness might in some way be the reverse of the golden coin Karen had shown me.

My heart almost failed me when I saw the school. It was one of those monstrosities that went up around the turn of the century. This one had been built for a boom town, but now all the upper windows were boarded up and obviously long out of use. The lower floor was blank, too, except for two rooms—though with the handful of children quietly standing around the door it was apparent that only one room was needed. And not only was the building deserted, the yard was swept clean from side to side, innocent of grass or trees—or playground equipment. There *was* a deep grove just beyond the school, though, and the glint of water down canyon.

"No swings?" I asked the three children who were escorting me. "No slides? No seesaws?"

"No!" Sarah's voice was unhappily surprised. Matt scowled at her warningly.

"No," he said, "we don't swing or slide—nor see a saw!" He grinned up at me faintly.

"What a shame!" I said. "Did they all wear out? Can't the school afford new ones?"

"We don't swing or slide or seesaw." The grin was dead. "We don't believe in it."

There's nothing quite so flat and incontestable as that last statement. I've heard it as an excuse for practically every type of omission, but, so help me, never applied to playground equipment. I couldn't think of a reply any more intelligent than "Oh," so I didn't say anything.

All week long I felt as if I were wading through knee-deep Jello or trying to lift a king-sized feather bed up over my head. I used up every device I ever thought of to rouse the class to enthusiasm—about anything, *anything!* They were polite and submissive and did what was asked of them, but joylessly, apathetically, enduringly.

Finally, just before dismissal time on Friday, I leaned in desperation across my desk.

"Don't you like *anything?*" I pleaded. "Isn't *anything* fun?"

Dorcas Diemus' mouth opened into the tense silence. I saw Matt kick quickly, warningly, against the leg of the desk. Her mouth closed.

"I think school is fun," I said. "I think we can enjoy all kinds of things. I want to enjoy teaching but I can't unless you enjoy learning."

"We learn," Dorcas said quickly. "We aren't stupid."

"You learn," I acknowledged. "You aren't stupid. But don't any of you *like* school?"

"I like school," Martha piped up, my first grade. "I think it's fun!"

"Thank you, Martha," I said. "And the rest of you—" I

90

glared at them in mock anger, "you're going to have fun if I have to beat it into you!"

To my dismay they shrank down apprehensively in their seats and exchanged troubled glances. But before I could hastily explain myself Matt laughed and Dorcas joined him. And I beamed fatuously to hear the hesitant rusty laughter spread across the room, but I saw ten-year-old Esther's hands shake as she wiped tears from her eyes. Tears—of laughter?

That night I twisted in the darkness of my room, almost too tired to sleep, worrying and wondering. What had blighted these people? They had health, they had beauty—the curve of Martha's cheek against the window was a song, the lift of Dorcas' eyebrows was breathless grace. They were fed—adequately, clothed—adequately, housed—adequately, but nothing like they could have been. I'd seen more joy and delight and enthusiasm from little campground kids who slept in cardboard shacks and washed—if they ever did—in canals and ate whatever edible came their way, but grinned, even when impetigo or cold sores bled across their grins.

But these lifeless kids! My prayers were troubled and I slept restlessly.

A month or so later things had improved a little bit, but not much. At least there was more relaxation in the classroom. And I found that they had no deep-rooted convictions against plants, so we had things growing on the deep window sills—stuff we transplanted from the spring and from among the trees. And we had jars of minnows from the creek and one drowsy horned toad that roused in his box of dirt only to flick up the ants brought for his dinner. And we sang, loudly and enthusiastically, but, miracle of miracles, without even one monotone in the whole room. But we *didn't* sing "Up, Up in the Sky" or "How Do You Like to Go Up in a Swing?" My solos of such songs were received with embarrassed blushes and lowered eyes!

There had been one dust-up between us, though—this matter of shuffling everywhere they walked.

"Pick up your feet, for goodness' sake," I said irritably one morning when the *shoosh, shoosh, shoosh* of their coming and going finally got my skin off. "Surely they're not so heavy you can't lift them."

Timmy, who happened to be the trigger this time, nibbled unhappily at one finger. "I can't," he whispered. "Not supposed to."

"Not supposed to?" I forgot momentarily how warily I'd been going with these frightened mice of children. "Why not? Surely there's no reason in the world why you can't walk quietly."

Matt looked unhappily over at Miriam, the sophomore who was our entire high school. She looked aside, biting her lower lip, troubled. Then she turned back and said, "It is customary in Bendo."

"To shuffle along?" I was forgetting any manners I had. "Whatever for?"

"That's the way we do in Bendo." There was no anger in her defense, only resignation.

"Perhaps that's the way you do at home. But here at school let's pick our feet up. It makes too much disturbance otherwise."

"But it's bad—" Esther began.

Matt's hand shushed her in a hurry.

"Mr. Diemus said what we did at school was my business," I told them. "He said not to bother your parents with our problems. One of our problems is too much noise when others are trying to work. At least in our schoolroom let's lift our feet and walk quietly."

The children considered the suggestion solemnly and turned to Matt and Miriam for guidance. They both nodded and we went back to work. For the next few minutes, from the corner of my eyes, I saw with amazement all the unnecessary trips back and forth across the room, with high-lifted feet, with grins and side glances that marked such trips as high adventure—as a delightfully daring thing to do! The whole deal had me bewildered. Thinking back I realized that not only the children of Bendo scuffled but all the adults did, too —as though they were afraid to lose contact with the earth, as though . . . I shook my head and went on with the lesson.

Before noon, though, the endless *shoosh, shoosh, shoosh* of feet began again. Habit was too much for the children. So

I silently filed the sound under "Uncurable, Endurable," and let the matter drop.

I sighed as I watched the children leave at lunchtime. It seemed to me that with the unprecedented luxury of a whole hour for lunch they'd all go home. The bell tower was visible from nearly every house in town. But instead they all brought tight little paper sacks with dull crumbly sandwiches and unimaginative apples in them. And silently with their dull scuffly steps they disappeared into the thicket of trees around the spring.

"Everything is dulled around here," I thought. "Even the sunlight is blunted as it floods the hills and canyons. There is no mirth, no laughter. No high jinks or cutting up. No preadolescent silliness. No adolescent foolishness. Just quiet children, enduring."

I don't usually snoop but I began wondering if perhaps the kids were different when they were away from me—and from their parents. So when I got back at twelve thirty from an adequate but uninspired lunch at Diemuses' house I kept on walking past the schoolhouse and quietly down into the grove, moving cautiously through the scanty undergrowth until I could lean over a lichened boulder and look down on the children.

Some were lying around on the short still grass, hands under their heads, blinking up at the brightness of the sky between the leaves. Esther and little Martha were hunting out fillaree seed pods and counting the tines of the pitchforks and rakes and harrows they resembled. I smiled, remembering how I used to do the same thing.

"I dreamed last night." Dorcas thrust the statement defiantly into the drowsy silence. "I dreamed about the Home."

My sudden astonished movement was covered by Martha's horrified "Oh, Dorcas!"

"What's wrong with the Home?" Dorcas cried, her cheeks scarlet. "There *was* a Home! There was! There was! Why shouldn't we talk about it?"

I listened avidly. This couldn't be just coincidence—a Group and now the Home. There must be some connection. . . . I pressed closer against the rough rock.

"But it's bad!" Esther cried. "You'll be punished! We can't talk about the Home!"

"Why not?" Joel asked as though it had just occurred to him, as things do just occur to you when you're thirteen. He sat up slowly. "Why can't we?"

There was a short tense silence.

"I've dreamed, too," Matt said. "I've dreamed of the Home —and it's *good*, it's good!"

"Who hasn't dreamed?" Miriam asked. "We all have, haven't we? Even our parents. I can tell by Mother's eyes when she has."

"Did you ever ask how come we aren't supposed to talk about it?" Joel asked. "I mean and ever get any answer except that it's bad."

"I think it has something to do with a long time ago," Matt said. "Something about when the Group first came—"

"I don't think it's just dreams," Miriam declared, "because I don't have to be asleep. I think it's remembering."

"Remembering?" asked Dorcas. "How can we remember something we never knew?"

"I don't know," Miriam admitted, "but I'll bet it is."

"I remember," volunteered Talitha, who never volunteered anything.

"Hush!" whispered Abie, the second-grade next-to-youngest who always whispered.

"I remember," Talitha went on stubbornly. "I remember a dress that was too little so the mother just stretched the skirt till it was long enough and it stayed stretched. 'Nen she pulled the waist out big enough and the little girl put it on and flew away."

"Hoh!" Timmy scoffed. "I remember better than that." His face stilled and his eyes widened. "The ship was so tall it was like a mountain and the people went in the high high door and they didn't have a ladder. 'Nen there were stars, big burning ones—not squinchy little ones like ours."

"It went too fast!" That was Abie! Talking eagerly! "When the air came it made the ship hot and the little baby died before all the little boats left the ship." He scrunched down suddenly, leaning against Talitha and whimpering.

"You see!" Miriam lifted her chin triumphantly. "We've all dreamed—I mean remembered!"

"I guess so," said Matt. "I remember. It's *lifting*, Talitha, not flying. You go and go as high as you like, as far as you want to and don't *ever* have to touch the ground—at all! At all!" He pounded his fist into the gravelly red soil beside him.

"And you can dance in the air, too," Miriam sighed. "Freer than a bird, lighter than—"

Esther scrambled to her feet, white-faced and panic-stricken. "Stop! Stop! It's evil! It's bad! I'll tell Father! We can't dream—or lift—or dance! It's bad, it's bad! You'll die for it! You'll die for it!"

Joel jumped to his feet and grabbed Esther's arm.

"Can we die any deader?" he cried, shaking her brutally. "You call *this* being alive?" He hunched down apprehensively and shambled a few scuffling steps across the clearing.

I fled blindly back to school, trying to wink away my tears without admitting I was crying, crying for these poor kids who were groping so hopelessly for something they knew they should have. Why was it so rigorously denied them? Surely, if they were what I thought them . . . And they could be! They could be!

I grabbed the bell rope and pulled hard. Reluctantly the bell moved and rolled.

One o'clock, it clanged. *One o'clock!*

I watched the children returning with slow uneager shuffling steps.

That night I started a letter:

"Dear Karen,

"Yep, 'sme after all these years. And, oh, Karen! I've found some more! Some more of the People! Remember how much you wished you knew if any other Groups besides yours had survived the Crossing? How you worried about them and wanted to find them if they had? Well, *I've* found a whole Group! But it's a sick unhappy group. Your heart would break to see them. If you could come and start them on the right path again . . ."

I put my pen down. I looked at the lines I had written and then crumpled the paper slowly. This was *my* Group. I had found them. Sure, I'd tell Karen—but later. Later, after —well, after *I* had tried to start them on the right path—at least the children.

After all I knew a little of their potentialities. Hadn't Karen briefed me in those unguarded magical hours in the old dorm, drawn to me as I was to her by some mutual sympathy that seemed stronger than the usual roommate attachment, telling me things no Outsider had a right to hear? And if, when I finally told her and turned the Group over to her, if it could be a joyous gift, then I could feel that I had repaid her a little for the wonder world she had opened for me.

"Yes," I thought ruefully, "and there's nothing like a large portion of ignorance to give one a large portion of confidence." But I did want to try—desperately. Maybe if I could break prison for someone else, then perhaps my own bars . . . I dropped the paper in the wastebasket.

But it was several weeks before I could bring myself to do anything to let the children know I knew about them. It was such an impossible situation, even if it was true—and if it wasn't what kind of lunacy would they suspect me of?

When I finally set my teeth and swore a swear to myself that I'd do something definite my hands shook and my breath was a flutter in my dry throat.

"Today—" I said with an effort, "today is Friday." Which gem of wisdom the children received with charitable silence. "We've been working hard all week, so let's have fun today." This stirred the children—half with pleasure, half with apprehension. They, poor kids, found my "fun" much harder than any kind of work I could give them. But some of them were acquiring a taste for it. Martha had even learned to skip!

"First, monitors pass the composition paper." Esther and Abie scuffled hurriedly around with the paper, and the pencil sharpener got a thorough workout. At least these kids didn't differ from others in their pleasure in grinding their pencils away at the slightest excuse.

"Now," I gulped, "we're going to write." Which obvious asininity was passed over with forbearance, though Miriam looked at me wonderingly before she bent her head and let her hair shadow her face. "Today I want you all to write about the same thing. Here is our subject."

Gratefully I turned my back on the children's waiting eyes and printed slowly:

I Remember the Home

I heard the sudden intake of breath that worked itself downward from Miriam to Talitha and then the rapid whisper that informed Abie and Martha. I heard Esther's muffled cry and I turned slowly around and leaned against the desk.

"There are so many beautiful things to remember about the Home," I said into the strained silence. "So many wonderful things. And even the sad memories are better than forgetting, because the Home was *good*. Tell me what you remember about the Home."

"We can't!" Joel and Matt were on their feet simultaneously.

"Why can't we?" Dorcas cried. "Why can't we?"

"It's bad!" Esther cried. "It's evil!"

"It ain't either!" Abie shrilled, astonishingly. "It ain't either!"

"We shouldn't." Miriam's trembling hands brushed her heavy hair upward. "It's forbidden."

"Sit down," I said gently. "The day I arrived at Bendo Mr. Diemus told me to teach you what I had to teach you. I have to teach you that remembering the Home is good."

"Then why don't the grownups think so?" Matt asked slowly. "They tell us not to talk about it. We shouldn't disobey our parents."

"I know," I admitted. "And I would never ask you children to go against your parents' wishes, unless I felt that it is very important. If you'd rather they didn't know about it at first, keep it as our secret. Mr. Diemus told me not to bother them with explanations or reasons. I'll make it right with your parents when the time comes." I paused to swallow and blink away a vision of me leaving town in a cloud of dust, barely ahead of a posse of irate parents. "Now, everyone, busy," I said briskly. " 'I Remember the Home.' "

There was a moment heavy with decision and I held my

breath, wondering which way the balance would dip. And then —surely it must have been because they wanted so to speak and affirm the wonder of what had been that they capitulated so easily. Heads bent and pencils scurried. And Martha sat, her head bowed on her desk with sorrow.

"I don't know enough words," she mourned. "How do you write '*toolas*'?"

And Abie laboriously erased a hole through his paper and licked his pencil again.

"Why don't you and Abie make some pictures?" I suggested. "Make a little story with pictures and we can staple them together like a real book."

I looked over the silent busy group and let myself relax, feeling weakness flood into my knees. I scrubbed the dampness from my palms with Kleenex and sat back in my chair. Slowly I became conscious of a new atmosphere in my classroom. An intolerable strain was gone, an unconscious holding back of the children, a wariness, a watchfulness, a guilty feeling of desiring what was forbidden.

A prayer of thanksgiving began to well up inside me. It changed hastily to a plea for mercy as I began to visualize what might happen to me when the parents found out what I was doing. How long must this containment and denial have gone on? This concealment and this carefully nourished fear? From what Karen had told me it must be well over fifty years—long enough to mark indelibly three generations.

And here I was with my fine little hatchet trying to set a little world afire! On which very mixed metaphor I stiffened my weak knees and got up from my chair. I walked unnoticed up and down the aisles, stepping aside as Joel went blindly to the shelf for more paper, leaning over Miriam to marvel that she had taken out her Crayolas and part of her writing was with colors, part with pencil—and the colors spoke to something in me that the pencil couldn't reach, though I'd never seen the forms the colors took.

The children had gone home, happy and excited, chattering and laughing, until they reached the edge of the school grounds. There, smiles died and laughter stopped and faces and feet grew heavy again. All but Esther's. Hers had never been light. I sighed and turned to the papers. Here was Abie's little book. I thumbed through it and drew a deep breath and went back through it slowly again.

A second grader drawing this? Six pages—six finished adult-looking pages. Crayolas achieving effects I'd never seen before—pictures that told a story loudly and clearly.

Stars blazing in a black sky, with the slender needle of a ship, like a mote in the darkness.

The vasty green cloud-shrouded arc of earth against the blackness. A pink tinge of beginning friction along the ship's belly. I put my finger to the glow. I could almost feel the heat.

Inside the ship, suffering and pain, heroic striving, crumpled bodies and seared faces. A baby dead in its mother's arms. Then a swarm of tinier needles erupting from the womb of the ship. And the last shriek of incandescence as the ship volatilized against the thickening drag of the air.

I leaned my head on my hands and closed my eyes. All this, all *this* in the memory of an eight-year-old? All *this* in the feelings of an eight-year-old? Because Abie knew—he *knew* how this felt. He knew the heat and strivings and the dying and fleeing. No wonder Abie whispered and leaned. Racial memory was truly a two-sided coin.

I felt a pang of misgivings. Maybe I was wrong to let him remember so vividly. Maybe I shouldn't have let him . . .

I turned to Martha's papers. They were delicate, almost spidery drawings of some fuzzy little animal (*toolas?*) that apparently built a hanging hammocky nest and gathered fruit in a huge leaf basket and had a bird for a friend. A truly out-of-this-world bird. Much of her story escaped me because first graders—if anyone at all—produce symbolic art and, since her frame of reference and mine were so different, there was much that I couldn't interpret. But her whole booklet was joyous and light.

And now, the stories . . .

I lifted my head and blinked into the twilight. I had finished all the papers except Esther's. It was her cramped writing, swimming in darkness, that made me realize that the day was gone and that I was shivering in a shadowy room with the fire in the old-fashioned heater gone out.

Slowly I shuffled the papers into my desk drawer, hesitated and took out Esther's. I would finish at home. I shrugged into my coat and wandered home, my thoughts intent on the papers I had read. And suddenly I wanted to cry—to cry for the wonders that had been and were no more. For the heritage of attainment and achievement these children had but couldn't use. For the dream-come-true of what they were capable of doing but weren't permitted to do. For the homesick yearning that filled every line they had written— these unhappy exiles, three generations removed from any physical knowledge of the Home.

I stopped on the bridge and leaned against the railing in the half dark. Suddenly I felt a welling homesickness. *That* was what the world should be like—what it *could* be like if only—if only . . .

But my tears for the Home were as hidden as the emotions of Mrs. Diemus when she looked up uncuriously as I came through the kitchen door.

"Good evening," she said. "I've kept your supper warm."

"Thank you." I shivered convulsively. "It *is* getting cold."

I sat on the edge of my bed that night, letting the memory of the kids' papers wash over me, trying to fill in around the bits and snippets that they had told of the Home. And then I began to wonder. All of them who wrote about the actual Home had been so happy with their memories. From Timmy and his "Shinny ship as high as a montin and faster than two jets," and Dorcas' wandering tenses as though yesterday and today were one: "The flowers were like lights. At night it isn't dark becas they shine so bright and when the moon came up the breeos sing and the music was so you can see it like rain falling around only happyer"; up to Miriam's wistful "On Gathering Day there was a big party. Everybody came dressed in beautiful clothes with *flahmen* in the girls' hair. *Flahmen* are flowers but they're good to eat. And if a girl felt her heart sing for a boy they ate a *flahmen* together and started two-ing."

Then, if all these memories were so happy, why the rigid

suppression of them by grownups? Why the pall of unhappiness over everyone? You can't mourn forever for a wrecked ship. Why a hidey hole for disobedient children? Why the misery and frustration when, if they could do half of what I didn't fully understand from Joel and Matt's highly technical papers, they could make Bendo an Eden?

I reached for Esther's paper. I had put it on the bottom on purpose. I dreaded reading it. She had sat with her head buried on her arms on her desk most of the time the others were writing busily. At widely separated intervals she had scribbled a line or two as though she were doing something shameful. She, of all the children, had seemed to find no relief in her remembering.

I smoothed the paper on my lap.

"I remember," she had written. "We were thirsty. There was water in the creek we were hiding in the grass. We could not drink. They would shoot us. Three days the sun was hot. She screamed for water and ran to the creek. They shot. The water got red."

Blistered spots marked the tears on the paper.

"They found a baby under a bush. The man hit it with the wood part of his gun. He hit it and hit it and hit it. I hit scorpins like that.

"They caught us and put us in a pen. They built a fire all around us. Fly 'they said' fly and save yourselfs. We flew because it hurt. They shot us.

"Monster 'they yelled' evil monsters. People can't fly. People can't move things. People are the same. You aren't people. Die die die."

Then blackly, traced and retraced until the paper split:

"If anyone finds out we are not of earth we will die.

"Keep your feet on the ground."

Bleakly I laid the paper aside. So there was the answer, putting Karen's bits and snippets together with these. The shipwrecked ones finding savages on the desert island. A remnant surviving by learning caution, suppression and denial. Another generation that pinned the *evil* label on the Home to insure continued immunity for their children, and now, a generation that questioned and wondered—and rebelled.

I turned off the light and slowly got into bed. I lay there

101

staring into the darkness, holding the picture Esther had evoked. Finally I relaxed. "God help her," I sighed. "God help us all."

Another week was nearly over. We cleaned the room up quickly, for once anticipating the fun time instead of dreading it. I smiled to hear the happy racket all around me, and felt my own spirits surge upward in response to the lightheartedness of the children. The difference that one afternoon had made in them! Now they were beginning to feel like children to me. They were beginning to accept me. I swallowed with an effort. How soon would they ask, "How come? How come you knew?" There they sat, all nine of them—nine, because Esther was my first absence in the year—bright-eyed and expectant.

"Can we write again?" Sarah asked. "I can remember lots more."

"No," I said. "Not today." Smiles died and there was a protesting wiggle through the room. "Today we are going to *do.* Joel." I looked at him and tightened my jaws. "Joel, give me the dictionary." He began to get up. "*Without leaving your seat!*"

"But I—!" Joel broke the shocked silence. "I can't!"

"Yes you can," I prayed. "Yes, you can. Give me the dictionary. Here, on my desk."

Joel turned and stared at the big old dictionary that spilled pages 1965 to 1998 out of its cracked old binding. Then he said, "Miriam?" in a high tight voice. But she shook her head and shrank back in her seat, her eyes big and dark in her white face.

"You can." Miriam's voice was hardly more than a breath. "It's just bigger—"

Joel clutched the edge of his desk and sweat started out on his forehead. There was a stir of movement on the bookshelf. Then, as though shot from a gun, pages 1965 to 1998 whisked to my desk and fell fluttering. Our laughter cut through the blank amazement and we laughed till tears came.

"That's a-doing it, Joel!" Matt shouted. "That's showing them your muscles!"

"Well, it's a beginning." Joel grinned weakly. "You do it, brother, if you think it's so easy."

So Matt sweated and strained and Joel joined with him, but they only managed to scrape the book to the edge of the shelf where it teetered dangerously.

Then Abie waved his hand timidly. "I can, teacher."

I beamed that my silent one had spoken and at the same time frowned at the loving laughter of the big kids.

"Okay, Abie," I encouraged. "You show them how to do it."

And the dictionary swung off the shelf and glided unhastily to my desk, where it came silently to rest.

Everyone stared at Abie and he squirmed. "The little ships," he defended. "That's the way they moved them out of the big ship. Just like that."

Joel and Matt turned their eyes to some inner concentration and then exchanged exasperated looks.

"Why, sure," Matt said. "Why, sure." And the dictionary swung back to the shelf.

"Hey!" Timmy protested. "It's my turn!"

"That poor dictionary," I said. "It's too old for all this bouncing around. Just put the loose pages back on the shelf."

And he did.

Everyone sighed and looked at me expectantly.

"Miriam?" She clasped her hands convulsively. "*You* come to me," I said, feeling a chill creep across my stiff shoulders. "*Lift* to me, Miriam."

Without taking her eyes from me she slipped out of her seat and stood in the aisle. Her skirts swayed a little as her feet lifted from the floor. Slowly at first and then more quickly she came to me, soundlessly, through the air, until in a little flurried rush her arms went around me and she gasped into my shoulder. I put her aside, trembling. I groped for my handkerchief. I said shakily, "Miriam, help the rest. I'll be back in a minute."

And I stumbled into the room next door. Huddled down in the dust and debris of the catchall storeroom it had become, I screamed soundlessly into my muffling hands. And screamed and screamed! Because after all—*after all!*

And then suddenly, with a surge of pure panic, I heard a

103

sound—the sound of footsteps, many footsteps, approaching the schoolhouse. I jumped for the door and wrenched it open just in time to see the outside door open. There was Mr. Diemus and Esther and Esther's father, Mr. Jonso.

In one of those flashes of clarity that engrave your mind in a split second I saw my whole classroom.

Joel and Matt were chinning themselves on nonexistent bars, their heads brushing the high ceiling as they grunted upward. Abie was swinging in a swing that wasn't there, arcing across the corner of the room, just missing the stove-pipe from the old stove, as he chanted, "Up in a swing, up in a swing!" This wasn't the first time *they* had tried their wings! Miriam was kneeling in a circle with the other girls and they were all coaxing their books up to hover unsupported above the floor, while Jimmy *vroomm-vroomed* two paper jet planes through intricate maneuvers in and out the rows of desks.

My soul curdled in me as I met Mr. Diemus' eyes. Esther gave a choked cry as she saw what the children were doing, and the girls' stricken faces turned to the intruders. Matt and Joel crumpled to the floor and scrambled to their feet. But Abie, absorbed in his wonderful new accomplishment, swung on, all unconscious of what was happening until Talitha frantically screamed, "Abie!"

Startled, he jerked around and saw the forbidding group at the door. With a disappointed cry, as though a loved toy had been snatched from him, he stopped there in midair, his fists clenched. And then, realizing, he screamed, a terrified panic-stricken cry, and slanted sharply upward, trying to escape, and ran full tilt into the corner of the high old map case, sideswiping it with his head, and, reeling backward, fell!

I tried to catch him. I did! I did! But I caught only one small hand as he plunged down onto the old wood-burning heater beneath him. And the crack of his skull against the ornate edge of the cast-iron lid was loud in the silence.

I straightened the crumpled little body carefully, not daring to touch the quiet little head. Mr. Diemus and I looked at each other as we knelt on opposite sides of the child. His lips opened, but I plunged before he could get started.

104

"If he dies," I bit my words off viciously, "you killed him!"

His mouth opened again, mainly from astonishment. "I—" he began.

"Barging in on my classroom!" I raged. "Interrupting classwork! Frightening my children! It's all your fault, your fault!" I couldn't bear the burden of guilt alone. I just had to have someone share it with me. But the fire died and I smoothed Abie's hand, trembling.

"Please call a doctor. He might be dying."

"Nearest one is in Tortura Pass," Mr. Diemus said. "Sixty miles by road."

"Cross country?" I asked.

"Two mountain ranges and an alkali plateau."

"Then—then—" Abie's hand was so still in mine.

"There's a doctor at the Tumble A Ranch," Joel said faintly. "He's taking a vacation."

"Go get him." I held Joel with my eyes. "*Go as fast as you know how!*"

Joel gulped miserably. "Okay."

"They'll probably have horses to come back on," I said. "Don't be too obvious."

"Okay," and he ran out the door. We heard the thud of his running feet until he was halfway across the schoolyard, then silence. Faintly, seconds later, creek gravel crunched below the hill. I could only guess at what he was doing—that he couldn't lift all the way and was going in jumps whose length was beyond all reasonable measuring.

The children had gone home, quietly, anxiously. And after the doctor arrived we had improvised a stretcher and carried Abie to the Peterses' home. I walked along close beside him watching his pinched little face, my hand touching his chest occasionally just to be sure he was still breathing.

And now—the waiting . . .

I looked at my watch again. A minute past the last time I looked. Sixty seconds by the hands, but hours and hours by anxiety.

"He'll be all right," I whispered, mostly to comfort myself. "The doctor will know what to do."

Mr. Diemus turned his dark empty eyes to me. "Why did

you do it?" he asked. "We almost had it stamped out. We were almost free."

"Free of what?" I took a deep breath. "Why did *you* do it? Why did you deny your children their inheritance?"

"It isn't your concern—"

"Anything that hampers my children is my concern. Anything that turns children into creeping frightened mice is wrong. Maybe I went at the whole deal the wrong way, but you told me to teach them what I had to—and I did."

"Disobedience, rebellion, flouting authority—"

"They obeyed *me*," I retorted. "They accepted *my* authority!" Then I softened. "I can't blame them," I confessed. "They were troubled. They told me it was wrong—that they had been *taught* it was wrong. I argued them into it. But oh, Mr. Diemus! It took so little argument, such a tiny breach in the dam to loose the flood. They never even questioned my knowledge—any more than you have, Mr. Diemus! All this—this *wonder* was beating against their minds, fighting to be set free. The rebellion was there long before I came. I didn't incite them to something new. I'll bet there's not a one, except maybe Esther, who hasn't practiced and practiced, furtively and ashamed, the things I permitted—demanded that they do for me.

"It wasn't fair—not fair at all—to hold them back."

"You don't understand." Mr. Diemus' face was stony. "You haven't all the facts—"

"I have enough," I replied. "So you have a frightened memory of an unfortunate period in your history. But what people *doesn't* have such a memory in larger or lesser degree? That you and your children have it more vividly should have helped, not hindered. You should have been able to figure out ways of adjusting. But leave that for the moment. Take the other side of the picture. What possible thing could all this suppression and denial yield you more precious than what you gave up?"

"It's the only way," Mr. Diemus said. "We are unacceptable to Earth but we have to stay. We have to conform—"

"Of course you had to conform," I cried. "Anyone has to when they change societies. At least enough to get them by

106

until others can adjust to them. But to crawl in a hole and pull it in after you! Why, the other Group—"

"Other Group!" Mr. Diemus whitened, his eyes widening. "Other Group? There are others? There are others?" He leaned tensely forward in his chair. "Where? Where?" And his voice broke shrilly on the last word. He closed his eyes and his mouth trembled as he fought for control. The bedroom door opened. Dr. Curtis came out, his shoulders weary.

He looked from Mr. Diemus to me and back. "He should be in a hospital. There's a depressed fracture and I don't know what all else. Probably extensive brain involvement. We need X rays and—and—" He rubbed his hand slowly over his weary young face. "Frankly, I'm not experienced to handle cases like this. We need specialists. If you can scare up some kind of transportation that won't jostle—" He shook his head, seeing the kind of country that lay between us and anyplace, and went back into the bedroom.

"He's dying," Mr. Diemus said. "Whether you're right or we're right, he's dying."

"Wait! Wait!" I said, catching at the tag end of a sudden idea. "Let me think." Urgently I willed myself back through the years to the old dorm room. Intently I listened and listened and remembered.

"Have you a—a—*Sorter* in this Group?" I asked, fumbling for unfamiliar terms.

"No," said Mr. Diemus. "One who could have been, but isn't."

"Or *any* Communicator? Anyone who can send or receive?"

"No," Mr. Diemus said, sweat starting on his forehead. "One who could have been, but—"

"See?" I accused. "See what you've traded for—for what? Who are the could-but-can'ts? Who are they?"

"I am," Mr. Diemus said, the words a bitterness in his mouth. "And my wife."

I stared at him, wondering confusedly. How far did training decide? What could we do with what we had?

"Look," I said quickly. "There *is* another Group. And they—they have all the persuasions and designs. Karen's been trying to find you—to find any of the People. She told me—oh, Lord, it's been years ago, I hope it's still so—every

107

evening they send out calls for the People. If we can catch it—if *you* can catch the call and answer it they can help. I know they can. Faster than cars, faster than planes, more surely than specialists—"

"But if the doctor finds out—" Mr. Diemus wavered fearfully.

I stood up abruptly. "Good night, Mr. Diemus," I said, turning to the door. "Let me know when Abie dies."

His cold hand shook on my arm.

"Can't you see!" he cried. "I've been taught, too—longer and stronger than the children! We never even dared *think* of rebellion! Help me, help me!"

"Get your wife," I said. "Get her and Abie's mother and father. Bring them down to the grove. We can't do anything here in the house. It's too heavy with denial."

I hurried on ahead and sank on my knees in the evening shadows among the trees.

"I don't know what I'm doing," I cried into the bend of my arm. "I have an idea but I don't know! Help us! Guide us!"

I opened my eyes to the arrival of the four.

"We told him we were going out to pray," said Mr. Diemus. And we all did.

Then Mr. Diemus began the call I worded for him, silently, but with such intensity that sweat started again on his face. *Karen, Karen, come to the People, come to the People.* And the other three sat around him, bolstering his effort, supporting his cry. I watched their tense faces, my own twisting in sympathy, and time was lost as we labored.

Then slowly his breathing calmed and his face relaxed and I felt a stirring as though something brushed past my mind. Mrs. Diemus whispered, "He remembers now. He's found the way."

And as the last spark of sun caught mica highlights on the hilltop above us Mr. Diemus stretched his hands out slowly and said with infinite relief, "There they are."

I looked around startled, half expecting to see Karen coming through the trees. But Mr. Diemus spoke again.

"Karen, we need help. One of our Group is dying. We have

108

a doctor, an Outsider, but he hasn't the equipment or the know-how to help. What shall we do?"

In the pause that followed I became slowly conscious of a new feeling. I couldn't tell you exactly what it was—a kind of unfolding—an opening—a relaxation. The ugly tight defensiveness that was so characteristic of the grownups of Bendo was slipping away.

"Yes, Valancy," said Mr. Diemus. "He's in a bad way. We can't help because—" His voice faltered and his words died. I felt a resurgence of fear and unhappiness as his communication went beyond words and then ebbed back to speech again.

"We'll expect you then. You know the way."

I could see the pale blur of his face in the dusk under the trees as he turned back to us.

"They're coming," he said, wonderingly. "Karen and Valancy. They're so pleased to find us—" His voice broke. "We're *not* alone—"

And I turned away as the two couples merged in the darkness. I had pushed them somewhere way beyond me.

It was a lonely lonely walk back to the house for me—alone.

They dropped down through the half darkness—four of them. For a fleeting second I wondered at myself that I could stand there matter-of-factly watching four adults slant calmly down out of the sky. Not a hair ruffled, not a stain of travel on them, knowing that only a short time before they had been hundreds of miles away—not even aware that Bendo existed.

But all strangeness was swept away as Karen hugged me delightedly.

"Oh, Melodye," she cried, "it *is* you! He said it was, but I wasn't sure! Oh, it's so *good* to see you again! Who owes who a letter?"

She laughed and turned to the smiling three. "Valancy, the Old One of our Group." Valancy's radiant face proved the Old One didn't mean age. "Bethie, our Sensitive." The slender fair-haired young girl ducked her head shyly. "And my brother Jemmy. Valancy's his wife."

"This is Mr. and Mrs. Diemus," I said. "And Mr. and Mrs.

Peters, Abie's parents. It's Abie, you know. My second grade."
I was suddenly overwhelmed by how long ago and far away
school felt. How far I'd gone from my accustomed pattern!

"What shall we do about the doctor?" I asked. "Will he
have to know?"

"Yes," said Valancy. "We can help him but we can't do
the actual work. Can we trust him?"

I hesitated, remembering the few scanty glimpses I'd had
of him. "I—" I began.

"Pardon me," Karen said. "I wanted to save time. I went
in to you. We know now what you know of him. We'll
trust Dr. Curtis."

I felt an eerie creeping up my spine. To have my thoughts
taken so casually! Even to the doctor's name!

Bethie stirred restlessly and looked at Valancy. "He'll be in
convulsions soon. We'd better hurry."

"You're sure you have the knowledge?" Valancy asked.

"Yes," Bethie murmured. "If I can make the doctor see—if
he's willing to follow."

"Follow what?"

The heavy tones of the doctor's voice startled us all as he
stepped out on the porch.

I stood aghast at the impossibility of the task ahead of us
and looked at Karen and Valancy to see how they would make
the doctor understand. They said nothing. They just looked
at him. There was a breathless pause. The doctor's startled
face caught the glint of light from the open door as he turned
to Valancy. He rubbed his hand across his face in bewilderment and, after a moment, turned to me.

"Do *you* hear her?"

"No," I admitted. "She isn't talking to me."

"Do you *know* these people?"

"Oh, yes!" I cried, wishing passionately it were true. "Oh,
yes!"

"And believe them?"

"Implicitly."

"But she says that Bethie—who's Bethie?" He glanced
around.

"She is," Karen said, nodding at Bethie.

110

"*She* is?" Dr. Curtis looked intently at the shy lovely face. He shook his head wonderingly and turned back to me.

"Anyway this one, Valancy, says Bethie can sense every condition in the child's body and that she will be able to tell all the injuries, their location and extent without X rays! Without equipment!"

"Yes," I said. "If they say so."

"You would be willing to risk a child's life—?"

"Yes. They know. They really do." And I swallowed hard to keep down the fist of doubt that clenched in my chest.

"You believe they can *see* through flesh and bone?"

"Maybe not see," I said, wondering at my own words. "But *know* with a knowledge that is sure and complete." I glanced, startled, at Karen. Her nod was very small but it told me where my words came from.

"Are *you* willing to trust these people?" The doctor turned to Abie's parents.

"They're *our* People," Mr. Peters said with quiet pride. "I'd operate on him myself with a pickax if they said so."

"Of all the screwball deals—!" The doctor's hand rubbed across his face again. "I know I needed this vacation, but this is ridiculous!"

We all listened to the silence of the night and—at least I —to the drumming of anxious pulses until Dr. Curtis sighed heavily.

"Okay, Valancy. I don't believe a word of it. At least I wouldn't if I were in my right mind, but you've got the terminology down pat as if you knew *something*— Well, I'll do it. It's either that or let him die. And God have mercy on our souls!"

I couldn't bear the thought of shutting myself in with my own dark fears, so I walked back toward the school, hugging myself in my inadequate coat against the sudden sharp chill of the night. I wandered down to the grove, praying wordlessly, and on up to the school. But I couldn't go in. I shuddered away from the blank glint of the windows and turned back to the grove. There wasn't any more time or direction or light or anything familiar, only a confused cloud of anxiety and a final icy weariness that drove me back to Abie's house.

I stumbled into the kitchen, my stiff hands fumbling at the doorknob. I huddled in a chair, gratefully leaning over the hot wood stove that flicked the semidarkness of the big homey room with warm red light, trying to coax some feeling back into my fingers.

I drowsed as the warmth began to penetrate, and then the door was flung open and slammed shut. The doctor leaned back against it, his hand still clutching the knob.

"Do you know what they did?" he cried, not so much to me as to himself. "What they made *me* do? Oh, Lord!" He staggered over to the stove, stumbling over my feet. He collapsed by my chair, rocking his head between his hands. "They made me operate on his brain! *Repair* it. Trace circuits and rebuild them. *You can't do that!* It can't be done! Brain cells damaged can't be repaired. No one can restore circuits that are destroyed! It can't be done. But I did it! *I did it!*"

I knelt beside him and tried to comfort him in the circle of my arms.

"There, there, there," I soothed.

He clung like a terrified child. "No anesthetics!" he cried. "*She* kept him asleep. And no bleeding when I went through the scalp! *They* stopped it. And the impossible things I did with the few instruments I have with me! And the brain starting to mend right before my eyes! Nothing was right!"

"But nothing was wrong," I murmured. "Abie will be all right, won't he?"

"How do I know?" he shouted suddenly, pushing away from me. "I don't know anything about a thing like this. I put his brain back together and he's still breathing, but how do I know!"

"There, there," I soothed. "It's over now."

"It'll never be over!" With an effort he calmed himself, and we helped each other up from the floor. "You can't forget a thing like this in a lifetime."

"We can give you forgetting," Valancy said softly from the door. "If you *want* to forget. We can send you back to the Tumble A with no memory of tonight except a pleasant visit to Bendo."

"You can?" He turned speculative eyes toward her. "You can," he amended his words to a statement.

"Do you want to forget?" Valancy asked.

"Of course not," he snapped. Then, "I'm sorry. It's just that I don't often work miracles in the wilderness. But if I did it once, maybe—"

"Then you understand what you did?" Valancy asked, smiling.

"Well, no, but if I could—if you would— There must be some way—"

"Yes," Valancy said, "but you'd have to have a Sensitive working with you, and Bethie is it as far as Sensitives go right now."

"You mean it's true what I saw—what you told me about the—the Home? You're extraterrestrials?"

"Yes," Valancy sighed. "At least our grandparents were." Then she smiled. "But we're learning where we can fit into this world. Someday—someday we'll be able—" She changed the subject abruptly.

"You realize, of course, Dr. Curtis, that we'd rather you wouldn't discuss Bendo or us with anyone else. We would rather be just people to Outsiders."

He laughed shortly, "Would I be believed if I did?"

"Maybe no, maybe so," Valancy said. "Maybe only enough to start people nosing around. And that would be too much. We have a bad situation here and it will take a long time to erase—" Her voice slipped into silence, and I knew she had dropped into thoughts to brief him on the local problem. How long is a thought? How fast can you think of hell—and heaven? It was that long before the doctor blinked and drew a shaky breath.

"Yes," he said. "A long time."

"If you like," Valancy said, "I can block your ability to talk of us."

"Nothing doing!" the doctor snapped. "I can manage my own censorship, thanks."

Valancy flushed. "I'm sorry. I didn't mean to be condescending."

"You weren't," the doctor said. "I'm just on the prod tonight. It has been *a day*, and that's for sure!"

"Hasn't it, though?" I smiled and then, astonished, rubbed my cheeks because tears had begun to spill down my face. I laughed, embarrassed, and couldn't stop. My laughter turned suddenly to sobs and I was bitterly ashamed to hear myself wailing like a child. I clung to Valancy's strong hands until I suddenly slid into a warm welcome darkness that had no thinking or fearing or need for believing in anything outrageous, but only in sleep.

It was a magic year and it fled on impossibly fast wings, the holidays flicking past like telephone poles by a railroad. Christmas was especially magical because my angels actually flew and the glory actually shone round about because their robes had hems woven of sunlight—I watched the girls weave them. And Rudolph the red-nosed reindeer, complete with cardboard antlers that wouldn't stay straight, really took off and circled the room. And as our Mary and Joseph leaned raptly over the manger, their faces solemn and intent on the miracle, I felt suddenly that they were really seeing, really kneeling beside the manger in Bethlehem.

Anyway the months fled, and the blossoming of Bendo was beautiful to see. There was laughter and frolicking and even the houses grew subtly into color. Green things crept out where only rocks had been before, and a tiny tentative stream of water had begun to flow down the creek again. They explained to me that they had to take it slow because people might wonder if the creek filled overnight! Even the rough steps up to the houses were being overgrown because they were so seldom used, and I was becoming accustomed to seeing my pupils coming to school like a bevy of bright birds, playing tag in the treetops. I was surprised at myself for adjusting so easily to all the incredible things done around me by the People, and I was pleased that they accepted me so completely. But I always felt a pang when the children escorted me home—with me, they had to walk.

But all things have to end, and one May afternoon I sat staring into my top desk drawer, the last to be cleaned out, wondering what to do with the accumulation of useless things in it. But I wasn't really seeing the contents of the drawer, I was concentrating on the great weary emptiness that pressed my shoulders down and weighted my mind. "It's not fair," I muttered aloud and illogically, "to show me heaven and then snatch it away."

"That's about what happened to Moses, too, you know."

My surprised start spilled an assortment of paper clips and thumbtacks from the battered box I had just picked up.

"Well, forevermore!" I said, righting the box. "Dr. Curtis! What are you doing here?"

"Returning to the scene of my crime," he smiled, coming through the open door. "Can't keep my mind off Abie. Can't believe he recovered from all that—shall we call it repair work? I have to check him every time I'm anywhere near this part of the country—and I still can't believe it."

"But he has."

"He has for sure! I had to fish him down from a treetop to look him over—" The doctor shuddered dramatically and laughed. "To see him hurtling down from the top of that tree curdled my blood! But there's hardly even a visible scar left."

"I know," I said, jabbing my finger as I started to gather up the tacks. "I looked last night. I'm leaving tomorrow, you know." I kept my eyes resolutely down to the job at hand. "I have this last straightening up to do."

"It's hard, isn't it?" he said, and we both knew he wasn't talking about straightening up.

"Yes," I said soberly. "Awfully hard. Earth gets heavier every day."

"I find it so lately, too. But at least you have the satisfaction of knowing that you—"

I moved uncomfortably and laughed.

"Well, they do say: those as can, do; those as can't, teach."

"Umm," the doctor said noncommittally, but I could feel his eyes on my averted face and I swiveled away from him, groping for a better box to put the clips in.

"Going to summer school?" His voice came from near the windows.

"No," I sniffed cautiously. "No, I swore when I got my Master's that I was through with education—at least the kind that's come-every-day-and-learn-something."

"Hmm!" There was amusement in the doctor's voice. "Too

bad. I'm going to school this summer. Thought you might like to go there, too."

"Where?" I asked bewildered, finally looking at him.

"Cougar Canyon summer school," he smiled. "Most exclusive."

"Cougar Canyon! Why that's where Karen—"

"Exactly," he said. "That's where the other Group is established. I just came from there. Karen and Valancy want us both to come. Do you object to being an experiment?"

"Why, no—" I cried, and then, cautiously, "What kind of an experiment?" Visions of brains being carved up swam through my mind.

The doctor laughed. "Nothing as gruesome as you're imagining, probably." Then he sobered and sat on the edge of my desk. "I've been to Cougar Canyon a couple of times, trying to figure out some way to get Bethie to help me when I come up against a case that's a puzzler. Valancy and Karen want to try a period of training with Outsiders—" he grimaced wryly, "—that's us—to see how much of what *they* are can be transmitted by training. You know Bethie is half Outsider. Only her mother was of the People."

He was watching me intently.

"Yes," I said absently, my mind whirling, "Karen told me."

"Well, do you want to try it? Do you want to go?"

"Do I want to go!" I cried, scrambling the clips into a rubber-band box. "How soon do we leave? Half an hour? Ten minutes? Did you leave the motor running?"

"Woops, woops!" The doctor took me by both arms and looked soberly into my eyes.

"We can't set our hopes too high," he said quietly. "It may be that for such knowledge we aren't teachable—"

I looked soberly back at him, my heart crying in fear that it might be so.

"Look," I said slowly. "If you had a hunger, a great big gnawing-inside hunger and no money and you saw a bakery shop window, which would you do? Turn your back on it? Or would you press your nose as close as you could against the glass and let at least your eyes feast? I know what I'd do." I reached for my sweater.

"And, you know, you never can tell. The shop door might open a crack, maybe—someday—"

IV

"I'D LIKE to talk with her a minute," Lea said to Karen as the chattering group broke up. "May I?"

"Why, sure," Karen said. "Melodye, have you a minute?"

"Oh, Karen!" Melodye threaded the rows back to Lea's corner. "That was wonderful! It was just like living it for the first time again, only underneath I knew what was coming next. But even so my blood ran cold when Abie——" She shuddered. "Bro—ther! Was that ever a day!"

"Melodye," Karen said, "this is Lea. She wants to talk with you."

"Hi, fellow alien," Melodye smiled. "I've been wanting to meet you."

"Do you believe——" Lea hesitated. "Was that really true?"

"Of course it was," Melodye said. "I can show you my scars—mental, that is—from trying to learn to lift." Then she laughed. "Don't feel funny about doubting it. I still have my 3 A.M.-ses when I can't believe it myself." She sobered. "But it *is* true. The People *are* the People."

"And even if you're not of the People," Lea faltered, "could they—could they help anyway? I don't mean anything broken. I mean, nothing visible——" She was suddenly covered with a sense of shame and betrayal as though caught hanging out a black line of sins in the morning sun. She turned her face away.

"They can help." Melodye touched Lea's shoulder gently. "And, Lea, they never judge. They mend where mending is needed and leave the judgment to God." And she was gone.

"Maybe," Lea mourned, "if I *had* sinned some enormous sins I could have something big to forgive myself so I could start over, but all these niggling nibbling little nothingnesses——"

"All these niggling little, nibbling little nothingnesses that

117

compounded themselves into such a great despair," Karen said. "And what is despair but a separation from the Presence—"

"Then the People do believe that there is—?"

"Our Home may be gone," Karen said firmly, "and all of us exiles if you want to look at it that way, but there's no galaxy wide enough to separate us from the Presence."

Later that night Lea sat up in bed. "Karen?"

"Yes?" Karen's voice came instantly from the darkness though Lea knew she was down the hall.

"Are you still shielding me from—from whatever it was?"

"No," Karen said. "I released you this morning."

"That's what I thought." Lea drew a quavering breath. "Right now it's all gone away, as though it had never been, but I'm still nowhere and going nowhere. Just waiting. And if I wait long enough it'll come back again, that I know. Karen, what can I do to—not to be where I am now when it comes back?"

"You're beginning to work at it now," Karen said. "And if it does come back we're here to help. It will never be so impenetrable again."

"How could it be?" Lea murmured. "How could I have gone through anything as black as that and survived—or ever do it again?"

Lea lay back with a sigh. Then, sleepily, "Karen?"

"Yes?"

"Who was that down at the pool?"

"Don't you know?" Karen's voice smiled. "Have you looked around at all?"

"What good would it do? I can't remember what he looked like. It's been so long since I've noticed anything—and then the blackness— But he brought me back to the house, didn't he? You must have seen him—"

"Must I?" Karen teased. "Maybe we could arrange to have him carry you again. 'Arms remember when eyes forget.'"

"There's something wrong with that quotation," Lea said drowsily, "But I'll skip it for now."

It seemed to Lea that she had just slipped under the edge of sleep when she heard Karen.

"What!" Karen cried. "Right now? Not tomorrow?"

"Karen!" Lea called, groping in the darkness for the light switch. "What's the matter?"

"The matter!" Karen laughed and shot through the window, turning and tumbling ecstatically in midair.

"Nothing's the matter! Oh, Lea, come and be joyful!" She grabbed Lea's hands and pulled her up from the bed.

"No! Karen! No!" Lea cried as her bare feet curled themselves away from the empty air that seemed to lick at them. "Put me down!" Terror sharpened her voice.

"Oh, I'm sorry!" Karen said, releasing her to plump gently down on her bed. She herself flashed again across the room and back in a froth of nightgowny ruffles. "Oh, be joyful! Be joyful unto the Lord!"

"What *is* it!" Lea cried, suddenly afraid, afraid of anything that might change things as they were. The vast emptiness began to cave away inside her. The blackness was a cloud the size of a man's hand on the far horizon.

"It's Valancy!" Karen cried, shooting away back through the window. "I have to get dressed! The baby's here!"

"The baby!" Lea was bewildered. "What baby?"

"Is there any other baby?" Karen's voice floated back, muffled. "Valancy and Jemmy's. It's here! I'm an aunt! Oh, dear, now I'm well on the way to becoming an ancestress. I thought they would never get around to it. It's a girl! At least Jemmy says he thinks it's a girl! He's so excited that it could be both, or even triplets! Well, as soon as Valancy gets back—" She walked back through the door, brushing her hair briskly.

"What hospital did she go to?" Lea asked. "Isn't this pretty isolated—"

"Hospital? Oh, none, of course. She's at home."

"But you said when she gets back—"

"Yes. It's a far solemn journey to bring back a new life from the Presence. It takes a while."

"But I didn't even notice!" Lea cried. "Valancy was there tonight and I don't remember—"

"But then you haven't been noticing much of anything for a long time," Karen said gently.

"But anything as obvious as that!" Lea protested.

"Fact remains, the baby's here and it's Valancy's—with a

little co-operation from Jemmy—and she *didn't* carry it around in a knitting bag!

"Okay, Jemmy, I'm coming. Hold the fort!" She flashed, feet free of the floor, out the door, her hairbrush hovering forlornly, forgotten, in midair, until it finally drifted slowly out the door to the hall.

Lea huddled on the tumbled bed. A baby. A new life. "I had forgotten," she thought. "Birth and death have still been going on. The world is still out there, wagging along as usual. I thought it had stopped. It *had* stopped for me. I lost winter. I lost spring. It must be summer now. Just think! Just think! There are people who found all my black days full of joyful anticipation—bright jewels slipping off the thread of time! And I've been going around and around like a donkey dragging a weight around a stake, winding myself tighter and tighter—" She straightened suddenly on the bed, spread-eagling out of her tight huddle. The darkness poured like a heavy flood in through the door—down from the ceiling—up from the floor.

"Karen!" she cried, feeling herself caught up to be crammed back into the boundaryless nothingness of herself again.

"No!" she gritted through her teeth. "Not this time!" She turned face down on the bed, clutching the pillow tightly with both hands. "Give me strength! Give me strength!" With an effort, almost physical, she turned her thoughts. "The baby—a new baby—crying. Do babies of the People cry? They must, having to leave the Presence for Earth. The baby—tiny fists clenched tightly, eyes clenched tightly shut. All powder and flannel and tiny curling feet. I can hold her. Tomorrow I can hold her. And feel the continuity of life—the eternal coming of God into the world. Rockabye baby. Sleep, baby, sleep. Thy Father watches His sheep. A new baby—tiny red fingers to curl around my finger. A baby—Valancy's baby—"

And by the time dawn arrived Lea was sleeping, her face smoothing out from the agony of the black night. There was almost triumph upon it.

That evening Karen and Lea walked through the gathering twilight to the schoolhouse. The softly crisp evening air was so clear and quiet that voices and far laughter echoed around them.

"Wait, Lea." Karen was waving to someone. "Here comes

Santhy. She's just learning to lift. Bet her mother doesn't know she's still out." She laughed softly.

Lea watched with wonder as the tiny five-year-old approached them in short abrupt little arcs, her brief skirts flattening and flaring as she lifted and landed.

"She's using more energy lifting than if she walked," Karen said softly, "but she's so proud of herself. Let's wait for her. She wants us."

By now Lea could see the grave intent look on Santhy's face and could almost hear the little grunts as she took off until she finally landed, staggering, against Lea. Lea steadied her, dropping down beside her, holding her gently in the circle of her arms.

"You're Lea," Santhy said, smiling shyly.

"Yes," Lea said. "How did you know?"

"Oh, we all know you. You're our new God-bless every night."

"Oh." Lea was taken aback.

"I brought you something," Santhy said, her hand clenched in a bulging little pocket. "I saved it from our 'joicing party for the new baby. I don't care if you're an Outsider. I saw you wading in the creek and you're pretty." She pulled her hand out of her pocket and deposited on Lea's palm a softly glowing bluey-green object. "It's a *koomatka*," she whispered. "Don't let Mama see it. I was s'posed to eat it but I had two—" She spread her arms and lifted up right past Lea's nose.

"A *koomatka*," Lea said, getting up and holding out her hand wonderingly, the glow from it deepening in the dusk.

"Yes," Karen said. "She really shouldn't have. It's forbidden to show to Outsiders, you know."

"Must I give it back?" Lea asked wistfully. "Can't I keep it even if I don't belong?"

Karen looked at her soberly for a moment, then she smiled. "You can keep it, or eat it, though you probably won't like it. It tastes like music sounds, you know. But you may have it —even if you don't belong."

Lea's hand closed softly around the *koomatka* as the two turned toward the schoolhouse. "Speaking of belonging—" Karen said, "it's Dita's turn tonight. She knows plenty about belonging and not belonging."

"I wondered about tonight. I mean not waiting for Valancy—" Lea shielded her eyes against the bright open door as they mounted the steps.

"Oh, she wouldn't miss it," Karen said. "She'll listen in from home."

They were the last to arrive. Invocation over, Dita was already in the chair behind the desk, her hands folded primly in front of her. "Valancy," she said, "we're all here now. Are you ready?"

"Oh, yes." Lea could feel Valancy's answer. "Our Baby's asleep now."

The group laughed at the capitals in Valancy's voice.

"You didn't *invent* babies," Dita laughed.

"Hah!" Jemmy's voice answered triumphantly. "*This* one we did!"

Lea looked around the laughing group. "They're happy!" she thought. "In a world like this they're happy anyway! What do they have as a touchstone?" She studied the group as Dita began, and under the first flow of Dita's words she thought, "Maybe this is the answer. Maybe this is the touchstone. When any one of them cries out the others hear—and *listen*. Not just with their ears but with their hearts. No matter who cries out—*someone* listens—"

"My theme," Dita said soberly, "is very brief—but oh, the heartbreak in it. It's 'And your children shall wander in the wilderness.'" Her clasped hands tightened on each other. "I was wandering that day . . ."

WILDERNESS

"WELL, HOW do you expect Bruce to concentrate on spelling when he's so worried about his daddy?" I thumbed through my second graders' art papers, hoping to find one lift out of the prosaic.

"'Worried about his daddy'?" Mrs. Kanz looked up from her spelling tests. "What makes you think he's worried about him?"

"Why, he's practically sick for fear he won't come home this time." I turned the paper upside down and looked again. "I thought you knew everything about everyone," I teased. "You've briefed me real good in these last three weeks. I feel like a resident instead of a newcomer." I sighed and righted the paper. It was still a tree with six apples on it.

"But I certainly didn't know Stell and Mark were having trouble." Mrs. Kanz was chagrined.

"They had an awful fight the night before he left," I said. "Nearly scared the waddin' out of Bruce."

"How do you know?" Mrs. Kanz's eyes were suddenly sharp. "You haven't met Stell yet and Bruce hasn't said a word all week except yes and no."

I let my breath out slowly. "Oh, no!" I thought. "Not already! Not already!"

"Oh, a little bird told me," I said lightly, busying myself with my papers to hide the small tremble of my hands.

"Little bird, toosh! You probably heard it from Marie, though how she—"

"Could be," I said, "could be." I bundled up my papers hurriedly. "Oops! Recess is almost over. Gotta get downstairs before the thundering herd arrives."

The sound of the old worn steps was hollow under my hurried feet, but not nearly so hollow as the feeling in my stomach.

Only three weeks and I had almost betrayed myself already. Why couldn't I *remember!* Besides, the child wasn't even in my room. I had no business knowing anything about him. Just because he had leaned so quietly, so long, over his literature book last Monday—and I had only looked a little. . . .

At the foot of the stairs I was engulfed waist-deep in children sweeping in from the playground. Gratefully I let myself be swept with them into the classroom.

That afternoon I leaned with my back against the window sill and looked over my quiet class. Well, quiet in so far as moving around the room was concerned, but each child humming audibly or inaudibly with the untiring dynamos of the young—the mostly inarticulate thought patterns of happy children. All but Lucine, my twelve-year-old first grader, who hummed briefly to a stimulus and then clicked off, hummed

123

again and clicked off. There was a short somewhere, and her flat empty eyes showed it.

I sighed and turned my back on the room, wandering my eyes up the steepness of Black Mesa as it towered above the school, trying to lose myself from apprehension, trying to forget why I had run away—nearly five hundred miles—trying to forget those things that tugged at my sanity, things that could tear me loose from reality and set me adrift. . . . Adrift? Oh, glory! Set me free! Set me free! I hooked my pointer fingers through the old wire grating that protected the bottom of the window and tugged sharply. Old nails grated and old wire gave, and I sneezed through the dry acid bite of ancient dust.

I sat down at my desk and rummaged for a Kleenex and sneezed again, trying to ignore, but knowing too well, the heavy nudge and tug inside me. That tiny near betrayal had cracked my tight protective shell. All that I had packed away so resolutely was shouldering and elbowing its way . . .

I swept my children out of spelling into numbers so fast that Lucine poised precariously on the edge of tears until she clicked on again and murkily perceived where we had gone.

"Now, look, Petie," I said, trying again to find a way through his stubborn block against number words, "this is the picture of two, but this is the name of two. . . ."

After the school buses were gone I scrambled and slid down the steep slope of the hill below the gaunt old schoolhouse and walked the railroad ties back toward the hotel-boarding house where I stayed. Eyes intent on my feet but brightly conscious of the rails on either side, I counted my way through the clot of old buildings that was town, and out the other side. If I could keep something on my mind I could keep ghosts out of my thoughts.

I stopped briefly at the hotel to leave my things and then pursued the single rail line on down the little valley, over the shaky old trestle that was never used any more, and left it at the tailings dump and started up the hill, enjoying fiercely the necessary lunge and pull, tug and climb, that stretched my muscles, quickened my heartbeat and pumped my breath up hard against the top of my throat.

Panting I grabbed a manzanita bush and pulled myself up the

last steep slope. I perched myself, knees to chest, on the crumbly outcropping of shale at the base of the huge brick chimney, arms embracing my legs, my cheek pressed to my knees. I sat with closed eyes, letting the late-afternoon sun soak into me. "If only this could be all," I thought wistfully. "If only there were nothing but sitting in the sun, soaking up warmth. Just being, without questions." And for a long blissful time I let that be all.

But I couldn't put it off any longer. I felt the first slow trickling through the crack in my armor. I counted trees, I counted telephone poles, I said timestables until I found myself thinking six times nine is ninety-six and, then I gave up and let the floodgates open wide.

"It's always like this," one of me cried to the rest of me. "You promised! You promised and now you're giving in again—after all this time!"

"I could promise not to breathe, too," I retorted.

"But this is insanity—you know it is! Anyone knows it is!"

"Insane or not, it's me!" I screamed silently. "It's me! It's me!"

"Stop your arguing," another of me said. "This is too serious for bickering. We've got problems."

I took a dry manzanita twig and cleared a tiny space on the gravelly ground, scratching up an old square nail and a tiny bit of sun-purpled glass as I did so. Shifting the twig to my other hand I picked up the nail and rubbed the dirt off with my thumb. It was pitted with rust but still strong and heavy. I wondered what it had held together back in those days, and if the hand that last held it was dust now, and if whoever it was had had burdens. . . .

I cast the twig from me with controlled violence and, rocking myself forward, I made a straight mark on the cleared ground with the nail. This was a drearily familiar inventory, and I had taken it so many times before, trying to simplify this complicated problem of mine, that I fell automatically into the same old pattern.

Item one. Was I really insane—or going insane—or on the way to going insane? It must be so. Other people didn't see sounds. Nor taste colors. Nor feel the pulsing of other people's emotions like living things. Nor find the weight of flesh so like a galling strait jacket. Nor more than half believe that the burden was lay-downable short of death.

"But then," I defended, "I'm still functioning in society and I don't drool or foam at the mouth. I don't act very crazy, and as long as I guard my tongue I don't sound crazy."

I pondered the item awhile, then scribbled out the mark. "I guess I'm still sane—so far."

Item two. "Then what's wrong with me? Do I just let my imagination run away with me?" I jabbed holes all around my second heavy mark. No, it was something more, something beyond just imagination, something beyond—what?

I crossed that marking with another to make an X.

"What shall I do about it then? Shall I fight it out like I did before? Shall I deny and deny and deny until—" I felt a cold grue, remembering the blind panic that had finally sent me running until I had ended up at Kruper, and all the laughter went out of me, clear to the bottom of my soul.

I crosshatched the two marks out of existence and hid my eyes against my knees again and waited for the sick up-gushing of apprehension to foam into despair over my head. Always it came to this. Did I *want* to do anything about it? Should I stop it all with an act of will? *Could* I stop it all by an act of will? Did I *want* to stop it?

I scrambled to my feet and scurried around the huge stack, looking for the entrance. My feet cried, No *no!* on the sliding gravel. Every panting breath cried, No *no!* as I slipped and slithered around the steep hill. I ducked into the shadowy interior of the huge chimney and pressed myself against the blackened crumbling bricks, every tense muscle shouting, No *no!* And in the wind-shuddery silence I cried, "No!" and heard it echo up through the blackness above me. I could almost see the word shoot up through the pale elliptical disk of the sky at the top of the stack.

"Because I could!" I shrieked defiantly inside me. "If I weren't afraid I could follow that word right on up and erupt into the sky like a Roman candle and never, never, never feel the weight of the world again!"

But the heavy drag of reason grabbed my knees and elbows and rubbed my nose forcibly into things-as-they-really-are, and I sobbed impotently against the roughness of the curving

126

wall. The sting of salty wetness across my cheek shocked me out of rebellion.

Crying? Wailing against a dirty old smelter wall because of a dream? Fine goings on for a responsible pedagogue!

I scrubbed at my cheeks with a Kleenex and smiled at the grime that came off. I'd best get back to the hotel and get my face washed before eating the inevitable garlicky supper I'd smelled on my way out.

I stumbled out into the red flood of sunset and down the thread of a path I had ignored when coming up. I hurried down into the duskiness of the cottonwood thicket along the creek at the bottom of the hill. Here, where no eyes could see, no tongues could clack at such undignified behavior, I broke into a run, a blind headlong run, pretending that I could run away —just away! Maybe with salty enough tears and fast enough running I could buy a dreamless night.

I rounded the turn where the pinky-gray granite boulder indented the path—and reeled under a sudden blow. I had run full tilt into someone. Quicker than I could focus my eyes I was grabbed and set on my feet. Before I could see past a blur of tears from my smarting nose I was alone in the dusk.

I mopped my nose tenderly. "Well," I said aloud, "that's one way to knock the nonsense out of me." Then immediately began to wonder if it was a sign of unbalance to talk aloud to yourself.

I looked back uphill when I came out of the shadow of the trees. The smelter stack was dark against the sky, massive above the remnants of the works. It was beautiful in a stark way, and I paused to enjoy it briefly. Suddenly there was another darkness up there. Someone had rounded the stack and stood silhouetted against the lighter horizon.

I wondered if the sound of my sorrow was still echoing up the stack, and then I turned shamefaced away. Whoever it was up there had more sense than to listen for the sounds of old sorrows.

That night, in spite of my outburst of the afternoon, I barely slipped under the thin skin of sleep and, for endless ages, clutched hopelessly for something to pull me down into complete forgetfulness. Then despairingly I felt the familiar tug and pull and, hopelessly, eagerly, slipped headlong into my dream that I had managed to suppress for so long.

There are no words—there are no words anywhere for my dream. Only the welling of delight, the stretching of my soul, the boundless freedom, the warm belongingness. And I held the dearness close to me—oh, so close to me!—knowing that awakening must come. . . .

And it did, smashing me down, forcing me into flesh, binding me leadenly to the earth, squeezing out the delight, cramping my soul back into finiteness, snapping bars across my sky and stranding me in the thin watery glow of morning so alone again that the effort of opening my eyes was almost too much to be borne.

Lying rigidly under the press of the covers I gathered up all the tatters of my dream and packed them tightly into a hard little knot way back of my consciousness. "Stay there. Stay there," I pleaded. "Oh, stay there!"

Forcing myself to breakfast I came warily into the dining room at the hotel. As the only female-type woman guest in the hotel I was somewhat disconcerted to walk into the place when it was full and to have every hand pause and every jaw still itself until I found my way to the only empty seat, and then to hear the concerted return to eating, as though on cue. But I was later this morning, and the place was nearly empty.

"How was the old stack?" Half of Marie's mouth grinned as she pushed a plate of hotcakes under my nose and let go of it six inches above the table. I controlled my wince as it crashed to the table, but I couldn't completely ignore the sooty thumbprint etched in the grease on the rim. Marie took the stiffly filthy rag she had hanging as usual from her apron pocket, and smeared the print around until I at least couldn't see the whorls and ridges any more.

"It was interesting," I said, not bothering to wonder how she knew I'd been there. "Kruper must have been quite a town when the smelter was going full blast."

"Long's I've been here it's been dyin'," Marie said. "Been here thirty-five years next February and *I* ain't never been up to the stack. I ain't lost nothing up there!"

She laughed soundlessly but gustily. I held my breath until

the garlic went by. "But I hear there's some girls that's gone up there and lost—"

"Marie!" Old Charlie bellowed from across the table. "Cut out the chatter and bring me some grub. If teacher wants to climb *up* that da-dang stack leave her be. Maybe she likes it!"

"Crazy way to waste time," Marie muttered, teetering out to the kitchen, balancing her gross body on impossibly spindly legs.

"Don't mind her," Old Charlie bellowed. "Only thing she thinks is fun is beer. Why, lots of people like to go look at worthless stuff like that. Take—well—take Lowmanigh here. He was up there only yesterday—"

"Yesterday?" My lifted brows underlined my question as I looked across the table. It was one of the fellows I hadn't noticed before. His name had probably been thrown at me with the rest of them by Old Charlie on my first night there, but I had lost all the names except Old Charlie and Severeid Swanson, which was the name attached to a wavery fragile-looking Mexicano, with no English at all, who seemed to subsist mostly on garlic and *vino* and who always blinked four times when I smiled at him.

"Yes." Lowmanigh looked across the table at me, no smile softening his single word. My heart caught as I saw across his cheek the familiar pale quietness of chill-of-soul. I knew the look well. It had been on my own face that morning before I had made my truce with the day.

He must have read something in my eyes, because his face shuttered itself quickly into a noncommittal expression and, with a visible effort, he added, "I watched the sunset from there."

"Oh?" My hand went thoughtfully to my nose.

"Sunsets!" Marie was back with the semiliquid she called coffee. "More crazy stuff. Why waste good time?"

"What do you spend your time on?" Lowmanigh's voice was very soft.

Marie's mind leaped like a startled bird. "Waiting to die!" it cried.

"Beer," she said aloud, half of her face smiling. "Four beers equal one sunset." She dropped the coffeepot on the table and went back to the kitchen, leaving a clean sharp, almost visible pain behind her as she went.

"You two oughta get together," Old Charlie boomed. "Liking the same things like you do. Low here knows more junk heaps and rubbish dumps than anybody else in the county. He collects ghost towns."

"I like ghost towns," I said to Charlie, trying to fill a vast conversational vacancy. "I have quite a collection of them myself."

"See, Low!" he boomed. "Here's your chance to squire a pretty schoolmarm around. Together you two oughta be able to collect up a storm!" He choked on his pleasantry and his last gulp of coffee and left the room, whooping loudly into a blue bandanna.

We were all alone in the big dining room. The early-morning sun skidded across the polished hardwood floor, stumbled against the battered kitchen chairs, careened into the huge ornate mirror above the buffet and sprayed brightly from it over the cracked oilcloth table covering on the enormous oak table.

The silence grew and grew until I put my fork down, afraid to click it against my plate any more. I sat for half a minute, suspended in astonishment, feeling the deep throbbing of a pulse that slowly welled up into almost audibility, questioning, "Together? Together? Together?" The beat broke on the sharp edge of a wave of desolation, and I stumbled blindly out of the room.

'No!" I breathed as I leaned against the newel post at the bottom of the stairs. "Not involuntarily! Not so early in the day!"

With an effort I pulled myself together. "Cut out this cotton-pickin' nonsense!" I told myself. "You're enough to drive anybody crazy!"

Resolutely I started up the steps, only to pause, foot suspended, halfway up. "That wasn't my desolation," I cried silently. "It was his!"

"How odd," I thought when I wakened at two o'clock in the morning, remembering the desolation.

"How odd!" I thought when I wakened at three, remembering the pulsing "Together?"

"How very odd," I thought when I wakened at seven and

slid heavy-eyed out of bed—having forgotten completely what Lowmanigh looked like, but holding wonderingly in my consciousness a better-than-three-dimensional memory of him.

School kept me busy all the next week, busy enough that the old familiar ache was buried almost deep enough to be forgotten. The smoothness of the week was unruffled until Friday, when the week's restlessness erupted on the playground twice. The first time I had to go out and peel Esperanza off Joseph and pry her fingers out of his hair so he could get his snub nose up out of the gravel. Esperanza had none of her Uncle Severeid's fragility and waveriness as she defiantly slapped the dust from her heavy dark braid.

"He calls me Mexican!" she cried. "So what? I'm Mexican. I'm proud to be Mexican. I hit him some more if he calls me Mexican like a bad word again. I'm proud to be—"

"Of course you're proud," I said, helping her dust herself off. "God made us all. What do different names matter?"

"Joseph!" I startled him by swinging around to him suddenly. "Are you a girl?"

"Huh?" He blinked blankly with dusty lashes, then, indignantly: "Course not! I'm a boy!"

"Joseph's a boy! Joseph's a boy!" I taunted. Then I laughed. "See how silly that sounds? We are what we are. How silly to tease about something like that. Both of you go wash the dirt off." I spatted both of them off toward the schoolhouse and sighed as I watched them go.

The second time the calm was interrupted when the ancient malicious chanting sound of teasing pulled me out on the playground again.

"Lu-cine is crazy! Lu-cine is crazy! Lu-cine is crazy!"

The dancing taunting group circled twelve-year-old Lucine where she stood backed against the one drooping tree that still survived on our playground. Her eyes were flat and shallow above her gaping mouth, but smoky flames were beginning to flicker in the shallowness and her muscles were tightening.

"Lucine!" I cried, fear winging my feet. "Lucine!"

I sent me ahead of myself and caught at the ponderous murderous massiveness of her mind. Barely I slowed her until I could get to her.

"Stop it!" I shrieked at the children. "Get away, quick!"

My voice pierced through the mob-mind, and the group dissolved into frightened individuals. I caught both of Lucine's hands and for a tense moment had them secure. Then she bellowed, a peculiarly animallike bellow, and with one flip of her arm sent me flying.

In a wild flurry I was swept up almost bodily, it seemed, into the irrational delirium of her anger and bewilderment. I was lost in the mazes of unreasoning thoughts and frightening dead ends, and to this day I can't remember what happened physically.

When the red tide ebbed and the bleak gray click-off period came I was hunched against the old tree with Lucine's head on my lap, her mouth lax and wet against my hand, her flooding quiet tears staining my skirt, the length of her body very young and very tired.

Her lips moved.

"Ain't crazy."

"No," I said, smoothing her ruffled hair, wondering at the angry oozing scratch on the back of my hand. "No, Lucine. I know."

"He does, too," Lucine muttered. "He makes it almost straight but it bends again."

"Oh?" I said soothingly, hunching my shoulder to cover its bareness with my torn blouse sleeve. "Who does?"

Her head tensed under my hand, and her withdrawal was as tangible as the throb of a rabbit trying to escape restricting hands. "He said don't tell."

I let the pressure of my hand soothe her and I looked down at her ravaged face. "Me," I thought. "Me with the outside peeled off. I'm crippled inside in my way as surely as she is in hers, only my crippling passes for normal. I wish I could click off sometimes and not dream of living without a limp—sweet impossible dream."

There was a long moist intake of breath, and Lucine sat up. She looked at me with her flat incurious eyes.

"Your face is dirty," she said. "Teachers don't got dirty faces."

"That's right." I got up stiffly, shifting the zipper of my skirt around to the side where it belonged. "I'd better go wash. Here comes Mrs. Kanz."

Across the play field the classes were lined up to go back inside. The usual scuffling horseplay was going on, but no one even bothered to glance our way. If they only knew, I thought, how close some of them had been to death . . .

"I been bad," Lucine whimpered. "I got in a fight again."

"Lucine, you bad girl!" Mrs. Kanz cried as soon as she got within earshot. "You've been fighting again. You go right in the office and sit there the rest of the day. Shame on you!"

And Lucine blubbered off toward the school building.

Mrs. Kanz looked me over. "Well," she laughed apologetically, "I should have warned you about her. Just leave her alone when she gets in a rage. Don't try to stop her."

"But she was going to *kill* someone!" I cried, tasting again the blood lust, feeling the grate of broken bones.

"She's too slow. The kids always keep out of her way."

"But someday—"

Mrs. Kanz shrugged. "If she gets dangerous she'll have to be put away."

"But why do you let the children tease her?" I protested, feeling a spasmodic gush of anger.

She looked at me sharply. "I don't 'let.' Kids are always cruel to anyone who's different. Haven't you discovered that yet?"

"Yes, I have," I whispered. "Oh, yes, yes!" And huddled into myself against the creeping cold of memory.

"It isn't good but it happens," she said. "You can't make everything right. You have to get calluses sometimes."

I brushed some of the dust off my clothes. "Yes," I sighed. "Calluses come in handy. But I still think something should be done for her."

"Don't say so out loud," Mrs. Kanz warned. "Her mother has almost beat her own brains out trying to find some way to help her. These things happen in the best of families. There's no help for them."

"Then who is—?" I choked on my suppressed words, belatedly remembering Lucine's withdrawal.

"Who is who?" asked Mrs. Kanz over her shoulder as we went back to the schoolhouse.

"Who is going to take care of her all her life?" I asked lamely.

"Well! Talk about borrowing trouble!" Mrs. Kanz laughed. "Just forget about the whole thing. It's all in a day's work. It's a shame your pretty blouse had to get ruined, though."

I was thinking of Lucine while I was taking off my torn blouse at home after school. I squinted tightly sideways, trying to glimpse the point of my shoulder to see if it looked as bruised as it felt, when my door was flung open and slammed shut and Lowmanigh was leaning against it, breathing heavily.

"Well!" I slid quickly into my clean shirt and buttoned it up briskly. "I didn't hear you knock. Would you like to go out and try it over again?"

"Did Lucine get hurt?" He pushed his hair back from his damp forehead. "Was it a bad spell? I thought I had it controlled—"

"If you want to talk about Lucine," I said out of my surprise, "I'll be out on the porch in a minute. Do you mind waiting out there? My ears are still burning from Marie's lecture to me on 'proper decorum for a female in this here hotel.'"

"Oh." He looked around blankly. "Oh, sure—sure."

My door was easing shut before I knew he was gone. I tucked my shirttail in and ran my comb through my hair.

"Lowmanigh and Lucine?" I thought blankly. "What gives? Mr. Kanz *must* be slipping. This she hasn't mentioned." I put the comb down slowly. "Oh. 'He makes it almost straight but it bends again.' But how can that be?"

Low was perched on the railing of the sagging balcony porch that ran around two sides of the second story of the hotel. He didn't turn around as I creaked across the floor toward the dusty dilapidated wicker settle and chair that constituted the porch furniture.

"Who are you?" His voice was choked. "What are you doing here?"

Foreboding ran a thin cold finger across the back of my neck. "We were introduced," I said thinly. "I'm Perdita Verist, the new teacher, remember?"

He swung around abruptly. "Stop talking on top," he said. "I'm listening underneath. You know as well as I do that you can't run away— But how *do* you know? Who are you?"

134

"You stop it!" I cried. "You have no business listening underneath. Who are *you?*"

We stood there stiffly glaring at each other until with a simultaneous sigh we relaxed and sat down on the shaky wickerware. I clasped my hands loosely on my lap and felt the tight hard knot inside me begin to melt and untie until finally I was turning to Low and holding out my hand only to meet his as he reached for mine. Some one of me cried, "My kind? My kind?" But another of me pushed the panic button.

"No," I cried, taking my hand back abruptly and standing up. "No!"

"No." Low's voice was soft and gentle. "It's no betrayal."

I swallowed hard and concentrated on watching Severeid Swanson tacking from one side of the road to the other on his way home to the hotel for his garlic, his two *vino* bottles doing very little to maintain his balance.

"Lucine," I said. "Lucine and you."

"Was it bad?" His voice was all on top now, and my bones stopped throbbing to that other wave length.

"About par for the course according to Mrs. Kanz," I said shallowly. "I just tried to stop a buzz saw."

"Was it bad!" his voice spread clear across the band.

"Stay out!" I cried. "Stay out!"

But he was in there with me and I was Lucine and he was I and we held the red-and-black horror in our naked hands and stared it down. Together we ebbed back through the empty grayness until he was Lucine and I was I and I saw me inside Lucine and blushed for her passionately grateful love of me. Embarrassed, I suddenly found a way to shut him out and blinked at the drafty loneliness.

". . . and stay out!" I cried.

"That's right!" I jumped at Marie's indignant wheeze. "I seen him go in your room without knocking and Shut the Door!" Her voice was capitalized horror. "You done right chasing him out and giving him What For!"

My inner laughter slid the barrier open a crack to meet his amusement.

"Yes, Marie," I said soberly. "You warned me and I remembered."

"Well, now, good!" Half of Marie's face smirked, gratified.

"I knew you was a good girl. And, Low, I'm plumb ashamed of you. I thought you was a cut above these gaw-danged muckers around here and here you go wolfing around in broad daylight!" She tripped off down the creaky hall, her voice floating back up the lovely curved stairway. "In broad daylight! Supper'll be ready in two jerks of a dead lamb's tail. Git washed."

Low and I laughed together and went to "git washed."

I paused over a double handful of cold water I had scooped up from my huge china washbowl, and watched it all trickle back as I glowed warmly with the realization that this was the first time in uncountable ages that I had laughed underneath. I looked long on my wavery reflection in the water. "And not alone," one of me cried, erupting into astonishment, "not alone!"

The next morning I fled twenty-five miles into town and stayed at a hotel that had running water, right in the house, and even a private bath! And reveled in the unaccustomed luxury, soaking Kruper out of me—at least all of it except the glitter bits of loveliness or funniness or niceness that remained on the riffles of my soul after the dust, dirt, inconvenience and ugliness sluiced away.

I was lying there drowsing Sunday afternoon, postponing until the last possible moment the gathering of myself together for the bus trip back to Kruper. Then sudden, subtly, between one breath and the next, I was back into full wary armor, my attention twanged taut like a tightened wire and I sat up stiffly. Someone was here in the hotel. Had Low come into town? Was he here? I got up and finished dressing hastily. I sat quietly on the edge of the bed, conscious of the deep ebb and flow of *something*. Finally I went down to the lobby. I stopped on the last step. Whatever it had been, it was gone. The lobby was just an ordinary lobby. Low was nowhere among the self-consciously ranch-style furnishings. But as I started toward the window to see again the lovely drop of the wooded canyon beyond the patio he walked in.

"Were you here a minute ago?" I asked him without preliminaries.

"No. Why?"

"I thought—" I broke off. Then gears shifted subtly back to the commonplace and I said, "Well! What are you doing here?"

"Old Charlie said you were in town and that I might as well pick you up and save you the bus trip back." He smiled faintly. "Marie wasn't quite sure I could be trusted after showing my true colors Friday, but she finally told me you were here at this hotel."

"But I didn't know myself where I was going to stay when I left Kruper!"

Low grinned engagingly. "My! You *are* new around here, aren't you? Are you ready to go?"

"I hope you're not in a hurry to get back to Kruper." Low shifted gears deftly as we nosed down to Lynx Hill bridge and then abruptly headed on up Lynx Hill at a perilous angle. "I have a stop to make."

I could feel his wary attention on me in spite of his absorption in the road.

"No," I said, sighing inwardly, visualizing long hours waiting while he leaned over the top fence rail exchanging long silences and succinct remarks with some mining acquaintance. "I'm in no hurry, just so I'm at school by nine in the morning."

"Fine." His voice was amused, and, embarrassed, I tested again the barrier in my mind. It was still intact. "Matter of fact," he went on, "this will be one for your collection, too."

"My collection?" I echoed blankly.

"Your ghost-town collection. I'm driving over to Machron, or where it used to be. It's up in a little box canyon above Bear Flat. It might be that it—" An intricate spot in the road —one small stone and a tiny pine branch—broke his sentence.

"Might be what?" I asked, deliberately holding onto the words he was trying to drop.

"Might be interesting to explore." Aware amusement curved his mouth slightly.

"I'd like to find an unbroken piece of sun glass," I said. "I have one old beautiful purple tumbler. It's in pretty good condition except that it has a piece out of the rim."

"I'll show you my collection sometime," Low said. "You'll drool for sure."

"How come you like ghost towns? What draws you to them? History? Treasure? Morbid curiosity?"

"Treasure—history—morbid curiosity—" He tasted the words slowly and approved each with a nod of his head. "I guess all three. I'm questing."

"Questing?"

"Questing." The tone of his voice ended the conversation. With an effort I detached myself from my completely illogical up-gush of anger at being shut out, and lost myself in the wooded wonder of the hillsides that finally narrowed the road until it was barely wide enough for the car to scrape through.

Finally Low spun the wheel and, fanning sand out from our tires, came to a stop under a huge black-walnut tree.

"Got your walking shoes on? This far and no farther for wheels."

Half an hour later we topped out on a small plateau above the rocky pass where our feet had slid and slithered on boulders grooved by high-wheeled ore wagons of half a century ago. The town had spread itself in its busiest days, up the slopes of the hills and along the dry creeks that spread fingerlike up from the small plateau. Concrete steps lead abortively up to crumbled foundations, and sagging gates stood fenceless before shrub-shattered concrete walks.

There were a few buildings that were nearly intact, just stubbornly resisting dissolution. I had wandered up one faint street and down another before I realized that Low wasn't wandering with me. Knowing the solitary ways of ghost-town devotees, I made no effort to locate him, but only wondered idly what he was questing for—carefully refraining from wondering again who he was and why he and I spoke together underneath as we did. But even unspoken the wonder was burning deep under my superficial scratching among the junk heaps of this vanished town.

I found a white button with only three holes in it and the top of a doll's head with one eye still meltingly blue, and scrabbled, bare-handed, with delight when I thought I'd found a whole sun-purpled sugar bowl—only to find it was just a handle and half a curve held in the silt.

I was muttering over a broken fingernail when a sudden soundless cry crushed into me and left me gasping with the unexpected force. I stumbled down the bank and ran clattering down the rock-strewn road. I found Low down by the old town dump, cradling something preciously in the bend of his arm.

He lifted his eyes blindly to me.

"Maybe—!" he cried. "This might be some of it. It was never a part of this town's life. Look! Look at the shaping of it! Look at the flow of lines!" His hands drank in the smooth beauty of the metal fragment. "And if this is part of it, it might not be far from here that—" He broke off abruptly, his thumb stilling on the underside of the object. He turned it over and looked closely. Something died tragically as he looked. " 'General Electric,' " he said tonelessly. " 'Made in the USA.' " The piece of metal dropped from his stricken hands as he sagged to the ground. His fist pounded on the gravelly silt. "Dead end! Dead end! Dead—"

I caught his hands in mine and brushed the gravel off, pressing Kleenex to the ooze of blood below his little finger.

"What have you lost?" I asked softly.

"Myself," he whispered. "I'm lost and I can't find my way back."

He took no notice of our getting up and my leading him to the fragment of a wall that kept a stunted elderberry from falling into the canyon. We sat down and for a while tossed on the ocean of his desolation as I thought dimly, "Too. Lost, too. Both of us." Then I helped him channel into speech, though I don't know whether it was vocal or not.

"I was so little then," he said. "I was only three, I guess. How long can you live on a three-year-old's memories? Mom told me all they knew but I could remember more. There was a wreck—a head-on collision the other side of Chuckawalla. My people were killed. The car tried to fly just before they hit. I remember Father lifted it up, trying to clear the other car, and Mother grabbed a handful of sun and platted me out of danger, but the crash came and I could only hear Mother's cry 'Don't forget! Go back to the Canyon,' and Father's 'Remember! Remember the Home!' and they were gone, even their bodies, in the fire that followed. Their bodies and every identification. Mom and Dad took me in and raised me like their own, but I've got to go back. I've got to go back to the Canyon. I belong there."

"What Canyon?" I asked.

"What Canyon?" he asked dully. "The Canyon where the People live now—my People. The Canyon where they located after the starship crashed. The starship I've been questing for, praying I might find some little piece of it to point me the way to the Canyon. At least to the part of the state it's in. The Canyon I went to sleep in before I woke at the crash. The Canyon I can't find because I have no memory of the road there.

"But *you* know!" he went on. "You surely must know! You aren't like the others. You're one of us. You must be!"

I shrank down into myself.

"I'm nobody," I said. "I'm not one of anybody. My mom and dad can tell me my grandparents and great-grandparents and great-great-grandparents, and they used to all the time, trying to figure out why they were burdened with such a child, until I got smart enough to get 'normal.'

"You think *you're* lost! At least you know what you're lost from. You could get un-lost. But I can't. I haven't *ever* been un-lost!"

"But you can talk underneath." He blinked before my violence. "You showed me Lucine—"

"Yes," I said recklessly. "And look at this!"

A rock up on the hillside suddenly spurted to life. It plowed down the slope, sending gravel flying, and smashed itself to powder against a boulder at the base.

"And I never tried this before, but look!"

I stepped up onto the crumbling wall and walked away from Low, straight on out over the canyon, feeling Earth fall away beneath my feet, feeling the soft cradling sweep of the wind, the upness and outness and unrestrainedness. I cried out, lifting my arms, reaching ecstatically for the hem of my dream of freedom. One minute, one minute more and I could slide out of myself and never, never, *never* . . .

And then . . .

Low caught me just before I speared myself on the gaunt stubby pines below us in the canyon. He lifted me, struggling and protesting, back up through the fragile emptiness of air, back to the stunted elderberry tree.

140

"But I did! I did!" I sobbed against him. "I didn't just fall. For a while I really *did!*"

"For a while you really did, Dita," he murmured as to a child. "As good as I could do myself. So you do have some of the Persuasions. Where did you get them if you aren't one of us?"

My sobs cut off without an after-echo, though my tears continued. I looked deep into Low's eyes, fighting against the anger that burned at this persistent returning to the wary hurting place inside me. He looked steadily back until my tears stopped and I finally managed a ghost of a smile. "I don't know what a Persuasion is, but I probably got it the same place *you* got that tilt to your eyebrows."

He reddened and stepped back from me.

"We'd better start back. It's not smart to get night-caught on these back roads."

We started back along the trail.

"Of course you'll fill in the vacancies for me as we go back," I said, barely catching myself as my feet slithered on a slick hump of granite. I felt his immediate protest. "You've got to," I said, pausing to shake the gravel out of one shoe. "You can't expect me to ignore today, especially since I've found someone as crazy as I am."

"You won't believe—" He dodged a huge buckbrush that crowded the narrow road.

"I've had to believe things about myself all these years that I couldn't believe," I said, "and it's easier to believe things about other people."

So we drove through the magic of an early twilight that deepened into a star-brilliant night, and I watched the flick of the stars through the overarching trees along the road and listened to Low's story. He stripped it down to its bare bones, but underneath, the bones burned like fire in the telling.

"We came from some other world," he said, wistful pride at belonging showing in his "we." "The Home was destroyed. We looked for a refuge and found this earth. Our ships crashed or burned before they could land. But some of us escaped in life slips. My grandparents were with the original Group that gathered at the Canyon. But we were all there, too, because our memories are joined continuously back into the Bright

Beginning. That's why I know about my People. Only I can't remember where the Canyon is, because I was asleep the one time we left it, and Mother and Father couldn't tell me in that split second before the crash.

"I've got to find the Canyon again. I can't go on living forever limping." He didn't notice my start at his echoing of that thought of mine when I was with Lucine. "I can't achieve any stature at all until I am with my People.

"I don't even know the name of the Canyon, but I do remember that our ship crashed in the hills and I'm always hoping that someday I'll find some evidence of it in one of these old ghost towns. It was before the turn of the century that we came, and somewhere, somewhere, there must be some evidence of the ship still in existence."

His was a well-grooved story, too, worn into commonplace by repetition as mine had been—lonely aching repetition to himself. I wondered for a moment, in the face of his unhappiness, why I should feel a stirring of pleased comfort, but then I realized that it was because between us there was no need for murmurs of sympathy or trite little social sayings or even explanations. The surface words were the least of our communication.

"You aren't surprised?" He sounded almost disappointed.

"That you are an out-worlder?" I asked. I smiled. "Well, I've never met one before and I find it interesting. I only wish I could have dreamed up a fantasy like that to explain me to me. It's quite a switch on the old 'I *must* be adopted because I'm so different.' But—"

I stiffened as Low's surge of rage caught me offguard.

"Fantasy! I *am* adopted. I remember! I thought you'd know. I thought since you surely must be one of us that you'd be—"

"I'm not one of you!" I flared. "Whatever 'you' are. I'm of Earth—so much so that it's a wonder the dust doesn't puff out of my mouth when I speak—but at least I don't try to kid myself that I'm normal by *any* standard, Earth-type or otherwise."

For a hostile minute we were braced stonily against each other. My teeth ached as the muscles on my jaws knotted. Then Low sighed and reaching out a finger he traced the line of my face from brow to chin to brow again.

142

"Think your way," he said. "You've probably been through enough bad times to make anyone want to forget. Maybe someday you'll remember that you *are* one of us and then—"

"Maybe, maybe, maybe!" I said through my weary shaken breath. "But I can't any more. It's too much for one day." I slammed all the doors I could reach and shoved my everyday self up to the front. As we started off I reopened one door far enough to ask, "What's this between you and Lucine? Are you a friend of the family or something that you're working with her?"

"I know the family casually," Low said. "They don't know about Lucine and me. She caught my imagination once last year when I was passing the school. The kids were pestering her. I never felt such heartbroken bewilderment in all my life. Poor little Earth kid. She's a three-year-old in a twelve-year-old body—"

"Four-year-old," I murmured. "Or almost five. She's learning a little."

"Four or five," Low said. "It must be awful to be trapped in a body—"

"Yes," I sighed. "To be shut in the prison of yourself."

Tangibly I felt again the warm running of his finger around my face, softly, comfortingly, though he made no move toward me. I turned away from him in the dusk to hide the sudden tears that came.

It was late when we got home. There were still lights in the bars and a house or two when we pulled into Kruper, but the hotel was dark, and in the pause after the car stopped I could hear the faint creaking of the sagging front gate as it swung in the wind. We got out of the car quietly, whispering under the spell of the silence, and tiptoed up to the gate. As usual the scraggly rosebush that drooped from the fence snagged my hair as I went through, and as Low helped free me we got started giggling. I suppose neither of us had felt young and foolish for so long, and we had both unburdened ourselves of bitter tensions, and found tacit approval of us as the world refused to accept us and as we most wanted to be; and, each having at least glimpsed a kindred soul, well, we suddenly bubbled over. We stood beneath the upstairs porch and tried to muffle our giggles.

143

"People *will* think we're crazy if they hear us carrying on like this," I choked.

"I've got news for you," said Low, close to my ear. "We *are* crazy. And I dare you to prove it."

"Hoh! As though it needed any proof!"

"I dare you." His laughter tickled my cheek.

"How?" I breathed defiantly.

"Let's not go up the stairs," he hissed. "Let's lift through the air. Why waste the energy when we can——?"

He held out his hand to me. Suddenly sober I took it and we stepped back to the gate and stood hand in hand, looking up.

"Ready?" he whispered, and I felt him tug me upward.

I lifted into the air after him, holding all my possible fear clenched in my other hand.

And the rosebush reached up and snagged my hair.

"Wait!" I whispered, laughter trembling again. "I'm caught."

"Earth-bound!" he chuckled as he tugged at the clinging strands.

"Smile when you say that, podner," I returned, feeling my heart melt with pleasure that I had arrived at a point where I could joke about such a bitterness—and trying to ignore the fact that my feet were treading nothing but air. My hair freed, he lifted me up to him. I think our lips only brushed, but we overshot the porch and had to come back down to land on it. Low steadied me as we stepped across the railing.

"We did it," he whispered.

"Yes," I breathed. "We did."

Then we both froze. Someone was coming into the yard. Someone who stumbled and wavered and smashed glassily against the gatepost.

"*Ay! Ay! Madre mía!*" Severeid Swanson fell to his knees beside the smashed bottle. "*Ay, virgen purísima!*"

"Did he see us?" I whispered on an indrawn breath.

"I doubt it." His words were warm along my cheek. "He hasn't seen anything outside himself for years."

"Watch out for the chair." We groped through the darkness into the upper hall. A feeble fifteen-watt bulb glimmered on the steady drip of water splashing down into the sagging

144

sink from the worn faucets that blinked yellow through the worn chrome. By virtue of these two leaky outlets we had bathing facilities on the second floor.

Our good nights were subvocal and quick.

I was in my nightgown and robe, sitting on the edge of my bed, brushing my hair, when I heard a shuffle and a mutter outside my door. I checked the latch to be sure it was fastened and brushed on. There was a thud and a muffled rapping and my doorknob turned.

"Teesher!" It was a cautious voice. "Teesher!"

"Who on earth!" I thought and went to the door. "Yes?" I leaned against the peeling panel.

"Lat—me—een." The words were labored and spaced.

"What do you want?"

"To talk weeth you, teesher."

Filled with astonished wonder I opened the door. There was Severeid Swanson swaying in the hall! But they had told me he had no English. . . . He leaned precariously forward, his face glowing in the light, years younger than I'd ever seen him.

"My bottle is broken. You have done eet. It is not good to fly without the wings. *Los ángeles santos, sí, pero* not the lovers to fly to kiss. It makes me drop my bottle. On the ground is spilled all the dreams."

He swayed backward and wiped the earnest sweat from his forehead. "It is not good. I tell you this because you have light in the face. You are good to my Esperanza. You have dreams that are not in the bottle. You have smiles and not laughing for the lost ones. But you must not fly. It is not good. My bottle is broken."

"I'm sorry," I said through my astonishment. "I'll buy you another."

"No," Severeid said. "Last time they tell me this, too, but I cannot drink it because of the wondering. Last time, like birds, all, all in the sky—over the hills—the kind ones. The ones who also have no laughter for the lost."

"Last time?" I grabbed his swaying arm and pulled him into the room, shutting the door, excitement tingling along the insides of my elbows. "Where? When? Who was flying?"

145

He blinked owlishly at me, the tip of his tongue moistening his dry lips.

"It is not good to fly without wings," he repeated.

"Yes, yes, I know. Where did you see the others fly without wings? I must find them—I must!"

"Like birds," he said, swaying. "Over the hills."

"Please," I said, groping wildly for what little Spanish I possessed.

"I work there a long time. I don't see them no more. I drink some more. Chinee Joe give me new bottle."

"*Por favor, señor,*" I cried, "*dónde—dónde—?*"

All the light went out of his face. His mouth slackened. Dead eyes peered from under lowered lids.

"*No comprendo.*" He looked around, dazed. "*Buenas noches, señorita.*" He backed out of the door and closed it softly behind him.

"But—!" I cried to the door. "But please!"

Then I huddled on my bed and hugged this incredible piece of information to me.

"Others!" I thought. "Flying over the hills! All, all in the sky! Maybe, oh maybe one of them was at the hotel in town. Maybe they're not too far away. If only we knew . . . !"

Then I felt the sudden yawning of a terrifying chasm. If it was true, if Severeid had really seen others lifting like birds over the hills, then Low was right—there *were* others! There *must* be a Canyon, a starship, a Home. But where did that leave me? I shrank away from the possibilities. I turned and buried my face in my pillow. But Mother and Dad! And Granpa Josh and Gramma Malvina and Great-granpa Benedaly and— I clutched at the memories of all the family stories I'd heard. Crossing the ocean in steerage. Starting a new land. Why, my ancestors were as solid as a rock wall back of me, as far back as—as *Adam,* almost. I leaned against the certainty and cried out to feel the stone wall waver and become a curtain stirring in the winds of doubt.

"No, *no!*" I sobbed, and for the first time in my life I cried for my mother, feeling as bereft as though she had died.

Then I suddenly sat up in bed. "It might not be *so!*" I cried. "He's just a drunken wino. No telling what he might conjure out of his bottle. It might not be *so!*"

"But it might," one of me whispered maliciously. "It might!"

The days that followed were mostly uneventful. I had topped out onto a placid plateau in my battle with myself, perhaps because I had something new to occupy my mind or perhaps it was just a slack place since any emotion has to rest sometime.

However, the wonder of finding Low was slow to ebb. I could sense his "Good morning" with my first step down the stairs each day, and occasionally roused in the darkness to his silent "Good night."

Once after supper Marie planted herself solidly in front of me as I rose to leave. Silently she pointed at my plate where I had apparently made mud pies of my food. I flushed.

"No good?" she asked, crossing her wrists over the grossness of her stomach and teetering perilously backward.

"It's fine, Marie," I managed. "I'm just not hungry." And I escaped through the garlicky cloud of her indignant exhalation and the underneath amusement of Low. How could I tell her that Low had been showing me a double rainbow he had seen that afternoon and that I had been so engrossed in the taste of the colors and the miracle of being able to receive them from him that I had forgotten to eat?

Low and I spent much time together, getting acquainted, but during most of it we were ostensibly sitting with the others on the porch in the twilight, listening to the old mining and cattle stories that were the well-worn coins that slipped from hand to hand wherever the citizens of Kruper gathered together. A good story never wore out, so after a while it was an easy matter to follow the familiar repetitions and still be alone together in the group.

"Don't you think you need a little more practice in lifting?" Low's silent question was a thin clarity behind the rumble of voices.

"Lifting?" I stirred in my chair, not quite so adept as he at carrying two threads simultaneously.

"Flying," he said with exaggerated patience. "Like you did over the canyon and up to the porch."

"Oh." Ecstasy and terror puddled together inside me. Then

147

I felt myself relaxing in the strong warmth of Low's arms instead of fighting them as I had when he had caught me over the canyon.

"Oh, I don't know," I answered, quickly shutting him out as much as I could. "I think I can do it okay."

"A little more practice won't hurt." There was laughter in his reply. "But you'd better wait until I'm around—just in case."

"Oh?" I asked. "Look." I lifted in the darkness until I sat gently about six inches above my chair. "So!"

Something prodded me gently and I started to drift across the porch. Hastily I dropped back, just barely landing on the forward edge of my chair, my heels thudding audibly on the floor. The current story broke off in mid-episode and everyone looked at me.

"Mosquitoes," I improvised. "I'm allergic to them."

"That's not fair!" I sputtered silently to Low. "You cheat!"

"All's fair—" he answered, then shut hastily as he remembered the rest of the quotation.

"Hmm!" I thought. "Hmm! And this is war?" And felt pleased all out of proportion the rest of the evening.

Then there was the Saturday when the sky was so tangily blue and the clouds so puffily light that I just couldn't stay indoors scrubbing clothes and sewing on buttons and trying to decide whether to repair my nail polish or take it all off and start from scratch again. I scrambled into my saddle shoes and denim skirt, turned back the sleeves of my plaid shirt, tied the sleeves of my sweater around my waist and headed for the hills. This was the day to follow the town water pipe up to the spring that fed it and see if all the gruesome stories I'd heard about its condition were true.

I paused, panting, atop the last steep ledge above the town and looked back at the tumbled group of weathered houses that made up this side of Kruper. Beyond the railroad track there was enough flatland to make room for the four new houses that had been built when the Golden Turkey Mine reopened. They sat in a neat row, bright as toy blocks against the tawny red of the hillside.

I brushed my hair back from my hot forehead and turned my back on Kruper. I could see sections of the town water

148

pipe scattered at haphazard intervals up among the hills—in some places stilted up on timbers to cross from one rise to another, in other places following the jagged contour of the slopes. A few minutes and sections later I was amusing myself trying to stop with my hands the spray of water from one of the numerous holes in one section of the rusty old pipe and counting the hand-whittled wooden plugs that stopped up others. It looked a miracle that any water at all got down to town. I was so engrossed that I unconsciously put my hand up to my face when a warm finger began to trace . . .

"Low!" I whirled on him. "What are you doing up here?"

He slid down from a boulder above the line.

"Johnny's feeling porely today. He wanted me to check to see if any of the plugs had fallen out."

We both laughed as we looked up-line and traced the pipe by the white gush of spray and the vigorous greenness that utilized the spilling water.

"I'll bet he has at least a thousand plugs hammered in," Low said.

"Why on earth doesn't he get some new pipe?"

"Family heirlooms," Low said, whittling vigorously. "It's only because he's feeling so porely that he even entertains the thought of letting me plug his line. All the rest of the plugs are family affairs. About three generations' worth."

He hammered the plug into the largest of the holes and stepped back, reaming the water from his face where it had squirted him.

"Come on up. I'll show you the spring."

We sat in the damp coolness of the thicket of trees that screened the cave where the spring churned and gurgled, blue and white and pale green before it lost itself in the battered old pipes. We were sitting on opposite sides of the pipe, resting ourselves in the consciousness of each other, when all at once, for a precious minute, we flowed together like coalescing streams of water, so completely one that the following rebound to separateness came as a shock. Such sweetness without even touching one another . . . ?

Anyway we both turned hastily away from this frightening new emotion, and, finding no words handy, Low brought me down a flower from the ledge above us, nipping a drooping leaf off it as it passed him.

"Thanks," I said, smelling of it and sneezing vigorously. "I wish I could do that."

"Well, you can! You lifted that rock at Macron and you can lift yourself."

"Yes, myself." I shivered at the recollection. "But not the rock. I could only move it."

"Try that one over there." Low lobbed a pebble toward a small slaty blue rock lying on the damp sand. Obligingly it plowed a small furrow up to Low's feet.

"*Lift* it," he said.

"I can't. I told you I can't lift anything clear off the ground. I can just move it." I slid one of Low's feet to one side.

Startled, he pulled it back.

"But you *have* to be able to lift, Dita. You're one of—"

"I am not!" I threw the flower I'd been twiddling with down violently into the spring and saw it sucked into the pipe. Someone downstream was going to be surprised at the sink or else one of the thousands of fountains between here and town was going to blossom.

"But all you have to do is—is—" Low groped for words.

"Yes?" I leaned forward eagerly. Maybe I could learn. . . .

"Well, just *lift!*"

"Twirtle!" I said, disappointed. "Anyway can you do *this?* Look." I reached in my pocket and pulled out two bobby pins and three fingernails full of pocket fluff. "Have you got a dime?"

"Sure." He fished it out and brought it to me. I handed it back. "Glow it," I said.

"Glow it? You mean blow it?" He turned it over in his hand.

"No, *glow* it. Go on. It's easy. All you have to do is glow it. Any metal will do but silver works better."

"Never heard of it," he said, frowning suspiciously.

"You must have," I cried, "if you are part of me. If we're linked back to the Bright Beginning you must remember!"

Low turned the dime slowly. "It's a joke to you. Something to laugh at."

150

"A joke!" I moved closer to him and looked up into his face. "Haven't I been looking for an answer long enough? Wouldn't I belong if I could? Would my heart break and bleed every time I have to say no if I could mend it by saying yes? If I could only hold out my hands and say, 'I belong . . .'" I turned away from him, blinking. "Here," I sniffed. "Give me the dime."

I took it from his quiet fingers and, sitting down again, spun it quickly in the palm of my hand. It caught light immediately, glowing stronger until I slitted my eyes to look at it and finally had to close my fingers around its cool pulsing.

"Here." I held my hand out to Low, my bones shining pinkly through. "It's glowed."

"Light," he breathed, taking the dime wonderingly. "Cold light! How long can you hold it?"

"I don't have to hold it. It'll glow until I damp it."

"How long?"

"How long does it take metal to turn to dust?" I shrugged. "I don't know. Do your People know how to glow?"

"No." His eyes stilled on my face. "I have no memory of it."

"So I *don't* belong." I tried to say it lightly above the wrenching of my heart. "It almost looks like we're simultaneous, but we aren't. You came one way. I came t'other." "Not even to him!" I cried inside. "I can't even belong to him!" I drew a deep breath and put emotion to one side.

"Look," I said. "Neither of us fits a pattern. You deviate and I deviate and you're satisfied with your explanation of why you are what you are. I haven't found my explanation yet. Can't we let it go at that?"

Low grabbed my shoulders, the dime arching down into the spring. He shook me with a tight controlled shaking that was hardly larger than a trembling of his tensed hands. "I tell you, Dita, I'm not making up stories! I belong and you belong and all your denying won't change it. We are the same—"

We stared stubbornly at each other for a long moment, then the tenseness ran out of his fingers and he let them slide down my arms to my hands. We turned away from the spring and started silently, hand in hand, down the trail. I looked back and saw the glow of the dime and damped it.

"No," I said to myself. "It isn't so. I'd know it if it were true. We aren't the same. But what am I then? What am I?" And I stumbled a little wearily on the narrow path.

During this time everything at school was placid, and Pete had finally decided that "two" could have a name *and* a picture, and learned his number words to ten in one day,

And Lucine—symbol to Low and me of our own imprisonment—with our help was blossoming under the delight of reading her second pre-primer.

But I remember the last quiet day. I sat at my desk checking the tenth letter I'd received in answer to my inquiries concerning a possible Chinee Joe and sadly chalking up another "no." So far I had been able to conceal from Low the amazing episode of Severeid Swanson. I wanted to give him back his Canyon myself, if it existed. I wanted it to be my gift to him—and to my own shaken self. Most of all I wanted to be able to know at least one thing for sure, even if that one thing proved me wrong or even parted Low and me. Just one solid surety in the whole business would be a comfort and a starting place for us truly to get together.

I wished frequently that I could take hold of Severeid bodily and shake more information out of him, but he had disappeared—walked off from his job without even drawing his last check. No one knew where he had gone. The last Kruper had seen of him was early the next morning after he had spoken with me. He had been standing, slack-kneed and wavering, a bottle in each hand, at the crossroads—not even bothering to thumb a ride, just waiting blankly for someone to stop for him—and apparently someone had.

I asked Esperanza about him, and she twisted her thick shining braid around her hand twice and tugged at it.

"He's a wino," she said dispassionately. "They ain't smart. Maybe he got losted." Her eyes brightened. "Last year he got losted and the cops picked him up in El Paso. He brang me some perfume when he came back. Maybe he went to El Paso again. It was pretty perfume." She started down the stairs. "He'll be back," she called, "unless he's dead in a ditch somewhere."

I shook my head and smiled ruefully. And she'd fight like a wildcat if anyone else talked about Severeid like that. . . .

I sighed at the recollection and went back to my disappointing letter. Suddenly I frowned and moved uneasily in my chair. What was wrong? I felt acutely uncomfortable. Quickly I checked me over physically. Then my eyes scanned the room. Petie was being jet planes while he drew pictures of them, and the soft *skoosh! skoosh! skoosh!* of the take-offs was about the only on-top sound in the room. I checked underneath and the placid droning hum was as usual. I had gone back on top when I suddenly dived back again. There was a sharp stinging buzz like an angry bee—a malicious angry buzz! Who was it? I met Lucine's smoldering eyes and I knew.

I almost gasped under the sudden flood of hate-filled anger. And when I tried to reach her, down under, I was rebuffed—not knowingly but as though there had never been a contact between us. I wiped my trembling hands against my skirt, trying to clean them of what I had read.

The recess bell came so shatteringly that I jumped convulsively and shared the children's laughter over it. As soon as I could I hurried to Mrs. Kanz's room.

"Lucine's going to have another spell," I said without preface.

"What makes you think so?" Mrs. Kanz marked "46½%" on the top of a literature paper.

"I don't think so, I know so. And this time she won't be too slow. Someone will get hurt if we don't do something."

Mrs. Kanz laid down her pencil and folded her arms on the desk top, her lips tightening. "You've been brooding too much over Lucine," she said, none too pleased. "If you're getting to the point where you think you can predict her behavior, you're pretty far gone. People are going to be talking about *your* being queer pretty soon. Why don't you just forget about her and concentrate on—on—well, on Low? He's more fun than she is anyway, I'll bet."

"He'd know," I cried. "He'd tell you, too! He knows more about Lucine than anyone thinks."

"So I've heard." There was a nasty purr to her voice that I didn't know it possessed. "They've been seen together out in the hills. Well, it's only her mind that's retarded. Remember, she's over twelve now, and some men—"

I slapped the flat of my hand down on the desk top with a sharp crack. I could feel my eyes blazing, and she dodged back as though from a blow. She pressed the back of one hand defensively against her cheek.

"I—" she gasped, "I was only kidding!"

I breathed deeply to hold my rage down. "*Are* you going to do anything about Lucine?" My voice was very soft.

"What can I do? What is there to do?"

"Skip it," I said bitterly. "Just skip it."

I tried all afternoon to reach Lucine, but she sat lumpish and unheeding—on top. Underneath violence and hatred were seething like lava, and once, without apparent provocation, she leaned across the aisle and pinched Petie's arm until he cried.

She was sitting in isolation with her face to the wall when the last bell rang.

"You may go now, Lucine," I said to the sullen stranger who had replaced the child I knew. I put my hand on her shoulder. She slipped out of my touch with one fluid quick motion. I caught a glimpse of her profile as she left. The jaw muscles were knotted and the cords in her neck were tensed.

I hurried home and waited, almost wild from worry, for Low to get off shift. I paced the worn Oriental rug in the living room, circling the potbellied cast-iron heater. I peered a dozen times through the lace curtains, squinting through the dirty cracked window panes. I beat my fist softly into my palm as I paced, and I felt physical pain when the phone on the wall suddenly shrilled.

I snatched down the receiver.

"Yes!" I cried. "Hello!"

"Marie. I want Marie." The voice was far and crackling. "You tell Marie I gotta talk to her."

I called Marie and left her to her conversation and went out on the porch. Back and forth, back and forth I paced, Marie's voice swelling and fading as I passed.

". . . well, I expected it a long time ago. A crazy girl like that—"

"Lucine!" I shouted and rushed indoors. "What happened?"

"Lucine?" Marie frowned from the telephone. "What's Lucine gotta do with it? Marson's daughter ran off last night with the hoistman at the Golden Turkey. He's fifty if he's a day and she's just turned sixteen." She turned back to the phone. "Yah, yah, yah?" Her eyes gleamed avidly.

I just got back to the door in time to see the car stop at the gate. I grabbed my coat and was down the steps as the car door swung open.

"Lucine?" I gasped.

"Yes." The sheriff opened the back door for me, his deputy goggle-eyed with the swiftness of events. "Where is she?"

"I don't know," I said. "What happened?"

"She got mad on the way home." The car spurted away from the hotel. "She picked Petie up by the heels and bashed him against a boulder. She chased the other kids away with rocks and went back and started to work on Petie. He's still alive, but Doc lost count of the stitches and they're transfusing like crazy. Mrs. Kanz says you likely know where she is."

"No." I shut my eyes and swallowed. "But we'll find her. Get Low first."

The shift bus was just pulling in at the service station. Low was out of it and into the sheriff's car before a word could be spoken. I saw my anxiety mirrored on his face before we clasped hands.

For the next two hours we drove the roads around Kruper. We went to all the places we thought Lucine might have run to, but nowhere, nowhere in all the scrub-covered foothills or the pine-pointed mountains, could I sense Lucine.

"We'll take one more sweep—through Poland Canyon. Then if it's no dice we'll hafta get a posse and Claude's hounds." The sheriff gunned for the steep rise at the canyon entrance. "Beats me how a kid could get so gone so fast."

"You haven't seen her really run," Low said. "She never can when she's around other people. She's just a little lower than a plane and she can run me into the ground any time. She just shifts her breathing into overdrive and takes off. She could beat Claude's hounds without trying, if it ever came to a run-down."

"Stop!" I grabbed the back of the seat. "Stop the car!"

The car had brakes. We untangled ourselves and got out.

"Over there," I said. "She's over there somewhere." We stared at the brush-matted hillside across the canyon.

"Gaw-dang!" the sheriff moaned. "Not in Cleo II! That there hell hole's been nothing but a jinx since they sunk the first shaft. Water and gas and cave-in sand, every gaw-dang thing in the calendar. I've lugged my share of dead men out of there—me and my dad before me. What makes you think she's in there, Teacher? Yuh see something?"

"I know she's somewhere over there," I evaded. "Maybe not in the mine but she's there."

"Let's get looking," the sheriff sighed. "I'd give a pretty to know how you saw her clear from the other side of the car." He edged out of the car and lifted a shotgun after him.

"A gun?" I gasped. "For Lucine?"

"You didn't see Petie, did you?" he said. "I did. I go animal hunting with guns."

"No!" I cried. "She'll come for us."

"Might be," he spat reflectively. "Or maybe not."

We crossed the road and plunged into the canyon before the climb.

"Are you sure, Dita?" Low whispered. "I don't reach her at all. Only some predator—"

"That's Lucine," I choked. "That's Lucine."

I felt Low's recoil. "That—that *animal?*"

"That animal. Did we do it? Maybe we should have left her alone."

"I don't know." I ached with his distress. "God help me, I don't know."

She *was* in Cleo II.

Over our tense silence we could hear the rattling of rocks inside as she moved. I was almost physically sick.

"Lucine," I called into the darkness of the drift. "Lucine, come on out. It's time to go home."

A fist-sized rock sent me reeling, and I nursed my bruised shoulder with my hand.

"Lucine!" Low's voice was commanding and spread all over the band. An inarticulate snarl answered him.

"Well?" The sheriff looked at us.

"She's completely crazy," Low said. "We can't reach her at all."

"Gaw-dang," the sheriff said. "How we gonna get her out?"

No one had an answer, and we stood around awkwardly while the late-afternoon sun hummed against our backs and puddled softly in the mine entrance. There was a sudden flurry of rocks that rattled all about us, thudding on the bare ground and crackling in the brush—then a low guttural wail that hurt my bones and whitened the sheriff's face.

"I'm gonna shoot," he said, thinly. "I'm gonna shoot it daid." He hefted the shotgun and shuffled his feet.

"No!" I cried. "A child! A little girl!"

His eyes turned to me and his mouth twisted.

"That?" he asked and spat.

His deputy tugged at his sleeve and took him to one side and muttered rapidly. I looked uneasily at Low. He was groping for Lucine, his eyes closed, his face tense.

The two men set about gathering up a supply of small-sized rocks. They stacked them ready-to-hand near the mine entrance. Then, taking simultaneous deep breaths, they started a steady bombardment into the drift. For a while there was an answering shower from the mine, then an outraged squall that faded as Lucine retreated farther into the darkness.

"Gotter!" The two men redoubled their efforts, stepping closer to the entrance, and Low's hand on my arm stopped me from following.

"There's a drop-off in there," he said. "They're trying to drive her into it. I dropped a rock in it once and never heard it land."

"It's murder!" I cried, jerking away, grabbing the sheriff's arm. "Stop it!"

"You can't get her any other way," the sheriff grunted, his muscles rippling under my restraining hand. "Better her dead than Petie and all the rest of us. She's fixing to kill."

"I'll get her," I cried, dropping to my knees and hiding my face in my hands. "I'll get her. Give me a minute." I concentrated as I had never concentrated before. I sent myself stumbling out of me into the darkness of the mine, into a heavier deeper uglier darkness, and I struggled with the darkness in Lucine until I felt it surging uncontrollably into my own mind. Stubbornly I persisted, trying to flick a fingernail of reason under the edge of this angry unreason to let a little sanity in. Low reached me just before the flood engulfed me. He reached me and held me until I could shudder myself back from hell.

Suddenly there was a rumble from inside the hill—a cracking crash and a yellow billow of dust from the entrance.

There was an animal howl that cut off sharply and then a scream of pure pain and terror—a child's terrified cry, a horrified awakening in the darkness, a cry for help—for light!

"It's Lucine!" I half sobbed. "She's back. What happened?"

"Cave-in!" the sheriff said, his jaws working. "Shoring gone—rotted out years ago. Gotter for sure now, I guess."

"But it's Lucine again," Low said. "We've got to get her out."

"If that cave-in's where I think it is," the sheriff said, "she's a goner. There's a stretch in there that's just silt. Finest slitheriest stuff you ever felt. Comes like a flood of water. Drowns a feller in dirt." His lips tightened. "First dead man I ever saw I dragged out of a silt-down in here. I was sixteen, I guess—skinniest feller in the batch, so they sent me in after they located the body and shored up a makeshift drift. Dragged him out feet first. Stubborn feller—sucked out of that silt like outa mud. Drownded in dirt. We'll sweat getting this body out, too.

"Well," he hitched up his Levi's, "might as well git on back to town and git a crew out here."

"She's not dead," Low said. "She's still breathing. She's caught under something and can't get loose."

The sheriff looked at him through narrowed eyes. "I've heard you're kinda tetched," he said. "Sounds to me like you're having a spell yourself, talking like that.

"Wanta go back to town, ma'am?" His voice gentled. "Nothing you can do around here any more. She's a goner."

"No, she isn't," I said. "She's still alive. I can hear her."

"Gaw-dang!" the sheriff muttered. "Two of them. Well, all right then. You two are deppytized to watch the mine so it don't run away while I'm gone." Grinning sourly at his own wit, he left, taking the deputy with him.

We listened to the echoes of the engine until they died away in the quiet quiet upsurging of the forested hills all around us. We heard the small wind in the brush and the far cry of some

158

flying bird. We heard the pounding of our own pulses and the frightened bewilderedness that was Lucine. And we heard the pain that began to beat its brassy hammers through her body, and the sharp piercing stab of sheer agony screaming up to the bright twanging climax that snapped down into unconsciousness. And then both of us were groping in the darkness of the tunnel. I stumbled and fell and felt a heavy flowing something spread across my lap, weighting me down. Low was floundering ahead of me. "Go back," he warned. "Go back or we'll both be caught!"

"No!" I cried, trying to scramble forward. "I can't leave you!"

"Go back," he said. "I'll find her and hold her until the men come. You've got to help me hold the silt back."

"I can't," I whimpered. "I don't know how!" I scooped at the heaviness in my lap.

"Yes, you do," he said down under. "Just look and see."

I scrambled back the interminable distance I hadn't even been conscious of when going in, and crouched just outside the mine entrance, my dirty hands pressed to my wet face. I looked deep, deep inside me, down into a depth that suddenly became a height. I lifted me, mind and soul, up, up, until I found a new Persuasion, a new ability, and slowly, slowly, stemmed the creeping dry tide inside the mine—slowly began to part the black flood that had overswept Lucine so that only the arch of her arm kept her mouth and nose free of the invading silt.

Low burrowed his way into the mass, straining to reach Lucine before all the air was gone.

We were together, working such a work that we weren't two people any more. We were one, but that one was a multitude, all bound together in this tremendous outpouring of effort. Since we were each other, we had no need for words as we worked in toward Lucine. We found a bent knee, a tattered hem, a twisted ankle—and the splintery edge of timber that pinned her down. I held the silt back while Low burrowed to find her head. Carefully we cleared a larger space for her face. Carefully we worked to free her body. Low finally held her limp shoulders in his arms—*and was gone! Gone completely, between one breath and another.*

"Low!" I screamed, scrambling to my feet at the tunnel's mouth, but the sound of my cry was drowned in the smashing crash that shook the ground. I watched horrified as the hillside dimpled and subsided and sank into silence after a handful of pebbles, almost hidden in a puff of dust, rattled to rest at my feet.

I screamed again and the sky spun in a dizzy spiral rimmed with sharp pine tops, and suddenly unaccountably Severeid Swanson was there joining the treetops and the sky and spinning with them as he said, "Teesher! Teesher!"

The world steadied as though a hand had been put upon it. I scrambled to my feet.

"Severeid!" I cried. "They're in there! Help me get them out! Help me!"

"Teesher," Severeid shrugged helplessly, "*no comprendo.* I bring a flying one. I go get him. You say you gotta find. I find him. What you do out here with tears?"

Before I was conscious of another person standing beside Severeid I felt another person in my mind. Before I could bring my gasping into articulation the words were taken from me. Before I could move I heard the rending of rocks, and turning I sank to my knees and watched, in terrified wonder, the whole of the hillside lift itself and arch away like a furrow of turned earth before a plowshare. I saw silt rise like a yellow-red fountain above the furrow. I saw Low and Lucine rise with the silt. I saw the hillside flow back upon itself. I saw Low and Lucine lowered to the ground before me and saw all the light fading as I fell forward, my fingertips grazing the curve of Low's cheek just before I drank deeply of blackness.

The sun was all. Through the thin blanket I could feel the cushioning of the fine sand under my cheek. I could hear the cold blowing overhead through the sighing trees, but where we were the warmth of the late-fall sun was gathered between granite palms and poured down into our tiny pocket against the mountain. Without moving I could reach Low and Valancy and Jemmy. Without opening my eyes I could see them around me, strengthening me. The moment grew too dear to hold. I rolled over and sat up.

"Tell me again," I said. "How did Severeid ever find you the second time?"

I didn't mind the indulgent smile Valancy and Jemmy exchanged. I didn't mind feeling like a child—if they were the measure of adults.

"The first time he ever saw us," Jemmy said, "was when he chose to sleep off his *vino* around a boulder from where we chose to picnic. He was so drunk, or so childlike, or both, that he wasn't amazed or outraged by our lifting and tumbling all over the sky. He was intrigued and delighted. He thought he had died and by-passed purgatory, and we had to restrain him to keep him from taking off after us. Of course, before we let him go we blocked his memory of us so he couldn't talk of us to anyone except others of the People." He smiled at me. "That's why we got real shook when we found that he'd told you and that you're not of the People. At least not of the Home. You're the third blow to our provincialism. Peter and Bethie were the first, but at least they were half of the People, but you—" he waggled his head mournfully, "you just didn't track."

"Yes," I shivered, remembering the long years I hadn't tracked with anyone. "I just didn't track—" And I relaxed under the triple reassurance that flooded in from Low and Jemmy and his wife Valancy.

"Well, when you told Severeid you wanted to find us he stumbled as straight as a wino string back to our old picnic grounds. He must have huddled over that tiny fire of his for several days before we found him—parched with thirst and far past his last memory of food." Jemmy drew a long breath.

"Well, when we found out that Severeid knew of what we thought were two more of us—we've been in-gathering ever since the ships first arrived—*well!* We slept him all the way back. He would have been most unhappy with the speed and altitude of that return trip, especially without a car or plane.

"I caught your struggle to save Lucine when we were still miles away, and, praise the Power, I got there in time."

"Yes," I breathed, taking warmth from Low's hand to thaw my memory of that moment.

"That's the quickest I ever platted anything," Jemmy said.

"And the first time I ever did it on a scale like that. I wasn't sure that the late sunlight, without the moonlight, was strong enough, so I was openmouthed myself at the way the mountain ripped open." He smiled weakly. "Maybe it's just as well that we curb our practice of some of our Persuasions. It was really shake-making!"

"That's for sure!" I shivered. "I wonder what Severeid thought of the deal?"

"We gave Severeid forgetfulness of the whole mine episode," Valancy said. "But, as Jemmy would say, the sheriff was considerably shook when he got back with the crew. His only articulate pronouncement was, 'Gaw-dang! Cleo II's finally gone!'"

"And Lucine?" I asked, savoring the answer I already knew.

"And Lucine is learning," Valancy said. "Bethie, our Sensitive, found what was wrong and it is mended now. She'll be normal very shortly."

"And—me?" I breathed, hoping I knew.

"One of us!" the three cried to me down under. "Earth born or not—one of us!"

"But what a problem!" Jemmy said. "We thought we had us all catalogued. There were those of us completely of the People and those who were half of the People and half of Earth like Bethie and Peter. And then *you* came along. Not one bit of the People!"

"No," I said, comfortably leaning against my ancestral stone wall again. "Not one bit of the People."

"You look like confirmation of something we've been wondering about, though," Valancy said. "Perhaps after all this long time of detour the people of Earth are beginning to reach the Persuasions, too. We've had hints of such developments but in such little bits and snippets in these research deals. We had no idea that anyone was so far along the way. No telling how many others there are all over the world waiting to be found."

"Hiding, you mean," I said. "You don't go around asking to be found. Not after the first few reactions you get. Oh, maybe in the first fine flush of discovery you hurry to share the wonder, but you learn quickly enough to hide."

"But so like us!" Valancy cried. "Two worlds and yet you're so like us!"

"But she can't inanimate-lift," Low teased.

"And you can't glow," I retorted.

"And you can't sun-and-moonlight-platt," Jemmy said.

"Nor you cloud-herd," I said. "And if you don't stop picking on me I'll do just that right now and snatch that shower away from—from Morenci and drench you all!"

"And she could do it!" Valancy laughed. "And we can't, so let's leave her alone."

We all fell silent, relaxing on the sun-warmed sand until Jemmy rolled over and opened one eye.

"You know, Valancy, Dita and Low can communicate more freely than you and I. With them it's sometimes almost involuntary."

Valancy rolled over, too. "Yes," she said. "And Dita can block me out, too. Only a Sorter is supposed to be able to block a Sorter and she's not a Sorter."

Jemmy waggled his head. "Just like Earthlings! Always out of step. What a problem this gal's going to be!"

"Yep," Low cut in underneath. "A problem and a half, but I think I'll keep her anyway." I could feel his tender laughter.

I closed my eyes against the sun, feeling it golden across my lids.

"I'm un-lost," I thought incredulously, aching with the sudden joy of it. "I'm really un-lost!"

I took tight hold of the hem of my dream, knowing finally and surely that someday I would be able to wrap the whole fabric of it not just around me but around others who were lost and bewildered, too. Someday we would all *be* what was only a dream now.

Softly I drowsed, Low's hand warm upon my cheek—drowsed finally, without dreading an awakening.

V

"OH, BUT! Oh, but!" Lea thought excitedly. "Maybe, maybe—!" She turned at the pressure of a hand on her shoulder and met Melodye's understanding eyes.

"No," she said, "we're still Outsiders. It's like the color of your eyes. You're either brown-eyed or you're not. We're not the People. Welcome to my bakery window."

"Seems to me you're fattening on just the sight and smell then." It was Dr. Curtis.

"Fattening!" Melodye wailed. "Oh, no! Not after all my efforts—"

"Well, perhaps being nourished would be a more tactful way of saying it, as well as being more nearly exact. You don't seem to be wasting away."

"Maybe," Melodye said, sobering, "maybe it's because knowing there can be this kind of communication between the People, and trying to reach it for myself, I have made myself more receptive to communication from a source that knows no Outsiders—no East or West—no bond or free—"

"Hmm," Dr. Curtis said. "There you have a point for pondering."

Karen and Lea separated from the happily chattering groups as they passed the house. The two girls lingered, huddling in their jackets, until the sound of the other voices died in shadowy echoes down-canyon. Lea lifted her chin to a sudden cool breeze.

"Karen, do you think I'll ever get straightened out?" she asked.

"If you're not too enamored of your difficulties," Karen said, her hand on the doorknob. "If you're not too firmly set

164

on remodeling 'nearer to *your* heart's desire.' We may think this is a 'sorry scheme of things' but we have to learn that our own judgment is neither completely valid nor the polestar for charting our voyage. Too often we operate on the premise that what *we* think just *has* to be the norm for all things. Really, you'd find it most comforting to admit that you aren't running the universe—that you can't be responsible for everything, that there are lots of things you can and must relinquish into other hands—"

"To let go—" Lea looked down at her clenched hands. "I've held them like this so much it's a wonder my nails haven't grown through my palms."

"Sneaky way to keep from having to use nail polish!" Karen laughed. "But come—to bed, to bed. Oh, I'll be so glad when I can take you over the hill!" She opened the door and went in, tugging at her jacket. "I just ache to talk it over with you, good old Outsider-type talking. I acquired quite a taste for it that year I spent Outside—" Her voice faded down the hall. Lea looked up at the brilliant stars that punctuated the near horizon.

"The stars come down," she thought, "down to the hills and the darkness. The darkness lifts up to the hills and the stars. And here on the porch is a me-sized empty place trying to Become. It's so hard to reconcile darkness and the stars—but what else are we but an attempt at reconciliation?"

Night came again. It seemed to Lea that time was like a fan. The evenings were the carefully carved, tangible bones of the fan that held their identity firmly. The days folded themselves meekly away between the nights—days containing patterns only in that they were bounded on each side by evenings—folded days scribbled on unintelligibly. She held herself carefully away from any attempt to read the scrawling scribbles. If they meant anything she didn't want to know it. Only so long as she could keep from reading meanings into anything or trying to relate one thing to another—only that long could she maintain the precarious peace of the folded days and active evenings.

She settled down almost gladly into the desk that had become pleasantly familiar. "It's rather like drugging myself on movies or books or TV," she thought. "I bring my mind empty to the Gatherings, let the stories flow through and take my mind empty home again." Home? Home? She felt the fist clench in her chest and twist sharply, but she stubbornly concentrated on the lights that swung from the ceiling. Her attention sharpened on them. "Those aren't electric lights," she whispered to Karen. "Nor Coleman lanterns. What are they?"

"Lights," Karen smiled. "They cost a dime apiece. A dime and Dita. She glowed them for us. I've been practicing like mad and I almost glowed one the other day." She laughed ruefully. "And she an Outsider! Oh, I tell you, Lea, you never know how much you use pride to keep yourself warm in this cold world until someone tears a hole in it and you shiver in the draft. Dita was a much-needed rip to a lot of us, bless her pointed little ears!"

"Greetings." Dr. Curtis slid into his seat next to Lea. "You'll like the story tonight," he nodded at Lea. "You share a great deal with Miss Carolle. I find it very interesting—the story, that is—well, and your similarity, too. Well, anyway, I find the story interesting because my own fine Italian hand—" He subsided as Miss Carolle came down the aisle.

"Why, she's crippled!" Lea thought in amazement. "Or has been," she amended. Then wondered what there was about Miss Carolle that made her think of handicaps.

"Handicaps?" Lea flushed. "I share a great deal with her?" She twisted the corner of her Kleenex. "Of course," she admitted humbly, ducking her head. "Handicapped—crippled—" She caught her breath as the darkness swelled—ripping to get in—or out—or just ripping. Before the tiny beads of cold sweat had time to finish forming on her upper lip and at her hairline she felt Karen touch her with a healing strength. "Thank you, my soothing syrup," she thought wryly. "Don't be silly!" she heard Karen think sharply. "Laugh at your Band-Aids after the scabs are off!"

Miss Carolle murmured into the sudden silence, "We are met together in Thy Name."

Lea let the world flow away from her.

"I have a theme song instead of just a theme," Miss Carolle said. "Ready?"

Music strummed softly, coming from nowhere and from

everywhere. Lea felt wrapped about by its soft fullness. Then a clear voice took up the melody, so softly, so untrespassingly, that it seemed to Lea that the music itself had modulated to words, voicing some cry of her own that had never found words before.

> "By the rivers of Babylon,
> There we sat down and wept,
> When we remembered Zion.
> We hanged our harps
> Upon the willows in the midst thereof.
> For there they that carried us away captive
> Required of us a song
> And they that wasted us
> Required of us mirth
> Saying, 'Sing us one of the songs of Zion.'
> How shall we sing the Lord's song
> In a strange land?"

Lea closed her eyes and felt weak tears slip from under the lids. She put her head down on her arms on the desk top to hide her face. Her heart, torn by the anguish of the music, was sore for all the captives who had ever been, of whatever captivity, but most especially for those who drove themselves into exile, who locked themselves into themselves and lost the key.

The crowd had become a listening person as Miss Carolle twisted her palms together, fingers spread and tense for a moment and then began. . . .

CAPTIVITY

I suppose many lonely souls have sat at their windows many nights looking out into the flood of moonlight, sad with a sadness that knows no comfort, a sadness underlined by a beauty that is in itself a pleasant kind of sorrow—but very few ever have seen what I saw that night.

I leaned against the window frame, close enough to the inflooding light so that it washed across my bare feet and the

167

hem of my gown and splashed whitely against the foot of my bed, but picked up none of my features to identify me as a person, separate from the night. I was enjoying hastily, briefly, the magic of the loveliness before the moon would lose itself behind the heavy grove of cottonwoods that lined the creek below the curve of the back-yard garden. The first cluster of leaves had patterned itself against the edge of the moon when I saw him—the Francher kid. I felt a momentary surge of disappointment and annoyance that this perfect beauty should be marred by any person at all, let alone the Francher kid, but my annoyance passed as my interest sharpened.

What was he doing—half black and half white in the edge of the moonlight? In the higgledy-piggledy haphazardness of the town Groman's Grocery sidled in at an angle to the back yard of the Somansons' house, where I boarded—not farther than twenty feet away. The tiny high-up windows under the eaves of the store blinked in the full light. The Francher kid was standing, back to the moon, staring up at the windows. I leaned closer to watch. There was a waitingness about his shoulders, a prelude to movement, a beginning of something. Then there he was—up at the windows, pushing softly against the panes, opening a dark rectangle against the white side of the store. And then he was gone. I blinked and looked again. Store. Windows. One opened blankly. No Francher kid. Little windows. High up under the eaves. One opened blankly. No Francher kid.

Then the blank opening had movement inside it, and the Francher kid emerged with both hands full of something and slid down the moonlight to the ground outside.

"Now looky here!" I said to myself. "Hey! Lookit now!"

The Francher kid sat down on one end of a twelve-by-twelve that lay half in our garden and half behind the store. Carefully and neatly he arranged his booty along the timber. Three Cokes, a box of candy bars, and a huge harmonica that had been in the store for years. He sat and studied the items, touching each one with a fingertip. Then he picked up a Coke and studied the cap on it. He opened the box of candy and closed it again. He ran a finger down the harmonica and then lifted it between the pointer fingers of his two hands. Holding it away from him in the moonlight he looked at it, his head swinging

168

slowly down its length. And, as his head swung, faintly, faintly, I heard a musical scale run up, then down. Careful note by careful note singing softly but clearly in the quiet night.

The moon was burning holes through the cottonwood tops by now and the yard was slipping into shadow. I heard notes riff rapidly up and cascade back down, gleefully, happily, and I saw the glint and chromium glitter of the harmonica, dancing from shadow to light and back again, singing untouched in the air. Then the moon reached an opening in the trees and spotlighted the Francher kid almost violently. He was sitting on the plank, looking up at the harmonica, a small smile on his usually sullen face. And the harmonica sang its quiet song to him as he watched it. His face shadowed suddenly as he looked down at the things laid out on the plank. He gathered them up abruptly and walked up the moonlight to the little window and slid through, head first. Behind him, alone, unattended, the harmonica danced and played, hovering and darting like a dragonfly. Then the kid reappeared, sliding head first out of the window. He sat cross-legged in the air beside the harmonica and watched and listened. The gay dance slowed and changed. The harmonica cried softly in the moonlight, an aching asking cry as it spiraled up and around until it slid through the open window and lost its voice in the darkness. The window clicked shut and the Francher kid thudded to the ground. He slouched off through the shadows, his elbows winging sharply backward as he jammed his fists in his pockets.

I let go of the curtain where my clenched fingers had cut four nail-sized holes through the age-fragile lace, and released a breath I couldn't remember holding. I stared at the empty plank and wet my lips. I took a deep breath of the mountain air that was supposed to do me so much good, and turned away from the window. For the thousandth time I muttered "I won't," and groped for the bed. For the thousandth time I finally reached for my crutches and swung myself over to the edge of the bed. I dragged the unresponsive half of me up onto the bed, arranging myself for sleep. I leaned against the pillow and put my hands in back of my head, my elbows fanning out on either side. I stared at the light square that was the window until it wavered and rippled before my sleepy eyes.

Still my mind was only nibbling at what had happened and showed no inclination to set its teeth into any sort of explanation. I awakened with a start to find the moonlight gone, my arms asleep and my prayers unsaid.

Tucked in bed and ringed about with the familiar comfort of my prayers, I slid away from awareness into sleep, following the dance and gleam of a harmonica that cried in the moonlight.

Morning sunlight slid across the boardinghouse breakfast table, casting alpine shadows behind the spilled corn flakes that lay beyond the sugar bowl. I squinted against the brightness and felt aggrieved that anything should be alive and active and so—so—hopeful so early in the morning. I leaned on my elbows over my coffee cup and contemplated a mood as black as the coffee.

". . . Francher kid."

I rotated my head upward on the axis of my two supporting hands, my interest caught. "Last night," I half remembered, "last night—"

"I give up." Anna Semper put a third spoonful of sugar in her coffee and stirred morosely. "Every child has a something —I mean there's *some* way to reach every child—all but the Francher kid. I can't reach him at all. If he'd even be aggressive or actively mean or actively *anything*, maybe I could do something, but he just sits there being a vegetable. And then I get so spittin' mad when he finally *does* do something, just enough to keep him from flunking, that I could bust a gusset. I can't abide a child who can and won't." She frowned darkly and added two more spoonfuls of sugar to her coffee. "I'd rather have an eager moron than a won't-do genius!" She tasted the coffee and grimaced. "Can't even get a decent cup of coffee to arm me for my struggle with the little monster."

I laughed. "Five spoonfuls of sugar would spoil almost anything. And don't give up hope. Have you tried music? Remember, 'Music hath charms—' "

Anna reddened to the tips of her ears. I couldn't tell if it was anger or embarrassment. "Music!" Her spoon clished against her saucer sharply. She groped for words. "This is

170

ridiculous, but I have had to send that Francher kid out of the room during music appreciation."

"Out of the room? Why ever for? I thought he was a vegetable."

Anna reddened still further. "He is," she said stubbornly, "but—" She fumbled with her spoon, then burst forth, "But sometimes the record player won't work when he's in the room."

I put my cup down slowly. "Oh, come now! This coffee is awfully strong, I'll admit, but it's not *that* strong."

"No, really!" Anna twisted her spoon between her two hands. "When he's in the room that darned player goes too fast or too slow or even backwards. I swear it. And one time—" Anna looked around furtively and lowered her voice, "one time it played a whole record and it wasn't even plugged in!"

"You ought to patent that! That'd be a real money-maker."

"Go on, laugh!" Anna gulped coffee again and grimaced. "I'm beginning to believe in poltergeists—you know, the kind that are supposed to work through or because of adolescent kids. If you had that kid to deal with in class—"

"Yes." I fingered my cold toast. "If only I did."

And for a minute I hated Anna fiercely for the sympathy on her open face and for the studied not-looking at my leaning crutches. She opened her mouth, closed it, then leaned across the table.

"Polio?" she blurted, reddening.

"No," I said. "Car wreck."

"Oh." She hesitated. "Well, maybe someday—"

"No," I said. "No." Denying the faint possibility that was just enough to keep me nagged out of resignation.

"Oh," she said. "How long ago?"

"How long?" For a minute I was suspended in wonder at the distortion of time. How long? Recent enough to be a shock each time of immobility when I expected motion. Long enough ago that eternity was between me and the last time I moved unthinkingly.

"Almost a year," I said, my memory aching to *this time last year I could* ...

"You were a teacher?" Anna gave her watch a quick appraising look.

"Yes." I didn't automatically verify the time. The immediacy of watches had died for me. Then I smiled. "That's why I can sympathize with you about the Francher kid. I've had them before."

"There's always one," Anna sighed, getting up. "Well, it's time for my pilgrimage up the hill. I'll see you." And the swinging door to the hall repeated her departure again and again with diminishing enthusiasm. I struggled to my feet and swung myself to the window.

"Hey!" I shouted. She turned at the gate, peering back as she rested her load of workbooks on the gatepost.

"Yes?"

"If he gives you too much trouble send him over here with a note for me. It'll take him off your hands for a while at least."

"Hey, that's an idea. Thanks. That's swell! Straighten your halo!" And she waved an elbow at me as she disappeared beyond the box elder outside the gate.

I didn't think she would, but she did.

It was only a couple of days later that I looked up from my book at the creak of the old gate. The heavy old gear that served as a weight to pull it shut thudded dully behind the Francher kid. He walked up the porch steps under my close scrutiny with none of the hesitant embarrassment that most people would feel. He mounted the three steps and wordlessly handed me an envelope. I opened it. It said:

"Dust off your halo! I've reached the !! stage. Wouldn't you like to keep him permanent-like?"

"Won't you sit down?" I gestured to the porch swing, wondering how I was going to handle this deal.

He looked at the swing and sank down on the top porch step.

"What's your name?"

He looked at me incuriously. "Francher." His voice was husky and unused-sounding.

"Is that your first name?"

"That's my name."

"What's your other name?" I asked patiently, falling into a first-grade dialogue in spite of his age.

"They put down Clement."

172

"Clement Francher. A good-sounding name, but what do they call you?"

His eyebrows slanted subtly upward, and a tiny bitter smile lifted the corners of his mouth.

"With their eyes—juvenile delinquent, lazy trash, no-good off-scouring, potential criminal, burden—"

I winced away from the icy malice of his voice.

"But mostly they call me a whole sentence, like— 'Well, what can you expect from a background like that?' "

His knuckles were white against his faded Levi's. Then as I watched them the color crept back and, without visible relaxation, the tension was gone. But his eyes were the eyes of a boy too big to cry and too young for any other comfort.

"What *is* your background?" I asked quietly, as though I had the right to ask. He answered as simply as though he owed me an answer.

"We were with the carnival. We went to all the fairs around the country. Mother—" his words nearly died, "Mother had a mind-reading act. She was good. She was better than anyone knew—better than she wanted to be. It hurt and scared her sometimes to walk through people's minds. Sometimes she would come back to the trailer and cry and cry and take a long long shower and wash herself until her hands were all water-soaked and her hair hung in dripping strings. They curled at the end. She couldn't get all the fear and hate and—and tired dirt off even that way. Only if she could find a Good to read, or a dark church with tall candles."

"And where is she now?" I asked, holding a small warm picture in my mind of narrow fragile shoulders, thin and defenseless under a flimsy moist robe, with one wet strand of hair dampening one shoulder of it.

"Gone." His eyes were over my head but empty of the vision of the weatherworn siding of the house. "She died. Three years ago. This is a foster home. To try to make a decent citizen of me."

There was no inflection in his words. They lay as flat as paper between us in our silence.

"You like music," I said, curling Anna's note around my forefinger, remembering what I had seen the other night.

"Yes." His eyes were on the note. "Miss Semper doesn't

173

think so, though. I hate that scratchy wrapped-up music."

"You sing?"

"No. I make music."

"You mean you play an instrument?"

He frowned a little impatiently. "No. I make music with instruments."

"Oh," I said. "There's a difference?"

"Yes." He turned his head away. I had disappointed him or failed him in some way.

"Wait," I said. "I want to show you something." I struggled to my feet. Oh, deftly and quickly enough under the circumstances, I suppose, but it seemed an endless aching effort in front of the Francher kid's eyes. But finally I was up and swinging in through the front door. When I got back with my key chain the kid was still staring at my empty chair, and I had to struggle back into it under his unwavering eyes.

"Can't you stand alone?" he asked, as though he had a right to.

"Very little, very briefly," I answered, as though I owed him an answer.

"You don't walk without those braces."

"I can't walk without those braces. Here." I held out my key chain. There was a charm on it: a harmonica with four notes, so small that I had never managed to blow one by itself. The four together made a tiny breathy chord, like a small hesitant wind.

He took the chain between his fingers and swung the charm back and forth, his head bent so that the sunlight flickered across its tousledness. The chain stilled. For a long moment there wasn't a sound. Then clearly, sharply, came the musical notes, one after another. There was a slight pause and then four notes poured their separateness together to make a clear sweet chord.

"You make music," I said, barely audible.

"Yes." He gave me back my key chain and stood up. "I guess she's cooled down now. I'll go on back."

"To work?"

"To work." He smiled wryly. "For a while anyway." He started down the walk.

"What if I tell?" I called after him.

174

"I told once," he called back over his shoulder. "Try it if you want to."

I sat for a long time on the porch after he left. My fingers were closed over the harmonica as I watched the sun creep up my skirts and into my lap. Finally I turned Anna's envelope over. The seal was still secure. The end was jagged where I had torn it. The paper was opaque. I blew a tiny breathy chord on the harmonica. Then I shivered as cold crept across my shoulders. The chill was chased away by a tiny hot wave of excitement. So his mother could walk through the minds of others. So he knew what was in a sealed letter—or had he got his knowledge from Anna before the letter? So he could make music with harmonicas. So the Francher kid was . . . My hurried thoughts caught and came to a full stop. What *was* the Francher kid?

After school that day Anna toiled up the four front steps and rested against the railing, half sitting and half leaning. "I'm too tired to sit down," she said. "I'm wound up like a clock and I'm going to strike something pretty darned quick." She half laughed and grimaced a little. "Probably my laundry. I'm fresh out of clothes." She caught a long ragged breath. "You must have built a fire under that Francher kid. He came back and piled into his math book and did the whole week's assignments that he hadn't bothered with before. Did them in less than an hour, too. Makes me mad, though—" She grimaced again and pressed her hand to her chest. "Darn that chalk dust anyway. Thanks a million for your assist. I wish I were optimistic enough to believe it would last." She leaned and breathed, her eyes closing with the effort. "Awful shortage of air around here." Her hands fretted with her collar. "Anyway the Francher kid said you'd substitute for me until my pneumonia is over." She laughed, a little soundless laugh. "He doesn't know that it's just chalk dust and that I'm never sick." She buried her face in her two hands and burst into tears. "I'm not sick, am I? It's only that darn Francher kid!"

She was still blaming him when Mrs. Somanson came out and led her into her bedroom and when the doctor arrived to shake his head over her chest.

So that's how it was that the first-floor first grade was hastily moved upstairs and the junior high was hastily moved down-

175

stairs and I once more found myself facing the challenge of a class, telling myself that the Francher kid needed no special knowledge to say that I'd substitute. After all I like Anna, I was the only substitute available, and besides, any slight—substitute's pay!—addition to the exchequer was most welcome. You *can* live on those monthly checks, but it's pleasant to have a couple of extra coins to clink together.

By midmorning I knew a little of what Anna was sweating over. The Francher kid's absolutely dead-weight presence in the room was a drag on everything we did. Recitations paused, limped and halted when they came to him. Activities swirled around his inactivity, creating distracting eddies. It wasn't only a negative sort of nonparticipation on his part but an aggressively positive not-doingness. It wasn't just a hindrance but an active opposition, without any overt action for any sort of proof of his attitude. This, along with my disappointment in not having the same comfortable rapport with him that I'd had before, and the bone-weariness of having to be vertical all day instead of collapsing horizontally at intervals, and the strain of getting back into harness, cold, with a roomful of teeners and subteeners, had me worn down to a nubbin by early afternoon.

So I fell back on the perennial refuge of harried teachers and opened a discussion of "what I want to be when I grow up." We had gone through the usual nurses and airplane hostesses and pilots and bridge builders and the usual unexpected ballet dancer and CPA (and he still can't add six and nine!) until the discussion frothed like a breaking wave against the Francher kid and stilled there.

He was lounging down in his seat, his weight supported by the back of his neck and the remote end of his spine. The class sighed collectively though inaudibly and waited for his contribution.

"And you, Clement?" I prompted, shifting vainly, trying to ease the taut cry of aching muscles.

"An outlaw," he said huskily, not bothering to straighten up. "I'm going to keep a list and break every law there is—and get away with it, too."

"Whatever for?" I asked, trying to reassure the sick pang inside me. "An outlaw is no use at all to society."

"Who wants to be of use?" he asked. "I'll use society—and I can do it."

"Perhaps," I said, knowing full well it was so. "But that's not the way to happiness."

"Who's happy? The bad are unhappy because they are bad. The good are unhappy because they're afraid to be bad—"

"Clement," I said gently, "I think you are—"

"I think he's crazy," said Rigo, his black eyes flashing. "Don't pay him no never mind, Miss Carolle. He's a screwball. He's all the time saying crazy things."

I saw the heavy world globe on the top shelf of the bookcase behind Rigo shift and slide toward the edge. I saw it lift clear of the shelf and I cried out, "Clement!" The whole class started at the loud urgency of my voice, the Francher kid included, and Rigo moved just far enough out of line that the falling globe missed him and cracked itself apart at his feet.

Someone screamed and several gasped and a babble of voices broke out. I caught the Francher kid's eyes, and he flushed hotly and ducked his head. Then he straightened up proudly and defiantly returned my look. He wet his forefinger in his mouth and drew an invisible tally mark in the air before him. I shook my head at him, slowly, regretfully. What could I do with a child like this?

Well, I had to do something, so I told him to stay in after school, though the kids wondered why. He slouched against the door, defiance in every awkward angle of his body and in the hooking of his thumbs into his front pockets. I let the parting noises fade and die, the last hurried clang of lunch pail, the last flurry of feet, the last reverberant slam of the outside door. The Francher kid shifted several times, easing the tension of his shoulders as he waited. Finally I said, "Sit down."

"No." His word was flat and uncompromising. I looked at him, the gaunt young planes of his face, the unhappy mouth thinned to stubbornness, the eyes that blinded themselves with dogged defiance. I leaned across the desk, my hands clasped, and wondered what I could say. Argument would do no good. A kid of that age has an answer for everything.

"We all have violences," I said, tightening my hands, "but we can't always let them out. Think what a mess things would be if we did." I smiled wryly into his unresponsive face. "If we gave in to every violent impulse I'd probably have slapped you with an encyclopedia before now." His eyelids flicked, startled, and he looked straight at me for the first time.

"Sometimes we can just hold our breath until the violence swirls away from us. Other times it's too big and it swells inside us like a balloon until it chokes our lungs and aches our jaw hinges." His lids flickered down over his watching eyes. "But it can be put to use. Then's when we stir up a cake by hand or chop wood or kick cans across the back yard or—" I faltered, "or run until our knees bend both ways from tiredness."

There was a small silence while I held my breath until my violent rebellion against unresponsive knees swirled away from me.

"There are bigger violences, I guess," I went on. "From them come assault and murder, vandalism and war, but even those can be used. If you want to smash things there are worthless things that need to be smashed and things that ought to be destroyed, ripped apart and ruined. But you have no way of knowing what those things are, yet. You must keep your violences small until you learn how to tell the difference."

"I can smash." His voice was thick.

"Yes," I said. "But smash to build. You have no right to hurt other people with your own hurt."

"People!" The word was profanity.

I drew a long breath. If he were younger . . . You can melt stiff rebellious arms and legs with warm hugs or a hand across a wind-ruffled head or a long look that flickers into a smile, but what can you do with a creature that's neither adult nor child but puzzlingly both? I leaned forward.

"Francher," I said softly, "if your mother could walk through your mind now—"

He reddened, then paled. His mouth opened. He swallowed tightly. Then he jerked himself upright in the doorway.

"Leave my mother alone." His voice was shaken and muffled. "You leave her alone. She's dead."

I listened to his footsteps and the crashing slam of the outside door. For some sudden reason I felt my heart follow him down the hill to town. I sighed, almost with exasperation. So this was to be a My Child. We teacher-types sometimes find them. They aren't our pets; often they aren't even in our

178

classes. But they are the children who move unasked into our hearts and make claims upon them over and above the call of duty. And this My Child I had to reach. Somehow I had to keep him from sliding on over the borderline to lawlessness as he so surely was doing—this My Child who, even more than the usual My Child, was different.

I put my head down on the desk and let weariness ripple up over me. After a minute I began to straighten up my papers. I made the desk top tidy and took my purse out of the bottom drawer. I struggled to my feet and glared at my crutches. Then I grinned weakly.

"Come, friends," I said. "Leave us help one another depart."

Anna was out for a week. After she returned I was surprised at my reluctance to let go of the class. The sniff of chalk dust was in my nostrils and I ached to be busy again. So I started helping out with the school programs and teen-age dances, which led naturally to the day my committee and I stood in the town recreation hall and looked about us despairingly.

"How long have those decorations been up?" I craned my neck to get a better view of the wilderness of sooty cobwebby crepe paper that clotted the whole of the high ceiling and the upper reaches of the walls of the ramshackle old hall that leaned wearily against the back of the saloon. Twyla stopped chewing the end of one of her heavy braids. "About four years, I guess. At least the newest. Pea-Green put it all up."

"Pea-Green?"

"Yeah. He was a screwball. He used up every piece of crepe paper in town and used nails to put the stuff up—big nails. He's gone now. He got silicosis and went down to Hot Springs."

"Well, nails or no nails we can't have a Hallowe'en dance with that stuff up."

"Going to miss the old junk. How we going to get it down?" Janniset asked.

"Pea-Green used an extension ladder he borrowed from a power crew that was stringing some wires up to the Bluebell Mine," Rigo said. "But we'll have to find some other way to get it down, now."

I felt a flick of something at my elbow. It might have been the Francher kid shifting from one foot to the other, or it

179

might have been just a thought slipping by. I glanced sideways but caught only the lean line of his cheek and the shaggy back of his neck.

"I think I can get a ladder." Rigo snapped his thumbnail loudly with his white front teeth. "It won't reach clear up but it'll help."

"We could take rakes and just drag it down," Twyla suggested.

We all laughed until I sobered us all with, "It might come to that yet, bless the buttons of whoever thought up twenty-foot ceilings. Well, tomorrow's Saturday. Everybody be here about nine and we'll get with it."

"Can't." The Francher kid cast anchor unequivocally, snapping all our willingness up short.

"Oh?" I shifted my crutches, and, as usual, his eyes fastened on them, almost hypnotically. "That's too bad."

"How come?" Rigo was belligerent. "If the rest of us can you oughta be able to. Ever'body's s'posed to do this together. Ever'body does the dirty work and ever'body has the fun. You're nobody special. You're on this committee, aren't you?"

I restrained myself from a sudden impulse to clap my hand over Rigo's mouth midway in his protest. I didn't like the quietness of the Francher kid's hands, but he only looked slantwise up at Rigo and said, "I got volunteered on this committee. I didn't ask to. And to fix this joint up today. I gotta work tomorrow."

"Work? Where?" Rigo frankly disbelieved.

"Sorting ore at the Absalom."

Rigo snapped his thumbnail again derisively. "That penny-picking stuff? They pay peanuts."

"Yes." And the Francher kid slouched off around the corner of the building without a glance or a good-by.

"Well, he's working!" Twyla thoughtfully spit out a stray hair and pointed the wet end of her braid with her fingers. "The Francher kid's doing something. I wonder how come?"

"Trying to figure that dopey dilldock out?" Janniset asked. "Don't waste your time. I bet he's just goofing off."

"You kids run on," I said. "We can't do anything tonight. I'll lock up. See you in the morning."

I waited inside the dusty echoing hall until the sound of their going died down the rocky alley that edged around the rim of the railroad cut and dissolved into the street of the town. I still couldn't reconcile myself to slowing their steps to match my uncertain feet. Maybe someday I would be able to accept my braces as others accept glasses; but not yet—oh, not yet!

I left the hall and snapped the dime-store padlock shut. I struggled precariously along through the sliding shale and loose rocks until suddenly one piece of shale shattered under the pressure of one of my crutches and I stumbled off balance. I saw with shake-making clarity in the accelerated speed of the moment that the only place my groping crutch could reach was the smooth curving of a small boulder, and, in that same instant, I visualized myself sprawling helplessly, hopelessly, in the clutter of the alley, a useless nonfunctioning piece of humanity, a drag and a hindrance on everyone again. And then, at the last possible instant, the smooth boulder slid aside and my crutch caught and steadied on the solid damp hollow beneath it. I caught my breath with relief and unclenched my spasmed hands a little. Lucky!

Then all at once there was the Francher kid at my elbow again, quietly waiting.

"Oh!" I hoped he hadn't seen me floundering in my awkwardness. "Hi! I thought you'd gone."

"I really will be working." His voice had lost its flatness. "I'm not making much but I'm saving to buy me a musical instrument."

"Well, good!" I said, smiling into the unusualness of his straightforward look. "What kind of instrument?"

"I don't know. Something that will sing like this—"

And there on the rocky trail with the long light slanting through the trees for late afternoon, I heard soft tentative notes that stumbled at first and then began to sing: "Oh, Danny Boy, the pipes, the pipes are calling—" Each note of this, my favorite, was like a white flower opening inside me in ascending order like steps—steps that I could climb freely, lightly. . . .

"What kind of instrument am I saving for?" The Francher kid's voice pulled me back down to earth.

"You'll have to settle for less." My voice shook a little. "There isn't one like that."

"But I've heard it—" He was bewildered.

"Maybe you have. But was anyone playing it?"

"Why yes—no. I used to hear it from Mom. She thought it to me."

"Where did your mom come from?" I asked impulsively.

"From terror and from panic places. From hunger and from hiding—to live midway between madness and the dream—" He looked at me, his mouth drooping a little. "She promised me I'd understand someday, but this is someday and she's gone."

"Yes," I sighed, remembering how once I had dreamed that someday I'd run again. "But there are other somedays ahead—for you."

"Yes," he said. "And time hasn't stopped for you either." And he was gone.

I looked after him. "Doggone!" I thought. "There I go again, talking to him as though he made sense!" I poked the end of my crutch in the damp earth three times, making interlacing circles. Then with quickened interest I poked the boulder that had rolled *up* out of the slight hollow before the crutch tip had landed there.

"Son-a-gun!" I cried aloud. "Well, son-a-gun!"

Next morning at five of nine the kids were waiting for me at the door to the hall, huddled against the October chill that the milky sun hadn't yet had time to disperse. Rigo had a shaky old ladder with two broken rungs and splashes of old paint gumming it liberally.

"That looks awfully rickety," I said. "We don't want any blood spilled on our dance floor. It's bad for the wax."

Rigo grinned. "It'll hold me up," he said. "I used it last night to pick apples. You just have to be kinda careful."

"Well, be so then," I smiled, unlocking the door. "Better safe than—" My words faltered and died as I gaped in at the open door. The others pushed in around me, round-eyed and momentarily silenced. My first wild impression was that the ceiling had fallen in.

"My gorsh!" Janniset gasped. "What hit this place?"

"Just look at it!" Twyla shrilled. "Hey! Just look at it!"

We looked as we scuffled forward. Every single piece of paper was gone from the ceiling and walls. Every scrap of paper was on the floor, in tiny twisted confetti-sized pieces like a tattered faded snowfall, all over the floor. There must have been an incredible amount of paper tangled in the decorations, because we waded wonderingly almost ankle-deep through it.

"Looky here!" Rigo was staring at the front of the bandstand. Lined up neatly across the front stood all the nails that had been pulled out of the decorations, each balanced precisely on its head.

Twyla frowned and bit her lip. "It scares me," she said. "It doesn't feel right. It looks like somebody was mad or crazy—like they tore up the paper wishing they was killing something. And then to put all those nails so—so even and careful, like they had been put down gently—that looks madder than the paper." She reached over and swept her finger sideways, wincing as though she expected a shock. A section of the nails toppled with faint pings on the bare boards of the stand. In a sudden flurry Twyla swept all the nails over. "There!" she said, wiping her finger on her dress. "Now it's all crazy."

"Well," I said, "crazy or not, somebody's saved us a lot of trouble. Rigo, we won't need your ladder. Get the brooms and let's get this mess swept out."

While they were gone for the brooms I picked up two nails and clicked them together in a metrical cadence: "Oh, Danny Boy, the pipes, the pipes are calling—"

By noon we had the place scrubbed out and fairly glistening through its shabby paint. By evening we had the crisp new orange-and-black decorations up, low down and with thumbtacks, and all sighed with tired satisfaction at how good the place looked. As we locked up Twyla suddenly said in a small voice, "What if it happens again before the dance Friday? All our work—"

"It won't," I promised. "It won't."

In spite of my hanging back and trying the lock a couple of times Twyla was still waiting when I turned away from the door. She was examining the end of her braid carefully as she said, "It was him, wasn't it?"

"Yes, I suppose so."

"How did he do it?"

"You've known him longer than I have. How did he do it?"

"Nobody knows the Francher kid," she said. Then softly, "He looked at me once, really looked at me. He's funny— but not to laugh," she hastened. "When he looks at me it—" her hand tightened on her braid until her head tilted and she glanced up slantingly at me, "it makes music in me.

"You know," she said quickly into the echo of her unorthodox words, "you're kinda like him. He makes me think things and believe things I wouldn't ever by myself. You make me say things I wouldn't ever by myself—no, that's not quite right. You *let* me say things I wouldn't dare to say to anyone else."

"Thank you," I said. "Thank you, Twyla."

I had forgotten the trembling glamor of a teen-age dance. I had forgotten the cautious stilted gait of high heels on loafer-type feet. I had forgotten how the look of maturity could be put on with a tie and sport jacket and how—how *peoplelike* teen-agers could look when divorced for a while from Levi's and flannel shirts. Janniset could hardly contain himself for his own splendor and turned not a hair of his incredibly polished head when I smiled my "Good evening, Mr. Janniset." But in his pleased satisfaction at my formality he forgot himself as he turned away and hoisted up his sharply creased trousers as though they were his old Levi's.

Rigo was stunning in his Latin handsomeness, and he and Angie so drowned in each other's dark eyes that I could see why our Mexican youngsters usually marry so young. And Angie! Well, she didn't look like any eighth grader—her strapless gown, her dangly earrings, her laughing flirtatious eyes—but taken out of the context and custom and tradition she was breath-takingly lovely. Of course it was on her "unsuitable for her age" dress and jewelry and make-up that the long line of mothers and aunts and grandmothers fixed disapproving eyes, but I'd be willing to bet that there were

184

plenty who wished their own children could look as lovely.

In this small community the girls always dressed up to the hilt at the least provocation, and the Hallowe'en dance was usually the first event of the fall that could serve as an excuse. Crinolined skirts belled like blossoms across the floor above the glitter of high heels, but it was only a matter of a few minutes before the shoes were kicked off, to toe in together forlornly under a chair or dangle from some motherly forefinger while unprotected toes braved the brogans of the boys.

Twyla was bright-cheeked and laughing, dance after dance, until the first intermission. She and Janniset brought me punch where I sat among the other spectators; then Janniset skidded off across the floor, balancing his paper cup precariously as he went to take another look at Marty, who at school was only a girl but here, all dressed up, was dawn of woman-wonder for him. Twyla gulped her punch hastily and then licked the corners of her mouth.

"He isn't here," she said huskily.

"I'm sorry," I said. "I wanted him to have fun with the rest of you. Maybe he'll come yet."

"Maybe." She twisted her cup slowly, then hastily shoved it under the chair as it threatened to drip on her dress.

"That's a beautiful dress," I said. "I love the way your petticoat shows red against the blue when you whirl."

"Thank you." She smoothed the billowing of her skirt. "I feel funny with sleeves. None of the others have them. That's why he didn't come, I bet. Not having any dress-up clothes like the others, I mean. Nothing but Levi's."

"Oh, that's a shame. If I had known—"

"No. Mrs. McVey is supposed to buy his clothes. She gets money for them. All she does is sit around and talk about how much she sacrifices to take care of the Francher kid and she doesn't take care of him at all. It's her fault—"

"Let's not be too critical of others. There may be circumstances we know nothing of—and besides—" I nodded my head, "he's here now."

I could almost see the leap of her heart under the close-fitting blue as she turned to look.

The Francher kid was lounging against the door, his face

closed and impassive. I noted with a flame of anger at Mrs. McVey that he was dressed in his Levi's, faded almost white from many washings, and a flannel shirt, the plaid of which was nearly indistinguishable except along the seams. It wasn't fair to keep him from being like the other kids even in this minor way—or maybe especially in this way, because clothes can't be hidden the way a mind or soul can.

I tried to catch his eye and beckon him in, but he looked only at the bandstand where the band members were preparing to resume playing. It was tragic that the Francher kid had only this handful of inexpertly played instruments to feed his hunger on. He winced back into the darkness at their first blare, and I felt Twyla's tenseness as she turned to me.

"He won't come in," she half shouted against the take-a-melody-tear-it-to-pieces-stick-it-back-together-bleeding type of music that was going on.

I shook my head regretfully. "I guess not," I mouthed and then was drawn into a half-audible, completely incomprehensible conversation with Mrs. Frisney. It wasn't until the next dance started and she was towed away by Grampa Griggs that I could turn back to Twyla. She was gone. I glanced around the room. Nowhere the swirl of blue echoing the heavy brown-gold swing of her ponytail.

There was no reason for me to feel apprehensive. There were any number of places she might have gone and quite legitimately, but I suddenly felt an overwhelming need for fresh air and swung myself past the romping dancers and out into the gasping chill of the night. I huddled closer inside my jacket, wishing it were on right instead of merely flung around my shoulders. But the air tasted clean and fresh. I don't know what we'd been breathing in the dance hall, but it wasn't air. By the time I'd got the whatever-it-was out of my lungs and filled them with the freshness of the night I found myself halfway down the path over the edge of the railroad cut. There hadn't been a train over the single track since nineteen-aught-something, and just beyond it was a thicket of willows and cottonwoods and a few scraggly piñon trees. As I moved into the shadow of the trees I glanced up at the sky ablaze with a skrillion stars that dissolved into light near the lopsided moon and perforated

186

the darker horizon with brilliance. I was startled out of my absorption by the sound of movement and music. I took an uncertain step into the dark. A few yards away I saw the flick of skirts and started to call out to Twyla. But instead I rounded the brush in front of me and saw what she was intent upon.

The Francher kid was dancing—dancing all alone in the quiet night. No, not alone, because a column of yellow leaves had swirled up from the ground around him and danced with him to a melody so exactly like their movement that I couldn't be sure there was music. Fascinated, I watched the drift and sway, the swirl and turn, the treetop-high rise and the hesitant drifting fall of the Francher kid and the autumn leaves. But somehow I couldn't see the kid as a separate Levied flannel-shirted entity. He and the leaves so blended together that the sudden sharp definition of a hand or a turning head was startling. The kid was just a larger leaf borne along with the smaller in the chilly winds of fall. On a final minor glissade of the music the Francher kid slid to the ground.

He stood for a moment, head bent, crumbling a crisp leaf in his fingers; then he turned swiftly defensive to the rustle of movement. Twyla stepped out into the clearing. For a moment they stood looking at each other without a word. Then Twyla's voice came so softly I could barely hear it.

"I would have danced with you."

"With me like this?" He gestured at his clothes.

"Sure. It doesn't matter."

"In front of everyone?"

"If you wanted to. I wouldn't mind."

"Not there," he said. "It's too tight and hard."

"Then here," she said, holding out her hands.

"The music—" But his hands were reaching for hers.

"Your music," she said.

"My mother's music," he corrected.

And the music began, a haunting lilting waltz-time melody. As lightly as the leaves that stirred at their feet the two circled the clearing.

I have the picture yet, but when I return to it my heart is emptied of adjectives because there are none for such enchantment. The music quickened and swelled, softly, richly full—the lost music that a mother bequeathed to her child.

Twyla was so completely engrossed in the magic of the moment that I'm sure she didn't even know when their feet no longer rustled in the fallen leaves. She couldn't have known when the treetops brushed their shoes—when the long turning of the tune brought them back, spiraling down into the clearing. Her scarlet petticoat caught on a branch as they passed, and left a bright shred to trail the wind, but even that did not distract her.

Before my heart completely broke with wonder the music faded softly away and left the two standing on the ragged grass. After a breathless pause Twyla's hand went softly, wonderingly, to Francher's cheek. The kid turned his face slowly and pressed his mouth to her palm. Then they turned and left each other, without a word.

Twyla passed so close to me that her skirts brushed mine. I let her cross the tracks back to the dance before I followed. I got there just in time to catch the whisper on apparently the second round, ". . . alone out there with the Francher kid!" and the gleefully malicious shock of ". . . and her petticoat is torn . . ."

It was like pigsty muck clotting an Easter dress.

Anna said, "Hi!" and flung herself into my one armchair. As the front leg collapsed she caught herself with the dexterity of long practice, tilted the chair, reinserted the leg and then eased herself back into its dusty depths.

"From the vagaries of the small town good Lord deliver me!" she moaned.

"What now?" I asked, shifting gears on my crochet hook as I finished another row of my rug.

"You mean you haven't heard the latest scandal?" Her eyes widened in mock horror and her voice sank conspiratorially. "They were out there in the dark—alone—doing *nobody knows what*. Imagine!" Her voice shook with avid outrage. "With the Francher kid!

"Honestly!" Her voice returned to normal. "You'd think the Francher kid was leprosy or something. What a to-do about a little nocturnal smooching. I'd give you odds that most of the other kids are being shocked to ease their own consciences of the same kind of carryings-on. But just because it's the Francher kid—"

"They weren't alone," I said casually, holding a tight rein on my indignation. "I was there."

"You were?" Anna's eyebrows bumped her crisp bangs. "Well, well. This complexions things different. What did happen? Not," she hastened "that I credit these wild tales about, my golly, Twyla, but what did happen?"

"They danced," I said. "The Francher kid was ashamed of his clothes and wouldn't come in the hall. So they danced down in the clearing."

"Without music?"

"The Francher kid—hummed," I said, my eyes intent on my work.

There was a brief silence. "Well," Anna said, "that's interesting, especially that vacant spot I feel in there. But you *were* there?"

"Yes."

"And they just danced?"

"Yes." I apologized mentally for making so pedestrian the magic I had seen. "And Twyla caught her petticoat on a branch and it tore before she knew it."

"Hmmm." Anna was suddenly sober. "You ought to take your rug up to the Sew-Sew Club."

"But I—" I was bewildered.

"They're serving nice heaping portions of Twyla's reputation for refreshments, and Mrs. McVey is contributing the dessert—the unplumbed depravity of foster children."

I stuffed my rug back into its bag. "Is my face on?" I asked.

Well, I got back to the Somansons' that evening considerably wider of eye than I had left it. Anna took my things from me at the door.

"How did it go?"

"My gorsh!" I said, easing myself into a chair. "If they ever got started on me what would I have left?"

"Bare bones," Anna said promptly. "With plenty of tooth marks on them. Well, did you get them told?"

"Yes, but they didn't want to believe me. It was too tame.

And of course Mrs. McVey didn't like being pushed out on a limb about the Francher kid's clothes. Her delicate hint about the high cost of clothes didn't impress Mrs. Holmes much, not with her six boys. I guess I've got me an enemy for life. She got a good-sized look at herself through my eyes and she didn't like it at all, but I'll bet the Francher kid won't turned up Levied for a dance again."

"Heaven send he'll never do anything worse," Anna intoned piously.

That's what I hoped fervently for a while, but lightning hit Willow Creek anyway, a subtle slow lightning—a calculated, coldly angry lightning. I held my breath as report after report came in. The Turbows' old shed exploded without a sound on the stroke of nine o'clock Tuesday night and scattered itself like kindling wood over the whole barnyard. Of course the Turbows had talked for years of tearing the shaky old thing down but— I began to wonder how you went about bailing a juvenile out of the clink.

Then the last sound timber on the old railroad bridge below the Thurmans' house shuddered and dissolved loudly into sawdust at eleven o'clock Tuesday night. The rails, deprived of their support, trembled briefly, then curled tightly *up* into two absurd rosettes. The bridge being gone meant an hour's brisk walk to town for the Thurmans instead of a fifteen-minute stroll. It also meant safety for the toddlers too young to understand why the rotting timbers weren't a wonderful kind of jungle gym.

Wednesday evening at five all the water in the Holmeses' pond geysered up and crashed down again, pureeing what few catfish were still left in it and breaking a spillway over into the creek, thereby draining the stagnant old mosquito-bearing spot with a conclusive slurp. As the neighbors had nagged at the Holmeses to do for years—but . . .

I was awestruck at this simple literal translation of my words and searched my memory with wary apprehensiveness. I could almost have relaxed by now if I could have drawn a line through the last two names on my mental roll of the club.

But Thursday night there was a crash and a roar and I

huddled in my bed praying a wordless prayer against I didn't know what, and Friday morning I listened to the shrill wide-eyed recitals at the breakfast table.

". . . since the devil was an imp and now there it is . . ."

". . . right in the middle, big as life and twice as natural . . ."

"What is?" I asked, braving the battery of eyes that pinned me like a moth in a covey of searchlights.

There was a stir around the table. Everyone was aching to speak, but there's always a certain rough protocol to be observed, even in a boardinghouse.

Ol' Hank cleared his throat, took a huge mouthful of coffee and sloshed it thoughtfully and noisily around his teeth before swallowing it.

"Balance Rock," he choked, spraying his vicinity finely, "came plumb unbalanced last night. Came a-crashing down, bouncing like a dang ping-pong ball an'nen it hopped over half a dozen fences an'nen *whammo!* it lit on a couple of the Scudders' pigs an'nen tore out a section of the Lelands' stone fence and now it's settin there in the middle of their alfalfa field as big as a house. He'll have a helk of a time mowing that field now." He slurped largely of his coffee.

"Strange things going on around here." Blue Nor's porchy eyebrows rose and fell portentously. "Never heard of a balance rock falling before. And all them other funny things. The devil's walking our land sure enough!"

I left on the wave of violent argument between proponents of the devil theory and the atom-bomb testing theory as the prime cause. Now I could draw another line through the list. But what of the last name? What of it?

That afternoon the Francher kid materialized on the bottom step at the boardinghouse, his eyes intent on my braces. We sat there in silence for a while, mostly I suppose because I could think of nothing rational to say. Finally I decided to be irrational.

"What about Mrs. McVey?"

He shrugged. "She feeds me."

"And what's with the Scudders' pigs?"

Color rose blotchily to his cheeks. "I goofed. I was aiming for the fence and let it go too soon."

"I told all those ladies the truth Monday. They knew they

had been wrong about you and Twyla. There was no need—"

"No need!" His eyes flashed, and I blinked away from the impact of his straight indignant glare. "They're dern lucky I didn't smash them all flat."

"I know," I said hastily. "I know how you feel, but I can't congratulate you on your restraint because however little you did compared to what you might have done, it was still more than you had a right to do. Especially the pigs and the wall."

"I didn't mean the pigs," he muttered as he fingered a patch on his knee. "Old man Scudder's a pretty right guy."

"Yes," I said. "So what are you going to do about it?"

"I don't know. I could swipe some pigs from somewhere else for him, but I suppose that wouldn't fix things."

"No, it wouldn't. You should buy—do you have any money?"

"Not for pigs!" he flared. "All I have is what I'm saving for my musical instrument and not one penny of that'll ever go for pigs!"

"All right, all right," I said. "You figure out something."

He ducked his head again, fingering the patch, and I watched the late sun run across the curve of his cheek, thinking what an odd conversation this was.

"Francher," I said, leaning forward impulsively, "do you ever wonder how come you can do the things you do?"

His eyes were quick on my face. "Do you ever wonder why you *can't* do what you can't do?"

I flushed and shifted my crutches. "I *know* why."

"No, you don't. You only know when your 'can't' began. You don't know the real why. Even your doctors don't know all of it. Well, I don't know the why of my 'cans.' I don't even know the beginning of them, only that sometimes I feel a wave of something inside me that hollers to get out of all the 'can'ts' that are around me like you-can't-do-this, you-can't-do-that, and then I *remember* that I can."

He flicked his fingers and my crutches stirred. They lifted and thudded softly down the steps and then up again to lean back in their accustomed place.

"Crutches *can't* walk," the Francher kid said. "But you—

192

something besides your body musta got smashed in that wreck."

"Everything got smashed," I said bitterly, the cold horror of that night and all that followed choking my chest. "Everything ended—everything."

"There aren't any endings," the Francher kid said. "Only new beginnings. When you going to get started?" Then he slouched away, his hands in his pockets, his head bent as he kicked a rock along the path. Bleakly I watched him go, trying to keep alive my flame of anger at him.

Well, the Lelands' wall had to be rebuilt and it was the Francher kid who got the job. He toiled mightily, lifting the heavy stones and cracking his hands with the dehydrating effect of the mortar he used. Maybe the fence wasn't as straight as it had been but it was repaired, and perhaps, I hoped, a stone had been set strongly somewhere in the Francher kid by this act of atonement. That he received pay for it didn't detract too much from the act itself, especially considering the amount of pay and the fact that it all went in on the other reparation.

The appearance of two strange pigs in the Scudders' east field created quite a stir, but the wonder of it was dulled by all the odd events preceding it. Mr. Scudder made inquiries but nothing ever came of them so he kept the pigs, and I made no inquiries but relaxed for a while about the Francher kid.

It was along about this time that a Dr. Curtis came to town briefly. Well, "came to town" is a euphemism. His car broke down on his way up into the hills, and he had to accept our hospitality until Bill Thurman could get around to finding a necessary part. He stayed at Somansons' in a room opposite mine after Mrs. Somanson had frantically cleared it out, mostly by the simple expedient of shoving all the boxes and crates and odds and ends to the end of the hall and draping a tarp over them. Then she splashed water across the barely settled dust and mopped out the resultant mud, put a brick under one corner of the bed, made it up with two army-surplus mattresses, one sheet edged with crocheted lace and one of heavy unbleached muslin. She

193

unearthed a pillow that fluffed beautifully but sighed itself to a wafer-thin odor of damp feathers at a touch, and topped the splendid whole with two hand-pieced hand-quilted quilts and a chenille spread with a Technicolor peacock flamboyantly dominating it.

"There," she sighed, using her apron to dust the edge of the dresser where it showed along the edge of the dresser scarf, "I guess that'll hold him."

"I should hope so," I smiled. "It's probably the quickest room he's ever had."

"He's lucky to have this at such short notice," she said, turning the ragrug over so the burned place wouldn't show. "If it wasn't that I had my eye on that new winter coat——"

Dr. Curtis was a very relaxing comfortable sort of fellow, and it seemed so good to have someone to talk to who cared to use words of more than two syllables. It wasn't that the people in Willow Creek were ignorant, they just didn't usually care to discuss three-syllable matters. I guess, besides the conversation, I was drawn to Dr. Curtis because he neither looked at my crutches nor not looked at them. It was pleasant except for the twinge of here's-someone-who-has-never-known-me-without-them.

After supper that night we all sat around the massive oil burner in the front room and talked against the monotone background of the radio turned low. Of course the late shake-making events in the area were brought up. Dr. Curtis was most interested, especially in the rails that curled up into rosettes. Because he was a doctor and a stranger the group expected an explanation of these goings-on from him, or at least an educated guess.

"What do I think?" He leaned forward in the old rocker and rested his arms on his knees. "I think a lot of things happen that can't be explained by our usual thought patterns, and once we get accustomed to certain patterns we find it very uncomfortable to break over into others. So maybe it's just as well not to want an explanation."

"Hmmm." Ol' Hank knocked the ashes out of his pipe into his hand and looked around for the wastebasket. "Neat way of saying you don't know either. Think I'll remember that. It might come in handy sometime. Well, g'night all."

He glanced around hastily, dumped the ashes in the geranium pot and left, sucking on his empty pipe.

His departure was a signal for the others to drift off to bed at the wise hour of ten, but I was in no mood for wisdom, not of the early-to-bed type anyway.

"Then there *is* room in this life for inexplicables." I pleated my skirt between my fingers and straightened it out again.

"It would be a poor lackluster sort of world if there weren't," the doctor said. "I used to rule out anything that I couldn't explain but I got cured of that good one time." He smiled reminiscently. "Sometimes I wish I hadn't. As I said, it can be mighty uncomfortable."

"Yes," I said impulsively. "Like hearing impossible music and sliding down moonbeams—" I felt my heart sink at the sudden blankness of his face. Oh, gee! Goofed again. He could talk glibly of inexplicables but he didn't really believe in them. "And crutches that walk by themselves," I rushed on rashly, "and autumn leaves that dance in the windless clearing—" I grasped my crutches and started blindly for the door. "And maybe someday if I'm a good girl and disbelieve enough I'll walk again—"

" 'And disbelieve enough'?" His words followed me. "Don't you mean 'believe enough'?"

"Don't strain your pattern," I called back. "It's 'disbelieve.' "

Of course I felt silly the next morning at the breakfast table, but Dr. Curtis didn't refer to the conversation so I didn't either. He was discussing renting a jeep for his hunting trip and leaving his car to be fixed.

"Tell Bill you'll be back a week before you plan to," said Ol' Hank. "Then your car will be ready when you do get back."

The Francher kid was in the group of people who gathered to watch Bill transfer Dr. Curtis' gear from the car to the jeep. As usual he was a little removed from the rest, lounging against a tree. Dr. Curtis finally came out, his .30-06 under one arm and his heavy hunting jacket under the other. Anna and I leaned over our side fence watching the whole procedure.

I saw the Francher kid straighten slowly, his hands leaving his pockets as he stared at Dr. Curtis. One hand went out tentatively and then faltered. Dr. Curtis inserted himself in the seat of the jeep and fumbled at the knobs on the dashboard. "Which one's the radio?" he asked Bill.

"Radio? In this jeep?" Bill laughed.

"But the music—" Dr. Curtis paused for a split second, then turned on the ignition. "Have to make my own, I guess," he laughed.

The jeep roared into life, and the small group scattered as he wheeled it in reverse across the yard. In the pause as he shifted gears, he glanced sideways at me and our eyes met. It was a very brief encounter, but he asked questions and I answered with my unknowing and he exploded in a kind of wonderment—all in the moment between reverse and low.

We watched the dust boil up behind the jeep as it growled its way down to the highway.

"Well," Anna said, "a-hunting we do go indeed!"

"Who's he?" The Francher kid's hands were tight on the top of the fence, a blind sort of look on his face.

"I don't know," I said. "His name is Dr. Curtis."

"He's heard music before."

"I should hope so," Anna said.

"*That* music?" I asked the Francher kid.

"Yes," he nearly sobbed. "Yes!"

"He'll be back," I said. "He has to get his car."

"Well," Anna sighed. "The words are the words of English but the sense is the sense of confusion. Coffee, anybody?"

That afternoon the Francher kid joined me, wordlessly, as I struggled up the rise above the boardinghouse for a little wideness of horizon to counteract the day's shut-in-ness. I would rather have walked alone, partly because of a need for silence and partly because he just couldn't ever keep his—accusing?—eyes off my crutches. But he didn't trespass upon my attention as so many people would have, so I didn't mind too much. I leaned, panting, against a gray granite boulder and let the fresh-from-distant-snow breeze lift my hair as I caught my breath. Then I huddled down into my coat, warming my ears. The Francher kid had a handful of pebbles and was lobbing them at the scattered rusty tin cans that dotted the hillside. After one pebble turned a square corner to hit a can he spoke.

"If he knows the name of the instrument, then—" He lost his words.

"What is the name?" I asked, rubbing my nose where my coat collar had tickled it.

"It really isn't a word. It's just two sounds it makes."

"Well, then, make me a word. 'Musical instrument' is mighty unmusical and unhandy."

The Francher kid listened, his head tilted, his lips moving. "I suppose you could call it a '*rappoor*,' " he said, softening the *a*. "But it isn't that."

"'*Rappoor*,'" I said. "Of course you know by now we don't have any such instrument." I was intrigued at having been drawn into another Francher-type conversation. I was developing quite a taste for them. "It's probably just something your mother dreamed up for you."

"And for that doctor?"

"Ummm." My mental wheels spun, tractionless. "What do you think?"

"I almost know that there are some more like Mother. Some who know 'the madness and the dream,' too."

"Dr. Curtis?" I asked.

"No," he said slowly, rubbing his hand along the boulder. "No, I could feel a faraway, strange-to-me feeling with him. He's like you. He—he knows someone who knows, but he doesn't know."

"Well, thanks. He's a nice bird to be a feather of. Then it's all very simple. When he comes back you ask him who he knows."

"Yes—" The Francher kid drew a tremulous breath. "Yes!"

We eased down the hillside, talking money and music. The Francher kid had enough saved up to buy a good instrument of some kind—but what kind? He was immersed in tones and timbres and ranges and keys and the possibility of sometime finding a something that would sound like a *rappoor*.

We paused at the foot of the hill. Impulsively I spoke.

"Francher, why do you talk with me?" I wished the words back before I finished them. Words have a ghastly way of shattering delicate situations and snapping tenuous bonds.

He lobbed a couple more stones against the bank and turned away, hands in his pockets. His words came back to me after I had given them up.

"You don't hate me—yet."

I was jarred. I suppose I had imagined all the people around the Francher kid were getting acquainted with him as I was, but his words made me realize differently. After that I caught at every conversation that included the Francher kid, and alerted at every mention of his name. It shook me to find that to practically everyone he was still juvenile delinquent, lazy trash, no-good off-scouring, potential criminal, burden. By some devious means it had been decided that he was responsible for all the odd happenings in town. I asked a number of people how the kid could possibly have done it. The only answer I got was, "The Francher kid can do anything—bad."

Even Anna still found him an unwelcome burden in her classroom despite the fact that he was finally functioning on a fairly acceptable level academically.

Here I'd been thinking—heaven knows why!—that he was establishing himself in the community. Instead he was doing well to hold his own. I reviewed to myself all that had happened since first I met him, and found hardly a thing that would be positive in the eyes of the general public.

"Why," I thought to myself, "I'm darned lucky he's kept out of the hands of the law!" And my stomach knotted coldly at what might happen if the Francher kid ever did step over into out-and-out lawlessness. There's something insidiously sweet to the adolescent in flouting authority, and I wanted no such appetite for any My Child of mine.

Well, the next few days after Dr. Curtis left were typical hunting-weather days. Minutes of sunshine and shouting autumn colors—hours of cloud and rain and near snow and raw aching winds. Reports came of heavy snow across Mingus Mountain, and Dogietown was snowed in for the winter, a trifle earlier than usual. We watched our own first flakes idle down, then whip themselves to tears against the huddled houses. It looked as though all excitement and activity were about to be squeezed out of Willow Springs by the drab grayness of winter.

Then the unexpected, which sometimes splashes our grayness with scarlet, happened. The big dude-ranch school, the Half Circle Star, that occupied the choicest of the range land in our area, invited all the school kids out to a musical splurge. They had imported an orchestra that played concerts as well as being a very good dance band, and they planned a gala weekend with a concert Friday evening followed by a dance for the teeners Saturday night. The ranch students were usually kept aloof from the town kids, poor little tikes. They were mostly unwanted or maladjusted children whose parents could afford to get rid of them with a flourish under the guise of giving them the advantage of growing up in healthful surroundings.

Of course the whole town was flung into a tizzy. There were the children of millionaires out there and famous people's kids, too, but about the only glimpse we ever got of them was as they swept grandly through the town in the ranch station wagons. On such occasions we collectively blinked our eyes at the chromium glitter, and sighed—though perhaps for different reasons. I sighed for thin unhappy faces pressed to windows and sad eyes yearning back at houses where families lived who wanted *their* kids.

Anyway the concensus of opinion was that it would be worth suffering through a "music concert" to get to go to a dance with a real orchestra, because only those who attended the concert were eligible for the dance.

There was much discussion and much heartburning over what to wear to the two so divergent affairs. The boys were complacent after they found out that their one good outfit was right for both. The girls discussed endlessly, and embarked upon a wild lend-borrow spree when they found that fathers positively refused to spend largely even for this so special occasion.

I was very pleased for the Francher kid. Now he'd have a chance to hear live music—a considerable cut above what snarled in our staticky wave lengths from the available radio stations. Now maybe he'd hear a faint echo of his *rappoor* and in style, too, because Mrs. McVey had finally broken down and bought him a new suit, a really nice one by the local standards. I was as anxious as Twyla to see how the Francher kid would look in such splendor.

So it was with a distinct shock that I saw the kid at the concert, lounging, thumbs in pockets, against the door of the room where the crowd gathered. His face was shut and dark, and his patched faded Levi's made a blotch in the dimness of the room.

"Look!" Twyla whispered. "He's in Levi's!"

"How come?" I breathed. "Where's his new suit?"

"I don't know. And those Levi's aren't even clean!" She hunched down in her seat, feeling the accusing eyes of the whole world searing her through the Francher kid.

The concert was splendid. Even our rockin'est rollers were caught up in the wonderful web of music. Even I lost myself for long lovely moments in the bright melodic trails that led me out of the gray lanes of familiarity. But I also felt the bite of tears behind my eyes. Music is made to be moved to, and my unresponsive feet wouldn't even tap a tempo. I let the brasses and drums smash my rebellion into bearable-sized pieces again and joined joyfully in the enthusiastic applause.

"Hey!" Rigo said behind me as the departing stir of the crowd began. "I didn't know anything could sound like that. Man! Did you hear that horn! I'd like to get me one of them things and blow it!"

"You'd sound like a sick cow," Janniset said. "Them's hard to play."

Their discussion moved on down the aisle.

"He's gone." Twyla's voice was a breath in my ear.

"Yes," I said. "But we'll probably see him out at the bus."

But we didn't. He wasn't at the bus. He hadn't come out on the bus. No one knew how he got out to the ranch or where he had gone.

Anna and Twyla and I piled into Anna's car and headed back for Willow Creek, my heart thudding with apprehension, my thoughts busy. When we pulled up at Somansons' there was a car parked in front.

"The McVey!" Anna sizzled in my ear. "Ah ha! Methinks I smell trouble."

I didn't even have time to take my coat off in the smothery

warmth of the front room before I was confronted by the monumental violence of Mrs. McVey's wrath.

"Dress him!" she hissed, her chin thrust out as she lunged forward in the chair. "Dress him so's he'll feel equal to the others!" Her hands flashed out, and I dodged instinctively and blinked as a bunch of white rags fluttered to my feet. "His new shirt!" she half screamed. Another shower of tatters, dark ones this time. "His new suit! Not a piece in it as big as your hand!" There was a spatter like muffled hail. "His shoes!" Her voice caught on the edge of her violence, and she repeated raggedly, "His *shoes!*" Fear was battling with anger now. "Look at those pieces—as big as stamps—*shoes!*" Her voice broke. "Anybody who can tear up *shoes!*"

She sank back in her chair, spent and breathless, fishing for a crumpled Kleenex to wipe the spittle from her chin. I eased into a chair after Anna helped me shrug out of my coat. Twyla huddled, frightened, near the door, her eyes big with fascinated terror.

"Let him be like the others," McVey half whispered. "That limb of Satan ever be like anyone decent?"

"But why?" My voice sounded thin and high in the calm after the hurricane.

"For no reason at all," she gasped, pressing her hand to her panting ribs. "I gave all them brand-new clothes to him to try on, thinking he'd be pleased. Thinking—" her voice slipped to a whining tremulo, "thinking he'd see how I had his best interest at heart." She paused and sniffed lugubriously. No ready sympathy for her poured into the hiatus so she went on, angrily aggrieved. "And he took them and went into his room and came out with them like that!" Her finger jabbed at the pile of rags. "He—he *threw* them at me! You and your big ideas about him wanting to be like other kids!" Her lips curled away from the venomous spate of words. "He don't want to be like nobody 'cepting hisself. And he's a devil!" Her voice sank to a whisper and her breath drew in on the last word, her eyes wide.

"But why did he do it?" I asked. "He must have said *something.*"

Mrs. McVey folded her hands across her ample middle and pinched her lips together. "There are some things a lady don't repeat," she said prissily, tossing her head.

"Oh, cut it out!" I was suddenly dreadfully weary of trying to be polite to the McVeys of this world. "Stop tying on that kind of an act. You could teach a stevedore—" I bit my lips and swallowed hard. "I'm sorry, Mrs. McVey, but this is no time to hold back. What did he say? What excuse did he give?"

"He didn't give any excuse," she snapped. "He just—just—" Her heavy cheeks mottled with color. "He called names."

"Oh." Anna and I exchanged glances.

"But what on earth got into him?" I asked. "There must be some reason—"

"Well," Anna squirmed a little. "After all what can you expect—?"

"From a background like that?" I snapped. "Well, Anna, I certainly expected something different from a background like yours!"

Anna's face hardened and she gathered up her things. "I've known him longer than you have," she said quietly.

"Longer," I admitted, "but not better. Anna," I pleaded, leaning toward her, "don't condemn him unheard."

"Condemn?" She looked up brightly. "I didn't know he was on trial."

"Oh, Anna." I sank back in my chair. "The poor kid's been on trial, presumed guilty of anything and everything, ever since he arrived in town, and you know it."

"I don't want to quarrel with you," Anna said. "I'd better say good night."

The door clicked behind her. Mrs. McVey and I measured each other with our eyes. I had opened my mouth to say something when I felt a whisper of a motion at my elbow. Twyla stood under the naked flood of the overhead light, her hands clasped in front of her, her eyes shadowed by the droop of her lashes as she narrowed her glance against the glare.

"What did you buy his clothes with?" Her voice was very quiet.

"None of your business, young lady," Mrs. McVey snapped, reddening.

"This is almost the end of the month," Twyla said. "Your check doesn't come till the first. Where did you get the money?"

"*Well!*" Mrs. McVey began to hoist her bulk out of the chair. "I don't have to stay here and have a sassy snip like this—"

202

Twyla swept in closer—so close that Mrs. McVey shrank back, her hands gripping the dusty overstuffed arms of the chair.

"You never have any of the check left after the first week," Twyla said. "And you bought a purple nylon nightgown this month. It took a week's pay—"

Mrs. McVey lunged forward again, her mouth agape with horrified outrage.

"You took *his* money," Twyla said, her eyes steely in her tight young face. "You stole the money he was saving!" She whirled away from the chair, her skirts and hair flaring. "Someday—" she said with clenched teeth, "someday I'll probably be old and fat and ugly, but heaven save me from being old and fat and ugly and a *thief!*"

"Twyla!" I warned, truly afraid that Mrs. McVey would have a stroke then and there.

"Well, she *is* a thief!" Twyla cried. "The Francher kid has been working and saving almost a year to buy—" she faltered, palpably feeling the thin ice of betraying a confidence, "to buy something. And he had almost enough! And she must have gone snooping around—"

"Twyla!" I had to stop her.

"It's true! It's true!" Her hands clenched rebelliously.

"Twyla." My voice was quiet but it silenced her.

"Good-by, Mrs. McVey," I said. "I'm sorry this happened."

"Sorry!" she snorted, rearing up out of her chair. "Sour old maids with never a chick or child of their own sticking their noses into decent people's affairs—" She waddled hastily to the door. She reached for the doorknob, her eyes narrow and venomous over her shoulder. "I got connections. I'll get even with you." The door shuddered as it emphasized her departure.

I let the McVey sweep out of my mind.

"Twyla," I took her cold hands in mine, "you'd better go on home. I've got to figure out how to find the Francher kid."

The swift movement of her hands protested. "But *I* want—"

"I'm sorry, Twyla. I think it'd be better."

"Okay." Her shoulders relaxed in acquiescence.

Just as she left, Mrs. Somanson bustled in. "Y' better come on out to the table and have a cup of coffee," she said. I straightened wearily.

"That McVey! She'd drive the devil to drink," she said cheerfully. "Well, I guess people are like that. I've had more teachers over the years say that it wasn't the kids they minded but the parents." She shooed me through the door and went to the kitchen for the percolator. "Now I was always one to believe that the teacher was right—right or wrong—" Her voice faded out in a long familiar story that proved just the opposite of what she'd said, as I stared into my cup of coffee, wondering despairingly where in all this world I could find the Francher kid. After the episode of the gossip I had my fears. Still, oftentimes people who react violently to comparatively minor troubles were seemingly unshaken by really serious ones—a sort of being at a loss for a proportionate emotional reaction.

But what would he do? Music—music—he'd planned to buy the means for music and had lost the wherewithal. Now he had nothing to make music with. What would he do first? Revenge —or find his music elsewhere? Run away? To where? Steal the money? Steal the music? *Steal!*

I snapped to awareness, my abrupt movement slopping my cold coffee over into the saucer. Mrs. Somanson was gone. The house was quiet with the twilight pause, the indefinable transitional phase from day to night.

This time it wouldn't be only a harmonica! I groped for my crutches, my mind scrabbling for some means of transportation. I was reaching for the doorknob when the door flew open and nearly bowled me over.

"Coffee! Coffee!" Dr. Curtis croaked, to my complete bewilderment. He staggered over, all bundled in his hunting outfit, his face ragged with whiskers, his clothes odorous of campfires and all out-of-doors, to the table and clutched the coffeepot. It was very obviously cold.

"Oh, well," he said in a conversational tone. "I guess I can survive without coffee."

"Survive what?" I asked.

He looked at me a moment, smiling, then he said, "Well, if I'm going to say anything about it to anyone it might as well be you, though I hope that I've got sense enough not to go around babbling indiscriminately. Of course it might be a slight visual hangover from this hunting trip—you should hunt with these friends of mine sometime—but it kinda shook me."

204

"Shook you?" I repeated stupidly, my mind racing around the idea of asking him for help in finding the Francher kid.

"A somewhatly," he admitted. "After all there I was, riding along, minding my own business, singing, lustily if not musically, 'A Life on the Ocean Waves,' when there they were, marching sedately across the road."

"They?" This story dragged in my impatient ears.

"The trombone and the big bass drum," he explained.

"The what!" I had the sensation of running unexpectedly into a mad tangle of briars.

"The trombone and the big bass drum," Dr. Curtis repeated. "Keeping perfect time and no doubt in perfect step, though you couldn't thump your feet convincingly six feet off the ground. Supposing, of course, you were a trombone with feet, which this wasn't."

"Dr. Curtis," I grabbed a corner of his hunting coat. "Please, please! What happened? Tell me! I've got to know."

He looked at me and sobered. "You are taking this seriously, aren't you?" he said wonderingly.

I gulped and nodded.

"Well, it was about five miles above the Half Circle Star Ranch, where the heavy pine growth begins. And so help me, a trombone and a bass drum marched in the air across the road, the bass drum marking the time—though come to think of it, the drumsticks just lay on top. I stopped the jeep and ran over to where they had disappeared. I couldn't see anything in the heavy growth there, but I swear I heard a faint Bronx cheer from the trombone. I have no doubt that the two of them were hiding behind a tree, snickering at me." He rubbed his hand across his fuzzy chin. "Maybe I'd better drink that coffee, cold or not."

"Dr. Curtis," I said urgently, "can you help me? Without waiting for questions? Can you take me out there? Right now?" I reached for my coat. Wordlessly he helped me on with it and opened the door for me. The day was gone and the sky was a clear aqua around the horizon, shading into rose where the sun had dropped behind the hills. It was only a matter of minutes before we were roaring up the hill to the junction. I shouted over the jolting rattle.

"It's the Francher kid," I yelled. "I've got to find him and make him put them back before they find out."

"Put who back where?" Dr. Curtis shouted into the sudden diminution of noise as we topped the rise, much to the astonishment of Mrs. Frisney, who was pattering across the intersection with her black umbrella protecting her from the early starshine.

"It's too long to explain," I screamed as we accelerated down the highway. "But he must be stealing the whole orchestra because Mrs. McVey bought him a new suit, and I've got to make him take them back or they'll arrest him, then heaven help us all."

"You mean the Francher kid had that bass drum and trombone?" he yelled.

"Yes!" My chest was aching from the tension of speech. "And probably all the rest."

I caught myself with barked knuckles as Dr. Curtis braked to a sudden stop.

"Now look," he said, "let's get this straight. You're talking wilder than I am. Do you mean to say that that kid is swiping a whole orchestra?"

"Yes, don't ask me how. I don't know how, but he can do it—" I grabbed his sleeve. "But he said you knew! The day you left on your trip, I mean, he said you knew someone who would know. We were waiting for you!"

"Well, I'll be blowed!" he said in slow wonder. "Well, dang me!" He ran his hand over his face. "So now it's *my* turn!" He reached for the ignition key. "Gangway, Jemmy!" he shouted. "Here I come with another! Yours or mine, Jemmy? Yours or mine?"

It was as though his outlandish words had tripped a trigger. Suddenly all this strangeness, this out-of-stepness became a mad foolishness. Despairingly I wished I'd never seen Willow Creek or the Francher kid or a harmonica that danced alone or Twyla's tilted side glance, or Dr. Curtis or the white road dimming in the rapid coming of night. I huddled down in my coat, my eyes stinging with weary hopeless tears, and the only comfort I could find was in visualizing myself twisting my hated braces into rigid confetti and spattering the road with it.

I roused as Dr. Curtis braked the jeep to a stop.

"It was about there," he said, peering through the dusk. "It's mighty deserted up here—the raw end of isolation. The kid's probably scared by now and plenty willing to come home."

"Not the Francher kid," I said. "He's not the run-of-the-mill type kid."

"Oh, so!" Dr. Curtis said. "I'd forgotten."

Then there it was. At first I thought it the evening wind in the pines, but it deepened and swelled and grew into a thunderous magnificent shaking chord—a whole orchestra giving tongue. Then, one by one, the instruments soloed, running their scales, displaying their intervals, parading their possibilities. Somewhere between the strings and woodwinds I eased out of the jeep.

"You stay here," I half whispered. "I'll go find him. You wait."

It was like walking through a rainstorm, the notes spattering all around me, the shrill lightning of the piccolos and the muttering thunder of the drums. There was no melody, only a child running gleefully through a candy store, snatching greedily at everything, gathering delight by the handful and throwing it away for the sheer pleasure of having enough to be able to throw it.

I struggled up the rise above the road, forgetting in my preoccupation to be wary of unfamiliar territory in the half-dark. There they were, in the sand hollow beyond the rise—all the instruments ranged in orderly precise rows as though at a recital, each one wrapped in a sudden shadowy silence, broken only by the shivery giggle of the cymbals which hastily stilled themselves against the sand.

"Who's there?" He was a rigid figure, poised atop a boulder, arms half lifted.

"Francher," I said.

"Oh." He slid through the air to me. "I'm not hiding any more," he said. "I'm going to be me all the time now."

"Francher," I said bluntly, "you're a thief."

He jerked in protest. "I'm not either—"

"If this is being you, you're a thief. You stole these instruments."

He groped for words, then burst out: "They stole my money! They stole all my music."

207

" 'They'?" I asked. "Francher, you can't lump people together and call them 'they.' Did I steal your money? Or Twyla—or Mrs. Frisney—or Rigo?"

"Maybe you didn't put your hands on it," the Francher kid said. "But you stood around and let McVey take it."

"That's a guilt humanity has shared since the beginning. Standing around and letting wrong things happen. But even Mrs. McVey felt she was helping you. She didn't sit down and decide to rob you. Some people have the idea that children don't have any exclusive possessions but what they have belongs to the adults who care for them. Mrs. McVey thinks that way. Which is quite a different thing from deliberately stealing from strangers. What about the owners of all these instruments? What have they done to deserve your ill will?"

"They're people," he said stubbornly. "And I'm not going to be people any more." Slowly he lifted himself into the air and turned himself upside down. "See," he said, hanging above the hillside. "People can't do things like this."

"No," I said. "But apparently whatever kind of creature you have decided to be can't keep his shirttails in either."

Hastily he scrabbled his shirt back over his bare midriff and righted himself. There was an awkward silence in the shadowy hollow, then I asked:

"What are you going to do about the instruments?"

"Oh, they can have them back when I'm through with them —if they can find them," he said contemptuously. "I'm going to play them to pieces tonight." The trumpet jabbed brightly through the dusk and the violins shimmered a silver obbligato.

"And every downbeat will say 'thief,' " I said. "And every roll of the drums will growl 'stolen.' "

"I don't care, I don't care!" he almost yelled. " 'Thief' and 'stolen' are words for people and I'm not going to be people any more, I told you!"

"What are you going to be?" I asked, leaning wearily against a tree trunk. "An animal?"

"No sir." He was having trouble deciding what to do with his hands. "I'm going to be *more* than just a human."

"Well, for a more-than-human this kind of behavior doesn't show very many smarts. If you're going to be more than human you have to be thoroughly a human first. If you're going to be better than a human you have to be the best a human can be, first—then go on from there. Being entirely different is no way to make a big impression on people. You have to be able to outdo them at their own game first and then go beyond them. It won't matter to them that you can fly like a bird unless you can walk straight like a man, first. To most people different is wrong. Oh, they'd probably say, 'My goodness! How wonderful!' when you first pulled some fancy trick, but—" I hesitated, wondering if I were being wise, "but they'd forget you pretty quick, just as they would any cheap carnival attraction."

He jerked at my words, his fists clenched.

"You're as bad as the rest." His words were tight and bitter. "You think I'm just a freak—"

"I think you're an unhappy person, because you're not sure who you are or what you are, but you'll have a much worse time trying to make an identity for yourself if you tangle with the law."

"The law doesn't apply to me," he said coldly. "Because I know who I am—"

"Do you, Francher?" I asked softly. "Where did your mother come from? Why could she walk through the minds of others? Who are you, Francher? Are you going to cut yourself off from people before you even try to find out just what wonders you are capable of? Not these little sideshow deals, but maybe miracles that really count." I swallowed hard as I looked at his averted face, shadowy in the dusk. My own face was congealing from the cold wind that had risen, but he didn't even shiver in its iciness, though he had no jacket on. My lips moved stiffly. "Both of us know you could get away with this lawlessness, but you know as well as I do that if you take this first step you won't ever be able to untake it. And, how do we know, it might make it impossible for you to be accepted by your own kind— if you're right in saying there are others. Surely they're above common theft. And Dr. Curtis is due back from his hunting trip. So close to knowing—maybe—

"I didn't know your mother, Francher, but I do know this is not the dream she had for you. This is not why she endured hunger and hiding, terror and panic places—"

I turned and stumbled away from him, making my way back to the road. It was dark, horribly dark, around me and in me as I wailed soundlessly for this My Child. Somewhere before I got back Dr. Curtis was helping me. He got me back into the jeep and pried my frozen fingers from my crutches and warmed my hands between his broad-gloved palms.

"He *isn't* of this world, you know," he said. "At least his parents or grandparents weren't. There are others like him. I've been hunting with some of them. He doesn't know, evidently, nor did his mother, but he *can* find his People. I wanted to tell you to help you persuade him—"

I started to reach for my crutches, peering through the dark, then I relaxed. "No," I said with tingling lips. "It wouldn't be any good if he only responded to bribes. He has to decide now, with the scales weighted against him. He's got to *push* into his new world. He can't just slide in limply. You kill a chick if you help it hatch."

I dabbled all the way home at tears for a My Child, lost in a wilderness I couldn't chart, bound in a captivity from which I couldn't free him.

Dr. Curtis saw me to the door of my room. He lifted my averted face and wiped it.

"Don't worry," he said. "I promise you the Francher kid will be taken care of."

"Yes," I said, closing my eyes against the nearness of his. "By the sheriff if they catch him. They'll discover the loss of the orchestra any minute now, if they haven't already."

"You made him think," he said. "He wouldn't have stood still for all that if you hadn't."

"Too late," I said. "A thought too late."

Alone in my room I huddled on my bed, trying not to think of anything. I lay there until I was stiff with the cold, then I crept into my warm woolly robe up to my chin. I sat in the darkness there by the window, looking out at the lacy ghosts of the cottonwood trees, in the dim moonlight. How long would it be before some kindly soul would come blundering in to regale me with the latest about the Francher kid?

I put my elbows on the window sill and leaned my face on my hands, the heels of my palms pressing against my eyes. "Oh, Francher My Child, My lonely lost Child—"

"I'm not lost."

I lifted a startled face. The voice was so soft. Maybe I had imagined . . .

"No, I'm here." The Francher kid stepped out into the milky glow of the moon, moving with a strange new strength and assurance, quite divorced from his usual teen-age gangling.

"Oh, Francher—" I couldn't let myself sob, but my voice caught on the last of his name.

"It's okay," he said. "I took them all back."

My shoulders ached as the tension ran out of them.

"I didn't have time to get them all back in the hall but I stacked them carefully on the front porch." A glimmer of a smile crossed his face. "I guess they'll wonder how they got out there."

"I'm so sorry about your money," I said awkwardly.

He looked at me soberly. "I can save again. I'll get it yet. Someday I'll have my music. It doesn't *have* to be now."

Suddenly a warm bubble seemed to be pressing up against my lungs. I felt excitement tingle clear out to my fingertips. I leaned across the sill. "Francher," I cried softly, "you *have* your music. Now. Remember the harmonica? Remember when you danced with Twyla? Oh, Francher. All sound is is vibration. You can vibrate the air without an instrument. Remember the chord you played with the orchestra? Play it again, Francher!"

He looked at me blankly, and then it was as if a candle had been lighted behind his face. "Yes!" he cried. "Yes!"

Softly—oh, softly—because miracles come that way, I heard the chord begin. It swelled richly, fully, softly, until the whole back yard vibrated to it—a whole orchestra crying out in a whisper in the pale moonlight.

"But the tunes!" he cried, taking this miracle at one stride and leaping beyond it. "I don't know any of the tunes for an orchestra!"

"There are books," I said. "Whole books of scores for symphonies and operas and—"

"And when I know the instruments better!" Here was the eager alive voice of the-Francher-kid-who-should-be. "Anything I hear—" The back yard ripped raucously to a couple of bars of the latest rock 'n' roll, then blossomed softly to an "*Adoramus Te*" and skipped to "The Farmer in the Dell." "Then someday

I'll make my own—" Tremulously a *rappoor* threaded through a melodic phrase and stilled itself.

In the silence that followed the Francher kid looked at me, not at my face but deep inside me somewhere.

"Miss Carolle!" I felt my eyes tingle to tears at his voice. "You've given me my music!" I could hear him swallow. "I want to give you something." My hand moved in protest, but he went on quickly, "Please come outside."

"Like this? I'm in my robe and slippers."

"They're warm enough. Here, I'll help you through the window."

And before I knew it I was over the low sill and clinging dizzily to it from the outside.

"My braces," I said, loathing the words with a horrible loathing. "My crutches."

"No," the Francher kid said. "You don't need them. Walk across the yard, Miss Carolle, all alone."

"I can't!" I cried through my shock. "Oh, Francher, don't tease me!"

"Yes, you can. That's what I'm giving you. I can't mend you but I can give you that much. Walk."

I clung frantically to the sill. Then I saw again Francher and Twyla spiraling down from the treetops, Francher upside down in the air with his midriff showing, Francher bouncing Balance Rock from field to field.

I let go of the sill. I took a step. And another, and another. I held my hands far out from my sides. Glorious freedom from clenched hands and aching elbows! Across the yard I went, every step in the milky moonlight a paean of praise. I turned at the fence and looked back. The Francher kid was crouched by the window in a tight huddle of concentration. I lifted onto tiptoe and half skipped, half ran back to the window, feeling the wind of my going lift my hair back from my cheeks. Oh, it was like a drink after thirst! Like food after famine! Like gates swinging open!

I fell forward and caught at the window sill. And cried out inarticulately as I felt the old bonds clamp down again, the old half-death seize hold of me. I crumpled to the ground beside the Francher kid. His tormented eyes looked into mine, his face pale and haggard. His forearm went up to wipe his sweat-drenched face. "I'm sorry," he panted. "That's all I can do now."

My hands reached for him. There was a sudden movement, so quick and so close that I drew my foot back out of the way. I looked up, startled. Dr. Curtis and a shadowy someone else were standing over us. But the surprise of their being there was drowned in the sudden upsurge of wonderment.

"It moved!" I cried. "My foot moved. Look! Look! It moved!" And I concentrated on it again—hard, hard! After laborious seconds my left big toe wiggled.

My hysterical laugh was half a shout. "One toe is better than none!" I sobbed. "Isn't it, Dr. Curtis? Doesn't that mean that someday—that maybe—?"

He had dropped to his knees and he gathered my frantic hands into his two big quiet ones.

"It might well be," he said. "Jemmy will help us find out."

The other figure knelt beside Dr. Curtis. There was a curious waiting kind of silence, but it wasn't me he was looking at. It wasn't my hands he reached for. It wasn't my voice that cried out softly.

But it was the Francher kid who suddenly launched himself into the arms of the stranger and began to wail, the wild noisy crying of a child—a child who could be brave as long as he was completely lost but who had to dissolve into tears when rescue came.

The stranger looked over the Francher kid's head at Dr. Curtis. "He's mine," he said. "But she's almost one of yours."

It could all have been a dream, or a mad explosion of imagination of some sort; but they don't come any less imaginative than Mrs. McVey, and I know she will never forget the Francher kid. She has another foster child now, a placid plump little girl who loves to sit and listen to woman-talk—but the Francher kid is indelible in the McVey memory. Unborn generations will probably hear of him and his shoes.

And Twyla—she will carry his magic to her grave, unless (and I know she sometimes hopes prayerfully) Francher someday goes back for her.

Jemmy brought him to Cougar Canyon, and here they are helping him sort out all his many gifts and capabilities—some of which are unique to him—so that he will be able, finally, to fit into his most effective slot in their scheme of things. They tell me that there are those of this world who are developing even now in the footsteps of the People. That's what Jemmy meant when he told Dr. Curtis I was almost one of his.

And I am walking. Dr. Curtis brought Bethie. She only touched me softly with her hands and read me to Dr. Curtis. And I *had* to accept it then—that it was mostly myself that stood in my own way. That my doctor had been right: that time, patience and believing could make me whole again.

The more I think about it the more I think that those three words are the key to almost everything.

Time, patience and believing—and the greatest of these is believing.

VI

Lea sat in the dark of the bedroom and swung her feet over the edge of the bed. She groped for and shrugged into a robe and huddled it around her. She went softly to the window and sat down on the broad sill. A lopsided moon rolled in the clouds above the hills, and all the Canyon lay ebony and ivory under its lights. Lea could see the haphazard dotting of houses that made up the community. All were dark except for one far window near the creek cliff.

Suddenly the whole scene seemed to take a sharp turn, completely out of focus. The hills and canyons became as strange as though she were looking at a moonscape or the hidden hills of Venus. Nothing looked familiar; even the moon suddenly became a leering frightening thing that could come closer and closer and closer. Lea hid her face in the bend of her elbow and drew her knees up sharply to support her shaking arms.

"What am I doing here?" she whispered. "What on earth am I doing here? I don't belong here. I've got to get away. What have I to do with all these—these—creatures? I don't believe them! I don't believe anything. It's madness. I've gone mad somewhere along the way. This must be an asylum. All these evenings—just pooling madnesses to see if a sanity will come out of it!"

She shuddered and lifted her head slowly, reluctantly opening her eyes. Determinedly she stared at the moon and the hills and the billowing clouds until they came back to familiarity. "A madness," she whispered. "But such a comforting madness. If only I could stay here forever—" Wistful tears blurred the moon. "If only, if only!

"Fool!" Lea buried her face fiercely on her knees again. "Make up your mind. Is this or isn't this insanity? You can't have it both ways—not at one time." Then the wistful one whispered, "If this is insanity—I'll take it anyway. Whatever it is it makes a wonderful kind of sense that I've never been able to find before. I'm so tired of suspecting everything. Miss Carolle said the greatest was believing. I've got to believe, whether I'm mistaken or not." She leaned her forehead against the cold glass of the window, her eyes intent on the far light. "I wonder what their wakefulness is," she sighed.

She shivered away from the chill of the glass and rested her cheek on her knees again.

"But it *is* time," she thought. "Time for me to take a hand in my drifting. That's all it is, my staying here. Drifting in the warm waters of prebirth. Oh, it's lovely here. No worries about earning a living. No worries about what to do. No wondering which branch of the Y in the road to take. But it can't last." She turned her face and looked up at the moon. "Nothing is forever," she smiled wryly, "though unhappiness comes pretty close to it.

"How long can I expect Karen to take care of me? I'm no help to anyone. I have nothing to contribute. I'm a drag on her whatever she does. And I can't—how can I ever get cured of anything in such a protected environment? I've got to go out and learn to look the world full in the face." Her mouth twisted. "And even spit in its eye if necessary."

"Oh, I can't, I can't," one of her wailed. "Pull the ground up over me and let me be quit of everything."

"Shut up!" Lea answered sternly. "I'm running things now. Get dressed. We're leaving."

She dressed hastily in the darkness beyond the reach of the moonlight, tears flooding down her face. As she bent over to slip her shoes on she crumpled against the bed and sobbed deep wrenching sobs for a moment, then finished dressing. She put on her own freshly laundered clothes. She shrugged into her coat —"nearly new"—and gathered up her purse.

"Money—" she thought. "I have no money—"

She dumped the purse on the bed. The few articles clinked on the bedspread. "I threw everything else away before I left—" able at last to remember leaving without darkness descending upon her, "and spent my last dollar—" She opened her billfold and spread it wide. "Not a cent."

She tugged out the miscellany of cards in the card compartment—little rectangles out of the past. "Why didn't I throw these out, too? Useless—" She started to cram them back blindly into the compartment, but her fingers hesitated on a projecting corner. She pulled out a thin navy-blue folder.

"Well! I did forget! My traveler's checks—if there's anything left." She unsnapped the folder and fingered the thin crisp sheaf. "Enough," she whispered. "Enough for running again—" She dumped everything back into her purse, then she opened the top dresser drawer. A faint blue light touched the outline of her face. She picked up the *koomatka* and turned it in her hand. She closed her fingers softly over it as she tore the margin from a magazine on the dresser top. She scrawled on it, "Thank you," and weighted the scrap of paper with the *koomatka*.

The shadows were so black, but she was afraid to walk in the light. She stumbled down from the house toward the road, not letting herself think of the miles and miles to be covered before reaching Kerry Canyon or anywhere. She had just reached the road when she started convulsively and muffled a cry against her clenched fists. Something was moving in the moonlight. She stood paralyzed in the shadow.

"Oh, hi!" came a cheerful voice, and the figure turned to her. "Just getting ready to leave. Didn't know anyone was going in, this trip. You just about got left. Climb in—"

Wordlessly Lea climbed into the battered old pickup.

"Some old jalopy, isn't it?" The fellow went on blithely, slamming the door and hooking it shut with a piece of baling wire. "I guess if you keep anything long enough it'll turn into an antique. This turned long ago! That's the only reason I can think of for their keeping it."

Lea made a vague noise and clutched the side of the car grimly as it took off and raced down the road a yard above the white gravelly surface.

"I haven't noticed you around," the driver said, "but then there's more people here than ever in the history of the Canyon with all this excitement going on. It's my first visit. It's comforting somehow, knowing there are so many of us, isn't it?"

"Yes, it is." Lea's voice was a little rusty. "It's a wonderful feeling."

"Nuisance, though, having to make all our trips in and out by night. They say that they used to be able to lift at least across Jackass Flat even in the daytime and then wheel in the rest of the way. But it's getting mighty close to dude season and we have to be more careful than during the winter. Travel at night. Wheel in from Widow's Peak. Lousy road, too. Takes twice as long. Have you decided yet?"

"Decided?" Lea glanced at him in the moonlight.

"Oh, I know I have no business asking," he smiled, "but it's what everyone is wondering." He sobered, leaning his arms on the steering wheel. "I've decided. Six times. Thought I'd finally decided for sure. Then comes a moonlight night like this—" He looked out over the vast panorama of hills and plains and far reaches—and sighed.

The rest of the trip was made in silence. Lea laughed shakily at her own clutching terror as the wheels touched down with a thud on the road near Widow's Peak. After that, conversation was impossible over the jolting bumping bouncing progress of the truck.

They arrived at Kerry Canyon just as the sunlight washed across the moon. The driver unhooked the door for her and let her out into the shivery dawn.

"We're in and out almost every morning and evening," he said. "You coming back tonight?"

"No." Lea shivered and huddled into her coat. "Not tonight."

"Don't be too long," the driver smiled. "It can't be much longer, you know. If you get back when no truck's in, just call. Mmm. Karen's Receptor this week. Bethie next. Someone'll come in to get you."

"Thank you," Lea said. "Thanks a lot." And she turned blindly away from his good-by.

The diner next to the bus stop was small and stuffy, clumsy still with the weight of the night, not quite awake in the bare drafty dawn. The cup of coffee was hot but hurried, and a little weak. Lea sipped and set it down, staring into its dark shaken depths.

"Even if this is all," she thought, "if I'm never to have any more of order and peace and sense of direction—why, I've at

218

least had a glimpse, and some people never get even that much. I think I have the key now—the almost impossible key to my locked door. Time, patience and believing—and the greatest of these is believing."

After a while she sipped again, not looking up, and found that the coffee had cooled.

"Hot it up for you?" A new waitress was behind the counter, briskly tying her apron strings. "Bus'll be along in just a little while."

"Thank you." Lea held out her cup, firmly putting away the vision of a cup of coffee that had steamed gently far into the morning, waiting, patient.

Time is a word—a shadow of an idea; but always, always, out of the whirlwind of events, the multiplicity of human activities or the endless boredom of disinterest, there is the sky —the sky with all its unchanging changeableness showing the variations of Now and the stability of Forever. There are the stars, the square-set corners of our eternities that wheel and turn and always find their way back. There are the transient tumbled clouds, the windy wisps of mares' tails, the crackling mackerel skies and the romping delightful tumult of the thunderstorms. And the moon—the moon that dreams and sets to dreaming—that mends the world with its compassionate light and makes everything look as though newness is forever.

On such a night as this . . .

Lea leaned on the railing and sighed into the moonlight. Was it two such moons ago or only one that she had been on the bridge or fainting in the skies or receiving in the crisp mountain twilight love's gift of light from a child? She had shattered the rigidness of her old time-pattern and had not yet confined herself in a new one. Time had not yet paced itself into any sort of uniformity for her.

Tomorrow Grace would be back from her appendectomy, back to her job at the Lodge, the job Lea had been fortunate enough to step right into. But now this lame little temporary refuge would be gone. It meant another step into uncertainty. Lea would be free again, free from the clatter of the kitchen and dining room, free to go into the bondage of aimlessness again.

"Except that I have come a little way out of my darkness

into a twilight zone. And if I take this next step patiently and believingly—"

"It will lead you right back to the Canyon—" The laughing voice came softly.

Lea whirled with an inarticulate cry. Then she was clutching Karen and crying, "Oh, Karen! Karen!"

"Watch it! Watch it!" Karen laughed, her arms tender around Lea's shaken shoulders. "Don't bruise the body! Oh, Lea! It's good to see you again! This *is* a better suicide-type place than that bridge." Her voice ran on, covering Lea's struggle for self-possession. "Want me to push you over here? Must be half a mile straight down. And into a river, yet—a river with water."

"Wet water," Lea quavered, releasing Karen and rubbing her arm across her wet cheeks. "And much too cold for comfortable dying. Oh, Karen! I was such a fool! Just because my eyes were shut I thought the sun had been turned off. Such a f-fool!" She gulped.

"Always last year a fool," Karen said. "Which isn't too bad if this year we know it and aren't the same kind of fool. When can you come back with me?"

"Back with you?" Lea stared. "You mean back to the Canyon?"

"Where else?" Karen asked. "For one thing you didn't finish all the installments—"

"But surely by now—"

"Not quite yet," Karen said. "You haven't even missed one. The last one should be ready by the time we get back. You see, just after you left— Well, you'll hear it all later. But I'm so sorry you left when you did. I didn't get to take you over the hill—"

"But the hill's still there, isn't it?" Lea smiled. "The eternal hills—?"

"Yes," Karen sighed. "The hill's still there but I could take anyone there now. Well, it can't be helped. When can you leave?"

"Tomorrow Grace will be back," Lea said. "I was lucky to get this job when I did. It helped tide me over—"

"As tiding-over goes it's pretty good," Karen agreed. "But it isn't a belonging-type thing for you."

Lea shivered, suddenly cold in the soul, fearing a change of pattern. "It'll do."

"Nothing will *do*," Karen said sharply, "if it's just a make-do, a time-filler, a drifting. If you won't fill the slot you were meant to you might as well just sit and count your fingers. Otherwise you just interfere with everything."

"Oh, I'm willing to try to fill my slot. It's just that I'm still in the uncomfortable process of trying to find out what rating I am in whose category, and, even if I don't like it much, I'm beginning to feel that I belong to something and that I'm heading somewhere."

"Well, your most immediate somewhere is the Canyon," Karen said. "I'll be by for you tomorrow evening. You're not so far from us as the People fly! Your luggage?"

Lea laughed. "I have a toothbrush now, and a nightgown."

"Materialist!" Karen put out her forefinger and touched Lea's cheek softly. "The light is coming back. The candle is alight again."

"Praised be the Power." The words came unlearned to Lea's lips.

"The Presence be with you." Karen lifted to the porch railing, her back to the moon, her face in shadow. Her hands were silvered with moonlight as she reached out to touch Lea's two shoulders in farewell.

Before moonrise the next night Lea stood on the dark porch hugging her small bundle to her, shivering from excitement and the wind that strained icily through the piñon trees on the canyon's rim. The featureless bank of gray clouds had spread and spread over the sky since sundown. Moonrise would be a private thing for the upper side of the growing grayness. She started as the shadows above her stirred and coagulated and became a figure.

"Oh, Karen," she cried softly, "I'm afraid. Can't I wait and go by bus? It's going to rain. Look—look!" She held her hand out and felt the sting of the first few random drops.

"Karen sent *me*." The deep amused voice shook Lea back against the railing. "She said she was afraid your toothbrush and nightgown might have compounded themselves. For some reason or other she seems to have suddenly developed a Charley horse in her lifting muscles. Will I do?"

"But—but—" Lea clutched her bundle tighter. "I can't lift! I'm afraid! I nearly died when Karen transported me last time. Please let me wait and go by bus. It won't take much longer. Only overnight. I wasn't even thinking when Karen told me last night." She squeezed her eyes shut. "I'm going to cry," she choked, "or cuss, and I don't do either gracefully, so please go. I'm just too darn scared to go with you."

She felt him pry her bundle gently out of her spasmed fingers. "It's not all that bad," he said matter-of-factly.

"Darn you People!" Lea wanted to yell. "Don't you ever understand? Don't you ever sympathize?"

"Sure we understand." The voice held laughter. "And we sympathize when sympathy is indicated, but we don't slop all over everyone who has a qualm. Ever see a little kid fall down? He always looks around to see whether or not he should cry. Well, you looked around. You found out and you're not crying, are you?"

"No, darn you!" Lea half laughed. "But honestly I really am too scared—"

"Well—say, my name is Deon in case you'd like to personalize your cussing. Anyway we have ways of managing. I can sleep you or opaque my personal shield so you can't see out—only you'd miss so much either way. I should have brought the jalopy after all."

"The jalopy?" Lea clutched the railing.

"Sure, you know the jalopy. They weren't planning to use it tonight."

"If you were thinking I'd feel more secure in that bucket of bolts—" Lea hugged her arms above the elbows. "I'd still be afraid."

"Look." Deon lifted Lea's bundle briskly. "It's going to rain in about half a minute. We're a long way from home. Karen's expecting you tonight and I promised her. So let's make a start of some kind, and if you find it unbearable we'll try some other way. It's dark and you won't be able to see—"

A jab of lightning plunged from the top of the sky to the depth of the canyon below them, and thunder shook the projecting porch like an explosion. Lea gasped and clutched Deon.

His arms closed around her as she buried her face against his shoulder, and she felt his face pressed against her hair.

"I'm sorry," she shuddered, still clinging. "I'm scared of so many things."

Wind whipped her skirts about her and stilled. The tumultuous threshing of the trees quieted, and Lea felt the tension drain out. She laughed a little and started to lift her head. Deon pressed it back to his shoulder.

"Take it easy," he said. "We're on our way."

"Oh!" Lea gasped, clutching again. "Oh, no!"

"Oh, yes," Deon said. "Don't bother to look. Right now you couldn't see anything anyway. We're in the clouds. But start getting used to the idea. We'll be above them soon and the moon is full. *That* you must see."

Lea fought her terror, and slowly, slowly, it withdrew before a faint dawning wonder. "Oh!" she thought. "Oh!" as Karen's forgotten words welled softly up out of memory—"arms remember when eyes forget." "Oh, my goodness!" And her eyes flew open only to wince shut again against the outpouring of the full moon.

"Wasn't it—didn't you—?" she faltered, peering narrowly up into Deon's moon-whitened face.

"That's just what I was going to ask you," Deon smiled. "Seems to me I should have recognized you before this, but remember, the first time I ever saw you you were neck-deep in water and stringy in the hair—one piece of it was plastered across your nose—and Karen didn't even clue me!"

"But look now! Just look now!"

They had broken out of the shadows, and Lea looked below her at the serene tumble of clouds—the beyond-words wonder of a field of clouds under the moon. It was a beauty that not only fed the eyes but made all the senses yearn to encompass it and comprehend it. It sorrowed her not to be able to fill her arms with it and hold it so tight that it would melt right into her own self.

Silently the two moved over acres and acres of the purity of curves, the ineffable delight of depth and height and changing shadows—a world, whole and complete in itself, totally unrelated to the earth below in the darkness.

Finally Lea whispered, "Could I touch one? Could I actually put my hands into one of those clouds?"

"Why, sure," Deon said. "But, baby, it's cold out there. We have considerable altitude to get over the storm. But if you like—"

"Oh, yes!" Lea breathed. "It would be like touching the hem of heaven!"

Not even feeling the bite of cold when Deon opened the shield, Lea reached out gently to touch the welling flank of the cloud. It closed over her hands, bodiless, beautiful, as intangible as light, as insubstantial as a dream, and, like a dream, it dissolved through her fingers. As Deon closed the shield again, Lea found herself gasping and shivering. She looked at her hands and saw them glisten moistly in the moonlight. She looked up at Deon, turning in his arms. "Share my cloud," she said, and touched his cheek softly.

It was hard to gauge time, moving above a wonderland of clouds like that below them, but it didn't seem very long before Deon's voice vibrated against Lea's cheek where it rested against his shoulder. "We're going down now. Stand by for turbulence. We'll probably get tossed around a little."

Lea stirred and smiled. "I must have slept. I'm only dreaming all this."

"Pleasant dreams?"

"Pleasant dreams."

"Here we go! Hang on!"

Lea gasped as they plunged down toward the whiteness. All the serenity and beauty was gone with the snuffing out of the moon. Darkness and tumult were all around them. Wind grabbed them roughly and tossed them raggedly through the clouds, up, impossibly fast, down, incredibly far, twisting and tumbling, laced about by lightning, shaken by the blare of thunder, deafened—even though protected—by the myriad shrieking voices of the wind.

"It's death!" Lea thought frantically. "Nothing can live! It's madness! It's chaos!"

And then, in the middle of the terrifying tumult, she became conscious of warmth and shelter and, more personally, the awareness of someone—the nearness of another's breathing, the strength of arms.

"This," she thought wistfully, "must be like that love Karen mentioned. Out there all the storms of the world. In here, strength, warmth and someone else."

A sudden down-draft flung them bodily out of the storm cloud, spinning them down to a staggering landing in the depth of Cougar Canyon, finally scraping them to a halt roughly against a yellow pine.

"Hoosh!" Deon leaned against the trunk and sagged. "Now I'm glad I *didn't* take the jalopy. That would have unscrewed every bolt in it. Thunderstorms are violent!"

"I should say so." Lea stirred in the circle of his arms. "But I wouldn't have missed it for the world. It'd be better than cussing or crying any time! Such wonderful slam-banging!" She stepped away from him and looked around.

"Where are we?" She prodded with her foot at the edge of a long indentation that ran darkly in the bright flush of lightning across the flat.

"Just over the hill from the schoolhouse."

"Over the hill?" Lea looked around her in startled interest. "But there's nothing here."

"How true." Deon kicked a small clod into the darkness. "Nothing here but me. And this time last week I'd have sworn — Oh, well—"

"You had me worried." The two jumped, startled at the sudden voice from the darkness above. "I thought maybe you might have been dumped miles away or maybe that Lea's toothbrush had slowed you down. Everyone's waiting." Karen touched down on the flat beside them.

"Then it came?" Deon surged forward eagerly. "Did it work? What was—?"

Karen laughed. "Simmer down, Deon. It arrived. It works. The Old Ones have called the Gathering and it's all ready to go except for three empty seats we're not filling. Alley-ooop!"

And Lea found herself snatched into the air and over the hill beyond the flat before she could gasp or let fear catch up with her. And she was red-cheeked and laughing, her hair sparkling with the first of a sudden shower, when they landed on the school porch and let the sudden snarl of thunder and shout of wind push them through the door. They threaded their way through the chattering groups and found seats. Lea looked over at the corner where she usually sat—almost afraid she might see herself still sitting there, hunched over the miserly counting of the coins of her misery.

She felt wonder and delight flood out into her arms and legs, and could hardly contain a wordless cry of joy. She spread her fingers on both hands, reaching, reaching openhanded, for what might be ahead.

"Darkness will come again," she admitted to herself. "This is just a chink in my prison—a promise of what is on the other side of me. But, oh! how wonderful—how wonderful!" She curled her fingers softly to hold a handful of the happiness and found it not strange that another hand closed warmly over hers. "These are people who will listen when I cry. They will help me find my answers. They will sustain me in the long long way that I must grope back to find myself again. But I'm not alone! Never alone again!"

She let everything but the present moment shudder away on a happy shaken sigh as she murmured with the Group, "We are met together in Thy Name."

No one was at the desk. In the middle of it was the same small gadget, or one very like it, that had always been there. Valancy, tenderly burdened on one arm with the flannelly bundle of Our Baby, leaned over and touched the gadget.

"I told you it would arrive okay." The voice came so lifelike that Lea involuntarily searched the front of the room for the absent speaker.

"And I'm to have the last say, after all.

"Well, I suppose you'd like a theme, just to round out things for you—so here it is.

" 'For ye shall pass over Jordan to go in to possess the land which the Lord your God giveth you and ye shall possess it and dwell therein. . . .' "

JORDAN

I GUESS I was the first to see it—the bright form among the clouds above Baldy. There seemed to be no interval of wondering or questioning in my mind. I knew the moment I caught the metallic gleam—the instant the curl-back of the clouds gave a brief glimpse of a long sleek curve. I knew and I gave a shout of delight. Here it was! What more direct answer to a prayer could any fellow want? Just like that! My release from rebellion, the long-awaited answer to my protests against restrictions! There above me was release! I emptied my two hands of the gravel I had made of two small rocks during the time I had brooded on my boulder, dusted my palms against my Levi's and lifted myself above the brush. I turned toward home, the tops of the underbrush ticking off the distance against my trailing toes. But oddly I felt a brief remote pang—almost of—regret?

As I neared the Canyon I heard the cry and saw one after another of the Group shoot upward toward Baldy. I forgot that momentary pang and shot upward with the rest of them. And my hands were among the first to feel the tingly hot-and-cold sleekness of the ship that was cooling yet from the heat of entry into the atmosphere. It was only a matter of minutes before the hands of the whole Group from the Canyon bore the ship downward from the clouds to the haven of the pine flats beyond Cougar—bore it rejoicing, singing an almost forgotten welcome song of the People.

Still tingling to the song I rushed to Obla's house, bringing, as always, any new event to her, since she could come to none.

"Obla! Obla!" I cried as I slammed in through her door. "They've come! They've come! They're here! Someone from the New Home— Then I remembered, and I went in to her mind. The excitement so filled my own mind that I didn't even have to verbalize for her before she caught the sight. Through my wordlessly sputtering delight I caught her faint chuckle. "Bram, the ship couldn't have rainbows around it and be diamond-studded from end to end!"

I laughed, too, a little abashed. "No, I guess not," I thought back at her. "But it should have a halo on it!"

Then for the next while I sat in the quiet room and relived every second of the event for Obla: the sights, the sounds, the smells, the feel of everything, including a detailed description of the—haloless—ship. And Obla, deaf, blind, voiceless, armless, legless, Obla who would horrify most any outsider, lived the whole event with me, questioned me minutely, and finally lifted her unheard voice with the rest of us in the song of welcome.

"Obla." I moved closer to her and looked down at the quiet scarred face, framed in the abundance of dark vigorous hair. "Obla, it means the Home, the real Home. And for you—"

"And for me—" Her lips tightened and her eyelids flattened. Then the curtain of her hair swirled across her face as she hid herself from my eyes. "Perhaps a kinder world to hide this hideous—"

"Not hideous!" I cried indignantly.

Her soft chuckle tickled my mind. "Well, *not*, anyway," she said. "You'll have to admit that the explosion didn't leave much of me—" Her hair flowed back from her face and spread across the pillow.

"The part of you that counts!" I exclaimed.

"On Earth you need a physical container. One that functions. And just once I wish that—" Her mind blanked before I could catch her wish. The glass of water lifted from the bedside stand and hovered at her mouth. She drank briefly. The glass slid back to its place.

"So you're all afire to blast off?" her thought teased. "Back to civilization! Farewell to the rugged frontier!"

"Yes, I am," I said defiantly. "You know how I feel. It's criminal to waste lives like ours. If we can't live to capacity here let's go Home!"

"To which Home?" she questioned. "The one we knew is gone. What is the new one like?"

"Well—" I hesitated, "I don't know. We haven't communicated yet. But it must be almost like the old Home. At least it's probably inhabited by the People, our People."

"Are you so sure we're still the same People?" Obla persisted. "Or that they are? Time and distance can change—"

"Of course we're the same," I cried. "That's like asking if a dog is a dog in the Canyon just because he was born in Socorro."

"I had a dog once," Obla said. "A long time ago. He thought he was people because he'd never been around other dogs. It took him six months to learn to bark. It came as quite a blow to him when he found out he was a dog."

"If you mean we've deteriorated since we came—"

"You chose the dog, not I. Let's not quarrel. Besides I didn't say that *we* were the dog."

"Yeah, but—"

"Yeah, but—" she echoed, amused, and I laughed.

"Darn you, Obla, that's the way most of my arguments with you end—yeah-but, yeah-but!"

"Why don't they come out?" I rapped impatiently against the vast seamless bulk, shadowy above me in the night. "What's the delay?"

"You're being a child, Bram," Jemmy said. "They have their reasons for waiting. Remember this is a strange world to them. They must be sure—"

"Sure!" I gestured impatiently. "We've *told* them the air's okay and there's no viruses waiting to snap them off. Besides they have their personal shields. They don't even have to *touch* this earth if they don't want to. Why don't they come out?"

"Bram." I recognized the tone of Jemmy's voice.

"Oh, I know, I know," I said. "Impatience, impatience. Everything in its own good time. But now, Jemmy, now that they're here, you and Valancy will have to give in. They'll make you see that the thing for us People to do is to get out completely or else get in there with the Outsiders and clean up this mess of a world. With this new help we could do it easily. We could take over key positions—"

"No matter how many have come—and we don't know yet how many there are," Jemmy said, "this 'taking over' isn't the way of the People. Things must grow. You only graft in extreme cases. And destroy practically never. But let's not get involved in all that again now. Valancy—"

Valancy slanted down, the stars behind her, from above the ship. "Jemmy." Their hands brushed as her feet reached the ground. There it was again. That wordless flame of joy, that completeness as they met, after a long ten minutes' separation. *That* made me impatient, too. I never felt that kind of oneness with anyone.

I heard Valancy's little laugh. "Oh, Bram," she said, "do you have to have your whole dinner in one gulp? Can't you be content to wait for anything?"

"It might be a good idea for you to do a little concentrated

229

thinking," Jemmy said. "They won't be coming out until morning. You stay here on guard tonight—"

"On guard against what?" I asked.

"Against impatience," Jemmy said, his voice taking on the Old One tone that expected obedience without having to demand it. Amusement had crept back into his voice before his next sentence. "For the good of your soul, Bram, and the contemplation of your sins, keep watch this whole night. I have a couple of blankets in the pickup." He gestured, and the blankets drifted through the scrub oak. "There, that'll hold you till morning."

I watched the two of them meet with the pickup truck above the thin trickle of the creek. Valancy called back, "Thinking *might* help, Bram. You should try it."

A startled night bird flapped dismally ahead of them for a while, and then the darkness took them all.

I spread the blankets on the sand by the ship, leaning against the smooth coolness of its outer skin, marveling anew at its seamlessness, the unbroken flow along its full length. Somewhere there had to be an exit, but right now the evening light ran uninterrupted from glowing end to glowing end.

Who was in there? How many were in there? A ship of this size could carry hundreds. Their communicator and ours had spoken briefly together, ours stumbling a little with words we remembered of the Home tongue that seemed to have changed or fallen out of use, but no mention of numbers was made before the final thought: "We are tired. It's a long journey. Thanks be to the Power, the Presence and the Name that we have found you. We will rest until morning."

The drone of a high-flying turbo-jet above the Canyon caught my ear. I glanced quickly up. Our un-light still humped itself up over the betraying shine of the ship. I relaxed on the blankets, wondering—wondering. . . .

It was so long ago—back in my grandparents' day—that it all happened. The Home, smashed to a handful of glittering confetti—the People scattered to every compass point, looking for refuge. It was all in my memory, the stream of remembrance that ties the People so strongly together. If I let myself I could suffer the loss, the wandering, the tedium and terror of the search for a new world. I could live again the shrieking in-

230

candescent entry into Earth's atmosphere, the heat, the vibration, the wrenching and shattering. And I could share the bereavement, the tears, the blinding maiming agony of some of the survivors who made it to Earth. And I could hide and dodge and run and die with all who suffered the settlement period—trying to find the best way to fit in unnoticed among the people of Earth and yet not lose our identity as the People.

But this was all the past—though sometimes I wonder if anything is ever past. It is the future I'm impatient for. Why, look at the area of international relations alone. Valancy could sit at the table at the next summit conference and read the truth behind all the closed wary sparring faces—truth naked and blinding as the glint of the moon on the edge of a metal door—opening—opening. . . .

I snatched myself to awareness. Someone was leaving the ship. I lifted a couple of inches off the sand and slid along quietly in the shadow. The figure came out, carefully, fearfully. The door swung shut and the figure straightened. Cautious step followed cautious step; then, in a sudden flurry of movement, the figure was running down the creek bed—fast! Fast! For about a hundred feet, and then it collapsed, face down into the sand.

I streaked over and hovered. "Hi!" I said.

Convulsively the figure turned over and I was looking down into her face. I caught her name—Salla.

"Are you hurt?" I asked audibly.

"No," she thought. "No," she articulated with an effort. "I'm not used to—" she groped, "running." She sounded apologetic, not for being unused to running but for running. She sat up and I sat down. We acquainted each other with our faces, and I liked very much what I saw. It was a sort of restatement of Valancy's luminously pale skin and dark eyes and warm lovely mouth. She turned away and I caught the faint glimmer of her personal shield.

"You don't need it," I said. "It's warm and pleasant tonight."

"But—" Again I caught the embarrassed apology.

"Oh, surely not always!" I protested. "What a grim deal. Shields are only for emergencies!"

She hesitated a moment and then the glimmer died. I caught the faint fragrance of her and thought ruefully that if I had a

—fragrance?—it was probably compounded of barnyard, lumber mill and supper hamburgers.

She drew a deep cautious breath. "Oh! Growing things! Life everywhere! We've been so long on the way. Smell it!"

Obligingly I did, but was conscious only of a crushed manzanita smell from beneath the ship.

This is a kind of an aside, because I can't stop in my story at every turn and try to explain. Outsiders, I suppose, have no parallel for the way Salla and I got acquainted. Under all the talk, under all the activity and busy-ness in the times that followed, was a deep underflow of communication between us. I had felt this same type of awareness before when our in-gathering brought new members of the Group to the Canyon, but never quite so strongly as with Salla. It must have been more noticeable because we lacked many of the common experiences that are shared by those who have occupied the same earth together since birth. That must have been it.

"I remember," Salla said as she sifted sand through slender unused-looking hands, "when I was very small I went out in the rain." She paused, as though for a reaction. "Without my shield," she amplified. Again the pause. "I got *wet!*" she cried, determined, apparently, to shock me.

"Last week," I said, "I walked in the rain and got so wet that my shoes squelched at every step and the clean taste of rain was in my mouth. It's one of my favorite pastimes. There's something so quiet about rain. Even when there's wind and thunder there's a stillness about it. I like it."

Then, shaken by hearing myself say such things aloud, I sifted sand, too, a little violently at first.

She reached over with a slender milky finger and touched my hand. "Brown," she said. Then, "Tan," as she caught my thought.

"The sun," I said. "We're out in the sun so much, unshielded, that it browns our skins or freckles them, or burns the living daylight out of us if we're not careful."

"Then you still live in touch of Earth. At Home we seldom ever—" Her words faded and I caught a capsuled feeling that might have been real cozy if you were born to it, but . . .

"How come?" I asked. "What's with your world that you

232

have to shield all the time?" I felt a pang for my pictured Eden. . . .

"We don't *have* to. At least not any more. When we arrived at the new Home we had to do a pretty thorough renovating job. We—of course this was my grandparents—wanted it as nearly like the old Home as possible. We've done wonderfully well copying the vegetation and hills and valleys and streams, but—" guilt tinged her words, "it's still a copy—nothing casual and—and thoughtless. By the time the new Home was livable we'd got into the habit of shielding. It was just what one did automatically. I don't believe Mother has gone unshielded outside her own sleep-room in all her life. You just—don't—"

I sprawled my arm across the sand, feeling it grit against my skin. Real cozy, but . . .

She sighed. "One time—I was old enough to know better, they told me—one time I walked in the sun unshielded. I got muddy and got my hands dirty and tore my dress." She brought out the untidy words with an effort, as though using extreme slang at a very prim gathering. "And I tangled my hair so completely in a tree that I had to pull some of it out to get free." There was no bravado in her voice now. Now she was sharing with me one of the most precious of her memories—one not quite socially acceptable among her own.

I touched her hand lightly, since I do not communicate too freely without contact, and saw her.

She was stealing out of the house before dawn—strange house, strange landscape, strange world—easing the door shut, lifting quickly out into the grove below the house. Her flame of rebellion wasn't strange to me, though. I knew it too well myself. Then she dropped her shield. I gasped with her because I was feeling, as newly as though I were the First in a brand-new Home, the movement of wind on my face, on my arms. I was even conscious of it streaming like tiny rivers between my fingers. I felt the soil beneath my hesitant feet, the soft packed clay, the outline of a leaf, the harsh stab of gravel, the granular sandiness of the water's edge. The splash of water against my legs was as sharp as a bite into lemon. And wetness! I had no idea that wetness was such an individual feeling. I can't remember when first I waded in water, or whether I ever felt wetness to know consciously, "This is wetness." The newness! It was like nothing I'd felt before.

Then suddenly there was the smell of crushed manzanita again, and Salla's hand had moved from beneath mine.

"Mother's questing for me," she whispered. "She has no idea I'm here. She'd have a *quanic* if she knew. I must go before she gets no answer from my room."

"When are you all coming out?"

"Tomorrow, I think, Laam will have to rest longer. He's our Motiver, you know. It was exhausting bringing the ship into the atmosphere. More so than the whole rest of the trip. But the rest of us—"

"How many?" I whispered as she glided away from me and up the curve of the ship.

"Oh," she whispered back, "there's—" The door opened and she slid inside and it closed.

"Dream sweetly," I heard soundlessly, then astonishingly, the touch of a soft cheek against one of my cheeks, and the warm movement of lips against the other. I was startled and confused, though pleased, until with a laugh I realized that I had been caught between the mother's questing and Salla's reply.

"Dream sweetly," I thought, and rolled myself in my blankets.

Something wakened me in the empty hours before dawn. I lay there feeling snatched out of sleep like a fish out of water, shivering in the interval between putting off sleep and putting on awakeness.

"I'm supposed to think," I thought dully. "Concentrated thinking."

So I thought. I thought of my People, biding their time, biding their time, waiting, waiting, walking when they could be flying. Think, *think*, what we could do if we stopped waiting and really got going. Think of Bethie, our Sensitive, in a medical center, reading the illnesses and ailments to the doctors. No more chance for patients to hide behind imaginary illnesses. No wrong diagnoses, no delay in identification of conditions. Of course there are only one Bethie and the few Sorters we have who could serve a little less effectively, but it would be a beginning.

Think of our Sorters, helping to straighten people out, able to search their deepest beings and pry the scabs off ancient cankers

234

and wounds and let healing into the suffering intricacies of the mind.

Think of our ability to lift, to transport, to communicate, to *use* Earth instead of submitting to it. Hadn't Man been given dominion over Earth? Hadn't he forfeited it somewhere along the way? Couldn't we help point him back to the path again?

I twisted with this concentrated restatement of all my questions. Why couldn't this all be so now, *now!*

But, "No," say the Old Ones. "Wait," says Jemmy. "Not now," says Valancy.

"But look!" I wanted to yell. "They're headed for space! Trying to get there on a Pogo stick. Look at Laam! He brought that ship to us from some far Homeland without lifting his hand, without gadgets in his comfortable motive-room. Take any of us. I myself could lift our pickup high enough to need my shield to keep me breathing. I'll bet even I in one of those sealed high-flying planes could take it to the verge of space, just this side of the escape rim. And any Motiver could take it over the rim and the hard part is over. Of course, though all of us can lift we have only two Motivers, but it would be a start!"

But, "No," say the Old Ones. "Wait," says Jemmy. "Not now," says Valancy.

All right, so it would be doing violence to the scheme of things, grafting a third arm onto an organism designed for two. So the Earth ones will develop along our line someday—look at Peter and Dita and that Francher kid and Bethie. So someday when it is earned they will have it. So—let's go, then! Let's find another Home. Let's take to space and leave them their Earth. Let's let them have their time—if they don't die of it first. Let's leave. Let's get out of this crummy joint. Let's go somewhere where we can be ourselves all the time, openly unashamed!

I pounded my fists on the blanket, then ruefully wiped the flecks of sand from my lips and tongue and grunted a laugh at myself. I caught my breath, then relaxed.

"Okay, Davy," I said, "what are you doing out so early?"

"I haven't been to bed," Davy said, drifting out of the shadows. "Dad said I could try my scriber tonight. I just got it finished."

"That thing?" I laughed up at him. "What could you scribe at night?"

"Well—" Davy sat down in the air above my blanket, rubbing his thumbs on the tiny box he was holding. "I thought it might be able to scribe dreams, but it won't. Not enough verbalizing in them. I checked my whole family and used up half my scribe tape. Gotta make some more today!"

"Nasty break," I said. "Back to the drawing boards, boy."

"Oh, I don't know," Davy said. "I tried it on your dreams—" He flipped up out of my casual swipe at him. "But I couldn't get anything. So I ran a chill down your spine—"

"You rat," I said, too lazy to resent it very much. "That's why I woke up so hard and quick."

"Yup," he said, drifting back over me. "So I tried it on you awake. More concentrated thought patterns."

"Hey!" I sat up slowly. "Concentrated thought?"

"Take this last part." Davy drifted up again. There was a quacking gabble. "Ope!" he said. "Forgot the slowdown. Thoughts are fast. Now—"

And clearly and minutely, the way a voice sometimes sounds from a telephone receiver, I heard myself yelling, "Let's leave, let's get out of this crummy joint—"

"Davy!" I yelled, launching myself upward, encumbered as I was with blankets.

"Watch it! Watch it!" he cried, holding the scriber away from me as we tumbled in the air. "Group interest! I claim Group interest! With the ship here now—"

"Group interest, nothing!" I said as I finally got my hands on the scriber. "You're forgetting privacy of thought—and the penalty for violation thereof." I caught his flying thought and pushed the right area on the box to erase the record.

"Dagnab!" said Davy, disgruntled. "My first invention and you erase my first recording on it."

"Nasty break!" I said. Then I tossed the box to him. "But say!" I reached up and pulled him down to me. "Obla! Think about Obla and this screwy gadget!"

"Yeah!" His face lighted up, then blanked as he was snatched along by the train of thought. "Yeah! Obla—no audible voice —" He had already forgotten me before the trees received him.

It wasn't that I had been ashamed of my thoughts. It was only that they sounded so—so naked, made audible. I stood there, my hands flattened against the beautiful ship and felt my conviction solidify. "Let's go. Let's leave. If there isn't room for us on this ship we can build others. Let's find a real Home somewhere. Either find one or build one."

I think it was at that moment that I began to say good-by to Earth, almost subconsciously beginning to sever the ties that bound me to it. Like the slow out-fanning of a lifting wing, the direction of my thoughts turned skyward. I lifted my eyes. "This time next year," I thought, "I won't be watching morning lighting up Old Baldy."

By midmorning the whole of the Group, including the whole Group from Bendo, which had been notified, was waiting on the hillside near the ship. There was very little audible speech and not much gaiety. The ship brought back too much of the past, and the dark streams of memory were coursing through the Group. I latched onto one stream and found only the shadows of the Crossing in it. "But the Home," I interjected, "the Home before!"

Just then a glitter against the bulk of the ship drew our attention. The door was opening. There was a pause, and then there were the four of them, Salla and her parents and another older fellow. The slight glintings of their personal shields were securely about them, and, as they winced against the down-pouring sun, their shields thickened above their heads and took on a deep blue tint.

The Oldest, his blind face turned to the ship, spoke on a Group stream.

"Welcome to the Group." His thought was organ-toned and cordial. "Thrice welcome among us. You are the first from the Home to follow us to Earth. We are eager for the news of our friends."

There was a sudden babble of thoughts. "Is Anna with you? Is Mark? Is Santhy? Is Bediah?"

"Wait, wait—" The Father lifted his arms imploringly. "I cannot answer all of you at once except by saying—there are only the four of us in the ship."

"Four!" The astonished thought almost lifted an echo from Baldy.

"Why, yes," answered—he gave us his name—Shua. "My family and I and our Motiver here, Laam."

"Then all the rest—?" Several of us slipped to our knees with the Sign trembling on our fingers.

"Oh no! No!" Shua was shocked. "No, we fared very well in our new Home. Almost all your friends await you eagerly. As you remember, ours was the group living adjacent to yours on the Home. Our Group and two others reached our new Home. Why, we brought this ship empty so we could take you all Home!"

"Home?" For a stunned moment the word hung almost visibly in the air above us.

Then, "Home!" The cry rose and swelled and broke to audibility as the whole Group took to the sky as one. It was such a jubilant ecstatic cry that it shook an echo sufficient to frighten a pair of blue jays from a clump of pines on the flat.

"Why they must all think the way I do!" I thought, astonished, as I joined in the upsurge and the jubilant chorus of the wordless Homeward song. Then I flatted a little as I wondered if any of them shared with me the sudden pang I had felt before. I tucked it quickly away, deep enough so that only a Sorter would be able to find it, and quickly cradled the Francher kid in my lifting—he hadn't learned to go much beyond the treetops yet, and the Group was leaving him behind. . . .

"There's four of them," I thought breathlessly at Obla. "Only four. They brought the ship to take us Home."

Obla turned her blind face to me. "To take us all? Just like that?"

"Well, yes," I replied, frowning a little. "I guess just like that—whatever that means."

"After all I suppose castaways are always eager for rescue," Obla said. Then, gently mocking, "I suppose you're all packed?"

"I've been packed almost since I was born. Haven't I always been talking about getting out of this bind that holds us back?"

"You have," Obla thought. "Exhaustively talked about it. Put your hand out the window, Bram. Take a handful of sun."

I did, filling my palm with the tingling brightness. "Pour

it out." I tilted my hand and felt the warm flow of escaping light. "No more Earth sun ever again," she said. "Not ever!"

"Darn you, Obla, cut it out!" I cried.

"You weren't so entirely sure yourself, were you? Even after all your protestations. Even in spite of that big warm wonder growing inside you."

"Warm wonder?" Then I felt my face heat up. "Oh," I said awkwardly. "That's only natural interest in a stranger—a stranger from Home!" I felt excitement mounting. "Just think, Obla! From Home!"

"A stranger from Home." Obla's thought was a little sad. "Listen to your words, Bram. A *stranger* from Home. Whenever have People been strangers to one another?"

"You're playing with words now. Let me tell you the whole thing—"

I have used Obla for a sounding board ever since I can remember. I have no memory of her physically complete. I became conscious of her only after her disaster and mine. The same explosion that maimed her took my parents. They were trying to get some Outsiders out of a crashed plane and didn't quite make it. Some of my most grandiose schemes have echoed hollow and empty against the listening receptiveness of Obla. And some of my shyest thoughts have grown to monumental strength with her uncritical acceptance of them. Somehow, when you hear your own ideas, crisply cut for transmission, they are stripped of anything extraneous and stand naked of pretensions, and *then* you can get a decent perspective on them.

"Poor child," she cut in when I told her of Salla's hair being caught. "Poor child, to feel that pain is a privilege—"

"Better that than having pain a way of life!" I flashed. "Who should know better than you?"

"Perhaps, perhaps. Who is to say which is better—to hunger and be fed, or to be fed so continuously that you never know hunger? Sometimes a little fasting is good for the soul. Think of a cold drink of water after an afternoon in the hayfield."

I shivered at the delicious recollection. "Well, *anyway . . .*" and I finished the account for her. I was almost out of the door before I suddenly realized that I hadn't mentioned Davy at all! I went back and told her. Before I was half through her face twisted and her hair swirled protectively over it. When I finished

I stood there awkwardly, not knowing exactly what to do. Then I caught a faint echo of her thought. "A voice again . . ." I think a little of my contempt for gadgets died at the moment. Anything that could pleasure Obla . . .

I thought I was troubled about whether we should go or stay, until the afternoon I found all the Blends and In-gathereds sitting together on the boulders above Cougar Creek. Dita was trailing the water from her bare toes, and all the rest were concentrating on the falling of the drops as though there were some answer in them. The Francher kid was making a sharp crystal scale out of their falling. I came openly so there was no thought of eavesdropping, but I don't think they were fully aware that I was there.

"But for me—" Dita drew her knees up to her chest and clasped her wet feet in her hands, "for me it's different. You're Blends, or all of the People. But I'm all of Earth. My roots are anchored in this old rock. Think what it would mean to me to say good-by to my world. Think back to the Crossing—" A ripple of discomfort moved through the Group. "You see? And yet, to stay—to watch the People go, to know them gone—" She laid her cheek against her knees.

The quick comfort of the others enveloped her, and Low moved to the boulder beside her.

"It'd be as bad for us to leave," he said. "Sure, we're of the People, but this is the only Home we've known. I didn't grow up in a Group. None of us did. All of our roots are firmly set here, too. To leave—"

"What has the New Home to offer that we don't have here?" Peter started a little whirlpool in the shallow stream below.

"Well—" Low stilled the whirlpool and spoke into a lengthening silence, "ask Bram. He's all afire to blast off." He grinned over his shoulder at me.

"The new Home is *our* world," I said, drifting over to them, gathering my scattered thoughts. "We would be among our own. No more concealment. No more trying to fit in where we don't fit. No more holding back, holding back, when we could be doing so much."

I could feel the surge and swirl of thoughts around me—each person aligning himself to the vision of the Home. Without any further word they all left the creek, absorbed in the problem. As they slowly scattered there was not an echo of a thought. Everyone was shutting himself up with his own reactions.

All the peace and tranquillity of Cougar Canyon was gone. Oh, sure, the light still slanted brightly through the trees at dawn, the wind still stirred the branches in the hot quiet afternoons and occasionally whipped up little whirlwinds to dance the dried leaves in a brief flurry of action, and the slender new moon was cleanly bright in the evening sky—but it was all overlaid with a big question mark.

I couldn't settle to anything. Halfway through ripping a plank at the mill I'd think, "Why bother? We'll be gone soon." And then the spasm of acute pleasure and anticipation would somehow turn to the pain of bereavement and I'd feel like clutching a handful of sawdust and—well—sobbing into it.

And late at night, changing the headgates to irrigate another alfalfa field, I'd kick the moss-slick wet boards and think exultantly, "When we get *there* we won't have to go through this mumbo-jumbo. We'll rain the water where and when we want it!"

Then again, I'd lie in the edge of the hot sun, my head in the shade of the cottonwoods, and feel the deep soaking warmth to my very bone, smell the waiting dusty smell of the afternoon, feel sleep wrapping itself around my thoughts and hear the sudden creaking cries of the red-winged blackbirds in the far fields, and suddenly *know* that I couldn't leave it. Couldn't give up Earth for any thing or any place.

But there was Salla. Showing her Earth was like nothing you could ever imagine. For instance it never occurred to her that things could hurt her. Like the day I found her halfway across Furnace Flat, huddled under a piñon pine, cradling her bare feet in her hands and rocking with pain.

"Where are your shoes?" It was the first thing I could think of as I hunched beside her.

"Shoes?" She caught the picture from me. "Oh, shoes. My—sandals—are at the ship. I wanted to *feel* this world. We shield so much at home that I couldn't tell you a thing about textures there. But the sand was so good the first night, and water is wonderful, I thought this black glowing smoothness and splin-

teredness would be a different sort of texture." She smiled ruefully. "It is. It's hot and—and—"

I supplied a word, "Hurty. I should think so. This shale flat
heats up like a furnace this time of day. That's why it's called
Furnace Flat."

"I landed in the middle of it, running. I was so surprised that
I didn't have sense enough to lift or shield."

"Let me see." I loosened her fingers and took one of her
slender white feet in my hand. *"Adonday Veeah!"* I whistled.
Carefully I picked off a few loose flakes of bloodstained shale.
"You've practically blistered your feet, too. Don't you know the
sun can be vicious this time of day?"

"I know now." She took her feet back and peered at the
sole. "Look! There's blood!"

"Yep. That's usual when you puncture your skin. Better come
on back to the house and get those feet taken care of."

"Taken care of?"

"Sure. Antiseptic for the germs, salve for the burns. You
won't go hunting for a day or two. Not with your feet, anyway."

"Can't we just no-bi and transgraph? It's so much simpler."

"Indubitably," I said, lifting sitting as she did and straightening up in the air above the path. "If I knew what you were
talking about." We headed for the house.

"Well, at Home the Healers—"

"This is Earth," I said. "We have no Healers as yet. Only in
so far as our Sensitive can help out those who know about healing. It's mostly a do-it-yourself deal with us. And who
knows, you might be allergic to us and sprout day lilies at every
puncture. It'll probably worry your mother—"

"Mother—" There was a curious pause. "Mother is annoyed
with me already. She feels that I'm definitely *undene*. She wishes
she'd left me Home. She's afraid I'll never be the same again."

"Undene?" I asked, because Salla had sent out no clarification
with the term.

"Yes," she said, and I caught at visualization until light finally
began to dawn.

"Well! We don't exactly eat peas with our knives or wipe
our noses on our sleeves! We can be pretty couth when we set
our minds to it."

242

"I know, I know," she hastened to say, "but Mother—well, you know some mothers."

"Yes, I know. But if you never walk or climb or swim or anything like that what do you do for fun?"

"It's not that we never do them. But seldom casually and unthinkingly. We're supposed to outgrow the need for childish activities like that. We're supposed to be capable of more intellectual pleasures."

"Like what?" I held the branches aside for her to descend to the kitchen door, and nearly kinked my shoulder trying to do that and open the door for her simultaneously. After several false starts and stops and a feeling of utter foolishness, like the one you get when you try to dodge past a person who tries to dodge past you, we ended up at the kitchen table with Salla gasping at the smart of the Merthiolate. "Like what?" I repeated.

"Hoosh! That's quite a sensation." She loosened her clutch on her ankles and relaxed under the soothing salve I spread on her reddened feet.

"Well, Mother's favorite—and she does it very well—is Anticipating. She likes roses."

"So do I," I said, bewildered, "but I seldom Anticipate in connection with them."

Salla laughed. I liked to hear her laugh. It was more nearly a musical phrase than a laugh. The Francher kid, the first time he heard it, made a composition of it. Of course neither he nor I liked it very much when the other kids in the Canyon, revved it up and used it for a dance tune, but I must admit it had quite a beat. . . . Well, anyway, Salla laughed.

"You know, for two people using the same words we certainly come out at different comprehensions. No—what Mother likes is Anticipating a rose. She chooses a bud that looks interesting—she knows all the finer distinctions—then she *makes* a rose, synthetic, as nearly like the real bud as she can. Then, for two or three days, she sees if she can anticipate every movement of the opening of the real rose by opening her synthetic simultaneously, or, if she's very adept, just barely ahead of the other." She laughed again. "It's one of our family stories—the time she chose a bud that did nothing for two

243

days, then shivered to dust. Somehow it had been sprayed with *destro*. Mother's never quite got over the humiliation."

"Maybe I'm being *undene*," I said, "but I can't see spending two days watching a rose bud."

"And yet you spent a whole hour just looking at the sky last evening. And four of you spent hours last night receiving and displaying cards. You got quite emotional over it several times."

"Umm—well, yes. But that's different. A sunset like that, and the way Jemmy plays—" I caught the teasing in her eyes and we laughed together. Laughter needs no interpreter, at least not our laughter.

Salla took so much pleasure in sampling our world that, as is usual, I discovered things about our neighborhood I hadn't known before. It was she who found the cave, because she was curious about the tiny trickle of water high on the slope of Baldy.

"Just a spring," I told her as we looked up at the dark streak that marked a fold in the massive cliff.

"Just a spring," she mocked. "In this land of little water is there such a thing as *just* a spring?"

"It's not worth anything," I protested, following her up into the air. "You can't even drink from it."

"It could ease a heart hunger, though. The sight of wetness in an arid land."

"It can't even splash," I said as we neared the streak.

"No," Salla said, holding her forefinger to the end of the moisture. "But it can grow things." Lightly she touched the minute green plants that clung to the rock wall and the dampness.

"Pretty," I said perfunctorily. "But look at the view from here."

We turned around, pressing our backs to the sheer cliff, and looked out over the vast stretches of red-to-purple-to-blue ranges of mountains, jutting fiercely naked or solidly forested or speckled with growth as far as we could see. And lazily, far away, a shaft of smelter smoke rose and bent almost at right angles as an upper current caught it and thinned it to haze. Below, fold after fold of the hills hugged protectively to themselves the tiny comings and goings and dwelling places of those who had lost themselves in the vastness.

"And yet," Salla almost whispered, "if you're lost in vast enough vastness you find yourself—a different self, a self that has only Being and the Presence to contemplate."

"True," I said, breathing deeply of sun and pine and hot granite. "But not many reach that vastness. Most of us size our little worlds to hold enough distractions to keep us from having to contemplate Being and God."

There was a moment's deep silence as we let our own thoughts close the subject. Then Salla lifted and I started down.

"Hey!" I called. "That's up!"

"I know it," she called. "And that's down! I still haven't found the spring!"

So I lifted, too, grumbling at the stubbornness of women, and arrived even with Salla just as she perched tentatively on a sharp spur of rock on the edge of the vegetation-covered gash that was the beginning of the oozing wetness. She looked straight down the dizzy thousands of feet below us.

"What beautiful downness!" she said, pleased.

"If you were afraid of heights—"

She looked at me quickly. "*Are* some people? Really?"

"Some are. I read one, one time. Would you care to try the texture of *that*?" And I created for her the horrified frantic dying terror of an Outsider friend of mine who hardly dares look out of a second-story window.

"Oh, no!" She paled and clung to the scanty draping of vines and branches of the cleft. "No more! No more!"

"I'm sorry. But it *is* a different sort of emotion. I think of it every time I read—'neither height nor depth nor any other creature.' Height to my friend is a creature—a horrible hovering destroyer waiting to pounce on him."

"It's too bad," Salla said, "that he doesn't remember to go on to the next phrase, and learn to lose his fear—"

By quick common consent we switched subjects in midair.

"This is the source," I said. "Satisfied?"

"No." She groped among the vines. "I want to see a trickle trickle, and a drop drop from the beginning." She burrowed deeper.

Rolling my eyes to heaven for patience, I helped her hold

back the vines. She reached for the next layer—and suddenly wasn't there.

"Salla!" I scrabbled at the vines. "Salla!"

"H-h-here," I caught her subvocal answer.

"Talk!" I said as I felt her thought melt out of my consciousness.

"I *am* talking!" Her reply broke to audibility on the last word. "And I'm sitting in some awfully cold wet water. Do come in." I squirmed cautiously through the narrow cleft into the darkness and stumbled to my knees in icy water almost waist-deep.

"It's dark," Salla whispered, and her voice ran huskily around the place.

"Wait for your eyes to change," I whispered back, and, groping through the water, caught her hand and clung to it. But even after a breathless sort of pause our eyes could not pick up enough light to see by—only faint green shimmer where the cleft was.

"Had enough?" I asked. "Is this trickly and drippy enough?" I lifted our hands and the water sluiced off our elbows.

"I want to see," she protested.

"Matches are inoperative when they're wet. Flashlight have I none. Suggestions?"

"Well, no. You don't have any Glowers living here, do you?"

"Since the word rings no bell, I guess not. But, say!" I dropped her hand and, rising to my knees, fumbled for my pocket. "Dita taught me—or tried to after Valancy told her how come—" I broke off, immersed in the problem of trying to get a hand into and out of the pocket of skin-tight wet Levi's.

"I know I'm an Outlander," Salla said plaintively, "but I thought I had a fairly comprehensive knowledge of your language."

"Dita's the Outsider that we found with Low. She's got some Designs and Persuasions none of us have. There!" I grunted, and settled back in the water. "Now if I can remember."

I held the thin dime between my fingers and shifted all those multiples of mental gears that are so complicated until

246

you work your way through their complexity to the under-lying simplicity. I concentrated my whole self on that little disc of metal. There was a sudden blinding spurt of light. Salla cried out, and I damped the light quickly to a more practical level.

"I did it!" I cried. "I glowed it first thing, this time! It took me half an hour last time to get a spark!"

Salla was looking in wonder at the tiny globe of brilliance in my hand. "And an Outsider can do *that?*"

"Can do!" I said, suddenly very proud of our Outsiders. "And so can I, now! There you are, ma'am," I twanged. "Yore light, yore cave—look to yore little heart's content."

I don't suppose it was much as caves go. The floor was sand, pale, granular, almost sugarlike. The pool—out of which we both dripped as soon as we sighted dry land—had no apparent source, but stayed always at the same level in spite of the slender flow that streaked the cliff. The roof was about twice my height and the pool was no farther than that across. The walls curved protectively close around the water. At first glance there was nothing special about the cave. There weren't even any stalactites or stalagmites—just the sand and the quiet pool shimmering a little in the light of the glowed coin.

"Well!" Salla sighed happily as she pushed back her heavy hair with wet hands. "This is where it begins."

"Yes." I closed my hand around the dime and watched the light spray between my fingers. "Wetly, I might point out."

Salla was scrambling across the sand on all fours.

"It's high enough to stand," I said, following her.

"I'm being a cave creature," she smiled back over her shoulder. "Not a human surveying a kingdom. It looks different from down here."

"Okay, troglodyte. How does it look down there?"

"Marvelous!" Salla's voice was very soft. "Bring the light and look!"

We lay on our stomachs and peered into the tiny tunnel, hardly a foot across, that Salla had found. I focused the light down the narrow passageway. The whole thing was a lacy network of delicate crystals, white, clear, rosy and pale green, so fragile that I held my breath lest they break. The longer I looked the more wonder I saw—miniature forests and snowflakelike laciness, flights of fairy steps, castles and spires, flowers terraced up gentle hill sides and branches of blossoms almost alive enough to sway. An arm's length down the tunnel a quietly bright pool reflected the perfection around it to double the enchantment.

Salla and I looked at each other, our faces so close together that we were mirrored in each other's eyes—eyes that stated and reaffirmed: *Ours—no one else in all the universe shares this spot with us.*

Wordlessly we sat back on the sand. I don't know about Salla, but I was having a little difficulty with my breathing, because, for some odd reason, it seemed necessary to hold my breath to shield from being as easily read as a child.

"Let's leave the light," Salla whispered. "It'll stay lighted without you, won't it?"

"Yeah. Indefinitely."

"Leave it by the little cave. Then we'll know it's always lighted and lovely."

We edged our way out of the cleft in the cliff and hovered there for a minute, laughing at our bedraggled appearance. Then we headed for home and dry clothes.

"I wish Obla could see the cave," I said impulsively. Then wished I hadn't because I caught Salla's immediate displeased protest.

"I mean," I said awkwardly, "she never gets to see—" I broke off. After all she wouldn't be able to see any better if she were there. I would have to be her eyes.

"Obla." Salla wasn't vocalizing now. "She's very near to you."

"She's almost my second self."

"A relative?"

"No. Only as souls are related."

"I can feel her in your thoughts so often. And yet—have I ever met her?"

"No. She doesn't meet people." I was holding in my mind the clean uncluttered strength of Obla; then again I caught Salla's distressed protest and her feeling of being excluded, before she shielded. Still I hesitated. I didn't want to share. Obla was more an expression of myself than a separate person. An expression that was hidden and precious. I was afraid to share—afraid that it might be like touching a finger to a fragile chemical fern in the little tunnel, that there wouldn't even be a *ping* before the perfection shivered to a shapeless powder.

Two weeks after the ship arrived a general Group meeting was called. We all gathered on the flat around the ship. It looked like a field day at first, with the flat filled with laughing lifting children playing tag above the heads of the more sedate elders. The kids my age clustered at one side, tugged toward playing tag, too, but restrained because after all you do outgrow some things—when people are looking. I sat there with them, feeling an emptiness beside me. Salla was with her parents.

The Oldest was not there. He was at home struggling to contain his being in the broken body that was becoming more and more a dissolving prison. So Jemmy called us to attention.

"Long-drawn periods of indecision are not good," he said without preliminary. "The ship has been here two weeks. We have all faced our problem—to go or to stay. There are many of us who have not yet come to a decision. This we must do soon. The ship will up a week from today. To help us decide we are now open to *brief* statements pro or con."

There was an odd tightening feeling as the whole Group flowed into a common thought stream and became a single unit instead of a mass of individuals.

"I will go." It was the thought of the Oldest from his bed back in the Canyon. "The new Home has the means to help me, so that the years yet allotted to me may be nearly painless. Since the Crossing—" He broke off, flashing an amused. "'Brief'!"

"I will stay." It was the voice of one of the young girls from Bendo. "We have only started to make Bendo a place fit to live in. I like beginnings. The new Home sounds finished, to me."

"I don't want to go away," a very young voice piped. "My radishes are just coming up and I hafta water them all the time. They'd die if I left." Amusement rippled through the Group and relaxed us.

"I'll go." It was Matt, called back from Tech by the ship's arrival. "In the Home my field of specialization has developed

249

far beyond what we have at Tech or anywhere else. But I'm coming back."

"There can be no free and easy passage back and forth between the Home and Earth," Jemmy warned, "for a number of very valid reasons."

"I'll chance it," Matt said. "I'll make it back."

"I'm staying," the Francher kid said. "Here on Earth we're different with a plus. There we'd be different with a minus. What we can do and do well won't be special there. I don't want to go where I'd be making ABC songs. I want my music to go on being big."

"I'm going," Jake said, his voice mocking as usual. "I'm through horsing around. I'm going to become a solid citizen. But I want to go in for—" His verbalization stopped, and all I could comprehend was an angular sort of concept wound with time and space as with serpentine. I saw my own blankness on the faces around me and felt a little less stupid. "See," Jake said. "That's what I've been having on the tip of my mind for a long time. Shua tells me they've got a fair beginning on it there. I'll be willing to ABC it for a while for a chance at something like that."

I cleared my throat. Here was my chance to broadcast to the whole Group what I intended to do! Apparently I was the only one seeing the situation clearly enough. "I—"

It was as though I'd stepped into a dense fog bank. I felt as though I'd gone blind and dumb at one stroke. I had a feeling of being torn like a piece of paper. I lost all my breath as I became vividly conscious of my actual thoughts. *I didn't want to go!* I was snatched into a mad whirlpool of thoughts at this realization. How could I stay after all I'd said? How could I go and know Earth no more? How could I stay and let Salla go? How could I go and leave Obla behind? Dimly I heard someone else's voice finishing:

". . . because Home or no Home, *this* is Home to me!"

I closed my gaping wordless mouth and wet my dry lips. I could see again—see the Group slowly dissolving—the Bendo Group gathering together under the trees, the rest drifting away from the flat. Low leaned across the rock. "S'matter, feller?" he laughed. "Cat got your tongue? I expected a blast of eloquence from you that'd push the whole Group up the gangplank."

"Bram's bashful!" Dita teased. "He doesn't like to make his convictions known!"

I tried a sort of smile. "Pity me, people," I said. "Before you stands a creature shorn of convictions, nekkid as a jay bird in the cold winds of indecision."

"Fresh out of long-johns," Peter said, sobering. "But there's plenty of sympathy available."

"Thanks," I said. "Noted and appreciated."

I couldn't take my new doubt and indecision, the new tumult and pain to Obla—not when she was so much a part of it, so I took them up into the hills. I perched like a brooding buzzard on the stone spur outside the little cave, high above the Canyon. Wildly, until my throat ached and my voice croaked, I railed against this world and its limitations. Hoarsely I whispered over all the lets and hindrances that plagued us— that plagued me. And, infuriatingly, the world and all its echoes placidly paced my every argument with solid rebuttal. I was hearing with both ears now, one for my own voice, one for the world's reply. And my voice got fainter and fainter, and Earth's voice wasn't a whisper any more.

"Nothing is the way it should be!" I hoarsely yelled my last weary assault at the evening sky.

"And never will be, short of eternity," replied the streak of sunset crimson.

"But we could do so much more—"

"Whoever heard of bread made only of leaven?" replied the first evening star.

"We're being wasted," I whispered.

"So is the wheat when it's broadcast in the field," answered the fringe of pines on the crest of a far hill.

"But Salla will go. She'll be gone—"

And nothing answered—only the wind cried and a single piece of dislodged gravel rattled down into the darkness.

"Salla!" I cried. "Salla will be gone! Answer *that* one if you can!" But the world was through with answers. The wind became very busy humming through the dusk.

"Answer me!" I had only a whisper left.

"I will." The voice was very soft but it shook me like a blast of lightning. "I can answer." Salla eased lightly down on the spur beside me. "Salla is staying."

"Salla!" I could only clutch the rock and stare.

"Mother had a *quanic* when I told her," Salla smiled, easing the tight uncomfortable emotion. "I told her I needed a research paper to finish my Level requirements and that this would be just perfect for it.

"She said I was too young to know my own mind. I said finishing high in my Level would be quite a feather in her cap—if you'll pardon the provincialism. And she said she didn't even know your parents." Salla colored, her eyes wavering. "I told her there had been no word between us. That we were not Two-ing. Yet. Much."

"It doesn't have to be now!" I cried, grabbing both her hands. "Oh, Salla! Now we can afford to wait!" And I yanked her off the spur into the maddest wildest flight of my life. Like a couple of crazy things we split and resplit the air above Baldy, soaring and diving like drunken lightning. But all the time part of us was moving so far, so fast, another part of us was talking quietly together, planning, wondering, rejoicing, as serenely as if we were back in the cave again, seeing each other in quiet reflective eyes. Finally darkness closed in entirely and we leaned exhausted against each other, drifting slowly toward the canyon floor.

"Obla—" I said, "let's go tell Obla." There was no need to shield any part of my life from Salla any more. In fact there was a need to make it a cohesive whole, complete with both Obla and Salla.

Obla's windows were dark. That meant no one was visiting her. She would be alone. I rapped lightly on the door—my own particular rap.

"Bram? Come in!" I caught welcome from Obla.

"I brought Salla," I said. "Let me turn the light on." I stepped in.

"Wait—"

But simultaneously with her cry I flipped the light switch.

"Salla," I started, "this is—"

Salla screamed and threw her arm across her eyes; a sudden overflooding of horrified revulsion choked the room, and Obla was fluttering in the far upper corner of the room—hiding

—hiding herself behind the agonized swirl of her hair, her broken body in the twisting of her white gown, pressing itself to the walls, struggling for escape, her startled physical and mental anguish moaning almost audibly around us.

I grabbed Salla and yanked her out of the room, snapping the light off as we went. I dragged her out to the edge of the yard where the canyon walls shot upward. I flung her against the sandstone wall. She turned and hid her face against the rock, sobbing. I grabbed her shoulders and shook her.

"How could you!" I gritted between my teeth, outraged anger thickening my words. "Is *that* the kind of people the Home is turning out now? Counting arms and legs and eyes more than the person?" Her tumbling hair whipped across my chin. "Permitting rejection and disgust for any living soul? Aren't you taught even common kindness and compassion?" I wanted to hit her—to hit anything solid to protest this unthinkable thing that had been done to Obla, this unhealable wounding.

Salla snatched herself out of my grasp and hovered just out of reach, wet eyes glaring angrily down at me.

"It's your fault, too!" she snapped, tears flowing. "I'd have died rather than do a thing like that to Obla or anyone else —if I had known! You didn't tell me. You never visualized her that way—only strength and beauty and wholeness!"

"Why not!" I shot back angrily, lifting level with her. "That's the only way I ever see her any more. And trying to shift the blame—"

"It *is* your fault! Oh, Bram!" And she was crying in my arms. When she could speak again between sniffs and hiccoughs she said, "We don't have people like that at Home. I mean, I never saw a—an incomplete person. I never saw scars and mutilation. Don't you see, Bram? I was holding myself ready to receive her, completely—because she was part of you. And then to find myself embracing—" She choked. "Look— look, Bram, we have transgraph and—and regeneration—and *no* one ever stays unfinished."

I let go of her slowly, lost in wonder. "Regeneration? Transgraph?"

"Yes, yes!" Salla cried. "She can have back her legs. She can have arms again. She can have her beautiful face again. She may even get back her eyes and her voice, though I don't know for sure about that. She can be Obla again, instead of a dark prison for Obla."

"No one told us."

"No one asked."

"Common concern."

"I'll ask then. Have you any *dobic* children? And cases of *cazerinea*? Any *trimorph semia*? It's not that we don't want to ask. How are we to know *what* to ask? We've never even heard of a—a basket case." She took the word from me. "It just didn't occur to us to ask."

"I'm sorry," I said, drying her eyes with the palms of my hands, lacking anything better. "I should have told you." My words were but scant surface indications of my deep abject apology.

"Come," she said, pulling away from me. "We must go to Obla—now—right now."

It was Salla who finally coaxed Obla back down to her bed. It was Salla who held the broken weeping face against her slight young shoulder and poured the healing balms of her sorrow and understanding over Obla's wounds. And it was Salla who told Obla of what the Home held for her. Told her and told her and told her, until Obla finally believed.

All three of us were limp and weary by then, and all three content just to sit for a minute, so the explosion of Davy into the room was twice the shock it ordinarily would have been.

"Hi, Bram! Hi, Salla! Hey, Obla! I got it fixed now. It won't hiss on the s's any more and you can trip the playback yourself. Here." He plopped onto her pillow the little cube I recognized as his scriber. "Try it out. Go on. Try it out on Bram."

Obla turned her face until her cheek felt the cube. Salla looked at me in wonderment and then at Obla. There was a brief pause and then a slight click and I heard, tiny but distinct, the first audible word I'd ever heard from Obla.

"Bram! Oh, Bram! Now I can go with you. I won't be left behind. And when we get to the Home I'll be whole again! Whole again!"

Through my shock I heard Davy say, "You didn't even use one s, Obla! Say something essy, so's I can check it."

Obla thought I was going to the Home! She expected me to go with her! She didn't know I'd decided to stay. That *we* were going to stay. I met Salla's eyes. Our communication was quick and complete before the small voice said, "Salla, my sweet sister! I trust that's sufficiently 'essy'!" And I heard Obla's laugh for the first time.

So, somewhere way back there, there is a tiny cave with a dime glowing in it, keeping in trust a preciousness between Salla and me—a candle in the window of memory. Somewhere way back there are the sights and sounds, the smells and tastes, the homeness of Earth. For a while I have turned my back on the Promised Land. For our Jordan was crossed those long years ago. My trouble was that I thought that wherever I looked, just because *I* did the looking, was the goal ahead. But all the time, the Crossing, shimmering in the light of memory, had been something completed, not something yet to reach. My yearning for the Home must have been a little of the old hunger for the fleshpots that haunts any pioneering effort.

And Salla . . . Well, sometimes when I'm not looking she looks at me and then at Obla. And sometimes when she isn't looking I look at her and then at Obla. Obla has no eyes, but sometimes when we aren't looking she looks at me and then at Salla.

Things will happen to all three of us before Earth swells again in the portholes, but whatever happens Earth *will* swell in the portholes again—at least for me. And *then* I will truly be coming Home.

THE BEST IN SCIENCE FICTION AND FANTASY FROM AVON ◆ BOOKS

URSULA K. LE GUIN

The Lathe of Heaven	43547	1.95
The Dispossessed	51284	2.50

ISAAC ASIMOV

Foundation	50963	2.25
Foundation and Empire	42689	1.95
Second Foundation	45351	1.95
The Foundation Trilogy (Large Format)	50856	6.95

ROGER ZELAZNY

Doorways in the Sand	49510	1.75
Creatures of Light and Darkness	35956	1.50
Lord of Light	44834	2.25
The Doors of His Face The Lamps of His Mouth	38182	1.50
The Guns of Avalon	31112	1.50
Nine Princes in Amber	51755	1.95
Sign of the Unicorn	30973	1.50
The Hand of Oberon	51318	1.75
The Courts of Chaos	47175	1.75

Include 50¢ per copy for postage and handling, allow 4-6 weeks for delivery.

Avon Books, Mail Order Dept.
224 W. 57th St., N.Y., N.Y. 10019